ENEMIES

TIJAN

Edited by Elaine York, Allusion Graphics, LLC

Proofread by Kara Hildebrand, Paige Smith, Chris O'Neil Parece, and Amy English

Beta read by Crystal Solis, Eileen Robinson, and Rochelle Paige

DEDICATION

I have a cousin named Dusty.
He is nothing like the female Dusty in this book, and he did not
inspire this character. I did not name her Dusty because of my
cousin Dusty, but because I know my cousin this book IS dedi-
cated to him.
There you go, bragging rights, Dud.
Though, it wasn't that cousin in the family who tailgated a cop
and got a ticket.

PROLOGUE

THE WINDOW SHATTERED.

I heard it.

It's supposed to be flight-or-fight. I did neither. I froze.

The funny thing, as I saw his silhouette approach the bedroom doorway, a part of my mind detached and all I thought about was how I had run the first time. Flight.

This was the second time.

If there was ever a third, maybe I'd fight then.

He came in, and my gaze shifted.

I left my body, my room, but I remembered the paperweight on my dresser.

I never stopped staring at that paperweight.

CHAPTER 1

THAT WAS A PARTY HOUSE.

Full out. No exceptions. That was a total party house.

Every room was lit up. People were on the front yard. The door was constantly opening and closing. People were running in and out. Girls. Guys. All Homo sapiens with those red cups in hand. A person didn't need to be a social outcast like myself to know what was in those cups. Beer. Booze. Alcohol. Liquor.

I checked my email again, and yep. This was not what I had signed up for. The rental ad read, *BORING! STUDIOUS! QUIET!* I clicked on it, and a person named 'Char' seemed only too eager for me, saying I was a 'perfect fit' and the rest had been history.

I mean, not totally.

There'd been the credit history, because mine wasn't so great since I had helped with family stuff, and she'd not been so regular on getting back to me, but the end result was all that mattered. Right? Right. I was answering myself and I was right. It was right.

But no, looking at the house that matched the address and matched the pictures, that was so not right.

Same house. Different context. The pictures she sent me told me it was a demure house. Boring, like her ad said. White-trimmed shutters. Freshly painted red on the house. A freaking blue door. The door might've sold it, or it might've been the promise that I'd have my own entrance and exit. My own parking spot.

She said quiet, studious, boring! Boring. Hello. A party with red Solo cups and people milling in and out the door, and those weren't even what I would consider normal party people. I was looking closer at them. I knew people from the higher echelon circles, and these people were definitely it.

That was not me. No way.

I had had a small scrape with someone from that world, and I walked away with a full body shiver.

Well. I was shivering again. A full body/full twitchy one.

I had two years left. Two freaking years. A thing happened and I had made the decision that life was short. I was going for what I truly loved, and apparently, what I truly loved took me almost five states away from my father and my stepmother.

I made my decision, applied, and when I was accepted a week later, even though I was late in the application process, I searched for a place to live while I was packing my car. The house was four blocks from college. I was changing my major from pre-law to marine biology, so I needed quiet, I needed studious, I needed boring because I knew what my next few years were going to be about. I would not have a life. That was okay with me. Fully. Totally.

It's what I wanted.

I let out a sigh and pulled my keys from the car. This was it. Do or die.

Well, not die. Not actually. That was too—I was shivering again—morbid.

My phone rang.

Fishing it out of my purse, I saw it was my stepmom and hit decline. Gail would need to wait, but I knew she was worried since I drove the whole way. I hadn't wanted to part with my car. My car meant independence, and I couldn't afford to ship it across state lines, so I texted her back.

Me: Just got here. Safe and sound. House looks cozy and quaint.

Lies. I tossed it back in my purse, grabbed my bag, and had to take another moment to compose myself.

I hated meeting people. Like, truly hated it. I was what you'd call an introvert extrovert. I was chatty once I got to know someone, but let's be honest here, because of a certain incident, I was very peopled-out.

Again. Noticing a theme here.

The less interaction with people, the better, which was why I was having a hard time making myself leave my car. I was safe here. I wasn't safe out there. I was shot-putting myself out of my sanctuary zone, but I had to go and face this.

I also had to pee. Badly.

The twenty-ounce coffee from the last gas station had been a great idea...then. Not so much now.

My hair was a road-trip mess. I tried pulling it back into a ponytail, but I knew some of the strands refused to obey. They kept slipping out, and I probably smelled. More like *definitely* smelled. I'd been driving since five that morning, and it was now evening. I wanted to just get here, and my six-hour pit stop at a motel hadn't been the most restful decision I'd ever made. But, alas, it was necessary. I'd been almost falling asleep behind the wheel, so I was forced to pull over. I was pretty sure the room next to me had been filming a porn—or auditioning for one—but I'd been so exhausted I'd even slept through that.

Until I woke up.

At five.

Because my body decided it was time to go, but now I was tired all over again.

With a backpack on, my purse hanging from the crook in my elbow, and a box in hand, I headed toward the house.

I was feeling a kindred spirit with *Dirty Dancing*'s Baby carrying that watermelon.

"Hey, man!"

A vehicle pulled up a few feet in front of me as I was trotting up the sidewalk. A circle of guys headed for the car.

I waited, breath held, thinking they'd look at me strange or say something that would draw attention to me.

They passed right by me. A few skimmed up and down, giving me the once-over, but for the most part, I was a ghost. Or mist. They went up to the car and pounded fists with the two guys who got out.

A couple girls went with them, darting past me, the same red cups in their hands. One of the girls almost ran into me. Her friend shrieked, pointing, and laughing at her other friend, "Look out!"

"Oh. Sorry." I tried to be invisible, wanted to be, at least.

Then they were both off, still laughing and almost tripping over their own feet.

Another group of girls remained near the house, sipping on their drinks, held close up to their mouths. They literally had formed a circle, but they were watching the guys. It was obvious the party wasn't a common occurrence to them. A few were hungry, watching. A few had slight panic in their eyes, like myself. And a few others looked irritated. They weren't dressed as skimpy as the two giggling girls. They actually wore clothes. Jeans. Shirt. Sandals. Hair in a blow-out. The gigglers only had a bikini top on and a miniskirt, clearly intoxicated in their state of almost undress.

It was hot down in Texas, especially the end of August. It was scorching, even late at night, so the bikini tops made sense. But with a miniskirt? Not so much.

Me. I still had my long-sleeve shirt on.

Driving from South Dakota, it was warm up there, as well, but it just wasn't the same. Still. Long sleeves were my comfort zone.

I moved past the female circle jerk, and like the others, they barely noticed me. The panic-stricken girls watched me, almost with envy. I didn't know why and kept my eyes downcast. Pausing at the door, I wasn't sure if I should ring the bell or knock, or just go in?

The door swung open toward me.

"Oomph!" I managed to swing backwards, out of the way, just as two more guys hotfooted it out of there. One was big and brawny and had a golden tan. He glanced back at me as he passed, his eyes cold, but neither of them stopped. The other one, I didn't even see. He jetted around his friends, out of sight, and my decision about ringing the bell or knocking was made for me.

I walked right in.

"Where'd Wyatt go?"

A girl with gazelle-length legs, Greek goddess hair, and the most porcelain complexion I'd ever seen was coming toward me. She was talking to someone behind her, and as her friend stepped to the side, she saw me and grabbed the Greek Gazelle. "Watch out!"

Too late.

The Greek Gazelle stepped forward...and on me. Well, more specifically, on my foot.

She stiffened and swung around. I was *right there*. Her arms smacked my box out of my arms and her body collided with me.

We both went down.

She screamed.

I oomphed again.

And cringed, hearing something snap.

Then the door opened behind me. I was lying prone now, and looking up at the same time the golden tan guy with cold eyes gazed down at me. He stared, his lip curled up in a smirk, and he drawled, "Always falling at my feet, Mia."

His eyes were on me, no emotion showing, but the Gazelle snapped, "Shut it, Wyatt. Help me up."

He did so, swooping quickly down to me. I almost thought he was going to help me up first, but he reached over me instead, grabbed her hand and simply lifted her up.

It was like he was lifting up a puppy or something, one-handed, by the back of its neck. But instead of a cute, cuddly neck, he was holding a slender arm, and instead of a cute puppy, the Gazelle was frothing at the mouth. If she could kill me with a look, I would've already died, been raised up, and ordered to bury myself again. It was that bad.

"Excuse you?!" she snapped as the guy set her on her feet, then threw his arm around her shoulders. She almost didn't notice. "This is a private party."

"Um." Her friend was biting her lip. She was eyeing my box that was now scattered all over the immediate real estate surrounding us as everything in there had spilled out.

Fuck.

Shit.

FUCK!

Okay.

Deep breath.

I was calm again, and I was reaching for the contents in the box.

The biting-lip friend knelt down, grabbing one of the picture frames. She lifted it up, pausing before handing it over. "Your mom?"

I swiped it from her, then hurried to grab the rest.

This was so embarrassing.

I'd literally been here less than two minutes and I'd already been knocked on my ass and snapped at by one of the mean girls. My worst nightmare come to life. Well, technically, I lived through my worst nightmare, hence the entire reason I was down here in the hella hot Texas heat, but you get my drift.

This. *Not* fun.

I didn't answer the question, though this girl seemed nicer. She spoke in a soft voice, her hair a little darker blonde than mine and laying in huge ringlets around her face. And she was almost as pretty as the mean Greek Gazelle. Cornflower eyes, a smattering of freckles over her cheeks, and a heart-shaped chin. She wasn't as tall as Gazelle, but as a guy stepped around the golden couple, he knelt down and helped grab the rest of my stuff from the floor. "Here, babe."

He handed my transfer papers and my high school yearbook to the nice girl.

Don't ask me why I had the diploma in that box. Random things had been grabbed and stuffed in a rush. And I'd only grabbed the box because I felt holding a backpack in front of me would've been a bit much, but seriously. I needed a shield between me and these people.

The girl sighed, handing over my stuff and then resting her palms on her legs. "You're Dusty, aren't you?"

My mom had a cousin named Dustin. He got in a lot of trouble, the kind that drank, crashed, and just kept on partying. The kind that got a tailgating ticket from a cop, because the cop was the one being tailgated.

Anyway, his kind of trouble got him dead young in life. He and my mom had had a special connection. They got into trouble together some of those times, and when I popped out of her, she said I had his gray eyes and I kept his dirty blond hair, so I became Dusty. Not Dustin. Dusty Gray. She always said I looked like him, too, though I was on the slender side and he'd not been. He'd been big, muscular, but those gray eyes were distinct. We had a kindred spirit. And he'd been handsome. My mom said I'd been pretty, long eyelashes, full lips, rosy cheeks, but since I never got a lot of male attention growing up, I was inclined to believe it'd been her love blinding her. She was a good mom. The best mom.

"Yeah. Hi."

The gorgeous guy next to her stood up, helping her up with a gentle hand behind her elbow. I was assuming these two were together, but unlike the golden couple, who were still standing, still glaring (her) and staring (him), both were giving me friendly vibes.

I added, "Char rented out her room to me. We talked and everything."

"Fucking hell!" The Gazelle threw her arms up, stalking off. "Fucking Char!"

I winced, literally.

Her golden bookend stayed, and his eyes grew a tad bit more interested, but he still only smirked. "Dude." Then he left, tipping his chin up to the other guy.

"I'm Savannah." Nice Girl was holding her hand out, tucking a ringlet behind her ears.

The guy gave me a lazy smile. "Noel."

They even had beautiful names. Of course.

I was dust. Literally.

"Hi." I tightened my grip on my box, now glancing around.

We were standing in the entryway that was between two rooms. One was a living room, a huge sixty-inch television hung up on the wall. Two couches in front of it. It looked almost like a theater room, and on the other end was another television. More couches. A few gamer chairs pulled up in front of the couches, and right then, a huge roar from somewhere close ripped through the air.

"TOUCHDOWN, REEEEEEEEEEEEEVES!"

Four guys surged to their feet, fists in the air, drinks raised high, their heads tipped back from the howls. A few girls shrieked, clapping along with them. A couple others were slower, looking over from where they'd been talking.

Both televisions were on the same game. They were watching the local pro football team, the Kings, and if anyone was anyone, which everyone was someone, then they knew who they were cheering for.

"Yes!" A guy pumped his fist in the air, spraying his drink.

He didn't care. The buddies he slapped hands with didn't care.

One girl who got most of it sprayed on her, however, *did* care.

No one cared about that either.

"Fucking Stone Reeves. He is the *man!*"

Stone Reeves.

Yes. Even I knew who he was. I picked Texas C&B because it was known for its marine biology program, but it was also known to house the newly rising in popularity pro football team, and we were smack in the beginning of that season.

I'd walked right into a football party.

Eyeing Savannah, I asked, "You guys do these parties often?" My box was slipping, so I transferred it to my hip and hiked it up.

Before she could answer, Noel dipped his head to her ear, saying something. She nodded, smiling, and pulled away. "Later."

He gave me a polite smile before heading over to one of the couches. The guys heralded him as if he'd been declared missing with posters and a local search and rescue. I thought it was all a bit much, but no one else blinked an eye. I was in the minority.

"I'll show you your room, yeah?"

Savannah ducked her head down, indicating past the two

living rooms and into what looked like the kitchen. I followed, holding my box still on my hip. I wanted to have a hand free. You never knew when you'd have to push another Mean Girl aside so she didn't trample you.

A few more people were in the kitchen. The dining room adjacent. An attached patio from there.

She led the way past the people standing by the sink. One was a shorter girl with sleek brown hair, bright brown eyes, and a wide smile. She saw Savannah, the smile remained, then her eyes tracked to me, to the box, to my backpack, and the smile dimmed. Dramatically. It was damn near gone as Savannah walked past her, reaching out, a hand tapping the girl's arm in hello. The girl had been talking to another guy, another meathead-type. He had on khaki shorts, a polo shirt, and a beer in hand. He reached forward, touching the girl's waist, but she stiffened. And hissing, she stormed past us, those frosty eyes on me. She almost clipped me at the shoulder, but I was ready. Free hand and all. It was a good thing she swung out of the way at the last minute, or I would've shoved her right into her guy.

Savannah turned toward what looked like the garage door.

My room was in the garage? For real?

She motioned to me, her smile now forced and pasted on. "Down here."

Down here was a door that went to the basement, and once we were down there, it was a lot quieter. I almost sagged in relief.

She noticed, her eyes crinkling. "Not one for parties?"

"Not one for people who don't want me here."

Had I... Oh shit. I had.

I clamped that free hand—see, I knew there was a practical use for it—over my mouth. I was blaming the lack of sleep and sheer will that had me driving across five states in two days. "I'm sorry," I said with my hand still over my mouth, so it was awkwardly moving with my lips. "I didn't mean that."

She snorted, turning to the right. "Why not? I would've said worse." She motioned ahead. "Come on. I'll show you your room."

She went through what looked like a section of the basement that had been turned into an apartment. There was a kitchenette area. A medium-sized fridge. A tiny sink. A tiny oven that my grandma might've used in the '30s. There were two tables. One was decked out with a red plaid plastic tablecloth, and another that was simply a brown round table. A few chairs around each. She motioned to a room attached to the kitchen, to the left of the stairs. "That's Lisa's room." Her eyes flicked upwards. "The one we just passed by."

Oh.

Lovely.

We'd braid each other's hair and exchange best friend beads, that much I was sure of.

Then Savannah was continuing on, going through the kitchen and into another room. It wasn't separated by a door, just a half-wall partition, and this room was obviously a game room. An old pool table. A foosball table. Even a bar tucked in the corner.

She kept straight, continuing on to a door on the other side of the room.

Dread lined my insides and she opened the door and stepped inside.

There was no more house to go.

I couldn't be in that room. It was literally right next to a party room. There was a bar, for fuck's sake.

But I stepped to the doorway and peeked in.

The room was bare. A bed in the corner. An empty nightstand.

"Come in."

I did, and she shut the door.

A desk was built into the wall behind the door with shelves above that. A dresser was beside it.

Another door was attached on the far end of the room. I assumed it was the closet.

It wasn't.

She opened it and stepped through. "Okay. So. I know this room sucks. I do. Char left and everyone shifted rooms. You got stuck with this one. And I'd like to say we never use that room, but we do. And I know I didn't answer your question above, but we do. Often. We're big into football." She seemed to hesitate, biting her lip, before rushing on. "But here's the upside of this room."

She stepped out of the way, pointing ahead. "You get your own bathroom." She knocked on the door to her left. "This is the furnace room/water heater room/your closet." She swept it open and there was a hanging rod put up. A lovely closet. Sort of.

"But..." She shut that door, and there was one last one (I was hoping) behind her. She opened it and I was looking up at a set of stairs. "You have your own entrance and exit as promised, and just beyond that door, down the fence line, is a parking spot that's all yours. Nicole, one of the roommates you didn't meet, her uncle owns this house. We've been living here every year since after our first semester freshman year. And Char leaving, it struck a chord. She never told us she wasn't coming back until she called last night."

"Last night?"

Was that my voice? That high-pitched squeak?

She nodded, her eyes heavy. "Yeah. And she informed us she got us a new roommate, a Dusty (we shouldn't make fun of her name because she seems lovely), and we were supposed to forward all her bills. Seems she decided to spend a semester abroad with a boyfriend none of us knew about."

I gulped. "I applied to come here two weeks ago."

She grimaced. "When'd you meet Char?"

Oh. Lovely. Again, so sarcastic here.

"I didn't. I answered an ad."

Her eyes bulged out. "An ad?" Her voice was squeaking like mine.

I nodded. This wasn't good. This so wasn't good.

"I didn't know I was walking into this."

Savannah clasped her arms over herself, hugging the ends of her elbows. "Us either. And Lisa and Mia's reactions, Char was the closest to them. They're not mad at you. They don't know you. They're mad at Char. You get it."

I did. I placed my box down, sitting on the edge of the bed. "Look. I don't know anyone else here. I'm transferring into my junior year. I get that you guys don't want me here, but I'm here. I'm good for the rent and I already paid Char for the first month's rent."

Her mouth clamped shut and her cheeks got red.

Oh no.

"Tell me she forwarded that to you guys?"

"She didn't. No."

No. Nope. I couldn't speak. "So I paid..."

I trailed off at her look, again.

"Char never sent us money. She lied to you. My guess, she kept the money."

Oh, now I was mad at Char, too.

I groaned. It was just my luck. Fuck's sake. Again.

"Um." Savannah edged toward the door. "So, yeah. You'll have to pay again. And I'll, uh, I'll leave you to it. I'll get your key, too." She paused, looking down. "Sorry about Char being a bitch, and a thief."

Sorry. Right. That wasn't super helpful for this month's rent.

Another roar sounded from above, and we could hear them yelling out, "INTERCEPTION! YES!"

She gave me an uneasy grin, pointing upwards. "Feel free to come and hang out. We've got lots of pizza and beer."

Then she beat it. I was fairly certain I saw her kicking up dust behind her, pun *so* not intended there. She couldn't get out of here fast enough. And to a degree, I got it. I understood it. I felt for her, but she left, shutting that door, and I let out the biggest sigh in my life. Or the second longest sigh in my life. But I guess it was better than tears.

Here I was. At a school I've never toured. In a house I've never seen. Living with people I've never met. In a state that I never thought I'd even visit.

Fuuuuuck.

My phone beeped at that moment.

Gail: You should look up Stone since you're there. I saw his mother in the supermarket, told her you were in the same city now. She didn't seem too keen, but I bet Stone would love to hear from you.

And, oh yeah.

Did I mention that I knew Stone Reeves? Personally.

No? Well, it didn't matter.

I hated him even more than I hated Char at this moment.

CHAPTER 2

IT WAS A LONG EVENING, followed by an even longer night.

Learning the way from my own entrance to my car, I pulled to the back where my parking spot was. The walk was slightly shorter, and noting how big this football party was, I was surprised I'd even gotten that spot. The backyard had people spilling out of it, but not as many. Two smaller circles and the same thing as the front yard. No one paid me a bit of attention.

That wasn't true. A few guys watched me. One started to come over to help, but Mia, the Gazelle Mean Girl, grabbed his arm and shook her head in a quick and savage motion. He resigned himself to sitting at their picnic table and just watching me. Every time I went back and forth, he took a drink. I noticed the whole table did that, too.

Great.

I'd been turned into a drinking game.

That was the only time Mean Gazelle had smiled for real. She was enjoying my humiliation.

Whatever. I trudged back and forth, shouldering my boxes

and bags. I didn't have a ton of stuff, but enough that it took five different trips, and once I was done, I eyed the shower and the bed. I was torn, but my stomach growled.

The coffee had been my breakfast and lunch, and I knew myself. If I took a shower, or lay down, I wouldn't want to get up till way later, and then I'd have a whole day go by without eating. Sighing, I washed up a tiny bit, then grabbed my purse and headed out to grab some food.

There was a fast food place a few blocks away, so I loaded up. I'd have to find a grocery store tomorrow, and get real food, but until then, I had two chicken sandwiches to tide me over.

After that, with their cheering and booing upstairs, I settled in.

I showered. I ate. I made my bed.

I began to unpack, and then around ten that night, I sat at my desk, hearing blissful silence above.

Well, that was following a bunch of yelling, feet stomping, doors opening and closing, then voices outside, and car doors shutting.

They had left the building.

What'd I do? Remain in my bedroom like a good little unwanted thing. It felt wrong going upstairs and checking out the rest of the house when I knew at least two of the girls didn't want me here, so I pulled out my school map and planned my day for tomorrow.

It was the first day of classes, and I was registered, but I still needed to go and do all the extra stuff like get my picture taken for my I.D. Actually, get the I.D. Set up a meal plan since they were requiring one because of my late acceptance. Get my books at the store. Find the library, that was the most important. And then just walk the campus, find where all my classes were going to be.

Since I was switching to marine biology, I was excited for the lab portion of the classes. I did the prerequisites at the community college near where I grew up, so those were all done and aced, but I knew it would be harder at this level. I was still surprised I'd gotten into Texas C&B, but I wasn't going to look a gift horse in the mouth.

I was here. I was doing it.

I'd always wanted to be a marine biologist since I was little, and this was the right time to pursue it. My other career choices fell away. Counseling. A language interpreter. A speech pathologist. They hadn't been the ones I really wanted, and life was short. I'd learned that a few times by now, so I was embracing it with both hands, but leaving my feet firmly planted on the ground.

Tired, but feeling an odd contentment, I crawled into bed at midnight.

⸺

Boom!

Thud!

"Fuck," someone yelled.

More feet shuffling above.

I could hear the laughter.

They were back. I was guessing they'd gone to a party or the nearest bar.

Rolling over in bed, pulling my sheet up around me, my fan pointed right on me, I waited and hoped. Maybe they'd eat, do whatever drunk people did, and then go to bed.

Boom, boom, boom!

They turned on music. Loud bass pounded through the floorboards. I could almost hear them rattling, so I rolled over and did what any girl in my place would do. I muffled a scream into my pillow. It was a full-body scream, too. Even my toes got into it, twitching. I needed sleep. Like bad. Like I would get sick if I went too many nights in a row without a full eight hours, and let's not get into why I wasn't getting my sleep. That tied into the whole reason I came to Texas, but I know people would say they could survive off four hours a night. Yes. I could, too, but not five nights in a row. I was on night six.

I. Needed. My. Sleep.

But really, what was I actually going to do? I was the interloper here. I'd have to endure, and I did. Until four in the morning. And even after that, the music was lowered but it was still a soft beat until finally, I drifted off to sleep. I swear, I went to sleep dreaming about Stone throwing his football down on my head each time, and it corresponded with the techno music blaring through my alarm clock.

My alarm clock.

It was going off.

And waking, realizing that particular dream had been a nasty one, I sat up and I was in pain. A supersonic nap would be needed later on. Pronto. Stat. Don't get me started. I was feeling a bit punchy here.

After showering and dressing, the phone started in. It was Gail. Again.

This time I accepted and knew this would take a while. I sat down. I needed to preserve my energy here.

"Hi, Gail."

"*Sweetie!*" Her voice was loud, and she was forcing a Southern accent. I didn't know why. She wasn't Southern. Never had been. "How *ahr y'all?*"

This was Gail. I didn't need to reply.

She was already onto the next question. "How *waas* your drive? I hoped you took it easy. That's a long way to drive by yourself. Your father left to have coffee with the men in town. You know how it is. He loves that coffee time. And how are *y'all* *feah*ling today? Excited? Your classes start *todaaay*. Have you gotten in touch with Stone yet? He's a big deal down there. I'm sure he'd be happy to show you the ropes, show *y'all* some places, maybe the best places to eat. You know."

One, Stone was a big deal everywhere in this state.

Two, he wouldn't be happy to show me the ropes. He loathed me more than I hated him, and that said a lot.

And three, I had a *fealing* my dad was sitting right next to her. He loathed going to get coffee with the men in town as much as Stone and I despised each other.

But, there was an upside to my relationship with Gail. I barely had to speak. It was mostly a one-sided dynamic, and to prove this, Gail kept right on chatting. She would exhaust herself, do both parts of our conversation so it went how *she* wanted it to go, and once she was happy *she'd* end the call.

Which is what she was doing right now.

"Stone is such a sweet boy."

He was an arrogant prick.

"And you know, that family. They fell on hard times, too."

His family was rich, and because he could, his dad fired mine shortly after turning their grocery store into a franchise.

"And Barb, she just looks so amazing. Her skin was glowing. She looks like she has trimmed down, too."

Barb was haggard looking.

Stone's mom was skinny because she smoked and drank champagne every day. Once every couple days, she'd throw in a piece of chicken, maybe a salad with that. And I knew this because we'd been their neighbors until we were forced to sell the house, and once upon a time, Stone and I had been great friends. I'd been at their house a lot growing up. All that changed once we hit puberty, of course, but Barb just kept getting skinnier and more gaunt-looking.

And people talked.

I mean, not Gail (in this circumstance.) She was almost the anti-gossiper here. She was literally spewing the opposite of what was true, but if she wanted to believe all of this, who was I to correct her? This was what she was choosing to think. So be it.

And by the end, after she was losing speed, I only murmured, "Sounds good, Gail. I should get going."

"Oh. Okay. Have a great day, *suh-weedie*! Your father and I are thinking about you today. Call tonight. Let us know how Stone is when you see him."

I wouldn't do any of that, and she knew that. My dad knew it. And she would call tomorrow, repeating all the same until she would've convinced herself that I *had* reached out to Stone, that he and I *were* friends again, and she would go on thinking how amazing I was doing in Texas.

CHAPTER 3

"YOU NEED A BIGGER MEAL PLAN."

The lady behind the desk wasn't getting it. Red-rimmed glasses. Just as red-rimmed lips, pursed together in a slight scowl, I could tell she'd already had her fill of new students, and it was only nine in the morning.

I pushed the paper back. "That's all I can afford."

Her eyes snapped back to mine, but there was no flicker of emotion. She pushed the paper right back. "You're a junior and you have off-campus housing. That's all fine, but since it's your first semester, you still have to abide by incoming freshman guidelines. You need to do either the meal plan above what you picked or the next one up. You cannot pick the option where you get one meal on campus a month."

"I live off-campus."

"I'm aware. It's in your file. You also were accepted late, and because of that, you've been put in the incoming freshman program. A daily meal plan is your only option."

She. Did. Not. Get. It.

I leaned forward, abundantly aware of how many students

behind me who were either annoyed because I was taking longer than the average two minutes allotted, or they were eavesdropping and enjoying my further humiliation. Either way, I wasn't taking the meal plan because I couldn't afford it.

I lowered my voice, my hands gripping my backpack straps that circled around my shoulders. "I can't afford to go higher."

She leaned forward, lowering her voice, too. "It's just a semester. You can have no meal plan next semester."

I closed my eyes, images of hitting my forehead on the counter flashing in my mind.

"I can't afford it," I said this through gritted teeth, my mind already flashing through my options and a whole new feeling of helplessness erupted inside of me because I knew what I'd have to do was going to hurt. A lot. More than a lot.

"You can't be a student here if you don't follow the rules. You can probably get through one week of classes, but the list is updated and faculty meetings happen. You'll be called out in every single class and told to come right back here to fulfill your meal plan program. Check this box." She did it for me and held out her hand. "And give me a form of payment, then you can be on your merry way."

This was going to hurt. So bad.

Swallowing over a lump the size of a boulder in my throat, I reached into my purse and pulled out my wallet. I had a credit card. It was only there for emergency reasons, and I hated using credit cards. Hated it with a passion. So many bad years of debt were running through my memories, but suppressing a chill, I pulled it out and handed it over.

She took it, eyeing me. "This will go through?"

I couldn't speak, but I dipped my head down in a nod.

"Okay." Her lips pressed together, and she ran the card.

It went through. I heard the beep, and I closed my eyes again to dam up the tears. They couldn't come, not again. I wouldn't allow them to spill. And fuck. I was screwed. I'd have to get a second job just to pay off this bill, and now job hunting was being added to my list of things to do today.

"Okay." She handed my card back, then pulled out my updated I.D. I'd already taken the picture and gave a bright and so-forced smile. "Welcome to Texas C&B."

I snatched both, glared at her, and waited until I was at least outside the office before muttering, "Bitch," under my breath.

"What'd you say?"

I looked up.

It was the Mean Gazelle, and seeing it was me, her eyes cooled, but the fight faded. "Never mind." There were others with her and her boyfriend, but I didn't recognize any of the girls. Not that I would. I only met Savannah and Lisa. You know those moments in life, the ones where you're walking, going about your life, and suddenly a whole herd of beautiful people walk past you? They're staring at you like you're the zoo animal on display, or the circus freak who's in their own unique tent. Well, that just happened, and Mean Gazelle was one of their leaders. If I had to guess, I was sure some of them had been at the house last night. One of the guys trailed behind and turned around, watching me, his mouth pursed in an odd smirk as if he were enjoying himself, as he continued walking backwards with his group.

"You survived a confrontation with Mia Catanna."

Turning, I saw a random girl had watched the whole thing, and she came over now, adjusting her own backpack. It was slung over one of her shoulders. Blonde hair. Glasses. She was petite, and like me, she wasn't wearing any makeup, but while some used it to highlight their beauty, this girl could've used it to not look like she was twelve.

"Her last name is Catanna?" For real? I grunted. "We had a Catanna Nursing Home back where I lived."

Her lips twitched. "I'm Siobhan."

Siobhan. Jesus. I waved. "My name doesn't make me think of an Irish model. I'm Dusty."

"Dusty?" Another lip twitch.

"Yep. Dusty Phillips, to be exact."

"Gotcha. If it makes you feel better, my sisters are all named Silver, Sinead, and Shavonia."

"Really? Shavonia?"

She laughed now. "Yeah. My mom liked cocaine during her child-birthing days. Not when she was pregnant. That was the only times she was sober, but don't worry. No pity needed. She kicked all the habits when I was twelve, moved us to a sober/hippy camp, and I spent the rest of my formidable years eating mostly plant-based food."

"Really?"

Yes. That was all I could manage at that time.

She nodded, shifting to stand closer as a group of students swarmed around us. "Need a fire started using only a paper clip and a match, and I'm the girl for you."

"That's good to know. Next time I go camping, I'm looking you up."

She laughed. "You go camping a lot?"

"Never."

"Yeah." She waved that off. "That's good because I was lying about everything."

I raised an eyebrow. "You really don't have a sister named Shavonia?"

"I do, actually. The names are the only thing I wasn't lying about. My name really is Siobhan, and you're going into the marine biology program?"

I tilted my head to the side. "You got that from me standing here?"

"No. I got that because I was three people behind you when you were in the administration building. Then I saw you leave the food office and figured I should introduce myself. I'm in the same program." She held her hand out, and we did the formal introductions once more.

Both of us were grinning by the end.

"I transferred in, so I don't know if we'll have the same classes."

She shrugged. "We'll have a few and we'll be in the same building. The higher-advanced classes take place at the marina. Who's your academic advisor?"

I looked down at my schedule. "It says Anna Anderson."

"Hmmm. She's a bitch. Hope you transferred from a good college."

My heart sank. "Community college."

She grimaced. "Well. If you're an independent student, the good news is that she's not going to care much about helping you. Bad news, if you're a student who needs a good relationship with your advisor, you might want to put a transfer in now."

"Transfer to a new school?" My voice broke. I couldn't have heard that right.

I just got here.

"No!" She barked out a laugh. "A new advisor. It sucks to say, but Dr. Anderson is one of those profs who only wants to mentor the brightest and most-promising students. If you're coming in from a community college, she's going to write you off as a D, maybe C student. She won't waste her time."

"Oh." That sucked. "Good to know, I guess. Who's your advisor?"

She grinned. "Dr. Anna Anderson. I'm her TA."

I almost choked. "Are you kidding?"

"No, that's how I know what I'm saying is true. She'll smile in your face and make you feel appreciated, then she'll hand off your folder to me and instruct me to draw up a generic letter of recommendation for you two years early. I've drawn up eight already for some summer students just last week."

"Damn."

Yeah. That huge pile of feeling helpless and hopeless, it was building.

But no.

I hadn't gone through what I went through, decided to go for what I really loved, only to be detoured by a jaded meal-plan office worker and a stuck-up academic advisor, or even mean roommates in a party house.

I would endure. That's the one quality us Phillips' had in abundance. We'd endured worse. This was just a blip in my life.

"Okay." Decision made. "Where do I put in for an advisor transfer?"

"Come on." She nodded back toward the building I just came out of. "I'll show you. Susan Cord is really nice, and she has a soft spot for the underdog students since she considers herself one."

God.

An underdog.

I'd already been painted that way.

Guess it was better than what happened at my last college. I suppressed a shiver. *Anything* was better than what happened there.

CHAPTER 4

SOMEONE KNOCKED on my door the next night, and I knew who it was. Not because it was a soft knock or any other reason, but because there was literally only one person who'd knock on my door.

My first day of classes was overwhelming. I had genetics, biostats, intro to cell biology, and I indulged with one marine class. Fundamentals of marine biology, though, okay, it wasn't a total indulge class. It was still the next level up from basic requirements, but I was getting close.

That meant something to me.

And finding out that Siobhan was in my genetics class, I felt a lot better. We planned to meet for lunch after class the next day, after all, I'd just paid for a meal plan I couldn't afford, but I was looking forward to the company.

Since then, just classes, just me time.

The house had been quiet last night when I got back from campus. I heard people arrive late, around ten, but they settled down around one in the morning. When I got back from my two classes today, I'd been surprised to find Lisa studying in the base-ment, but that was it.

She was at the table, and seeing me coming out of my room, she cursed and shoved her books closed. Storming into her room, her door was slammed shut just as I got to the fridge.

Well, then.

I still wasn't going anywhere, and I was just now figuring I should try finding a grocery store when that knock came.

Standing to open the door, I already had my polite smile on my face. "Hi, Savannah."

It wasn't Savannah.

A girl with brown hair, shoulder-length, and almond eyes, a smaller frame, but with meat on her was there instead. She tipped her head down, looking at me. "You're the new roommate."

I was guessing this was Nicole. "Hi. Your uncle owns the house?"

A short nod. "Yep."

She observed me the same time I was observing her.

I'd dressed simply that night. Jeans. A Texas C&B tank top and flip flops.

She was dressed similarly, and both of us were trying to hide a grin.

She cleared her face, her eyes cooling, though I thought it looked like she needed to put in some effort to do that. "Look, the house is technically my uncle's, I felt like I should properly intro-duce myself. Sav said you arrived Sunday night. I wasn't around yesterday."

She came in, noting my textbook out on the desk. "Genetics, huh?"

"Um. Yeah."

I left the door wide and resumed my seat behind my desk.

She nodded, swinging her leg back and forth, her toe

anchored on the ground. "That's cool. Lisa had that class last year. She's in the nursing program." She flashed me a grin. "I'm not as ambitious. I'm in education. Gonna be a teach like my ma, but I am ambitious because I'm specializing in middle school. Gonna crack those adolescent pubescents one at a time."

"What about Savannah?"

"Sav's going into sports medicine. It's how she met Noel, actually, and how most of us met any of the guys."

"What do you mean?"

"Noel." She waited, expecting a reaction.

I had nothing. "Oh. Oh, yeah! Noel."

She cracked up again. "You have no clue, do you?"

Not a one. But I just shrugged. "Noel and Savannah seem nice."

She snorted. "They're *the* couple on campus. If we had royalty here, it'd be them. Noel's starting quarterback for our school, and everyone loves Sav. She's considered C&B's princess, but Mia hates it. She likes to think she's the school's queen bitch instead."

It was worse than I thought, and I was following everything she just said. This house wasn't just a football-frenzy house. It *was* football. They *were* football.

"Are you kidding?" I was feeling the blood draining from my face. It was going to pool at my feet. There'd be a mess, and another reason they would hate me, and want to kick me out.

Nicole grinned. "Not a football fan? Sav mentioned you asked if we had a lot of football parties."

I'd moved into my nightmare house. Straight up. I had to start looking for a new place to live. Stat.

"It's okay."

She burst out laughing. "Well, at least I know now you're a shit liar. Good to know." She took pity on me. "Wyatt's one of the wide receivers. Nacho's a halfback. Dent's a defensive end."

All these football terms. I was being pelted.

"Really. Wow. That's super impressive."

She was still snickering. "Listen, I know Mia and Lisa are kinda being bitches about you being here, but you're here. It is what it is. Char was a bitch for what she did, and most of it was a middle finger to Mia and Lisa for things they were saying last semester. You seem nice. You're quiet. I already know that. If you want to stay, you can stay. Rent's due the first of the month. My uncle rigged a rent box in the back of the house, just put your check in there and it'll be fine." She paused a beat. "Sav told me what Char did. I'd like to say it's cool, but no one can cover you. The only redeeming thing I can say is that Char'll be back, and we'll get the money *then*."

"What about utilities?"

"We only pay cable and Internet. You just need to chip in for those."

"Who do I pay for that?"

"Mia's in charge of paying those bills, so you gotta give your money to her. It's usually only fifty dollars."

"When's that due?"

"You're good for this month, so not till end of next month."

More money, but I had a fund set aside just for bills. I had planned for this. "Okay."

"Um." She stood up, and we heard more footsteps going over my ceiling above. "That's probably the group. We're heading out for dinner. You want to come?"

I couldn't move. I wasn't sure if this was the beginning of a set-up or not. I'd been observing them by now, and they were social creatures. So were killer whales. I was not a killer whale. I was more a spotfin lionfish, but you know, without the venom and the beautiful dorsal fins. But I was antisocial. That was my point, and I was that way for a reason.

"Mia's at Wyatt's and Lisa's at the library. It's just me, Sav, Noel, and a few others."

A few others. I already knew that probably meant close to ten people.

I was torn. This was an olive branch, I was thinking. Or assuming. Or just hoping. She said the two girls who hated me wouldn't be there, but I did have a crap ton of studying to do already.

Shit.

What should I do?

She took pity on me again. "Listen, come. If it's not the scene for you, we can Uber back? I'll order the Uber, on me. I'll make sure we go somewhere small. I think they mentioned the bar on campus."

With an offer like that, I knew I had to go. She was making so many concessions just to get me to hang out with them.

This was so a set-up. I was the outcast seal swimming to my slaughter. They just wanted to play with me a bit before eating me.

I nodded and grabbed my purse. "I'm game." What else could I do?

"Great."

———

My roommate was a liar.

I knew there was a bar on campus. It was a small pub. Quaint. I saw it once walking past it, but I didn't know there were two bars on campus, and the one their group went to was the opposite of small. It was huge. Sixteen large screens were mounted around the place. It was an on-campus version of Wild Wings. It was a total sports hangout, and when we walked in, *they* were heralded as long-lost family members. A collective greeting came up from everywhere, but I'd been prepared for that. A D1 school, and Noel was the starting quarterback, he was a big deal. A really big deal. Savannah was next to him. And Nicole had introduced me to Nacho and Dent. Dent was the guy who had been going to help me the first night until Mia stopped him.

He had dark eyes and he'd been watching me the whole time. He sat next to me when we all piled into a huge booth in the corner. It was one that seated up to twelve people. Nicole was on my left and Dent was on my right. Reaching for the menu, his arm grazed mine.

I pulled my arm away, not to be rude, but because I had a thing with personal space and people invading it.

"Sorry."

"It's me. I have a personal bubble issue."

He chuckled. "Not for that, for the first night. We should've helped you bring in your boxes. It would have been the right thing to do."

Oh. That.

I shrugged. "It's fine. It's cool."

"No, really. We should've helped. Not all of us are like Liss and Mia. Some of us are cool. Friendly, even."

Yeah. He was being friendly now, but the jaded part of me, the side of me that knew I was living in a kill or be killed kinda world wondered if he'd keep it up when and if Mia was around. I was thinking not.

"They're—" I didn't know what to say. And I only had enough money for a small order of wings, so I didn't need to peruse the menu anymore. I settled for picking at my napkin. "They're fine."

"They're being bitches."

The guy next to Dent heard and choked back a laugh. "You're just pissy because Lisa shot you down hard last night."

And that put him in a whole new light.

I shifted back just as his gaze whipped back to mine. His eyebrows rose. "It's not like that."

No. I was getting what it was like exactly.

"It's cool."

But fuck. For real.

Nicole and Savannah, I could get them. I was the new roommate. They hadn't kicked me out, so I was figuring the two had taken pity on me. I mean, I was looking around. There were people galore around them, and others still on the periphery. Girls who would've been my replacement. Why Char did what she did...yeah, that was a bitch move. To them and myself, but it was done. I couldn't afford my own place yet. No way. They were only making me pay three hundred a month, and I knew that was a steal where the house was located, that it actually *was* a house. I'd resigned myself to the fact that I'd put up with the loud and the football, if only for a semester.

But this guy, he didn't have to pretend to be nice to me.

I saw him start to offer to help, then he was stopped. I thought for just the briefest of seconds that maybe I'd found another ally. A person needed to try to get along with their roommates, right? Their friends?

I was an idiot, and another realization hit me.

I shouldn't have been there, especially when every channel was turned to a sports channel and half of the screens were raving about Stone.

And just then, because it seemed the universe was against me, my phone chimed a text.

Gail: Here's Stone's phone number. I made your father ask Charles.

A contact alert came through and fuuuck. My thumb moved to delete it, but I waited. I mean, I hated him. With every bone in my body, but he literally was the only person from back home that I knew in the city. Then again, he probably had a filter for callers. He wouldn't know my number. He wouldn't take it, and even if he did know it or have mine programmed into his phone, he *really* wouldn't take it.

The hatred was mutual and that was the only thing we could both bond over.

Why was Gail doing this to me? Was my dad really letting her go down this path of delusions? He knew I hated Stone as much as I knew he hated Charles and Barb. There was literally no love lost between our foursome.

But still, I didn't delete it.

I could come back to it, in case something happened. An emergency of some sort, like if I had to get ahold of him.

"It's not like that."

I jerked my head up just as he started to look at my phone.

I clicked the button, turning my screen off, and I waited, my breath held, frozen, hoping he hadn't read Stone's name when Gail shared the contact with me. That was absolutely the last thing I wanted to happen here.

"That your mom?"

He was so sweet, assuming the only person who'd text me would be by my mom. "My mom's dead."

He jerked back in his seat, his eyes widening.

I kept it to myself that it had been my stepmom as I put my phone away. It was then that I knew it was time to cut and run before I got in deeper. Consider the outcasted seal wising up and learning killer whales were not the herd to swim with.

"Mind if I head to the bathroom?"

"Hey. I'm sorry about—"

I waved that off. "She died a long time ago. It's no big. Can you let me out? I gotta piss."

He wavered, but the guy beside him was already shifting out. So did Dent, and then I was free. They didn't wait for me to take off. Both got back in the booth, and I moved a few steps, watching. No one noticed I'd left. They weren't paying attention, and even after going to the bathroom, then coming back, I lingered before deciding if I truly should ditch or try to get ahold of Nicole and let her know I was going.

She was leaning into Dent, who had his arm around the back of her seat. They were all laughing, and observing the tables around them, I wasn't the only one watching. This was their group. This was what happened when they went out. I was starting to get that. They were watched by everyone, and a bunch of people came and went from talking to them, returning to their own tables after they'd been seen interacting with them. Others replaced them.

With the ease they all portrayed, this was an everyday thing for them.

Yeah.

I eased backwards.

They wouldn't even remember that I'd gone with them, so with that decided, I headed for the exit.

I used my money for the cab instead.

CHAPTER 5

THE REST of the week passed without much incident.

Classes were hard, but I knew they would be. I already had a short paper due in two of them, and we had quizzes in my other two classes. Nicole and Savannah never came back down to my room, but I didn't blame them. I used my own exit to come and go, so the only times I left my room were to venture to the fridge in the basement. I'd grab my food and head right back to my room. Wash, rinse, repeat.

But I heard them all in the house. Traipsing around.

I heard the guys, too. They seemed to be here anytime the girls were, and after that one time of running into Lisa downstairs, I never saw her again. Her door remained shut at all times. And Gail called me two more times, but I didn't pick up. And it wasn't that I had to guess what she was calling about. She told me in great detail. In my voicemail. Both times. Lengthy messages.

All about me calling Stone.

Had I reached out yet? He had a Sunday game, was I watching it? She bet he'd give me tickets. She bet he'd give all my friends tickets, too. Apparently, Barb had told him I was here.

Apparently, Barb had told him Charles gave his phone number to my dad, who gave it to Gail, who gave it to me. So apparently, Stone was waiting for me to call him. Or text him. Or even email, because she sent me his email address last night.

I was getting a pounding headache from the constant reminders about Stone. My dad knew it was all bullshit. Why was he not stepping in?

I was listening to another voice message from her when I walked into my room that night. My last class had been brutal. Intro to Marine Biology might've been titled an introductory class, but it was still an advanced one, and my head was swimming with all the different classifications of planktonic species. So it took me an hour to realize it was Friday night, and all I heard was nothing. It was completely silent upstairs. I almost felt like rejoicing and throwing a party of my own because I was certain they'd be living it up, but then I remembered.

The football team had an away game tomorrow. That's where they went. They must've traveled all together, so they took their party on the road. Thank God.

That was...a flash of jealousy sliced through me, followed by other emotions, feelings I had no reason feeling, and I stuffed it all down. Completely. I stomped on it. With both feet. And I did a one-two-kick, then a jump and down again. It was pushed as far to the bottom as I could muster, and once my head was free, I figured it was the perfect night to indulge my solitude. Chipotle it would be.

My phone rang as I was emptying out my backpack.

Seeing an unknown number flash, I paused a second, then cursed at myself. How old was I? Twelve. Jesus. My stepmom was the only call I skirted, so I hit the accept button. "Hello?"

"Is this... Dusty?"

I sat up straighter. "Siobhan?"

"Yeah!" A relieved laugh. "Sorry. I didn't want you to think

I'm a stalker, but I got your number from Dr. Anderson, not that she knows that. I really hope that's okay?"

I relaxed, slouching back down. "Oh, yeah. We should've exchanged numbers this week, anyway."

Our last class today had been a quiz, and once that was done, everyone shot out of there. The quiz had been brutal.

"Um..." She got quiet. "So, why do I feel like I'm asking you out on a date?" A nervous hiccup. "Oh. Sorry. But, yeah. What are you doing tonight? Do you already have plans?"

I eyed my keys and frowned. "To be honest, I was going to hit up Chipotle. That. That's my exciting college life Friday night plans."

She laughed. "Well, I wouldn't mind Chipotle myself, but want to head over here? My roommate and I were going to settle in for a movie marathon. We were thinking *Harry Potter* or *Fifty Shades*. We haven't decided."

I was gripping my phone so tightly. "What? No football game?"

"That's tomorrow, isn't it?"

"Yeah."

"And no." Her nervous hiccup was back. "We're not big football watcher people. I mean, our lives are spent in biology labs. The most sporting things we do is trying to grab different kinds of fish to tag them. When it's the weekend, we're either studying or we're relaxing. You know what I mean?"

I didn't, not yet, but I lied. "Yeah. Totally."

"We've got some wine here, too. You can sleep over, if you want. We have a super comfortable couch."

My decision was made. I didn't have to force myself to be a lionfish. I stood, reaching for my keys. "What's your address?"

I picked up Chipotle for her, myself, and her roommate. They were supplying the place to hang out at and the wine, so the food was on me. I'd just skim back on a couple meals later that week. It was doable. The body was a great adapter, one or two missed meals wasn't a big deal.

So it was all worth it, and when I rang their bell, both were in Harry Potter pajamas and I knew I'd found my people. Her roommate's name was Emily, and within ten minutes of the first movie, we were all fast friends.

I'd been feeling guilty about ditching my roommates the other night, like maybe I was wrong to do it.

Was I? My feelings got hurt. Dent didn't even matter. Nicole. Savannah. I was thinking I'd been too quick to judge before I shut them down. Maybe? But I also couldn't help but wonder...did they even notice I was gone? If they hadn't noticed, then I had nothing to feel guilty about.

But the last two days, I'd been thinking it was me in the wrong and I was the problem, yet here I was. I was sitting with a new friend and had made another friend, so maybe I wasn't actually the problem.

And that was making me feel all sorts of better. On a Friday night, no less.

My phone rang right then. I knew without looking it was Gail, and I'd ditched her enough this week.

I rose, gesturing to their patio with my phone. "Mind if I go out there to take this?"

"No, no." Siobhan waved a hand. "Go for it. We'll pause and make some margaritas."

I only grinned. They had a whole discussion if they should indulge in wine or margaritas. Emily wanted margaritas. Siobhan wanted wine. Emily had won out, and she sent me a tiny grin and a thumbs up as she followed her roommate into the kitchen.

Stepping outside, on the third ring I answered as I shut the door behind me. "Hello?"

"Your stepmom has been harassing my mom." A low, gravelly voice greeted me.

I cursed under my breath. That's what I get for not saving his number in my contacts.

"Yeah," he bit out. "Fucking A, Dust."

Dust.

That pissed me off.

He didn't get to call me out of the fucking blue, then use that nickname he used when we actually were friends. Oh-to-the-hell-fuck-no.

"Fuck you."

He was silent, hearing me, then a low and savage growl came from the other end. "Are you kidding me? Your stepmom has some delusion that you and I are fucking destined to be or something. Where's she getting that piece of shit story?"

He didn't say it outright, didn't point a finger in my direction, but I felt slapped in the face by his accusation anyway.

I bit out, my blood boiling, "Trust me, asshole. It's not because of me."

"Put her in her place. You and I, we ain't anything. Got that?"

"Abundantly." And because I knew where he was going, and I was petty and I wanted to get there first, I hung up on him. Bastard.

Then, a moment.

I couldn't breathe.

Dust.

Fuuuuuck him.

We built a fort together.

We played in the woods together and in the river that ran through both our properties.

We had a whole maze put in place.

I never did the dolls thing growing up.

I was outside. Dirty. Rough. We played tag and we pretended to hunt shit.

His dog was the friendliest German shepherd alive and he'd been horrible at protecting us. We pretended he was our guard dog anyway.

My mom baked for us.

His mom cooked for us.

We were best friends until sixth grade, until puberty hit, and suddenly Stone was too fucking cool for me.

Rage, long and deep, rose up in me, and grabbing ahold of the bannister, I bent over, letting out a scream like I'd never yelled before.

Hearing a clambering behind me, I remembered where I was, and a whole new litany of curses flashed in my mind.

I'd forgotten.

Real shit and private shit just went public, and turning, wiping all of it away, I waved a hand with an awkward smile on my face. "I'm good," I said as soon as the door opened again. "Sorry. Just an annoying call from home."

They both seemed concerned, but were polite about not being pushy. I could tell they were either weirded out by me, my reaction, or I don't know what else, but the easygoing and care-free vibes of our Friday night was gone. My outburst of anger had ended that, so maybe it *was* me? All my problems with other people. Maybe I needed to really decide what I wanted? If I wanted friends, I might need to seek some professional help and figure out what I was doing wrong...or if I didn't want friends, then I was good.

I left halfway through the second movie, and when I say I left, I mean that I felt it was in the most awkward way ever.

Emily and Siobhan seemed more relaxed when the first one ended. The margaritas might've helped, but there were quite a few sideways glances my way, and once during the second movie, Emily gave up all discreetness and openly stared at me. I knew right then that I needed to go.

Saying my goodbyes, Siobhan walked me to the door. Emily remained on the couch, giving me a wave, but I could tell she was relieved I was going. I was crushing their Friday night chill sesh and I didn't want to be responsible for that.

"Dr. Anderson is doing a research study. I have to go to the marine lab and check on her seahorses tomorrow. You want to come with?"

I almost did a double-take.

"Are you serious?" Not because this was awkward, she wanted me to go, and why would she invite me for another outing? But in the way that I was already preening because she was talking about seahorses. The males were the ones who carried the eggs, and what other species did that? Also, they lived the life of mostly resting and eating, and well hiding, but seriously. Resting. Eating. The guys carried the babes.

I was so in.

Siobhan grinned. "Yeah. The little things are kinda cute. Then I was going to meet Trent at the Quail to study. Want to come to that, too? I figure we always have something we can be studying."

I almost had to take a step back.

The Quail was the name of the campus pub, the one that I first thought was the only one on campus. Small. Cozy. I liked it immediately, but I hadn't known the name. The Quail seemed fitting for some reason, and also, I raised an eyebrow. "Trent?"

Her face went from a blush red to lobster red. She picked at her doorframe, her eyes jutting away. "Yeah. I mean. We're friends. He's a good guy."

"That's the guy in our genetics class? The cute blond you sit by?"

I hadn't thought it was possible, but her face was getting even redder.

I couldn't stop myself from teasing. "The guy who looks like a six-foot-one model? Who wears glasses, but he has high cheekbones and he could be the definition of a gorgeous nerd? That Trent?"

She was eyeing the air like she wanted a black hole to open up and she could step through it. "Yeah. Him."

I was starting to feel bad. "I'm just teasing. You know the guy is into you, right?"

Her eyes swung to mine. "You think he is?"

I nodded. "My knowledge might not be vast, but I can't imagine a guy meeting a girl in a bar, on a Saturday night, wanting to study, unless he also wants to get in her pants."

Her eyes bulged out at that one. Her mouth puckered. Her lips moved, but no sound came. Then, quietly, "You think so?"

It was like basic math. I only smiled softly. "I'm pretty sure. I thought he was your boyfriend."

"Oh my God."

"Whad's going on over thrd?" Emily yelled from the couch.

The slurring had commenced.

"You're going to have fun tonight with that one." From me.

"Hey." Her tone got serious. Her eyes went past mine, and I was pretty certain it wasn't on her roommate, but instead lingering on the patio. "From before. Are you okay?"

I shrugged that off.

The anger and resentment and all that annoying stuff was locked up tight. It was just carefree me who enjoyed teasing a new friend. I could do these next two years like this. Nothing would get in and hurt me that way.

"It's nothing. Just someone from back home."

"An old boyfriend?"

I could almost hear Stone's growl again. It would've been erupting at volcanic decibel levels at hearing that from her.

I swallowed over a lump. "No. Just—family stuff."

"Oh." Why did her smile turn sad after that? That wasn't my intention. "Okay, but I know you're new here and I don't have a lot of friends myself, so I'm here. For anything. You know?"

I knew. And I reached forward on an impulse, giving her a hug.

She hugged me back, surprised at first, then clasped me back.

"See you tomorrow then?" I stepped into the hallway.

She nodded. "Yeah. I usually go around nine in the morning. Is that too early?"

I had an empty house and I was usually knocked out by midnight. "I'll probably already be up for an hour before that, so it's perfect."

"Okay. I'll text you where to meet me? Or I can pick you up?"

Oh, shoot.

Would she recognize the party house for who lived there? I didn't think I was going out on a limb to worry about how Siobhan would think of my roommates. People like them and people like us didn't mix, not if we had a healthy self-preservation instinct.

My smile was tight. "I'll meet you there. And then if you really want a tagalong tomorrow night, I'll come, too, but only if you want a remora fish to tag along."

She laughed. "Okay. Sounds good. Though, that makes me the shark?"

I began to walk down the hallway. "We can figure that out tomorrow." I waved.

"Okay. See you. I'll text you in the morning." She waved back.

━━━

The house was dark when I got back, but for some reason it felt right to me. It was peaceful. And when I slid into bed, I was more than a little excited to see some seahorses in the morning.

Then a text came through, and I rolled over, grabbing it.

Unknown: This shit has to stop.

Unknown: *image attached*

I sat up, dread sinking low in my gut, and I clicked the image. It was a screen shot.

Gail: We know what your family did to mine. If your son doesn't reach out and make things right with my daughter, I'm going to the press. We have nothing to lose now, but you do, and your son does. How do you feel about that, Barb?

I cursed. Even typing a threatening and crazy text and my stepmother was using perfect grammar. There had to be a joke in there.

I hadn't put Stone's number in my phone, but I knew it was him, and I hit the call button.

He answered with, "Call off your crazy stepmom. We *will* sue. And I don't know what the fuck your stepmom is talking about, but my family did nothing to yours."

A surge of fury was rolling in my belly, but I waited. I counted to ten, and then I said through gritted teeth, "One. That's not true. Two. I *will* call her, but not because you're telling me to. Three. I also don't know where she's getting this idea from because trust me, dealing with you is the *last* thing I want." After a beat. I clipped out, "Do *me* a favor? Lose my number."

I hung up on him. Again. And it felt damn good.

CHAPTER 6

THE HISTORY with Stone wasn't completely between him and me. It was more between his father and mine, or to be more accurate, between my dad's employer and my father. The timing was all suspect, but my dad was the manager for their grocery store. Then my mom was diagnosed with cancer and we tried to keep it under wraps, but rumor got out, and within a week my dad was served his walking papers.

While my dad was trying to find another job, my mom was about to start chemo when we lost our health insurance due to my father getting the boot. A month went by. Nothing. He wasn't getting hired. Another month. Nothing. Three. Four. We were going on six months when finally, someone three towns over confided to a friend of a friend that word of mouth was saying not to hire Mitch Phillips.

He'd been blacklisted by Stone's dad. Why? We had no idea.

We tried to find out the reason, but no one was fessing up until a friend of my mom's overheard a man talking in the local bar. The guy was ranting about how Charles Reeves knew it was bad what he did, firing a man whose wife was just diagnosed with cancer, and he wanted to push the Phillips family out of town to stem any bad gossip.

It backfired.

This was all happening my senior year of school. Stone had gone on to join a D1 school and he was a rising football star, but he'd always been a superstar on the field. Another reason why Charles Reeves wanted to get my family out of town, in case media came sniffing around for a feel-good story about a local boy getting drafted by fancy colleges and maybe even the NFL down the road. He didn't want us to give them a scandal instead, or so the gossip mill was saying.

Because we were so in debt from the cancer treatments, we lost the house.

We moved into an apartment close to the hospital so I could remain in school that last year, and then we found out three months later that the Reeves family bought our house and land from the bank for a steal. They renovated it into a local Airbnb.

Stone scored the winning touchdown for his football championship game, and that night my mom died. We had spiraled so far into debt, there was no getting out for us. I don't think anyone could fault my family for the resentment that we held for the Reeves family. I knew there was some on my part. I expected equal amount on my dad's part.

I hadn't known there was some on Gail's part.

And the next day, after I went with Siobhan to check on some seriously cute seahorses, I knew the time for my phone call had come. I would've signed up for anything else instead of having to call Gail and deal with this. Even spending time with Stone. Gasp. Shrinks in horror, but yes. Even spending time with Stone would be preferable than doing this.

All that said, I couldn't stall anymore.

If they were threatening a lawsuit, I knew they'd go through with it. They had money. We did not. They'd already almost buried us. I didn't want to give them another chance to dig that shovel down any further into our despair. I wasn't sure how much more we could take, so I was sitting in my car, in my parking spot behind the house, as I made the call.

The house was still empty and I was assuming it would be until everyone returned the next day, or tonight, but I still didn't want to chance being overheard.

"Honey! What a pleasant surprise."

God. I ached inside. She was so happy.

"Your father and I are just moving out to the patio with a cup of coffee. I know you're off, pursuing your dream, but I was just wishing you were here. A phone call is the best surprise yet."

Christ.

This was going to be hard.

I closed my eyes, readying myself. "I got a phone call from Stone."

She was quiet on her end.

I waited.

I heard my dad ask, "What'd she say?"

Still, she was quiet. Then, a soft, "Oh, honey. I didn't want you to have to deal with that."

My voice was low, gravelly, like Stone's had been. "He sent me the text you sent to Barb."

"Oh, dear."

That was so not what I wanted to hear.

"Oh, dear?" I repeated her words to her. "What were you thinking?"

"I thought since Stone is down there, and you're there, and I've heard so many stories about how close the two of you were—"

I couldn't. I just couldn't.

Her words were twisting around in my head, mixing with my own memories, and all of it was bad. All of it was tainted. I could feel my mom. I could feel when her hand went slack. I was back there instead, in the room when she died, and Gail was on the phone instead of her.

"Stop," I yelled, my voice hoarse. I was so raw, so fucking raw. "Just. Stop."

My mom.

She'd been there.

Then she was gone.

The chemo hadn't worked. The cancer progressed too fast.

I watched my mother die.

"Dusty, honey."

My dad's rough voice broke out, "Let me talk to her! I'll handle this."

"No!" Gail snapped back with a voice I had never heard before from her. She said harshly, "You'll make it worse." Then she was back, and quieter, soft again. "Honey. I'm sorry. I just thought he's down there. You're there. I've seen you both suffer so much, and his family owes us. His family owes you."

"No!" I couldn't stomach anymore. Gail came into the picture after my mom was buried. She heard the stories, and I was now realizing she'd been getting ideas that I did not want her to have. "Let me explain this." I was speaking in a voice I had never heard before myself. My skin had been turned inside out. There was nothing to hide behind now. I felt like everything was scraped off of me. That's what enduring that year had done to me. "You *really* need to hear me."

I waited. I needed a moment to gather myself.

I felt like I was crumbling.

"I hate Stone Reeves."

I heard her gasp on the other end.

I kept on, "I hate him with a passion I didn't even know I possessed, and I was already hating him long before what his father did to us. I moved down here *because* my mom told me to reach for my dreams. I moved down here *because* I went through something; well, something that taught me life is actually short and I need to be making decisions for me. And saying that, it was something that I hadn't already learned through losing my mother. But having said *that*, life is not short enough where I would ever want Stone Reeves back in it."

She was sniffling now.

I refused to. "Let it go. Let whatever notion you have in your head about how this is going to resolve itself because it's not going to happen."

"But—"

"He called me. He texted me. He said they'll sue if you don't stop. Gail, please. Don't put my father and me through more pain."

I was there again, holding my mom's hand.

"I can't survive another round with that family."

I felt her hand go, again. It was always again. Over and over again, and I worked so hard to push that memory away, but it was back.

It was going to haunt me.

"Please." A whisper from me.

I heard more sniffling on her end, and then a pause before she said, so quietly, "Okay."

I felt dead inside. "Tell my father I love him." Then I hung up and texted Stone.

Me: It's done.

I didn't give him a chance to respond. I blocked his number.

As far as I was concerned, Stone Reeves was out of my life for good.

CHAPTER 7

STUDYING with Siobhan and Trent was more about drinking beer and avoiding the television because it was set to the football game. And watching the two of them flirt without really flirting, but both totally knowing they were flirting.

It was fun to watch, but I was also cold to it.

I didn't like that I was like that, but I was. Romance. Sexual chemistry. Even the fun at the beginning, like what they're going through right now, I was turned off to it. There was a firm wall built in me, and Siobhan whispered at one point that Trent had a roommate and if I was interested, he'd invite him out for me. She asked and nothing. Stone cold—crap. Wrong phrase. Deadness inside.

That's what I was, but I knew that wasn't normal. I mean, it made sense to me why I was like that. The event I went through before coming here...yeah, my throat was swelling up. Emotions that I didn't want to deal with swept up at a startling rate and I felt my throat choking up.

I pushed it down. Another firm shove, just like with all the other uncomfortable and painful stuff.

Fine. I'd be this way. But I'd fake it. I'd have to. Give me a course in marine mammals and I'd be happy as a clam. Offer to set me up, and full on arctic blast inside of me. No one likes someone who is apathetic to the excitement going on in their lives, though. That's the problem. That wasn't a good way to make and keep friends, and I wanted Siobhan to be my friend. I almost needed it, desperately. If I didn't have one friend, then who was I and what was my purpose?

I'd have to travel back to the worry from before that there was something truly unfixable about me.

I gripped my glass just thinking about that, and glancing down, I thought belatedly that I needed to loosen my grip. My fingers were white. I was either going to shatter the glass, or I was going to break my fingers. One or the other.

Expelling a harsh breath, I forced myself to stop thinking. That's how I'd get through life right now. No thoughts about personal stuff. Just academia. Marine biology. I could recite the forty-four species of dolphins frontwards and backwards in my sleep, and I salivated over learning more. That was my goal. Eye on the prize. That's what I'd do, and clipping my head in a firm nod to myself, feeling all rallied from my own pep-talk, I crossed the bar back to where Trent and Siobhan were leaning with their heads angled toward the other.

Crap.

Maybe I should make my exit? I told her I would if she gave me the word, but we'd never discussed what the code word would be.

I tried to wordlessly ask Siobhan as I slid onto my stool, but she lifted her head up with a welcoming smile. And some relief. The lines around her mouth slackened at me coming back from getting a refill. Okay. I'd be staying a bit longer.

"It's picking up in here."

Trent was looking over my shoulder toward the door and the

rest of the bar. We were in a corner, but I noticed the expanding crowd as well on the way back. A surge of customers came in just as I was getting my beer.

Siobhan frowned. "Well, it is eight, and it's the campus bar. The game probably finished and everyone's making their way back into town."

Trent cursed, shoving up his glasses. He frowned. "You're right. I forgot the first official game was today."

Siobhan explained to me. "The other bar is the normal hangout when there's an off campus game, and now this one will be at full capacity. The team usually comes back after and sometimes they stop here before going wherever they go. Both places will be swamped the rest of the night." She was looking around. "I forgot. I mean, I knew, but I forgot." Her eyes lingered on Trent a moment, almost apologetic.

He looked, caught her, and both turned away quickly.

I would've been amused, or felt I should've been amused, if I wasn't thinking about how my house would probably be party central tonight. If the team was coming back, I knew my roommates would be, too.

"Let's get out of here!" My outburst surprised even me.

Both blinked at me a moment, then Trent started grabbing his stuff. "I second that. We can go to my house. No football game. We can study, or..." he paused, his gaze warming and holding on Siobhan, "just hang out."

Her eyes got wide. "Is your roommate there?"

Her quick glance my way told me what she was thinking and shit, damn, fuck. I didn't need that. I was so beyond needing that. Panic and claustrophobia and sheer terror rained down on me, and I had to stop. I had to breathe. I had to remain for a second, and then, another moment. It was still with me.

I was paralyzed, but I knew my face didn't show it.

I'd perfected that bit over the last year. *He* couldn't see me scared. I never gave him the satisfaction. I wouldn't give anyone the satisfaction, and then I wasn't there anymore. I was back at the Quail and I was in a college five states away.

I.

Could.

Be.

Just be.

The cement grip that overtook me loosened and I blinked. I was past it, and I was the only one not putting my stuff in my bag.

"You gonna drink that?" Siobhan referenced my drink.

Drink. Alcohol. Right. "Can I ride with you?"

"Yeah. Sure."

I downed my beer. All of it. A full sixteen-ounce glass.

Even Trent looked taken aback. A guy next to our table whistled, "Way to go! You open that throat, baby."

I reacted without a thought, snarling at him, "Shut the fuck up." And sweeping my stuff into my bag, I was off my stool and ready to go.

The guy's face was clouding with anger, but he'd been there the whole time we were. He'd been drinking and watching the football game, and I knew he was too slow to react. And I'd been paying attention to his entire table in the back of my mind because that's what someone like me does. We pay attention.

And once I got to my feet, I could see the words forming.

He started to reach out.

Nope. Not today.

I evaded him, but then he had my bag.

He wasn't thinking clearly, and to an extent, past haunts were clouding my own thoughts, so I didn't hesitate to twist out from my bag, then bring my elbow down hard on his arm. He dropped the bag. I caught it, and before he could react to that, I stomped down hard on his foot.

He howled, grabbing for it, but that brought his head to the table, and he cursed again.

His buddies were dumbfounded. Two started to get up, but I pointed at them and clipped out, "Not a move. He made an offensive remark. I replied. Then he grabbed me. I defended myself. You say one word, I'll call the cops and I have witnesses and video to back me up." I snapped my fingers, pointing to the corners of the ceiling. There were no video cameras there, but there were televisions, and the guys would be too confused to investigate.

Trent and Siobhan were almost gawking behind me. I didn't wait. I'd handled this scene stronger than I should've and I knew the quicker you got free, the better.

I got free.

Siobhan and Trent stared at me outside the bar, both with owl-like expressions. Eyes blinking. Mouth pursed tight.

I didn't like that I'd done that. I showed a side of myself I didn't like to expose.

Coming here, five states away, was to start new. Not remember the old me. Me reacting to that guy just now, that was the old me. And I really didn't want to get into why I had to be that way in the past. No way. No how. No, siree.

"That beer's going to hit me in about two minutes. Can I still ride with you?"

Siobhan jerked awake, startling forward. "Yeah. Uh. My car's over here."

"Sha, you know how to get to my place?"

She was crossing the parking lot but nodded. "I remember. Last Biofest, remember?"

Trent's face brightened. "Oh, yeah! I forgot. Yeah, okay. See you guys there. AJ's there. You can ring up. I might stop and grab a few things on the way."

I noticed the little grin on Siobhan's face as we got to her car and got inside. And because I knew a friend would say it, I teased, "He's getting a few things. Like condoms?"

"Shut up!"

But she was blushing and blushing hard.

Starting and reversing out of the parking spot, she moved around until we were following Trent out of the parking lot.

She waited until a stoplight before muttering, "Besides, I'm not that kind of girl."

"What kind? The kind who likes sex?"

Back to the blushing. She was full-on red sea star. "You know." She moved around in her seat, her cheek suddenly pulling in. "The kind who has sex on the first night."

"How long have you known Trent?"

"It's not the same thing."

I wasn't following. This I wasn't faking. I said it almost tenderly, "Having sex with someone you have feelings for, no matter how many hours you've spent together, isn't a bad thing."

She swallowed, shoving upright in her seat. Her hands tightened on the wheel. "It is if he thinks you're a slut after."

The question wasn't if she knew a guy who'd do that. Guys did that. It was a question if she thought Trent would do that.

"For what it's worth, I'm pretty certain, and by certain I mean I'm like 99.8% sure that Trent is completely into you." I nudged her arm, lightly. "I get the double standards, but if you like sex and you like Trent, then what's really stopping you? I've known relationships that start that way. And honestly, life's too short to worry about that stuff."

A gnawing and hollow ache was forming in my chest, rooting and digging deep in there. My words hitting a little close to home.

I continued, faint even to my own ears, "French angelfish love should be cherished. Indulge while you can still feel those emotions."

Yes, I was talking about myself.

Yes, I wish I could feel that again.

But yes, I believed in what I said.

You never knew when your time was up. Then what would you do? Die with regrets of not trying something? That'd be worse than dying having tried and been rejected. Who cared about rejection? That stuff was never remembered. But not living, that was remembered till someone's death bed.

"Live, Sha." I used his nickname on purpose. "Regret will eat you alive if you don't."

She was quiet, then burst out laughing. "Okay. Yeah. Where'd that philosophical side come from? And it's not for sure that French angelfish mate for life, you know."

I half grinned. "That's my side major. Deep thinker here. Didn't you know? And let's just go with the analogy, yeah?"

She thought I was half-joking.

I wasn't.

CHAPTER 8

SIOBHAN AND TRENT played footsie all night. Literally.

We went to his apartment. Those two started on the couch together, their feet touching, while we watched a movie. Then we moved to their kitchen table with some wine poured and a game of Sequence. They sat across from each other, but the sly looks, flushed faces, and hushed giggling mixed with the constant squirming on their seats told me if they didn't get it on that night, they were idiots. Or that I'd be in for a looong semester with them.

AJ wasn't anything like Trent. A dad-bod, more than a dad-bod with a cut-off tee that had 'Trees are old. Go digital.' and hair that was sticking up in an almost adorable way, he was my cosigner on how Trent and Siobhan were cute, but verging on the line of being annoying.

I caught him watching them, a slight grin, but a slight grimace at the same time. The two weren't hiding it anymore, and when I said my goodbyes after two games of Sequences, I was wondering if Siobhan was going to follow my advice and just live. Either way, I figured I'd get a call the next day or an earful on Monday in class.

I was looking forward to both.

Feeling good that I had a friend, at least *one*, my mood didn't diminish when I got to the house to find a full party going. The house was busy, literally every room except mine had light streaming from the windows. The backyard light was dimmed, but a group of ten or so was standing around the picnic table. I recognized Mia and heard Nicole laughing as I walked past them, heading to my door.

None of them looked at me.

Well, glancing over, I was wrong. Dent was eyeing me, but his arm was around Nicole's shoulders and she was half in his lap. One of her legs was thrown over his and her hand was splayed out on his chest. As I watched, his hand slid down around her back, cupping the other side of her hip so he was half-cradling her to him now and his head was bent down to hers.

I just kept going, but as I went down the stairs to my door and unlocked it, I couldn't help wondering if I'd acted too quickly the other night at the bar? If I should've stuck it out, sat with them longer? Nicole technically hadn't done anything to me. Just Mia and Lisa had been bitches, but Sav and Nicole hadn't.

Remembering my own advice, I figured what would it hurt? Be nice. Apologize for ditching. I mean, they could laugh at me and do exactly the reasons why I left in the first place, but it wasn't sitting well with me. Maybe invite them to meet for lunch on campus, or at the very least, a coffee somewhere. Even just sitting and having a coffee at the house together, except the problem is that I didn't feel comfortable venturing upstairs, and neither of them came down to the basement. I heard Lisa slam her door every now and then, always followed with her stampeding feet up the stairs as if she couldn't get away from being on the same floor as me fast enough. With her and Mia, I definitely hadn't acted too harsh or quick, but still, with Sav and Nicole another try was warranted.

Tomorrow. I'd do it tomorrow.

I was determined to tune out the yelling from the room next to me. They must've had a pool game going because I kept hearing 'Eight ball, motherfucker.' But, making sure my door was locked — I'd even went as far to add an extra chain lock on my door during the week — I turned my fan on full blast. It was a box fan, rivaling ones that could be in a barn (not really, but I liked to pride myself that I'd found a gem like that), but I was fooling myself, I was too jacked up to head to bed.

Opening my laptop, plugging in my headphones, I typed in Texas C&B job classifieds. I'd been putting off finding a job all week, but my bank account was dwindling every day and I'd skipped lunch today to use my money for beer at the Quail. Thank God they had a two dollar tap deal until eight.

Trent and AJ had brought out a charcuterie board of meat, cheese, crackers, and dip back at their place. There were other things on there, along with chips and salsa and yes, I ate to my heart's content. I knew I had enough money for a couple things of ramen the next day, so I was taking advantage of their excellent hosting skills.

My full belly greatly appreciated it, but yes. Back to the matter at hand.

I needed a job. I couldn't put it off anymore, so I was searching the classifieds.

There was a lab assistant job, but reading more on it, it looked like it was for a graduate student. No-can-do for me, then. At least, not yet.

I kept going.

A library aide. I'd done that job before, and while I loved books, I knew I'd hate it. I'd gotten a look at the staff in there this week, and they were a whole new level of stuck-up. Serious.

Sometimes you ran into that, where they looked down on people who read outside what was considered the greatest literary works of arts like *Pride and Prejudice* or *War and Peace*. Don't get me wrong, those books were amazing, but there were novels and even textbooks outside the 'literary masterpieces' that were equally as enjoyable, too.

But that wasn't a literary battle I wanted to take on, so I kept looking.

Kitchen attendants.

Janitorial staff.

A custodian position.

I wasn't sure the difference between the last two.

A babysitter/nanny job, but looking more into it...they wanted longer hours than I could promise. And I'd have to be available during my classroom times.

Tech support.

Tech assistant.

Tech internships.

Maybe I was picking the wrong major?

I kept on until between the experience needed and the hours they were asking for, either weekends or evenings, I was down to two positions. A barback or waitressing job at the Quail or I could work concessions at the sporting events.

I clicked on the applications because I'd have to try for both. If I got one of them, I'd be happy. If I got both, I'd be ecstatic. They said their hours were flexible, would 'work with student schedules', so I was hoping they weren't lying like on my room rental details, because as I was filling out the applications, I was completely lying. Yes, I did, in fact, have an iota of job experience. Which was true, somewhat. I'd volunteered for a few bake sales. And yes, the time I bagged for a very short term, like a week, at Stone's parents' store before we became enemies might've been a lot shorter than I was admitting.

It was for a college position. I had a feeling they wouldn't be too picky, or I was hoping.

With that task checked off my to-do list, after that, I got ready for bed. Hearing a couple thuds in the wall and loud voices, I opted for falling asleep with my headphones on and my music blasting.

Let's face it, at this rate I'd be deaf by the end of this semester.

"You worked at Reever's Market?"

The Quail moved fast, calling me the next day and scheduling a job interview. I was sitting in the empty bar, an hour before it was open and luckily right smack in the break between two of my classes. I had exactly forty minutes for my early lunch, but I used my meal plan to fill up on breakfast for the day so I could take this interview.

I was allowed one meal per day, which I was now kicking myself. I should be taking advantage of what I was paying for over the weekend, too. I'd forgotten that it was for seven days a week, not five.

Note to self: become one with the freshman.

The guy, he introduced himself as Joe, who had called and met me this morning was bald, with a round face, dimples in his cheeks, and a solid, athletic build. He was maybe five feet nine, but I was emphasizing the solid part. His biceps bulged as he held his notes in his hands as he moved them closer to the tabletop.

"Yes."

Had they called and checked up on me? I listed the manager as my reference, but I knew that manager wasn't working there anymore. She'd liked me, said I was a good bagger for the week I'd been there.

Hell. Would she even remember me?

I took the job when I was first starting my teenage work career, and my hours had been low because it was during the time period where it was before you could legally even work. But once I hit sixteen, I got a full-time job at the local nursing home. My skills at turning down beds and collecting laundry had come in handy when my mom had her stint in the hospice facility years later.

"You know that's the same place that Stone Reeves' parents own, right?"

Understanding flooded me.

He was almost glaring at me, and I got it then. He thought I was lying, that I put that on purpose. If only he'd known it was the other way around.

I sat up straighter, feeling my entire back and neck muscles tighten. "I wasn't aware you knew that."

"He's a football god here in town. I'm a dude. I'm an athlete, too. You think I wouldn't know that?" His eyes turned cold and he put his notes down. "Are you lying on the application to get this job?"

I sucked in my breath. The preposterousness of that whole statement.

Lying? Me? Maybe over-exaggerated, but full-out lying... Okay. I did. Well. I bent the truth, a lot. But I had enough truth on my side to murmur and not feel bad about it, "To be honest, I was hoping you wouldn't know they're the owners."

His eyes got dark, then I saw the hope starting to light up.

"I see what you're thinking, and I have to stop you before you even get started."

His eyes went flat and his mouth turned down.

"I never met Stone. I know *of* him, how could you not going to our school together? But he was always in football camps and he was a different year than me." I was hoping he wouldn't do the math. Stone got drafted by Texas as soon as he could, which was a year ago. And if this guy was decent with numbers, he'd connect that I was younger than Stone. It wasn't hard, but I hadn't put that I was a transfer junior on the application. I pushed on, "And I don't really know his parents. I gave you the number for my manager. She's the one I worked with the most. She'd remember me. Stone—" Shit! I caught myself. "Mr. and Mrs. Reeves wouldn't even remember me, but I did work there."

He stared at me, long and hard.

I didn't move. I was afraid if I did, he'd either not buy my story or call my bluff. I didn't want to deal with the fallout of that, but after another thirty seconds of both of us sitting frozen in place, he nodded and looked back down to his notes.

"Okay. I got ya."

I exhaled so sharply that I had to quickly suck it right back in. Gah! What would he think then? It'd be obvious I was holding my breath.

He looked back up and I coughed, smoothing a hand over my hair. I was fine here. Nothing to see.

His eyes passed over me, and I was glad to report he'd lost all interest. His tone was even monotone now, "Tell me more about your job experience. Starting with your most current job."

Well, that was easy. If it was ever a question if I was a good worker or not, I always aced it. Just had to get in the door first, compliments of my over-exaggeration skillz.

CHAPTER 9

"YOU DON'T KNOW WHAT YOU'RE TALKING ABOUT!"

The screaming jerked me upright. I'd been awake, lying in bed and reading about population dynamics of Asteroidea. Eavesdropping was bad. So was gossip. Overhearing roommate drama, bad move. I was going anyway. Easing my door open, the basement was dark. Lisa's door was closed, though that didn't tell me if she was in the house or not. She was still avoiding me like the plague, but I moved through the game room, closer to the stairs.

"Wyatt! OMG! Don't!"

It was Mia screaming.

"What is going on?!"

That was Nicole, so she was home, and she was annoyed.

"Nothing. It's nothing!" Feet stomped over my head, they were coming close to the kitchen doorway.

The basement door must've been left open, or I wouldn't be able to hear so well. Lisa must've been up there because no one else would come down here.

"Hey! What the hell."

"It's nothing." A more calmer Wyatt, but he was restraining himself.

I could almost imagine him gritting his teeth.

"It's not nothing!"

And I could imagine Mia tossing her hair, throwing her hand to her hip.

"My God. Calm down. You guys were fine a minute ago."

"That was before he—" Silence. I didn't know what she was doing, but I could hear her huffing. "—started lecturing me on reaching out to Char, but he doesn't know what he's talking about. Guys are different. There's no beef. They all fight and get over it—"

"Not completely," a low mutter from Wyatt, but still calm. I was giving him props for that. "We compartmentalize more. Will I probably need to see this dude again in the future? If yes, get over it. If no, then throw a punch. Or throw a punch no matter the answer. Sometimes that's just more fun, but you never know. Some guys lately are weasels—"

"Wyatt!"

"Right. You don't care about what I'm saying." He sighed, now I heard his irritation. "What a surprise. Nothing new there."

"What does that mean?"

And judging by how snippy her tone turned, I could imagine her crossing her arms over her chest. Maybe a defiant tilt of her chin to complete the look?

"Mia." He was trying to smooth things over, but I heard the creak of a foot above. He was going toward her. His voice was calm, almost too calm. I couldn't have remained calm like him in that situation. "You are hurt by your friend. Char left you, she left everyone, and all I'm saying—"

"What?! That I'm being a bitch?!"

"Christ's sake." He snapped back, "You ARE!"

I heard an audible gasp. Mia's? Nicole's? It was the name game.

"Wyatt. Dude. Maybe—"

"No! She's being a bitch, and instead of picking up the fucking phone and chewing out the friend she should be chewing out, I've had to listen to her all fucking week talk shit about someone she doesn't even know."

A sick laugh from Mia. "Yeah. Right. I don't need to know the reject roommate to know a few things about her. She's—"

My heart sank. She was talking about me. This whole thing was about me. What the hell?

"YOU DON'T KNOW HER!"

My heart picked back up at Wyatt's roar.

He kept on, "You don't know her! You have no idea if she's nice or mean or poor or anything. You have no clue, except it's obvious she's quiet because you never know if she's here and she's fucking desperate. Why the hell would someone stay in the situation with you and Lisa actively hating her unless she had nowhere else to go." A pause. "And she's not heard eighty percent of the bullshit you've been spewing about her."

"WHY IS THIS YOUR PROBLEM?!"

"BECAUSE I DON'T WANT A HATEFUL FUCKING MEAN GIRLFRIEND!"

Wyatt's stock just skyrocketed to me. I wouldn't have believed it if I hadn't heard him. But hearing Mia had remained on the Hate New Roommate Train wasn't a surprise to me. Just confirmed everything I'd been feeling, and to think I almost considered trying again with them.

"She ditched Nicole and the group," Mia was still trying, but she was losing some of her momentum. "What kind of person does that? I mean, that's so mean and rude and disrespectful. Nicole didn't have to invite her at all in the first place."

"Yeah. You know, it was kind of shitty what she did, but put yourself in her shoes. She told Savannah she had driven across the nation to come here. She told Savannah she didn't know anyone else in town. You are a bitch to her within two seconds of stepping inside this new place. You're surrounded by all your friends. She's alone. She was set up by Char, too, and yeah, that was an insanely bitchy move on Char's part, but it's Char. Then, what I hear is that Lisa was a bitch to her. Sorry, but I'd probably ditch, too, because you never know when the tide is going to turn."

Silence. Total and complete silence.

Then, a hiccupping sob. "I'm not a mean person."

"No, you're not, but you're acting like one."

"Wyatt," a soft gasp. I don't know from who.

"Look, you can hate the girl all you want, but at least make it be for a good reason. You're hurt and mad at Char. Take it out on Char! That's the kind of girlfriend I fell in love with, someone who had a problem and took it up with that problem. You can't take it up with this girl because you know it's not really about her. And you're scared to deal with Char. I don't get why because you know that Char's gonna wake up and come back crawling and begging to be let back into this house, so you actually have the upper-hand with your old bestie."

I was firmly team Wyatt here.

"If you want to rip into the new girl, fine. I'm with you, but make sure it's because she's done something that deserves it."

My team allegiance was slipping.

Then the doorbell rang. Followed by a fist pounding against it.

"What the—"

Someone gasped again.

And then I heard my worst nightmare happening in real life, in real time, and I was frozen to stop it.

"Is Dusty here?"

Low. Angry. Irritated. Frustrated. A hint of savage impatience, too, and then as I swooned, but not in a good way, the fainting way because this was not happening. No way because I couldn't deal if it was—and then Wyatt went, "DUDE! You're Stone Reeves!"

There was a moment here.

It was the beginning of the storm. The air is thick, heavy. Hair sticking to the back of your neck. Your hands are oddly clammy. Your pulse is racing. You know a train is coming your way. You know you're on the tracks. You know you should jump off, but you can't. You're frozen because it's not just a flight or fight response. There's the whole freezing response, and as your heart picks up in force, in speed, in sound, you know you're about to get pummeled.

Yeah. Because that's what was about to happen.

Then a door slammed upstairs and I heard a gasp, "Stone Reeves is here?"

Another pounding of feet.

Shit. They were coming from everywhere.

"Oh my God."

That was Nicole. I recognized her voice just as I heard a growl rip from Stone.

"Hi. Yeah. I really need to talk to Dusty first, and then I can come back and chill for a while."

"Chill. He said chill." That was Wyatt. I could almost hear the face-splitting smile through those words.

A giggle. That was Mia.

She'd been screaming seconds ago, beside herself with anger, and now she was giggling.

I wanted to vomit.

The door in front of me opened and Lisa came out, her hair in a mess and her eyes soft from sleeping. Her face looked a little puffy. She stopped in the doorway, seeing me, and for a split second, we weren't enemies.

She frowned, hearing the chaos above. "What's happening?"

Um.

I said the first thing I thought, "Fire!"

And with that, I could move. The paralysis broke from me, and as Lisa yelled and rushed upstairs, I turned and sprinted for my room.

Thank God I hadn't changed into pajamas yet. It was nearing eight that night, so with my heart trying to pummel its way out of my chest, I grabbed everything I thought I'd need. I had no plan, other than maybe sleeping in my car, but I was running. As far away as I could.

He sounded furious.

Yeah.

Running was the best course of action and the only thing that could save me right now. I was embracing my inner sailfish.

CHAPTER 10

PURSE. Books for tomorrow. Phone. Keys. I checked—I had a bra on. I toed on my sandals, and I threw my arm through my backpack, pulling it on without stopping, and I was out the back door. Wait. Backtrack—I grabbed my toothbrush and paste from the bathroom, then I was running up the stairs.

Out the door.

"*Fuck* no, you don't!"

A cement arm grabbed me around the waist, and just like we were kids, Stone had me up in the air.

"No!"

Everything was turned upside down. Me included.

My purse was open and all my stuff fell to the ground. My backpack went down, hitting my head, then falling off my arm and thudding next to my purse. My phone fell out of my pocket. My keys rained down from my hands because I was trying to grab onto Stone's shoulders so I didn't land on my head, too, even though I knew he was more than capable of lifting me over his head.

But I was kicking and out of control, and I swung, hitting something.

He grunted, ducking, then putting me on my feet. "Jesus. I forgot how solid you are."

Solid.

My ass, I was solid.

Red in the face, hair literally everywhere, I shoved him back from me. "Get off me!"

"I'm off! Fuck's sake. Chill the fuck out."

He held his hands up, taking a step back, and then it was time to assess.

I was refusing to look at him. I knew how Stone looked. His face and physique was on the television on any given sports channel almost every day, or on the Internet, or people were talking about him on the radio. The team was local. I knew when I applied here that I'd have to deal with going into Stone-Land, but I hadn't realized it would be this bad.

So, no.

I did not need to know how he looked like a walking, well-cut ad for the Marines. He was a professional athlete. He and his teammates could walk and nuns would swoon. No joke. I heard one once, and that'd been when he was in college and I'd been visiting my mom in Hospice before she was sent home to die.

The memory was like a bucket of cold water.

I was drenched with reality, and fuck that. I looked up, seeing him still taking me in, a look in his eye I didn't want to identify, a hand at his jaw, and I snarled. "What are you doing here?"

Shit.

Now I was looking right at him, and I hadn't been prepared.

He was gorgeous, with his ripped, lean body, and his crew cut, and those hazel eyes that were darkening, taking me in. Even his face had morphed into an athletic machine. I didn't know that was possible, but his cheekbones were wide and slanting upwards. His jawline was so pronounced, ending in a strong square and fuuuuuuck, he was hawt.

Holy crapshitastic, he was hot.

I blinked a few times, needing to get myself together.

He had picked me up like I was nothing, and then told me I was solid, but I knew in Stone's world, that meant I was strong. Because I wasn't solid in the other way, but my body was freakishly strong. It was from my grandpa's genes. The women, though they might've looked tiny and weighed nothing, were almost as strong as the men. It came in handy if I needed something moved, because as long as I didn't twist my back, I could move almost anything. Might take some finagling and me being smart, but I rarely needed to ask for help.

It was a skill I prided myself on. Didn't need a man.

"Fuck, Dust." He grunted, shifting back.

At that, another bucket of water was tossed in my face.

I remembered where we were and looking around, I saw my roommates standing at the front of the house. Thankfully, they hadn't moved down the alley to where we were, giving us a modicum of privacy, but I was livid. Word was out. Secret was blown. They all fucking knew now, and I'd have to deal with damage control after this. The fallout was going to be freaking epic.

Horrified, feeling a sob working its way up my throat, I clamped that shit down and dropped to my knees.

I was grabbing blindly, just seeing red. The edges of my eyesight were blurring. I could only see what was literally in front of me, and so I focused there. Forcing deep breaths out through my nose, because if I opened my mouth, I'd either start crying or I'd start shouting.

Keys. Check.

Phone. Check.

What next?

My toothbrush was on the ground. That'd have to be tossed. More money coming out of my account.

What else? What else? What else?

I was slightly hysterical. I grabbed a textbook at the same time I felt Stone kneeling beside me. He began grabbing my things, too.

I lost it. I snapped.

"NO!" I shoved him backwards, pushing him off his feet.

His eyes widened, shock infiltrating his own anger. "I was trying to help!"

"I don't need your help!" I was on my feet.

People might think I was overreacting, but I wasn't. I really and truly wasn't. He had no idea what I went through because I knew him, because the wrong person found out I knew him. I was here because of that sick and twisted someone.

"Get gone, Stone! I don't want you here."

He stopped, taking me in, and a soft, "Shit," left him. He let out a sigh. "Dust."

"Don't! Don't 'Dust' me. I swear to God, don't."

He wasn't leaving.

I waited, but he wasn't going.

"LEAVE!"

He took a step back, flinching. But stopped. He looked torn, his hand going back to that strong jaw that could cut metal. "Dusty, I—"

"What do you want?" I flung my arms out wide. "I talked to Gail. I told her to stop whatever she was doing and thinking. She got the message. It's done. Your family. My family. We'll cease to exist to each other. I blocked your number because I never want to hear from you or see you ever again. Yet, here you are. Leave *me* alone. Please!"

And then, with words so soft that I'd never forget them, his face shuddered as he said, "Your parents were in an accident."

I—

I—

No.

No.

I hadn't heard him right.

A strangled laugh from me. "What?" That wasn't right. I'd just talked to Gail a few days ago.

I had told her—God. I had gotten upset with her. I'd been more heated than I should've been, and Dad—Dad.

"What?"

I was shaking my head. That wasn't right.

I must have heard him wrong.

He wasn't looking at me like my old best friend. This was all totally wrong.

Right?

"Dust." This one was even softer, filled with regret. And those eyes of his. The hostility was gone. Sympathy and something else? Mourning. NO! Who did he get to mourn?

But...

No. No. Just no.

"They're fine, right?"

They just couldn't call. I hadn't given my new number to anyone else but them. Stone had it, ironically. That's why he was here.

"What hospital?"

He still wasn't saying anything.

Whatever. I'd find out myself.

I went back to grabbing everything from my purse. I'd need all of that. And my emergency fund. I'd use that to fly back. I'd drop out of school. I'd have to. Then again, maybe they weren't that bad. Maybe they weren't even in a hospital.

I'd just have to call them.

Grabbing my phone, I tried Gail's number first.

"Dust." Stone stepped toward me.

I backed away.

"No, no. I'll just..." She wasn't picking up.

"Dusty."

Okay. "Her phone was damaged. Is that what happened?" Okay. I'd try my dad's cell, but he rarely used it. He hated the thing. He used Gail's.

I pulled him up, hitting the call button.

It rang.

And rang.

"Dusty, stop." Stone's hand covered mine. He took the phone away from me, and then ended the call.

He had the update. That's why he was here. I couldn't avoid this anymore.

So I stopped and I stared at him, but I did not cry.

I would not cry.

Not in front of him, or in front of my housemates. In front of no one.

"Just tell me, Stone."

He closed his eyes again, then opened them and I saw the tormented look flash there. It didn't leave. It stayed and it just made this all that much worse.

"They were driving to see your stepbrother's football game. Three deer were in the road. Right by Sidewinder Curve, you know the place."

Oh God.

My chest was hurting, like really badly hurting.

I felt something squeezing in there, not letting go.

That curve was aptly named.

"Three deer?" I whispered.

He nodded. "I'm really sorry. One deer would've been a smashed-up car. But three—"

I winced as if he'd hit me. Three. I knew the damage three

could do. It was rare, but not unheard of where we lived. Deer were everywhere.

"Their car rolled. Gail went through the front window. Your dad—"

I had to know.

I gutted out, "Say it."

"Your dad was pinned under the truck. The steering wheel cut into him, and he died just as the ambulance got there. Gail died on impact."

I...

...couldn't...

...

"No." I slid down to my knees, right in the middle of all my things.

A part of my brain, the rational part, was watching from outside of me. It was telling me to get it together, go somewhere private, stop being entertainment for these people. But that part wasn't controlling me right now. It wasn't the irrational part either. Or the feelings part. It was a part I wasn't entirely familiar with, a part that I'd only come to know one other time, so the tinge of familiarity wasn't as strong.

There's a pocket in your mind where you go when you feel unsafe, where you can't handle whatever is happening in real life, and you lock yourself in there because you feel protected. Self-preservation.

I was there, but I wasn't completely there.

And I couldn't quite grasp what Stone was telling me. Not completely, but I asked, "Jared?"

"Your stepbrother is with friends. He has a best friend, Apollo?"

That was good. That was the best place for him. Apollo was like family to Jared.

"I know you don't have any relatives in the area."

He was kneeling by me, talking so gently to me, this was so not Stone.

"I need to know what you want me to do to help. I want to help."

"Why?" A flash of anger burst in me. White. Hot. Seething. "Why are you still here? You delivered the message. Now go."

His face closed off, but he didn't stand up. He didn't back away. He didn't leave.

"GO!"

He stood now. A hand went to his jaw. "Dust—"

"I'm not Dust to you. That died a long time ago. My mom died, Stone! Your father fired mine so he didn't have to pay the medical insurance and my mother died so your dad could keep more money in his pockets."

He was backing away now. Flinching as I kept going.

"Then he blacklisted him, hoping we'd move out of town. He tried to run us out of town! In my senior year. But we stayed. They stayed. Because of me. I wasn't 'Dust' then. I haven't been 'Dust' since you were in sixth grade. Remember the last time I was 'Dust' to you? We watched a movie at the drive-in, shared a blanket, popcorn, and a soda, and then the next day you walked past me on the bike trail with Gibbons, Mark, Tony, and right then I was nothing to you. Remember? I do. You were laughing about Megan Parturges. You looked. Saw me. And then said, 'Yeah, I'd fuck Parturges,' and you kept walking by as if I were a stranger. That's when this," I pointed between him and me, "died. It died. And you gave me the message, now fucking leave me alone."

"Dust...y." His entire face shuddered. "Let me help you. I can fly you back."

"Get AWAY FROM ME!"

I hated him.

I loathed him.

His entire family.

His fame.

The power of his fame, how it could get inside a person and bring out their rotten insides. I especially hated that part of him.

I wanted him gone.

I wanted everyone gone, but he wasn't going. They weren't going.

I could see them back there, still watching, but I wasn't looking. They were nothing to me, too.

Okay. So fine. No one was leaving, I would.

I came out of that protected part of my brain, moving into the irrational side that was now merging with my rational side, and I just felt pain. Gut-wrenching pain, but then—a blessed relief—numbness. I couldn't handle what was happening and I was going numb. It was traveling up from my feet, so quickly, until it rose, blanketing over my mind, and silence.

Inside of me, total stillness.

Finally, I could move again. Finally, I could breathe again. Finally, I could function again.

I knelt and finished grabbing everything that had fallen. Piece by piece, I put it back in my purse. My backpack. It was as if Stone wasn't there. As if no one was there. As if he hadn't just told me how my life as I knew it had ended that day. It was as if none of those events happened, and standing, I just turned and went to my car.

"Dusty." Stone came after me.

I ignored him.

Walking out of the fence, going to my car, I glanced up at him as I unlocked my car.

A stranger. That's what he was to me now. And he saw it, too, because he reared back on his feet, a curse falling swiftly from his lips.

Then I got in my car, started it, and backed up, all the while staring at a stranger.

I kept backing up, and then I heard a shout before I felt the impact, followed by metal crunching, glass shattering, screams, and then blessed, blessed darkness.

Peace.

CHAPTER 11

THE BEEPING WOKE ME UP.

Then the pain really woke me up.

I jolted, immediately screamed from the pain, but it was muffled and I realized I had something gagging me.

Reaching up, breaking off whatever was holding my arm in place, I reached for whatever was in my throat and I started to pull it out.

Up. Up.

Then—out, and I was gagging. My body pitched forward. I was going to puke, but no, I was going to pass out. And then, air. My lungs drew it in, and I couldn't see past the tears in my eyes.

"What—oh my God!" I heard the squeak of shoes coming toward me, then a harsh exclamation. Panic in her voice. She rushed to me and I felt hands going to whatever I was still holding in my hand. "Oh no, no, no. You need this!"

I didn't. She didn't know that, though. I was shaking my head, trying to tell her I didn't want that, but then I heard someone come running and a, "Holy—get off her. Get off her."

That someone shoved between me and the nurse.

It was a him.

He was helping me. "She's good. She's good. Look at her."

"Mr. Reeves."

It was Stone.

I froze, but I think I knew it had been him. I'd never be able to not recognize his voice, no matter how much pain I was in.

"Oh no." From the nurse.

"What?!" A savage growl from Stone.

"She didn't get—oh no." She rushed away.

Stone went after her. "She didn't what?"

The nurse came back, a doctor behind her, and I still couldn't see. I could see shapes, but everything was blurred and it was the damn tears. I hated crying. I had to stop. Suck it up. Move forward. And feeling the impending doom that was about to crash over me, I did just that.

I went still.

I pushed past the pain, icing it all down, welcoming that same numbness from before again.

And then, as it all moved up, rising, covering me, I stopped crying.

I stopped feeling.

I grabbed whatever I was wearing and used it to wipe my tears clear, and then, I saw Stone's back. He was turned toward me, his hips half angled to me, but he was twisted around, paying attention to the doctor and nurse, who I saw were looking over my chart.

The nurse pointed.

The doctor nodded. "Change it out now, especially if she's awake." With that, his eyes jerked to mine, went back to the chart. Then. He stopped. He backtracked and his eyes widened in horror. I saw it for a split second before he masked it. The professional coming forth, and he cleared his throat, standing upright, his hands folded over his chest. "Miss Phillips. You're awake."

Stone whipped back around to me.

I didn't look at him. I didn't want to see what was there because my memory was coming back, and I knew what news I'd still have to deal with, but not yet. Not yet. Not until I could walk out of here.

"I know you're probably in a lot of pain, but we'll get you handled and taken care of real quick."

He looked at the nurse who was stringing something up, and she reached for a tube going into my arm, switching it out.

No, no, no. I knew what that was, and I started shaking my head, but my God. It hurt so bad. Everything hurt.

"No!"

Stone looked at me, his hand grasping the nurse's in the next flash.

She froze from his quickness.

I did, too, but then I said with my lips hurting and my mouth feeling just weird. "No morphine."

The nurse's eyes enlarged. "But you must be in so much pain."

"No." It hurt to talk. "Morphine."

"But—"

Stone let out a roar. "She said no fucking morphine. No fucking morphine." Then, casting me an apologetic look, he quieted his voice, "She doesn't usually drink or do drugs. She hates not feeling clearheaded."

I did.

I gave him a questioning look because I didn't think anyone knew that about me. I never drank or partied in school, or got high, and living where we did, so many went that route out of boredom. It was either that or trying to half kill yourself doing stupid stunts like Peter Mills who climbed the top of a crane to hide a flag for flag football and fell.

He didn't survive.

People did stupid things where we grew up, and I had, too, with Stone when we were kids, but that all stopped.

"Sandy." From the doctor. He seemed resigned. "If that's Miss Phillips' wish, then we need to adhere to it."

She let go of the tubing and took the new morphine bag with its stand and wheeled it out of the room as the doctor came forward. A grave look in his eyes, and I knew what that was about. I was trying not to flinch, trying not to feel, but the pain was slipping in through the numb shell I pulled over me. Still. I'd deal.

I'd have to.

"Miss Phillips, do you remember what happened to you?"

I couldn't speak, but my eyes went to Stone, and with a heaviness in his, he answered for me. "She remembers." He told me, "You backed up and a moving truck hit you. Your car was totaled. The truck just had scrapes. I've taken care of that, though."

My car.

"Your head hit your dashboard pretty hard, and we had to put you in a medically induced coma. We needed to gauge your injuries and determine if there'd be swelling on your brain. When the results came back with positive findings this morning, we decided to bring you out of the coma. And now that you're awake, I need to conduct a few more exams. Are you up for that?"

No.

I nodded, just the slightest movement.

"You'll be able to speak again by tomorrow. We needed to intubate you for the coma, just in case. Other than the hard hit to your head, you came out of the accident without any big injuries. No broken bones, but your body is still healing from the trauma. You will be in pain for a few days."

Checking my pupils. My vitals. The doctor left, saying he'd return to discuss departure plans with me about going home from the hospital. He glanced in Stone's direction as he added, "You will need to go somewhere that you can be cared for. One more person will need to be there, and we can't allow you to drive yourself home."

Stone cleared his throat, looking up from where he'd been standing, his arms folded over his chest. "She'll stay with me. I'll drive her there."

I opened my mouth to argue, but no sound came out as Stone sent me a withering look. "All your shit's already been moved."

Well. That shut me up.

"There you go. Problem solved." The doctor touched my foot, a reassuring smile on his face. "Rest, Dusty. Your body needs to heal. One day at a time right now."

He gave Stone a nod before leaving, pulling the door shut behind him.

Then it was just me and Stone, and his hands went up to his head. He let out a sharp breath. "Fucking hell!" Bending over, touching his elbows to his knees, he swiftly jerked back up, his hands falling, and a stark look was there.

Anger. Frustration. Pity. A whole mix of other things, but he was shaking his head. "Jesus Christ, Dusty. You know how the last few days have been?"

Anger sliced through my chest, and since I couldn't speak, I mouthed at him, "Fuck. Off."

He read it, and then his lip twitched before a full laugh left him. "Shit. There you are. Still fucking fighting while you're literally bed-ridden. I have no clue why I've stayed away." His tone turned mocking, a hardness lining his words, and I felt slapped by his words, but also comforted because that felt like familiar ground for us.

He groaned, slumping into the chair on the other side of my

bed. "Okay. You have two options. I can tell you everything that's happened because you've been in your coma for four days. Or we can wait until you can talk and ream me out and I can tell you then. Which option do you want because the outcome will be the same?" His eyes latched onto mine, still so hard and half glaring.

Dickhead.

I lifted my middle finger for number one.

"The first option?" He grinned at my finger.

I nodded, just the slightest bit.

With his hands going into his hoodie's front pocket, he pulled it low. "Since you are unable to travel by vehicle, train, or plane, a funeral was put together for your parents. Gail's sister traveled from New York to help facilitate everything, and Jared was asked what he'd like to do. If he wanted to remain at his best friend's house, go to New York with his aunt, or come down here to be with you."

Pain. Excruciating. Dizzying. Blinding pain punctured me as he kept on. Every word he said was another knife being thrust into me, but I had to hear everything. I had to know everything.

"Since Apollo's parents are open to fostering Jared the rest of his senior year, he opted to stay with them."

A tear fell, slipping down my cheek.

It was how it should be. Jared spent more time there than at his own home, more time spent with his best friend to even get to know me. Not that I'd really been around. I'd been in school except for a few months when Gail and my father had started dating.

"I notified your parents' lawyer and he's traveling down here to go over your father's will with you. Jared's six months from being eighteen. Apollo's parents are open to the idea of adopting him, if you and your aunt are okay with that. Technically, I believe the aunt has the option first. She agreed to the adoption, and so that goes to you, if you're okay with them starting the process."

I moved my head in a nod, more than I should've. A primal and head-splitting pain ripped through me, but I made no sound. I let no more tears fall. I swallowed and dealt with it. I knew Apollo's parents, Bud and Georgia. They were a happy couple, and Apollo with his little sister were both blossoming. Good kids, from good parents. A good family. Jared would be lucky to be taken in by them permanently.

"Okay." Stone took in another deep breath, his hand coming out of his hoodie pocket and smoothing down his leg. "I'll let them know, and Jared's social worker will reach out. She might need to talk to you, or meet you somehow. There are papers to sign, too."

Of course.

I couldn't voice my question, so I motioned toward where his phone was on the nightstand.

He frowned. "You can't talk at all."

I made a writing gesture with my hand.

"Oh!"

He grabbed his phone, pulling up a notepad app, and handed it to me.

I typed out, "Where are they buried?" And handed it to him.

"By your mom."

Relief tamped down some of the pain. It was a little more manageable.

I reached for his phone again, then typed, "Costs?"

He took his phone back, blacking the screen, and put his phone in his pocket. He looked away and sat back in his chair.

He wasn't going to answer.

I hit my hand on my bed rail, a wince leaving me because it was too unbearable, but I had to know.

He swung those stormy eyes back my way, hot and angry.

"What? What do you want me to say? You're going to freak the fuck out when I answer you, but I don't even care." He shot forward, scooting to the edge of his seat. "I don't give a fuck. You want to know about the costs? There are none. Wanna know why?" His chest was rising up and down, his eyes almost going wild. "Because I fucking paid for everything. Hospital, too. No. Not my parents. No, not your aunt. And goddammit, no way in hell, not you. Because after you lit all that shit up for me about what happened, I did my own digging and found out what my father did to yours. And I'm sorry, okay?!" He was almost shouting.

A nurse came to the door, peeking in, worried.

He shoved back in the chair, sending it scraping against the floor a few inches. "I paid for goddamn everything, and you don't get to sit there and hate me because of it. Not another thing on the list. You want to pay me back? Because I know you probably will keep a fucking tally till the day you end up in an old folks' home, fine. You can pay me back. I'll set it up with my lawyer, but you don't have to pay me back. I know you hate me. Fine. Dandy. Whatever the fuck. I'm not the biggest fan of yours either, but it's done. So now you do your thing and heal. Get better, then we'll deal with everything else."

I...had nothing.

No words.

No emotions, angry or sad, or even relieved.

I was just empty and after hearing all of that, I closed my eyes and lay there. Stone remained, and for the next hour until I fell asleep, we sat together in silence.

CHAPTER 12

"NO."

"Fuck's sake. Why not?"

Same dance. Different day.

It was the day I was being released from the hospital. They kept me another day, just to be safe, but I got the clear bill of health, and now here we were. On the front steps of the hospital. A crowd was starting to gather, more than a few recognized Stone, and based on conversations I'd overheard with the nurses, word had been building that he was a frequent visitor. The nurses wanted to know who I was, and the nurses who worked with me directly bit their tongue because they knew I wasn't a fan. In fact, more than a few times when Stone tried to help me, and I snapped at him to give me space, a nurse had to leave the room.

I got it. I did.

They thought I was being ungrateful and rude and I'm sure they had worse names to call me behind my back. Whatever. That was my attitude.

Whatever to them.

Fuck 'em.

They didn't have the history I did with Stone's family, and yeah, an argument could've been made that it hadn't been Stone who fired my dad, who blacklisted him, who tried to push him out of town when we were starting chemotherapy. That'd been his dad, but there'd been six years prior to that where Stone had been cold to me growing up, where I hadn't been 'good enough' for him, and I sat and watched my former best friend become this entirely new person.

Arrogant. Wealthy. Privileged.

A jackass.

And no one knew what I'd had to endure to put me in this position where I decided to pursue a dream I never thought I could go after, and now here we were. Again.

I was sans my dad. There were no more annoying texts or calls from Gail, and I was three seconds from losing it.

"I don't need you to take care of me."

We were standing outside the opened back door of his truck. I was able to stand from my wheelchair, because that was their policy, but I needed to be driven home by someone. The nurse left. I was free and clear to grab a taxi, and I was trying to do that when Stone started in.

"You're the most stubborn bitch I have ever dealt with."

I ignored him, my hand in the air. There was a taxi two cars down. Stone just needed to move his vehicle and the cab would have a clear path to me.

Stone saw my dilemma, too. "I'm not fucking moving. Get in my truck."

"No."

A few guys waiting to grab Stone's autograph heard the exchange, and a couple of them chuckled. One cheered Stone on. A passing lady cheered me on, saying, "You tell him, Missy. We don't need no men." And still there were a few other women who

I knew thought I'd completely lost my head. I heard one whispering, "I'll take her spot." Her friend laughed back. "Me, too. I'm feeling faint right now and I'll gladly get into his truck to recuperate."

Stone   growled,   ignoring   our   growing   audience. "Dusty. Now."

I just raised my hand higher for the taxi driver, pushing up on my tiptoes.

"Do not think I won't pick you up and throw you in my truck, head first and everything. I'm two seconds away."

I stopped and stared at him.

Shit. He meant business. He was glaring at me with eyes that said, "Do not fucking fuck with me, you fucking twit."

Well. Then.

I sighed. I'll try reasoning instead. "You're going to drive me to your house, and then I'll pack whatever I need and call a cab to take me all the way back to where I'm paying rent. It's not worth it. Just let me grab a cab now."

A savage curse bit out, and then his eyes flashed.

His singular warning had been when he told me he was two seconds away. In a flash, he grabbed me, and I was airborne, right into the back of his truck. But he wasn't done. He leapt up, grabbing the seatbelt over me, and pulled it around me, clicking it in place. He had the door shut, locked, and he was already going around the front before I could even push myself upright and then start to reach for my seatbelt.

By then, he was inside, the engine on, and he shoved off into traffic.

"This is stupid."

"You're right. You're being stupid." Cursing, he ducked down as a car sped past us. They knew he was driving because they came up on his driver's side, their phones up and ready to go. It was a car full of teenage girls. "Dammit."

"Where do you live?"

He opened his mouth, then caught himself. His eyes narrowed in the rearview mirror. "Why?"

I just smiled. "No reason."

He continued to study me in between still watching the road, and with a soft growl, he shook his head. "I'm not buying it. What? You're going to tell those girls who are trying to get a picture of me?"

"What's the difference? I'll know when you take me to your house. What's stopping me from posting it on Twitter, or even posting your phone number?"

A litany of curses spewed from him, and the back of his neck was getting red. I was having a heyday with this. It was more fun than I could remember having in a long time.

Until he announced it, "I liked your mom."

"What?"

"Your mom." He moved into the far lane, settling back.

I was thinking we had a bit of drive from here, and he settled an arm back on the passenger seat headrest.

"I always liked her. She made me cookies and muffins. And I remember when she tried to teach us to bake cakes from scratch. You were horrible and your cakes tasted terrible, but we'd lie to you. Both of us."

"You did not—" But I was remembering, and even I hadn't wanted to taste my cakes.

A tug at my mouth. "She'd wear that ugly yellow apron. She hated that apron."

"What? I loved that apron. Always felt like it was sunshine. Made me feel warm, even in the winter."

I noted softly, "That's why she wore it. For you."

His eyes lifted to the rearview mirror, holding mine a second again. He swallowed, his Adam's apple bobbing up and down. "Yeah." His voice came out raspy. "She was a good woman, and a good mom. She was a good wife. I could always tell."

I snorted. "Why? Because she wasn't wasting away like yours?" Then, I winced. That sounded even bitchier to my own ears, more than I thought it would be. "Shit. I'm sorr—"

"Because you guys laughed." He kept on talking about my family, ignoring what I'd so blatantly pointed out about his own, his face hard. "My parents laughed when they were drunk, and only when they had a party. When there were other people there to laugh with, never the two of them, never the three of us. I was their only kid. I wouldn't have known better except I half grew up in your home, too, and what I remember the most about growing up was that you guys laughed."

My throat burned.

"Yeah, we did." I looked out the window. A hollow feeling starting to dig in my chest. "Until she died. We didn't laugh much after that."

"You laughed until then?"

I nodded. I felt the chinks in my armor widening.

I remembered how he did adore my mom. The two acted as if they were conspiring together during our baking lessons, and any time he was in the house. He congregated around her. She congregated closer to him.

"You're the son she never had." Then, feeling bad about my shot at his mom, "Your mom cooked for us. I remember that one time she tried to teach us to make lasagna."

He cracked a grin, barking a laugh. "You sucked at that, too. I never knew lasagna noodles could come out hard like rocks until yours."

Fuck him, but I was grinning. I couldn't help myself.

Those were good times, good memories before the shit ones came. And they came soon after that lasagna disaster.

He quieted. "It wasn't the same. My mom versus yours. We

had baking lessons at your house once a month, every first Sunday. My mom tried to teach us how to make Caesar salad, the only second cooking session she gave us, and that one we all got fine. It's hard to screw up."

"Says you. You're perfect at everything."

He didn't reply.

I didn't expect him to. It was true. He knew it. I knew it. The entire nation knew it.

Then from him, "Not at being a friend."

My stomach kicked.

Hell no. No way. He wasn't getting back in. No fucking way.

"Oh. God." I groaned, throwing a hand up to hit my forehead. "Can we not? Can we save the dramatics until I'm able to call a cab to take me back to my place? For real. Enough bonding or whatever it is we were just doing."

He growled, "You are such a goddamn bitch."

I retorted, "And you are such a goddamn prick. Drop me the fuck off!"

"With fucking pleasure!"

He gunned the engine, shooting forward in traffic, and weaving until we were nearing my exit. When he took it, I relaxed. The rest of the way was tense and silent, and I knew both of us couldn't wait to be rid of the other. Then he pulled over to the curb. He didn't make a move, his only action just unlocking the door.

His head was turned halfway to me, his jaw clenching over and over again.

Fine.

I shoved forward, my head only swimming a little bit as I climbed out of his truck. Once I shut the door and turned around, he'd already hit the engine, tearing away from the curb.

I only had the clothes on my back, on the side of the street, but I'd never been so fucking grateful to be away from him.

Now, turning to the house I wasn't sure I was still invited to live in, I saw that all the lights were off. Lovely. It was then I remembered the day—Saturday. Game day. They'd be gone the entire day, but I had two things working in my favor. It was hella hot out, so I wouldn't freeze in only my shirt, jeans, and flip flops. Stone had all my things at his house. I had nothing with me. And it was a home game, so they wouldn't be staying overnight somewhere.

Slinking to the backyard, I climbed over the fence and took a seat on the picnic table. I'd wait it out here, maybe even nap stretched out on top if need be. Either way, I was just fine on my own.

CHAPTER 13

"DUSTY?"

I saw black when I opened my eyes. No. Stars. I was seeing stars.

It took a bit, then turning my head—I reared upright, scrambling backwards. I was on the edge of the picnic table. My head was woozy, and I was seeing two of someone.

No. Wait.

It was Savannah and Mia? Both were staring at me, eyebrows raised, and looks of confusion on their faces. Both were decked out in Texas C&B gear, the white and blue colors displayed loud and proud, seventeen and thirty-seven on their cheeks in sparkly blue paint. That's right. Their boyfriends were on the team. I'd forgotten.

And what was I doing here?

Oh, yeah.

Stone. Me being a bitch. Him charging off from the curb, and a part of me couldn't blame him. I'd be frustrated with me, too, if I were him.

"What are you doing?"

Mia was staring at my feet.

I looked, too. The flip flops had fallen off.

"Sorry. I was sleeping and…" I sat up, but whoa. The blood didn't go with me. It rushed downwards instead, making me light-headed and I was teetering on the edge of the table.

Savannah rushed forward, grabbing my arm.

Mia's top lip just lifted even more in a sneer.

"No. Like, what are you doing here?"

"Am I not living here anymore?" I put a hand to my forehead. I was fairly certain the pounding I was feeling up there wasn't a good sign. Neither was sleeping in the sun all afternoon long because Stone picked me up from the hospital at three. It was dark out. Looking over my shoulder, the lights were on in the house. I frowned. No one had seen me out here? "What time is it?"

"It's ten-thirty. Everybody's coming here from the Quail." That was Mia's flat response, like I'd irritated her that she even had to respond to a question.

The Quail.

Oh no.

"I had a job interview there. Oh no."

"Helllooooo. What are you doing here?" Savannah waved her hand in front of my face to get my attention. There was a bit more edge to her voice, and I couldn't blame her either. I'd be frustrated with myself.

Wait.

I was repeating my thoughts.

That *really* wasn't good.

"I don't have my phone or my keys, or anything. I couldn't get in the house." And they hadn't answered my question. "Did you guys kick me out?"

They shared a look, a dumbfounded expression, and I could just tell. Their mouths were hanging open. Their eyes were saying, 'wtf?' And their eyebrows were all the way up into their foreheads.

I was a keen observer of the human body.

That and I heard Mia whisper, "W-T-F?"

"You're..." Savannah had to stop, shake her head, clear her thoughts. "You were in an accident."

"Yes."

Noted. I knew that.

They shared another look.

I tried again. "So, the room? Is it still mine?"

And Savannah was trying to get me to understand again, too. "You totaled your car. A truck took you out."

"Girl," Mia snapped. "You were in a coma all week."

Yes. And yes.

But why were they not answering my question?

"So... I *don't* still have the room? Or do I?"

"OH MY GOD!" Mia burst out. "No! All your shit was picked up by Stone Fucking Reeves. You KNOW STONE FUCKING REEVES! Why are you HERE and not with HIM?!"

I flinched, frowning. "You don't need to yell at me. I have a splitting headache."

Savannah's face flashed to horror. "You do? You should be in the hospital. You shouldn't be here. What are you doing here? Sleeping outside?"

I was really trying to focus here. I was, but the headache was increasing by the minute, and Mia's shouting only made it worse. I literally had nothing to my name right now except the clothes on my back and I just needed to know where to go.

"Will you please just tell me?" My voice was dipping low, hoarse, and to an alarming sound that I knew was concerning, but I was losing normal thought function as to why I should be alarmed about how I was sounding. "Doahhafdaroomstll?"

"You're slurring your words." Savannah pointed out.

"She's slurring her words." Mia was always the smartest.

A disgusted sigh from her again, "Fucking hell."

"What are you doing?" That was Savannah again.

My eyes had closed.

I was getting so sleepy again.

I just had a long nap. I shouldn't be so tired so soon after, right? Right?

Mia snapped in a huff, "I'm calling 911 again. This bitch's death is not going to be on our hands."

"Oh dear."

I just thought this picnic table was so comfortable. Why'd I ever use a bed? That was my last, somewhat coherent thought until splendid peace.

CHAPTER 14

THE DOCTOR WAS MUCH MORE STERN the next time.

The ambulance came again.

I was taken to the ER again.

I was treated for the same concussion as before. Again. This time I was told to make sure I stayed hydrated, and if I fell asleep, to do it indoors and out of the sun.

And Stone was called, once again.

But this time, I was being released that same night, and as he stalked into the room, murder in his eyes, he refused to say a word. The doc was doing it all for him.

"You are *only* being released into the care of Mr. Reeves."

I was the petulant child, and my doctor was the aggravated second-grade teacher. He was close to his wit's end, but not quite there. I knew the type well. And Stone, he was the pissed-off older brother who hated his little sister, but the parents were dead so...

God.

I swallowed hard. I'd just thought that, hadn't I?

Stone would never look at me like we had a brother/sister relationship. One of us would've murdered the other long ago.

And yep, I was content with keeping the snarky jokes to myself. I didn't think anyone else would appreciate my sense of comedy, though I was rolling in it myself.

"I had a job interview at the Quail."

The awkward silence that filled the room told me something had happened. I'd done something. Then the doctor closed his mouth and I clued in. I'd completely interrupted him and that was a no-no.

Stone moved to rest his shoulder against the doorframe, his arms still folded over his chest. "That bar on your campus?"

"Yes." Eureka. He knew what I was talking about.

The doctor and nurse shared a look over my head. I didn't want to look. I was pretty sure it wasn't favorable to my recovery.

"They hired me. I think." I frowned. How would I know if I'd been hired or not? My phone. I focused on Stone. "Do you have my phone?"

He nodded, resigned to whatever was going to happen. It wasn't a happy look of resignation, but you know, the actual definition of resignation. A reluctant acceptance of what shit show was to come. I was the shit show, and he knew it.

He added, "I have all your shit at my place."

"My keys?"

He nodded.

"My phone?"

"You already asked that."

The doctor moved forward, bending to peer in my eyes again. "How many fingers do you see?" He was holding up three.

I said, "Four."

I was lying.

Instant concern filled his gaze.

A deep, aggravated sigh left Stone again. "She's fucking with you. She used to do the same thing when she skinned her knee as a kid. Her mom played along and it drove her dad nuts."

My dad.

I felt punched at the mention.

Stone shoved off from the doorway and strode forward, getting in front of the doctor and bent down to peer at me, face to face. "Stop fucking around. Stop hiding. Stop lying to yourself. All your shit's at my place. I know you. We have ties. Come to my house. I will help you through this. I promise." He wasn't being gentle as he was saying all this. It was being delivered in a matter-of-fact way, but then he faltered, and he lightened his tone. "I never went to your mom's funeral and I've always regretted it. She'd want me to help you, and I can right now. Stop fighting me."

He didn't get it.

I was already crumbling, though.

I felt it happening.

But I still whispered out, "I fight you, I fight *them*."

He got it immediately. Understanding dawned, and he nodded. His eyes clouding a second, then he straightened, but his hand came out to touch my face. Fingertips tucked a strand of hair behind my ear, and his words undid me.

"Let's go to my house. You can yell at me all you want there."

I was falling. Slipping. Tumbling.

The tears were coming, but my God, no. I didn't cry in public.

He saw them, and he chided softly, almost mocking me, "Pull yourself together, Phillips."

It worked.

I sucked them in but nodded to the doctor. "I'll go home with Stone."

This time it was late, after midnight when he rolled me out in the wheelchair. His truck was there, and I didn't fight. Standing, climbing into the front seat of his truck this time. Before he could, I did my own seatbelt saying quietly, "I got it."

He nodded, stepping back.

A few guys were outside, waiting, because I was realizing this was Stone's life. He put the wheelchair away, then paused to sign autographs. A few pictures were taken. He waved them goodbye before climbing behind the wheel.

"The pharmacy?" There was a list of meds they wanted me on.

"I already filled them." He was pulling out onto the interstate soon after. "You hungry?"

"I can eat?"

"Unless something's wrong with your stomach, and in that case, I'm turning right back to the ER, but yeah. They didn't say you couldn't."

I pondered it. I felt my stomach growling, but I shook my head. "I'm not hungry."

"You sure? You haven't eaten since they pulled the feeding tube out of you yesterday."

Yesterday. Was it wrong to wish I could go back to that coma? No? Well, then. I might keep that one to myself.

"No," I said faintly, watching the city lights flashing by me. "I'm not hungry."

Then I remembered something about Stone. "Shouldn't you be in bed? When do you have to be at the stadium tomorrow?"

"I have time."

Oh, yeah. That was right.

I settled back, beginning to feel my eyelids growing heavy, but I didn't fight it. At this point, I was hungry for any amount of sleep I could get. It was my only escape from this new reality.

Stone's house was huge. I wasn't surprised.

He hit a button and the gate opened, then he drove into an underground garage for his own house. He parked next to a Hummer and between a G Wagon on the other side. The rest of his garage was spacious and clean. He noticed my looks concerning both vehicles and grinned. "I indulged. My signing advance." Then he was walking, opening the door to a back room. This was where he helped me take off a sweater a nurse gave me because I got chilled. He tossed it on a clothes washer and turned the lights on in the next room, proceeding into the house.

We went into the largest kitchen I've ever seen. A full island was in the middle.

There was another counter off of the side of the kitchen with eight barstools lined up along it. A huge, curved wooden table that I instantly loved, but our journey wasn't finished. The grand tour continued. He gestured toward a darkened room on the left as we passed by. "That's the more formal sitting area if guests come over." But we were going up a set of half stairs.

He turned, going down a hallway.

He was leading me farther into the house, almost to a whole other section until he paused, and hit the lights in a room. "Guest quarters." He pushed the door open farther and went in. He narrated as he pointed to each section, going in a circle. "Kitchen." That was obvious by the setup with a fridge and everything. It was the size of the kitchen we had growing up. He kept going in a circle. "You got your own gym there."

Really? A gym?

He didn't wait, still going in the circle. "Your own living room area." And still going. "Bedroom one." A hallway was next. "Bedrooms two and three are farther down."

He went to a door, opening it, and repeating the motion of hitting the lights. "And if you're feeling motivated, you can do your own laundry."

He flashed me a grin, then paused.

I was back to crumbling. He saw it and grunted, "A little bit longer, Phillips. Keep it together."

On it. I could do that.

I shoved all the shit down, way down, and pulled up the numbness once again. The silly/fighting mood had gone. It wasn't helping me hold back what I knew was going to hit me like a tsunami. It'd be relentless.

He turned the light off, closed the door, and gently touched my shoulders, turning me back to the stairs.

"I got a bit more to show you. Hold on."

It was like he went on warp speed after that, rushing through the rest of the house.

He showed me a television room. A theater room. As he explained, they were different.

He had another gym in the basement, and it was attached to the garage. He showed me the door connecting them, then we were back and heading up into the house.

He ended by a different set of stairs and just pointed up. "I'm up there."

"The tour is done?"

"Tour's done."

Got it. I dipped my head in a nod. "Can you show me how to get to my section again?"

Chuckling, he said, "You're still not hungry?" He tapped my arm lightly. "I know how to make a mean Caesar salad, or you know, I might have some lasagna to heat up."

He was teasing. He was being kind. And it was the worst thing he could've done.

I couldn't hold them off anymore. They were slipping, so I turned so he couldn't see my face and I made my voice like steel, "Forget it. I'll find it."

"Hey. Hey." His hands touched my shoulder.

I pulled away from him, hurrying off. I'd find the fucking stairs myself.

Fuck him.

Fuck this house.

Fuck everything he had gained and I had lost.

Fuck it all.

He still had his shitty parents, and mine—a sob ripped from me. I felt it rising, burning on the way, and I tried to quiet it, but I couldn't. Stopping right at the stairs going to my section, I couldn't hold them back anymore, and I couldn't go any farther myself.

I bent over, right there, at the bottom stairs. My forehead went to my knees. I wrapped my arms around my legs, and I sobbed.

Deep. Guttural. Straight from the soul sobs.

He must've let me cry for a few minutes until I felt his hands on my back. "Fucking Christ, Phillips." But he didn't sound frustrated, and his hands were gentle. He knelt, his arms moving under me, and he picked me up.

He carried me to my room, going to turn the light on.

"No! Please."

I couldn't bear it. It was bad enough he was here, he was hearing me. If he saw evidence of my destruction, too?

I couldn't. I just couldn't.

"Okay." A soft whisper from him.

"I need you to hate me."

"I will." He sank down on a chair in the corner, toeing the curtains out of the way so he could see outside his window, and there he held me. "Tomorrow we can go back to hating each other."

I hiccupped on a sob. "Deal."

So the rest of the night, he cradled me.

The rest of the night, I cried.

The rest of the night, we didn't hate each other.

CHAPTER 15

"THOUGHT you didn't know Stone Reeves?" That was Joe's greeting when I called him the next day.

I frowned, sitting in Stone's living room. Alone. He'd gone in earlier for his game. "I don't."

He snorted. "Yeah, right. The dude himself stopped in this morning, told me about what's going on with you and asking if I'd hold a job for you."

I did nothing. I didn't know if I should get mad or breathe easier. Guess it'd depend on his answer.

"So are you?"

"Fuck yeah, I am. He said you're a damn hard worker and I'd be stupid not to make room for you, but I gotta tell it straight. I have to fill that position I hired you for. Way he was talking, you might be out awhile."

"I won't. I'll be in tomorrow."

"He said you were in a coma."

What's with all this coma talk? "I'm fine. It's just a headache."

"You were out all week for a headache?"

I was praying Stone hadn't said anything. "Yes. I'm good. For real. I can start tomorrow." Make that, I *need* to start tomorrow.

Even a day being here, with only my homework that somehow Stone got for me, wasn't enough. I fell asleep from sobbing so hard, and when I woke, Stone was gone. He left a note in my kitchen quarters saying he'd be back a bit after midnight. There were instructions how to use the remote to the television if I wanted to watch his godliness-level score. His exact words.

I snorted, then crumpled up the instructions, only to pause, think about it, and I smoothed them back out. One never knew when one needed to turn one's brain off and sink into one's oblivion, and I really needed to stop talking about myself as 'one'.

Today.

Man.

I did not want to handle today.

My mind was swimming, and I knew I wasn't acting rational.

Jared.

I needed to call my stepbrother...was he still a stepbrother?

God.

Gail.

I—no. I wasn't going to crumble. I couldn't.

What was I doing again?

I blinked.

I just called for my job.

I should make a list. What to get done. I would forget otherwise, like basic things such as showering. I sniffed in my armpit. Yeah. I should shower first.

Then call Jared.

Then I didn't know. I'd make a list for that, too.

Lists.

This was how I got through my mom, how I got through what happened before. I—no, no, no. I couldn't think like that. Stop thinking. That helped me, too.

Brain, turn off.

━━━

I showered.

After showering, I made coffee.

After coffee, I sat on the couch.

I didn't know the time.

My stomach was growling, but I wasn't hungry.

Water. I should drink water. I needed to stay hydrated.

So I wrote that on my list.

Shower. Coffee. Water.

What else did I need to do?

I added:

1. Shower

2. Coffee

3. ~~Water~~ Stay hydrated.

4. Call Jared.

What else?

5. Homework

6. Job

7. Call Gail's sister?

I needed to find out anything. I'd been in that coma. What had Stone said? Oh, yes. They were already buried. Next to my mom. I sagged in relief. That was good. She would've liked Gail. And the funeral was already done.

The costs?

Stone said my bills were covered, but what about my parents'? My mind was fuzzy. He said the lawyer was traveling here. Maybe there was some money left, enough to cover all those expenses? But no. If any was left, it should go to Jared. I'd cover the funerals and burial costs. That was my job.

What else?

I sat, that list in front of me, and I stared at the wall.

What time was it? I looked. It was six in the evening. When had the time gone by? I woke around ten.

But this was what I did before, after the event. I hadn't known how to process anything, so I sat, I stared, I lost time. I'd been a zombie then. I hadn't totally been a zombie after mom. My dad needed me. The bills needed me. School needed me.

School.

I could do that again.

Reaching for my phone, I pulled up Siobhan's number. I didn't have my housemates' numbers. I needed to have my housemates' numbers.

I hit call, and a second later, I heard, "Dusty?"

"Hi."

I felt lame saying that, but...hi.

"Oh, wow. You missed the entire second week of classes. Susan was fielding calls about you. She was all griping about 'missing transfer community college students', then suddenly she got a call and her attitude completely changed. I was instructed to take notes for you, make copies, and hand them to her at the end of each day. What happened? Are you okay?"

"Um."

Maybe I should've called the school first? But what office would I call? Probably the general administrative office?

My head was swimming again. I was on overload.

"Um."

Why had I called Siobhan again?

"I was in a coma."

Silence.

"YOU WERE IN A COMA?! WHAT?"

I grimaced, holding the phone away from me. That didn't help with the whole mind-swimming thing. For real. Why had I called Siobhan?

"What happened? Are you okay? Are you in the hospital? Do you need me to bring you anything? I'm totally here, anything you need. Are you okay now?"

There were too many questions.

"Uh, I'm at someone's house."

"Whose house? I didn't know you knew someone else down here."

"Can—" It was hitting me just then. I didn't have a car.

Because I totaled the car.

Stone said he handled the car.

But I had no car.

I had no way to get back to Jared.

I needed to call Jared.

Jared.

It was just him and me. We were almost strangers.

The pressure was building.

Building.

BUILDING!

BUILDING—I was hyperventilating.

My dad.

Gail.

They were gone.

And I had no car.

And Jared was no longer my brother.

I told Stone that Apollo's parents could adopt him.

What was I doing?

Where was I?

I had no parents.

I had no one.

I was alone.

Totally.

They were gone.

I couldn't breathe.

I heard someone saying my name, but it was from a distance, down a tunnel it sounded.

What was I doing?

I mumbled something to that someone, but I wasn't sure who it was.

Then I dropped something.

I was falling.

Yeah. That was a good idea.

I could sit.

Sit here. Not think.

Everything would be okay.

I just needed to sit a bit.

CHAPTER 16

THERE WAS A POUNDING SOMEWHERE.

I was waking up slowly.

Ouch.

My head was hurting.

What happened?

Everything was dark. Flashes of red and yellow were lighting up the walls. What the hell was going on?

More pounding.

A doorbell was ringing.

Whoever was there—it came back to me.

Shit.

I'd had a panic attack, and then I fell asleep.

Someone was yelling for me. Siobhan.

She'd been on the phone with me. She must've called an ambulance, but how had they known where to come?

Standing, wincing because everything was hurting, I tried to find the front door. Stone hadn't shown me this way, so I followed the sound of the doorbell ringing. Then, standing on the other side of it, I swept open the curtain and two paramedics were there, along with a cop.

"OPEN THE DOOR!" The cop motioned for the door.

I unlocked the door and opened it and—

ALARM! SIREN! ALARM! SIREN!

A strange, almost robotic voice filled the house, "YOU HAVE VIOLATED A PROTECTED AREA. LEAVE IMMEDI-ATELY. THE POLICE HAVE BEEN CALLED. YOU HAVE VIOLATED A PROTECTED AREA..."

I groaned.

The cop came in, looking around. "You have a way to turn that off?"

I shook my head. "It's not my house."

"According to records, Stone Reeves lives here?" I didn't know why he put that as a question. Ohhh, understanding flooded me.

I straightened upright. "I know Stone. I'm just staying here." I guess.

A phone started ringing. It was the house one, and I answered it. A woman's voice came over, "Are you in need of assistance?"

"No," I sighed. A panic attack, then I fell asleep. I didn't think I could explain all this away, though.

"Do you have the code?"

Fuck. Double fuck.

The woman didn't even hesitate. "Thank you, ma'am." A dial tone hit me next.

Pretty sure that wasn't good, but I turned back toward the door. The cop and paramedics had come in. All three were regarding me with suspicion.

I heard more ringing, but this one, I recognized. I had left my phone up in the guest area and I started to go for it, but the cop took my arm. "Let me grab it."

I gestured, feeling a sense of impending doom and the general wish that an entire mountain would drop on me. "It's probably Stone wondering what the hell is going on."

He nodded. "I'll get your phone."

He went in search of the electronic perpetrator and the female paramedic approached. "Ma'am? My name is Jill. We had a call that someone might need assistance?"

"Yeah."

The paramedic touched my arm. "Was that you, Miss? Are you in need of help?" Her hand slid down to my wrist, and she was taking my pulse.

I turned to her. "How'd you know where I was?"

The cop was returning, talking on my phone.

She was counting, but her partner stepped forward. He went to grab a chair, and brought it up behind me. "If you could have a seat?"

I did. My knees were about to give out anyway.

The male paramedic knelt beside me, unpacking his bag. "We had a call from a Susan Anderson, your academic advisor. She gave us this address."

But how'd she know this address? Wait. Stone. He must've been in contact with the university, too. Jesus, was there anything he hadn't already taken care of?

The cop stepped forward and handed my phone over. "He'd like to speak to you."

I took it but had the foresight to ask the time first.

"It's eleven-ten."

Whoa.

When had I called Siobhan? Earlier. Right? Time was slipping away, but this was how it'd been before. I had sat and stared into nothing until somehow my brain told me to stand, to move, to eat, to walk, to wash, to keep going.

It was now after eleven and I had no sense of any one

moment over the past couple of hours. I put the phone to my ear. "Did you win?" He had his game. It would've been done by now.

Silence. Then, "Are you fucking kidding me?"

I winced, but I couldn't blame him for being angry.

"I'm sorry, Stone. I—"

"Are you okay?" he cut me off, asking roughly.

"I will be."

The female paramedic was shining a light in my eye. I blinked, trying to turn away, but she overrode me, saying, "Ma'am, you need to keep still for us."

I did, trying to. "I had a panic attack, and then I fell asleep. That's it. I swear."

"Is your head okay?"

"Yeah." This was embarrassing. "I just got overwhelmed and I forget things and—"

"It's okay. It's okay. As long as you're okay. You are, right?"

The paramedics were still checking me over, now watching my chest. They'd already finished with my blood pressure. I was talking so my airway wasn't blocked. I was fine.

I told them and Stone at the same time, "Yes. I'm fine. I am."

At that moment, the alarm cut off. I saw the cop on the house-line, and he hung up a second later, coming back to us.

"Yeah," the female paramedic said, shifting back on her feet. "I tend to agree. A panic attack?"

The cop said, "Mr. Reeves said you recently experienced your own car accident after finding out—"

"Yes!" I almost shouted that word. I didn't want him to say the words. I couldn't—that was part of the problem. I lowered my head, unable to look up, seeing the pity in his gaze. "Yes, but I'm fine. I just got overwhelmed."

"You were in an accident?" female paramedic questioned.

"She was put in a coma, came out of it Thursday, and was

released from the hospital yesterday. Mr. Reeves said you'd gone back to the ER yesterday."

"Yeah. I..." They were making a bigger deal out of everything, more than it was. I was losing steam. Why was everything so hard? Why'd everything take so much energy? Why'd I want to just go to sleep again?

Trauma.

That's what he said. That was true. The body needed to do double work to heal after a trauma, and that went for both mental and physical trauma. I knew this. I knew this, but God. I sucked in a breath. My chest was hurting. My throat was hurting. I felt like my insides were pulling apart, one organ at a time was being ripped to pieces.

Trauma. Yes. I suppose that's the best word to describe it.

"Ma'am?"

The cop said, "Mr. Reeves said he was on his way back. He can answer any questions, but she doesn't seem to be in need of medical assistance right now."

At his words, a shift came over both paramedics. They began packing but stood.

I remained sitting, my head lowered, and as if just sensing I wanted my space, they moved over to where the cop was. I heard the guy ask, "Are we really talking about the actual Stone Reeves?"

"Seems like." The cop's tone turned almost cheerful. Upbeat. "Sounded like him on the phone."

"They won tonight, right?"

"Reeves ran in two of the three touchdowns himself."

The female. "He's a future Hall-of-Famer. Has to be."

They kept talking while I sat, listening. We all waited.

Stone got there and I swear I saw fury riding behind on his coat-tails. He strode in. His gaze went to me, and he was growling instantly. "Jesus! She's freezing."

Someone cursed.

I was fine. I started to tell him, but something was thrown around me, and someone was tucking it in front of me. Kneeling. Stone dropped in front of me. Gentle hands touched my face. "You okay?"

He was furious but concerned. And he looked tired. He was so tired. And smelly.

A second cop had joined the mix, and the paramedics were at the door. Their bags gone and their heads down, almost like they'd been caught stealing candy. The female was holding a piece of paper. The guy had a pen.

The two cops had migrated closer.

I was about to tell him I was fine when a cop started, "She never said a word."

Stone whirled on him, his back to me. "She lost her fucking parents, got into her own car accident, just came out of a four-day coma. You expect her to know when she's cold or not? I'm surprised she's been able to remain sitting this whole time."

The cop opened his mouth, then closed it. The second cop turned away. Both paramedics looked admonished.

Another growl came from Stone again, and he clipped out, "If she's not dying, I want you all to fucking leave. And no, I'm not in the mood to sign autographs."

Cop one stiffened. "Now, see—"

"Out!" he thundered.

The cops left, glaring at both of us. The paramedics remained, but the male one nudged the female, head nodding toward the piece of paper in her hand. He handed her the pen and slipped outside behind the cops. If Stone needed to talk to them, I was assuming he'd already said what he needed.

Once all were gone, the female waited a second. Approaching, she cleared her throat. "When we arrived, she was upright and walking. Her baseline was fine, and we checked a few more rounds while waiting for you to arrive. All sets of vitals were normal. You said she fainted again yesterday, but was released, and considering her history, you might still want to have her checked out again. Call to the hospital said you could make that decision. If you'd like, we can take her in with our wagon, or you can take her in yourself."

Stone was silent. His shirt was molded to him, so much so that I could see every muscle in his back was rigid and tense. He was right in front of me.

Without thinking, I lifted a hand and placed it to his back.

He sucked in a harsh breath, then turned, some of the tension leaving him. "What do you want to do?"

"I'm fine. It's the..." that word stuck in my throat, "trauma. I'm okay. Really."

His eyes were taking me in, sliding over my face, my body, studying every single detail. Whatever he saw, he relaxed and jerked his head in a nod. "Okay," he said to the woman, "We'll stay." He pointed to the paper. "I'm assuming that's for me to sign?"

Her eyes lit up. "Would you mind? To my partner and me both." She handed it over.

Stone took it, taking it over to the nearest table. "What are your names?"

"Cassie. Frank."

He scrawled over the piece of paper, writing a few words, and handed it over.

She read it, a pleased smile lighting her face up. "Thank you. It's been a pleasure to meet you." Her eyes fell to mine, and some of that smile dimmed. "Not under the best circumstances, but you know. And congratulations on your win tonight, the two touchdowns. We're lucky to have gotten you, I can say that much. If we didn't have you and Doubard, we'd be hurting this year." She went to the door. "You think we can do it? Make it to the Super Bowl?"

Stone didn't follow, just watched her, and I could sense his irritation rising.

He didn't respond, and clueing in, the woman's cheeks reddened. "Right. Well. If anything happens, don't hesitate to call. Get well, Miss."

I didn't respond.

Stone didn't respond.

She wasn't expecting acknowledgement and left, closing the door behind her. Stone let out a guttural curse before walking forward and hitting the locks. He bypassed me, going back to the kitchen area, and a few minutes later I heard a soft beeping sound.

Then he came back and regarded me. "I see you had an eventful day."

I closed my eyes. "Sorry."

"No." He shook his head, running a tired hand over his face. "It's my fault. I should've had someone here when you woke up, or at least told you about the security system. About shit my pants when one of the trainers brought my phone over, telling me it wouldn't stop ringing. Had calls from your college, and then the security system."

"Sorry."

That's all I had in me, just that one word.

He was watching me, reading me. "You woke up today, huh?"

I knew he wasn't asking about the actual physical act of waking, more like the mental version. "Yeah. I woke up." My voice trembled.

"Right. Okay." He pulled a chair forward, sitting and resting his elbows on his knees. He was sitting, facing me. "What do you want to do?"

"How much were the funeral costs?"

"What?"

"My parents died." All three of them now. "There was an accident. The car would've needed to be towed. The funeral costs. Coffins. The burial sites. Headstones. You said you covered my costs, but what about those?"

"I meant *everything.*" A soft curse under his breath. "Dusty, you don't need to worry about that."

I looked at him, really looked at him. So much was weighing on him. He'd taken all of my shit on without a second thought to what exactly that entailed. Why? We hated each other.

"Why are you doing all this for me?"

His head lifted. The torment there cleared into wonder. His eyebrows dipped together. "Because I considered you family at one point. And I liked your mom."

My mom. Right.

That was why.

Some of the confusion cleared. "I need to know how much everything costs, Stone. I have to know."

He was saying one thing, but he wasn't being honest. I could feel it. It was driving me nuts.

"Your aunt took care of it all."

Another lie.

"Bullshit." I knew there'd been a contentious relationship between Gail and her sister. She had called twice asking Gail for money, and I knew Gail turned her down both times. "Did my aunt even travel for the funeral?"

I was watching him, and I saw it. His nostrils flared. Guilt flared before he swallowed, dipping his head a little. "No. She was contacted by your parents' lawyer, said she wasn't in the will, and when asked about Jared, she couldn't have given him away quicker than she did."

That sounded right this time.

"Who took care of everything? I know you're lying."

He hesitated.

"TELL ME!"

His chair jerked back, but a deep wariness just passed over his face. "My parents did. My father, to be exact."

Fuck. It was worse than I thought.

"Why?"

"Because I made him. Because I threatened to never come home again unless he manned up and righted every fucking wrong he ever did to your family. My dad took care of mostly everything, and no, you will never know how much any of it cost. He also took care of your schooling for the next two years. Your campus got a sizeable donation in your name, along with a check for your schooling costs." He shoved out of his chair, his eyes flashing. His face hard. "Consider it done, and honestly, I don't want to hear another goddamn word about it again. It's the least my family could do."

His phone started blaring, but he looked down on me. "And with all that said, I'm going to make myself something to eat, head into the theater room, and put on something mindless to watch. You're welcome to join me, or not. I don't give a shit, just don't leave, because in your state, you'd probably walk into oncoming traffic."

He wasn't wrong.

But it would've been on accident, not intentional, and admitting that much to myself, I found my room and curled under the covers again.

I'd call Jared in the morning.

CHAPTER 17

STONE WAS SHIRTLESS.

Stone was only wearing sweatpants.

Those sweatpants were hanging seriously low over his hips.

And, he had a *lot* of bruises on his back. I was guessing they were from his game.

Oh, and he was making breakfast when I walked into the kitchen.

He stopped, his coffee cup in hand, the other manning the toaster, and glanced at the clock. "It's five in the morning."

"You say that like I've not been awake most of the night." I grunted, sliding onto one of those many barstools of his. He was clear across the counter and the island. I noted, "Kitchens shouldn't be this big. Who else lives here? What's the need for this much size?"

He stared at me, his mouth flattening. "Good morning to you, too."

Another grunt from me. "Sorry. I'm a bit bitchy."

He hid a grin. "That a new development or...?"

"Fuck off."

He didn't hide the grin this time, laughing as the toast popped up. "You want one?"

I considered it. I did, but I shook my head. "Coffee?"

He paused, his eyes narrowed on me. "When's the last time you ate?"

"When did that feeding tube get pulled out of me?"

He swore under his breath, buttering one of the pieces of toast for me. Placing it in front of me with a firm thud, he leaned over the counter. "Eat. Now."

"I'm not hung—"

"I don't give a shit." He pointed at it. "You don't eat, you'll end up right back in the hospital. I, for one, am sick of picking you up there. The nurses got more forward the second time I was there."

Now I hid a grin. "The hardships of being a football god."

And it was his turn to grunt, finishing the other toast for himself. "There's the perks, but trust me, there's cons, too. A shitty pic of you is on Page Nine's website today."

"You're lying." But I was pulling my phone out, typing in Page Nine, and then swearing. He hadn't minced words. It was a shitty pic of me. I was pale. My hair a mess. I groaned. "You look like you're picking up a drug rehab reject."

The headlines weren't far off. Mysterious New Love Interest for Reeves? And the article went on to detail how he'd been a regular visitor at the hospital, spotted several times going in and out. Half my face was hidden by his truck, but enough they caught enough of me where it made me think hospitals needed to offer a spa day to patients before allowing them to be released.

"I'm surprised they didn't get the other shot. That would've been better."

He poured my coffee, took it to his fridge and glanced back. "You still like milk in your coffee?"

"I never drank coffee when we were friends. How'd you know that?"

"I might've had a conversation one time with your mom in the grocery store. I was picking up flowers for graduation and she was there." He lifted his milk from his fridge. "Buying this for you."

I—I swallowed over a lump. "You have a lot of secret conversations with my mom?" I took the cup as he handed it over, then watched as he poured some green juice in a glass and placed it right next to me.

He pointed at it. "You can't have coffee if you don't drink that, too, and maybe a couple more. Random times I saw her. We liked to buy groceries at the same time."

"Saturday morning."

He added, "Nine in the morning." Leaning his back against his counter, he sipped his own coffee. "Course once I realized that was her usual time, I might've made sure to always have to pick something up for my mom during that time."

I wasn't sure how I felt about that. "It's like you had a secret affair with my mom, hopefully in a platonic sense."

He barked out a laugh, his hands going to his shoulders, making his entire chest area bulge up.

Jesus. Those biceps. They flexed just as I was watching them.

Then I stepped into the equivalent of a cold shower as he said, "Your lawyer is coming this morning."

Right.

Because for thirty minutes there, the image of a shirtless Stone had distracted me from what plagued me all night. "Right."

"You want me here?"

"Yes." I said it almost before he finished. I not only wanted him here, I needed him here, too.

I was past trying to be prideful.

A soft chuckle from him. "Can I make more food for you?"

I shook my head. I still hadn't started on the toast. "Why are you up this early? Isn't the day after your games for resting?"

"Technically, but I usually get up and head to the gym. I gotta run into the stadium today, too. And speaking of," He moved to his phone, hitting the screen and scrolling. "Your lawyer will be here around nine this morning, so I'll plan on going in after that." He paused, tilting his head to the side. "You want to come with me?"

"Where?"

"To the stadium. I just gotta go in and talk to my coach, then do a few other things. I won't be there long."

"Um..."

He cleared his throat, setting his coffee aside and coming to lean over the counter across from me. He was almost staring down at me. "Let me put it this way, both times I've left you, I've not enjoyed the myriad of phone calls I got later. You're coming with me where I know you probably won't get into trouble."

It was yes, sir. Right away, sir. No, I can't talk back, sir.

I lifted up the toast, nibbling at the end. My stomach was growling and protesting, but I took a few bites. I knew there'd be a time I'd look back at this day with fondness, where I was trying to make myself eat. Not about all the other stuff, all the reasons why I didn't feel like eating to begin with.

Except maybe a shirtless Stone, or a stern-talking Stone. I'd make sure to memorialize those moments.

Good Lord. I had a concussion. I was finding Stone attractive. I pondered that, and no. Not at all related. Finding someone attractive and being attracted to someone were totally different. I could recognize Mia and Savannah from the house were both gorgeous, but I didn't want to jump either of them. It was the same deal here.

And speaking of my housemates, "How long am I staying here?"

"You're here until I deem you're able to function in the real world again."

He was saying that all imposing-like. Two days ago I would've considered his face smirking and arrogant and pompous, but now I saw the thinly veiled concern.

He stood and straightened away from the counter. His eyes flashed, dropping from my face. "Listen. You have a concussion, and that shit's no joke. That means ensuring you have the least amount of stimuli as possible. After today, no homework. No phone. Try to keep the television stuff to a minimum. I feel bad that I even invited you to watch a movie with me last night. Just until you're okay to travel, stay put. I already cleared everything with your job and your college. They all know the deal. If you want it, they said you could take a leave of absence for the first semester and there'd be no penalty or impact to your tuition or your GPA."

My heart sank. I'd already lost so much, I couldn't lose a semester of school.

"No way."

I'd have to restart all over again. I could only handle so many restarts. "I can't do that."

"You lost your father. You lost your stepmother. I know you still haven't called your stepbrother yet. You are barely managing to get through a day here. And yeah, your job called me, said some bullshit that you'd be in tomorrow. I told 'em to fire you if you tried that shit again."

"What? Stone, you can't—"

"I can and I will!"

I was wrong. It was evident we were back to the 'I hate you' phase.

I shouted, "Why is this your business?!"

He didn't answer, his face twisting, his mouth snapping shut. He stared at me, something fierce flashing in those eyes until he backed down. I felt it in the air. He eased back and I was at a loss. What just happened here?

But he was saying, more quietly, a lot more restrained, "Your lawyer. Then the stadium. If you're hungry, we can stop and grab food on the way back. You need to head to your house, pick up anything left there?"

Maybe it was the concussion, but I wasn't able to keep up with him. He was soft, hard, soft, hard, and yeah. Were we now not back to the 'I hate you' stage? Damn, this revolving door was making me dizzy.

I slunk down in my chair, suddenly more exhausted than I'd ever felt. "I thought you got all my stuff?"

He shrugged. "I don't know. I just asked those girls to pack a bag. We can swing by, make sure you have everything you might need. Then after that, your ass doesn't leave this house. It's my one day I can drive you around, so I'm offering to make a pit stop."

Yeah. Okay. But he was already walking out of the kitchen.

CHAPTER 18

THERE WAS NO HOUSE.

I gaped at the lawyer. He was all trussed up, a black suit, black tie. Even a black suit jacket. Black briefcase. Black shoes. Black fucking socks. The only thing not black was the shirt. That was a cream color and I knew the quality was expensive. And there was not one iota of hesitation as he nodded to my question.

"Indeed, Miss Phillips. Your father was behind on his mortgage for the last year. He was going into foreclosure. We'd already had a meeting the week before..." Now he seemed to remember to be human, hesitating, "before the accident."

I had no words. Nothing. This wasn't as bad as when we lost the house the first time because of my mom's chemo treatments, but it seemed similar. No. It seemed worse. I had Dad with me then.

Stone leaned forward, sitting next to me. His leg pressed against mine, and he left it there. His elbows went to his knees. "What was owed on the house?"

"Seventy-five percent of it."

I sucked in my breath.

I had no idea they owed that much on it.

Stone gazed at me. "You want the house?"

The lawyer straightened. "Mr. Reeves, I don't know..."

"No." I was thinking, concussion be damned. "If you take the house back, what do they still owe?"

He hesitated again, the second time acting like a human. "They still owe us a hundred thousand. They took out a second loan to pay for some items for her son, I believe." His mouth pressed in before he said, "There's no money for you. There was a small amount they set aside for Jared, a fund that Gail had separate. His father's not in the picture, correct?"

I nodded. "Uh. Yeah. She never talked about him. I don't think he had parental rights to him. But I wasn't around that often. I was at college, then I moved here. Jared never mentioned him either. It was a secret. I guess. I never thought to wonder about it."

He frowned, pulling out some papers from his briefcase. "Paternal rights were taken away when Jared was two. There was a domestic abuse issue."

Jesus. My chest stopped working for a moment.

Two? What happened to my stepbrother and Gail?

I whispered, "Two years old?"

"Hmmm, yes." He put the papers back. "The file's closed. I don't believe Jared even knows what happened, but in my career, if rights were taken away at that age, it's with good reason."

I needed to call Jared. I'd been putting it off for too long.

"So." He read through the last of his papers and handed me the last one, along with a pen. "As for your father's personal effects. They've been put in a storage facility and I have the key for you. Mr. Reeves has said you've been ill yourself. The storage's been rented out for the next three months. Once those months are done, you'll have to take over the payments, or his effects will be sold. All rights revert back to the storage owners."

He reached into his pocket, pulling out a key on a keychain, and slid it over the table to me.

Stone took the key, asking, "You have their business card?"

"Oh, yes. Here it is."

Stone took that, as well, standing up from the table. "I'll be right back."

I already knew what he was doing. He was taking over payment after the ninety-days were up, but once I was better, I was traveling there and going through everything. I'd have to do it over a weekend because no matter what, I wasn't missing out on any more college classes.

"If you can sign here, Miss Phillips?" He pointed to the bottom of the paper. "This just says that I've gone over the last will and testament of your father." As I signed, he stood and collected the rest of his stuff, putting it into his briefcase. "I truly am sorry that we met under these circumstances. Your father spoke very highly of you the few times I met him. I looked up to him as a man, and as the kind of father I'd like to be one day."

The words sounded nice, but after signing, he almost bolted for the door.

"What a dick." Came from the side.

I grinned but looked down. It was all so neat and tidy. He'd left me a copy of everything and told me the extent of my father's belongings were in a storage shelter.

"I took care of the payments, and what was still owed. I'll set up everything tomorrow."

I had nothing to even fight him on that. A hundred thousand was too much, and I knew that it would take me probably my entire life to pay him back. But I would. I would.

"Thank you."

Stone didn't respond, and I was grateful.

I could hear my mom's laughter. It was faint, but I heard it and I was back there. "She liked to twirl sometimes." I looked up.

"When she was baking with us. She'd wear that yellow apron, especially when she was making something for you. I don't have those memories of him." Those memories were the hard ones. "We survived together after she died. We were roommates in that apartment. I went to school and worked. He worked. We just survived side by side. Then he met Gail three months after we buried Mom, and he was with Gail after that."

Then I graduated. Then I went to community college, but I had to take time to work before starting classes.

There were other memories. Had to be. "I don't have those same memories of him. He taught me to ride a bike. And throw a baseball."

Stone said, "I taught you to throw a baseball."

"Oh." That was right. "Yeah. He went fishing with me—"

"I took you fishing. I hated the worms, remember? You didn't care. You hooked the bait for us."

Another memory I got wrong. I flashed him a smile, feeling the back of my neck heating up. "My concussion. Fucks with the head."

He grunted. "That's the definition of a concussion." Checking his phone, he looked up. "I should head in. You ready to go?"

Change of subject. Thank God. Someone else might've done it to save me from the embarrassment of remembering how little I had with my father, but I could tell with Stone, he was done with the conversation. Sometimes he was thoughtful. This giving side was a throwback to our childhood, to the friend I used to remember, but right now, knowing he truly wanted to get going, this was the newer Stone. And his change of subject had nothing to do with me and was completely all about him.

I almost loved him for it, too. Almost.

"Yes. Let me change clothes and I'm ready to go."

I started for the guest area, but he caught the back of my

jeans. "You're good. You look hot anyway." He nodded for the back door. "Let's go. I told my coach I'd be there by now. I know he's waiting."

Stone thought I was hot. What. The. Hell.

I paused, that thought flashing through my body, but then it was numb again. Gone. That brief spark vanished.

So, we left. I had time to grab my phone, then dash out to the garage.

Stone powered his window down. "You set the code?"

I backtracked, setting the code he told me earlier, and then dashed out to his truck. The drive there was actually peaceful. For some reason, I liked riding in the passenger seat with Stone driving. He wasn't too reckless, but he drove how he played. Wild at times. Reckless. But also smart and controlled, too. Efficient. When we were at a stoplight, I half expected the people right next to us to recognize him.

They didn't.

"You have tinted windows?"

He nodded, easing forward as the light turned green. "Yeah. I had a scary incident last year, and since then, I'll never not have tinted windows again. Only reason that one photographer got you was because you hadn't totally shut the door yet."

"Good to know."

We went to where he worked.

He parked in a back lot, and we walked in through an off-door. A few other workers were around, and they raised their hand up, saying hello to Stone as he walked by. The orange and brown colors from the Kings displayed everywhere.

We went down one hallway and he paused outside a door, pushing it open. He stuck his head in, then backed up. "You can hang out in here." It was a waiting room. There were couches. A television. A kitchenette area. He went to the fridge and opened it. "You can help yourself, and I'll be about an hour. Two, tops.

That okay?" He went to a closed door and toed it open. It was a bathroom. Then he went to the exit and glanced back. "You're going to still be here and alive when I come back?"

I had my phone. I waved it. "I'll call 911 and give them your credit card number if I need anything."

He stared at me, gauging my intent, then rolled his eyes. "Har, har."

Yeah. Har, har back.

It was a weird dynamic between us. Moments of kindness, moments of caring and then moments of strain and sarcasm and bitterness. This time it was all on me. I knew the next would be his. Cursing me as I'm in the hospital, totally something Stone would do. And me being bitter when he's bringing me into this sanctum, where I knew so many would pay in blood to switch places—yeah. That was Stone and me.

I made some coffee while he was gone. I drank some of the water. I ate a yogurt, and had settled in, an HBO movie on when my phone started blowing up.

I picked it up, hitting one of the alerts.

Childhood Sweethearts? Mystery Woman Identified!

Say It Isn't So! Is Reeves Off The Market?

And another headline, this one with a bigger kick than the others.

Recent Trauma Brought Them Together?

Shit. Shit. Shit. Shit. I could repeat that forever and ever and ever and etcetera here because fuuuuuuuuck. Every single article had me tagged, and the last one brought up my car accident. I was skimming, but none of the others had the information about my dad and Gail.

I didn't know if this could get back and affect Jared's life, but I was hoping it wouldn't.

Then my phone started ringing, and my stomach really did turn inside out. Jared's name was flashing on the screen. Wow, that was quite the coincidence, him calling me at same time I'd just thought about him.

I hit accept and stood, already instantly nervous. "Hi."

He was quiet on the other end, just a second. "You kidding? That's the first thing you have to say to me?"

"Jared..."

"Mom and Dad died a week ago, and nothing. Apollo's mom and dad told me that they're adopting me today. Where are you? You don't want me?"

Oh.

God.

I collapsed down in a chair. "No, Jared. It's not like that."

"Then what is it like? Where the fuck are you?"

"This isn't because of the news?"

"Yeah. I mean, that's another thing. You hanging with Stone Reeves? I thought you were like mortal enemies and what? Now you're fucking?"

Shit. I frowned. "Is this how high schoolers speak now?"

"They are when their parents are dead and their only family has been absent every minute since they died. The funeral. Everything."

My heart squeezed. There was ahold on it, crushing it inch by inch.

"Jared. I was in a car accident. I've been in a coma." Had no one told him? I should've told him. I should've figured it out.

Silence. Again. And I didn't know how he was reacting, but I was painfully aware the other people we both loved had also been in a car accident.

His voice was strained, "You okay?"

"I..." This was hard. I was swallowing tears almost as fast as they were slipping down my face. "I got the news and got in my car, and a moving truck totaled me. I backed out in front of them."

"Fuck."

"They were worried about swelling on my brain, so they put me in a medically induced coma. I just got pulled out of it a few days ago, and since then, I haven't been handling anything the best way."

I should've called by now.

I should've called him the instant I heard.

"I'm so sorry, Jared. I'm so sorry."

"Yeah, well." His own voice broke. "Do you not want me, Dusty?"

I sat still, holding that phone so tight, and making sure I heard him right. Logically, I knew there were ways to think about this situation with us, but I wasn't thinking logically. I was thinking with all emotion, and that question pierced straight through my chest, finding my heart. Bullseye. Without missing a beat, I said the words that had haunted me about Jared since I woke up from the coma, "Do you want me?"

"Yes! I mean, shit. You're my only family. You're my sister."

This day. Right here. Right now. I would be better. I would no longer be an okay person, or a good person. I would be a fucking great person, and I'd have to google how to do that because I knew it'd be a lot of work.

I breathed into the phone, "Yes. Yes. I thought Apollo's parents would be the best for you. They have a stable house. They have jobs." I didn't. "You don't have to leave school. You could finish the year out there—"

"I don't give a shit about any of that. I want you. You're my family. The only person on this Earth I have left who cares about me."

I was nodding, and crying, not knowing how I was going to do any of this. "Okay. Yeah. Okay. Um," I stood. I couldn't figure out how to be this new person sitting down. That made no sense. "Okay. Just, okay."

"You have any idea what you're going to do?" I could hear a bell sound where he was. Lockers opening, shutting. Conversations. Laughter. Shouts. A 'what's up, man?' Followed by a 'pound my fist, dude.' He'd left his class early to call me.

"Not a goddamn clue." My head still felt woozy. "I think the concussion is affecting me."

"Coach says to take that stuff seriously. You shouldn't even be on your phone right now."

"Yeah. Well. I'm glad I am. I'm glad I had it, or I would've missed your call."

I heard his laugh, and everything righted for a split second. I could do this. I could keep going. Right? I was asking myself. Right? I just answered myself. I was feeling inspired.

"Okay. Well. You let me know."

I was nodding and smiling to myself and beaming like a fool. "I will. Right. Have a good rest of the day."

"Er. Okay. Bye."

"Bye!" I was waving, to the microwave. "Lov—"

That word stuck in my throat. I hated that it was there, but it was. Jared hung up.

I stood there.

I didn't move.

I almost felt the microwave was going to start heckling me, and then I heard from behind me, "You did not just do what I heard you just do?"

Stone was there. Stone was furious. Stone was probably back to being my enemy after this.

I gave him a weak smile. "I blame my concussion."

He growled, fixing me with a heated glare. "You are so fucking stupid."

Yep. I *so* knew that. But on the flipside, I was now a single mother-figure. So, yay that?

CHAPTER 19

WELL. The joke was on me.

Apollo's mom called me thirty minutes later. I was just leaving the stadium with Stone beside me. Seeing Georgia's name on the screen, I glanced at Stone before answering. "Georgia. Hi."

She started right in. "I am so sorry. Apollo called me and told me what Jared said to you. Now, you have to understand that I am in no way trying to get between a stepbrother and sister. You both lost your parents, and if I thought there was even a small inkling that Jared meant what he said, I wouldn't even be making this call. But having said all of that, Apollo told me last night that Jared has an alert set so any stories about Stone Reeves go right to his phone. He got the alert that Page Nine sent out a day ago, and he recognized you. Jared has…" She hesitated. "Jared's been a bit difficult the last couple days, with reason. We get it. We can't imagine his pain, but he was talking to Apollo last night and said that he wants to 'hook up' with his sister and score free Kings tickets."

She paused, her voice cracking.

"I am so sorry that he actually called, and I am so sorry that he even did this because you lost your father, too, and my heart is just breaking for both of you." Her voice grew hoarse.

I had stopped. We were right in front of the exit doors of the stadium.

Stone was watching me, moving in closer with his eyebrows raised. He was dressed in jeans with a Kings blazer on, and a Kings ballcap pulled low. His head inclined toward me and his mouth was flat, so I knew he could hear Georgia.

"He's such an avid fan of Stone Reeves. I think it stemmed because of his family's connection to yours, and it only got worse the last six months, and now with losing your parents and seeing that you're actually down there and with him, well, I'm just so sorry about this all."

I couldn't speak.

My body had rooted itself in place.

Noting all of this, Stone muttered a curse and took the phone. He turned away. "You're saying all that bullshit on the phone was for what? To get free tickets to one of my games?"

I couldn't hear her, but Stone was listening. He had the phone pressed so tight to his ear. I didn't know if he was doing it on purpose, to block me out and shield me, or because he was that pissed off. I was guessing it was for both reasons.

"Yeah." Stone.

Pause.

A longer pause.

"Yeah." He turned back to me, his eyes holding mine, but his face gave nothing away. "Yeah." And then, a sigh. "Yeah, I'm sorry, too. I will. Text me your information and I'll have my manager reach out. Thank you."

The call ended and he tossed the phone my way.

I caught it at the same time his hand came to the back of my neck. He gripped me and tugged me toward him. Bending down, so his forehead was almost touching mine, he said, "That kid is hurting and he's thinking of every possible way to avoid feeling even more hurt, so he fixated on me. That fixation grew after the accident, and what you heard from the mom was accurate. What you didn't hear from the mom is that he does want a relationship with you, but he doesn't want to actually leave their home. She said they'd put off the adoption if you wanted to wait and see if you did want to take him in. Knowing that, though, you gotta go up there and live there because that boy is adamant that he doesn't want to leave his hometown."

His jaw clenched.

His hand tightened on my neck. "All that said, most of that call was to get free tickets to my next Kings game. How are you feeling about that?"

I shook my head, whispering, "I have no idea."

He stared at me, long and hard, and let go of my neck. He stepped back, his arms going back to his pockets, hunching his shoulders forward. His head inclined again, but he could still see me just under the brim of his hat. "You're still in college. You're a kid. So's he. You take him on now, you got his college debt to take on. I know my dad paid for yours, but I didn't go three rounds with him just to see you take on debt that isn't your responsibility. Want my advice?" He cracked a grin, and I swear, the sight actually made my heart skip.

What the fuck was that?

I scowled, more at myself, but nodded. "Yeah."

"Call him later. Talk to him. Let Apollo's parents take him on as their own, and then work in a regular relationship with you. I talked to her and she seems legit. Had a few calls put out last week about them, too, and they all said what you said. Bud and Georgia Montrose are good people, good family, genuine. They ain't bullshitters, and I think her tears were the real deal. Be clearheaded about the future."

He tipped my head up, making sure I was looking him in the eye. He said, "Promise me."

My mouth dried.

I didn't know how to promise, because I didn't know what was in my head anymore. But I whispered, "Promise."

He waited, making sure, then let me go. "Good. Now, did you eat in there?"

Finally. Something I had done right. "I had a yogurt. And coffee." Score for me.

He scowled, "Fucking hell." He took my arm, walking me out the doors and back to where he'd parked. "Come on. Let's get food in you before going to that house."

It was the day after a game, so I hadn't expected to see a lot of people at the stadium, but there were enough workers milling about, all saying hello to Stone, that it was slow in hitting me. And I got that Stone was a new star in the football world, but seeing all these peoples' reactions, feeling the curious gazes as they paused wondering who was with him, a couple women shot me dirty looks—Stone was Famous Stone. He was only a year older than me, but acted ten years older. And it was because of this world, because of his career, that he'd grown up faster than most.

He'd barely come back once he left for college. I knew there had been some time off, but the rumor mill said he spent it at other athletes' houses and in pre-training programs. This was a different world than even the college football team.

Here, there was a relaxed but professional vibe in the air. Also, a no-nonsense feel, too. Like, there was no room for tries and missteps. You either did whatever you did, or you were replaced by someone who would.

I was a little in awe, but also I knew in the back of my mind that if this had been a normal day for me, no recent trauma or loss happening, that I'd be way more intimidated by Stone—and the

Stone in this world—than I was now. I was taking note of every-thing, almost like I was protected in an invisible car and the frame was made of firm, unbreakable glass.

Sounded weird, but it was what it was. I felt a layer of some-thing that I couldn't place all around me, so I wasn't really experi-encing every moment to the fullest. I didn't know if that was good or bad. And I wasn't going to question it.

He swung through a drive-thru and pulled away with enough food to feed a six-person family. Chicken sandwiches, minus the buns. Fries that he said were for me. Salads galore. A couple burgers, but mostly chicken. Also, grilled chicken.

The attendant fainted when she saw who was at the wheel, and a bunch of other employees came over. Stone handled it all with a polite smile, signing napkins for them, and a hat that had the fast food's logo printed on it.

I asked when we pulled away, "Is it always like that?"

"No. Nah. Just it's the day after a win and I don't usually stop during the day. I'm usually coming or going at odd hours. Team's local, too. I might get recognized only a third of the time if I were somewhere else, you know?"

I didn't, no.

He wasn't waiting for a response, and twenty minutes after that, he was pulling into my neighborhood. I almost sighed a little because finally I could recognize something.

"Forgot how stressful new things are."

I was half-musing to myself. He spoke up, "What?"

"Coming here. I didn't know anyone before I got here, and just now, I recognized the street. It made me feel comfort or something. Is that weird?"

"Makes sense to me. A lot of work goes into learning new things, places, people, and that's not even counting your school-ing. My mom said you came down here to study marine biology?"

I felt my face getting warm. It was so far from where we'd come from.

"Yeah."

He was side-eyeing me, slowing down to park in front of my house. A few other cars were already there, and those were more things I was recognizing. Like Noel's car. Wyatt's car. The girls' cars were all in the driveway and mine—I had a clear line of sight to my own parking spot from where we were parked. It was completely empty.

"Shit." I forgot about the car. "I have to get a new car."

His eyes flicked over, shutting the engine off. "I might know someone who's looking to get rid of a car. Nice car. He'll give you a deal."

"What? You're not going to buy me one?"

He stilled, his eyebrows pulling low. He had reached inside one of the bags and his hand paused before slowly pulling out one of the chicken sandwiches. "I could... Your debt, your school-ing, the funeral costs, that was on Dad to make things right for what he did to your family. Hospital bills, paying for the towing, I took care of that. Those bills aren't anything anyone in your posi-tion should take on, not when someone like me is there and knows you, and it just seems the right thing to do. But actually, buying you a car, I can. Thought that'd be personal, though? You'd like to pick out what you want. I know you have hang-ups about accepting financial help from someone who's not a bank or a scholarship grant."

His words touched me. "Thank you, and no. I was kidding. I want to do it myself."

Just would take me a bit to save up.

I frowned. "How long do I have to take it easy with this concussion?"

"Two weeks. And if you push to be let out of the house, you and I are going to go a few rounds. You're still struggling with remembering things." He nodded to my lap. "Case in point, I've told you three times to start eating those, and you had no clue I was even talking."

I looked down. There I was, clutching the small wrapper of fries, and I did faintly remember him telling me to eat them. I also faintly remember saying I would, and meaning to do just that because I liked fries, and then...Yeah. Distraction.

A Jeep zoomed past us, braking suddenly and wheeling into the house's driveway. All four doors opened and out streamed Nacho, Dent, Nicole, and Lisa. Bags of food were in their arms and they were starting to head to the house when Lisa looked up, saw our truck, then saw me. Her eyes narrowed, and she paused in mid-step, but a second's hesitation and she kept going.

Stone leaned forward. "The fuck?"

But Dent, who noticed Lisa's hesitation, looked over. And his eyes lit on Stone immediately, then went round. His eyebrows shot up and his arms opened in a flash. His bag of food was shoved into Nacho's chest, who took it as an automatic reflex.

Dent was already walking toward us, his head back. "Dude! Dude!" He saw me. "Dudette!"

A big smile came over Nicole's face, which seeing that relaxed me a little. If anyone could be mad at me, it'd be her since the big ol' ditch day. I never got the chance to apologize before the whole coma thing. Nacho, Dent, Nicole all came over, but Stone and I didn't move.

Lisa remained by the house, even after the front door opened and Wyatt and Noel came out. Savannah and Mia weren't far behind, but as I watched, both girls remained beside Lisa. Savannah's face was blank, but Mia still held a grimace.

The guys were rounding to Stone's side, but he waited, and when I looked back, he was watching me. "You and me. We got a few new things to talk about."

"Hey, man!" That was Dent, waving at Stone.

I just sighed, reaching to open my door.

All the guys went around to Stone's side. Nicole was the only one at my side. She stepped back as I got out of the truck. "Hey."

Another knot of tension loosened. She looked and sounded friendly.

"Hey, back."

She hesitated, her smile still big. "Can I hug you? How are you feeling?"

A hug? That was a good sign.

I nodded. "You can hug me."

She opened her arms and I stepped in, hugging her back.

Savannah broke from Mia and Lisa, crossing the lawn. She gave me a small grin and wave. "You're feeling better?"

I nodded, stepping back, and then Mia was moving in. Her hug wasn't as tight as Nicole's, but still. She seemed friendly-ish, too. More a lukewarm friendly, but I was taking it.

"Yeah." I spoke after we both stepped back, just continuously nodding. I'm surprised I wasn't getting concussion symptoms, at least being dizzy, so I stopped and tucked my hands behind my back. "No hospital stay after that last time."

The guys were still on the other side of Stone's truck, he was surrounded by them all.

Savannah glanced over, and stepped closer. "You're still at his place?"

I glanced, too, noting that Stone was waiting for me to look at him. He was talking to Wyatt, but his eyes were on me. He raised an eyebrow in question, and I nodded. I was okay. I didn't need him to step in. That's what he was asking. And how I knew that, I didn't know. I just did.

"Yeah. For the next two weeks until my head is better."

"That accident was so scary." Nicole touched my arm. "You have no idea. I've had nightmares. You were backing up and boom, the truck hit you and then you were gone in the ambulance. They were done for the day so they were speeding out of the alley."

"Yeah. I'll never look at a moving truck the same."

I almost grinned.

"Stone said he asked you guys to pack a bag the other day? Is there more of my stuff downstairs?"

Nicole said, "Mia threw a bunch of stuff into a bag for you, but I'm sure she didn't get everything. Are you... Well, Mia and Sav mentioned you kept asking if you could live here. You know the room's yours. Are you staying? Going back home?"

Oh. God.

Did they not know? I would've assumed they had heard Stone that night.

"Home?"

Nicole further clarified, "Yeah. Your parents. Were they mad about your car?"

Savannah was shaking her head, her eyes wide. "My dad would've freaked if I trashed my car. My mom would've gotten mad at him for getting mad at me."

Nicole laughed. "And you'd have a new convertible in about a week."

Savannah's eyes lit up. "Yeah. Probably."

I felt the back of my neck growing warm and looked, more from reflex. Stone was coming around the truck. I recognized the look on his face. It was set in a pissed-off expression, his eyes flashing and hard. He was going to say something. Either about my dad and Gail or about Lisa seeing me and trying to pretend she hadn't. Either way, Stone was done with this little side-trip.

And I didn't want to deal with the aftermath.

I stepped to him, my hand on his arm, and I spoke before he could, "Uh." I shot him a look, saying to the girls, "Yeah. My dad was furious about the car, but he was more concerned that I was okay."

Please. I was trying to convey to Stone. *Please don't say anything.*

I didn't want to see their pity. I didn't want to be treated with kid gloves, or worse, with extra cruelty. I just wanted the status quo to remain. Those blogs hadn't found out about my dad and Gail. They only talked about my car accident.

His jaw clenched, but he drew to a halt next to me. He stepped in, so my shoulder was brushing against his chest, but he didn't touch me otherwise. He was just there if I needed him.

"Oh, good. That's good, right? So you think you'll stick around?" It was one of the guys talking. His eyes were more on Stone, but his question was directed at me.

Stone shifted back, taking point behind me.

It was now all on me to steer the rest of the conversation.

It was a move he did when we were kids. I'd forgotten about that, and the memory almost brought tears to my eyes. Another sense of familiarity, and I was starting to cling to every moment of those.

"Will you?" That was from Savannah.

"Uh." I couldn't stay at Stone's forever, and I'd come to Texas for a reason. And I'd have to see about Jared, but was I a horrible person for wanting to stay? Wanting to keep going with my studies?

I didn't know.

"I'm not sure, but I'd like to hold onto to the room until I know for sure?"

"Of course." Nicole reached forward, squeezing my hand. "All semester. That was the original deal, and we can see later what you're thinking, too." She was looking from me to Stone, a slight gleam there, and it hit me then.

She thought Stone and I were together together.

"Oh—OH!" I stiffened, jackknifing away from Stone. "He and I, we're not like that. No. No way."

Stone started laughing behind me.

Nicole was frowning.

The guys mostly had blank expressions on their face.

Had I been wrong?

Nicole clarified, "No. I know. I was just letting you know the room is still considered yours."

"Wanna come in and have a beer?" That was from Wyatt.

Stone looked at me, waiting.

"I need to get things from my room."

I started to push through the crowd until I felt Stone's hand on my shoulder. "I'll come with, make sure you don't pass out on the stairs or something."

I glared at him. "I'm not that bad."

"Last seventy-two hours begs to differ. Don't know if you'll come back from the room with a kid in tow."

I shot him another glare, huffing and pushing forward.

Stone was half-guiding me, but he didn't need to do that either.

Once inside, I said over my shoulder, "You know I actually lived here. I know how to get through the house. You don't have to 'guide.'" And I stepped left into a hallway, when I should've gone through the kitchen.

I paused. Cursed. And backtracked.

Stone started laughing again. "You were saying?"

"Shut up. Concussion, remember?" I hissed right as the guys were all coming in behind us.

Stone threw them an easy grin. "Don't mind us. Apparently, Dust knows exactly where she's going, but just in case we take another wrong turn, how do you get to the basement again?" He poked me. "You know how to get to your room once we get down those stairs, right?"

"I said shut up!"

I swung through the kitchen, wrenching open the door, and

huffed all the way to the basement until it hit me what he'd done. He was needling me, knowing I'd get mad, and then I'd forget all the extra stuff I felt around those guys. Insecure. Doubt. Self-conscious. Embarrassed. That was the general smorgasbord of emotions for me.

He waited until we were in the game room and I was opening my door before he asked, "Those two always so welcoming to you?"

I breathed easier at the sight of my bed. My blanket. My books, not just my textbooks which most were at Stone's. The rest of my clothes. My shower caddy.

My picture frames...

"Holy shit. You have this?" Stone was pulling out the yearbook I stashed.

"No. Don't—"

But he was already opening it, falling to my bed. "Wow. This was your senior year?"

I knew what page it was on.

And I knew it, but I couldn't stop him, and a part of me didn't want to. A part of me needed one more person to read what was written on the very back page, the one page I kept just for her.

Going through the entire book, he laughed, smiled, cursed. He was shaking his head at some points. "Man. I remember those guys from football. I always thought they were dicks."

Funny. He was pointing to the guys he had partied with his last year, the same guys who went on to 'rule the school' after he and his friends left. The same guys who idolized him because he was 'making it big.'

It took fifteen minutes. Stone took his time, lingering on pages of people he remembered. He stopped, found me in the normal school section, then flipped around. "What the hell? Weren't you on mock trial or some shit like that?"

I sat in my desk chair. "Yearbook Committee. I was the junior editor when you were a senior." That's what he'd been thinking of.

He turned, thumbing through the pages until he found the yearbook staff. I wasn't there. "What the hell, Dust?"

He wasn't going to find it. It'd explain everything.

And I couldn't believe I was going to tell him, but I said with a slight nod, "Last page."

He frowned at me, then bent his head and flipped to the back of the yearbook.

He saw it, stilling. "Dusty." A soft one from him.

"I was never popular, but small town, small school. Last year. Everyone was sentimental, so I was surprised that I had to even reserve an entire page for her. But I did."

I didn't tell him the sad truth about what he read...the truth that she actually didn't write that in there. I had.

"Fuck." Another soft curse from him, his head bent and he was reading.

I knew the entire thing by heart. It's why I brought the yearbook with me

I moved to the floor, leaning back against the wall and pulling my knees up to my chest. "She always told me she wanted to sign my senior yearbook. Not the junior one. Sophomore one. Freshman one. My last one. It was a big deal to her."

"Your mom died in January."

I nodded. "The night you won the football championship."

"Yearbooks don't get printed till end of April."

Yeah...

I looked up, locking eyes with him. "I traced her letter in there. She asked me to."

His eyes closed. His head fell. His shoulders slumped. "Shit, Dusty. Shit." He moved in a flash. The yearbook was set on my desk and he had me up in the air, his arms around me. He moved back to my bed, and I was on his lap. His arms folded around me, and his head bent down to my shoulder. He breathed out, his air tickling my neck.

We sat there.

This hug wasn't for me. It was for him. And it was the most intimate hug or touch I'd had from Stone, but it didn't make my skin crawl. It felt oddly...nice. Familiar again. Like a memory that propelled us back to our childhoods, and I didn't know why I kept thinking about that stuff. It was so long ago. We'd moved past all that, but his chin was propped on my shoulder when there was a knock on my door.

I started to stand up. His hand tightened on me, holding me in place.

I tried again. He kept me in place again.

Sagging back down, I admitted defeat. "Yeah?"

The door opened. Nicole's head popped in and her eyes almost popped out. "Oh, sorry. I didn't mean to intrude—"

"You're not." Stone spoke almost lazily, no trace of the brief moment we'd just had. "What's up?"

She hesitated, biting her lip. Her hand gripped on the doorknob, and she kept looking over her shoulder. Coming to a decision, she shot inside and shut the door, turning the lock. "Sorry." She flashed us a grin, right at the same time as we heard footsteps running to the door and banging.

"Hey!" That was Dent. Or Nacho. I couldn't decipher their voices yet.

Nicole yelled through the door. "Let me talk to her, yeah? Stone went out the back door. He's not even in here."

Dent/Nacho harrumphed. "Bullshit."

Stone was grinning, tucking his head behind me and rubbing the bridge of his nose to my shoulder blade. It was sending tingles down my back. Goosebumps were breaking out over my arms, too. But enduring the shivers, I remained.

"I'm not lying, and she's crying. Back off."

"She's crying?" We all heard a soft curse muttered. "Okay. Sorry about your car, Dusty." A brief moment later, we heard his footsteps going up the stairs.

Nicole fixed us with a look, one eyebrow raised. She eased down into my desk chair. "Nacho came down because he wanted to invite Stone to hang out, watch the game tonight."

Stone cursed. "I should be watching that at my place."

Nicole went on, "And I came down to warn you that they have invited everyone. Literally everyone. You guys might want to sneak out in the next three minutes, or you'll get swarmed by fans."

Stone nodded, his hands easing on me and then starting to lift me off of him.

I stood.

He said to me, "Grab the rest of your stuff." He was looking around. "You have an extra bag? I can stuff whatever you need in that."

I didn't really have much, but since I couldn't bring myself to look at them, I pointed to the pictures on the wall. "Those." I turned for the bathroom.

"All of them?"

His voice dipped low, an edge to it.

I paused just in the doorway. "All of them."

I knew who was in the pictures. My dad. Gail. Jared. My mom. A picture of my dad, my mom, and myself. Another picture of my dad, Gail, Jared, and just me. And a last picture of me in my graduation gown after high school.

"Dust."

I looked back, not sure if I wanted to. I didn't know if I wanted to see whatever picture he could be holding.

It was my graduation one. He held it up. "You weren't this thin when I left. What happened?"

I lost thirty pounds that year. Pulling my gaze from it and back to his, I shrugged. "You know what happened that year."

His jaw clenched and he looked back down at the photo. I went to the bathroom, grabbing the rest of my things that Mia had left behind.

I could hear Stone and Nicole talking, but both were murmuring softly, and for a moment, I hoped he wasn't telling her about my dad and Gail. I was *still* mourning my mom. I hadn't even allowed myself to think about everything else I'd lost since then.

I was finishing up when my phone started ringing.

Going back to my room, I was looking at the screen.

"Who is it?"

I held it up. Screen said Jared.

He muttered a curse, then reached for it.

I wavered, but Stone was who Jared really wanted to talk to. Why fight it? I handed it over.

Stone took my phone, my bag over his shoulder, and headed up the back exit. "Jared, hey, man..." The door closed behind him, and I could only hear the faint trace of the call before that too faded.

"Wow." Nicole gulped. "So, you like, really know Stone Reeves?"

"Uh..."

"That night he came, everyone was in shock. He asked if there was a back exit, and when Mia said yes, he took off. It was like he just knew, and we came around the corner and you both were wrestling. Then your stuff got dumped and he tried to help you and you shoved him away. Everyone kept talking in the background and I was getting so irritated with them. I wanted to hear what you guys were saying, but I couldn't. The guys wouldn't shut the fuck up. Then you were getting in your car. He seemed like he wanted to stop you and bam!" She clapped her hands together.

I winced.

"You were out, like out out when we got to the car. Mia started screaming. And Lisa, you know she's in the nursing program, right?"

A faint memory surfaced being told that.

"She took charge. Started yelling no one could touch you. Stone was on the phone, already calling 911 and I swear, if Lisa hadn't looked ready to ream him, he would've yanked you out of the car and drove you to the hospital himself. The Rampage Reeves we see in the games sometimes, he was here. He was going nuts, cursing, threatening. Once he realized Lisa wasn't letting anyone touch you, he was on the phone, yelling at whoever would pick up. I lost track, but Lisa felt for your pulse and said you were breathing, too. Ambulance got here quick. I think that was one of the places Stone called to yell at, since it took them twelve minutes to show up." She had to stop for oxygen. "Wow. Just wow. He asked us for a bag. Mia's the one who packed it and gave it to him, then he took off with the ambulance. He came back later, and I'm pretty sure one of the other wide receivers dropped him off to get his truck. The guys were half-watching cause it was so late, but he looked absolutely wiped."

Stone hadn't told me any of this. Then again, I hadn't asked.

"I didn't realize all that happened."

"Just so you know, we all took a vow. We didn't tell anyone what happened. Nothing. No one knows about you knowing Stone Reeves."

"Really?" The 'we' she talked about was probably twenty-plus people. That seemed to be the core of their partying group. The football team. Them. And they had a few extra girls sprinkled in. I'd paid attention the two weeks I was there.

"Yeah. I mean, our group, but we didn't say anything to anyone else."

"Well, I got three Google alerts. I think it's out there."

"I'm just letting you know that since you're big on privacy, there's probably a whole sector of nerds on campus who don't know. So you know that much."

That was comforting. "Thank you."

"But I mean, like the regular sixty percent of campus probably knows. And when you come back, only maybe thirty percent will remember. And from even that, ten percent will recognize you. From *that*, maybe three percent will say something."

Around sixty-nine-thousand students went to our school. I got to look forward to a little over two thousand of them mentioning something about Stone and myself.

Two weeks in isolation at his house suddenly started to look good.

"So, yeah." Nicole's smile was still awed. "I just, I can't get over how much you know Stone. I mean, coming in and seeing you in his lap, and I know you said you and he aren't, you know, but man. Mia and Lisa are such bitches. They were saying you sucked his cock somewhere, but this—" She motioned to the bed where she'd seen me in his lap. "That's not what they're saying. I don't think they know how to handle this. It's awesome."

Awesome.

My dad and Gail died.

So awesome.

"Right."

There was nothing else to say. I was fine letting Nicole think what she thought, and I picked up the rest of my stuff. "Okay. I'm going to go."

"You need homework gathered for you or anything?"

I went to the door, but looked back. I thought about it, really thought about it. "No. I don't need that, but I do need to come back here after these two weeks are done. I need to be a normal student, and I need Mia and Lisa to continue being bitchy to me. I need that because—well, I don't know why, I just need it. Please don't say anything about me being in Stone's lap. We have a weird history."

"Oh." She blinked. "Yeah. Yeah, okay. No problem. I won't say a word."

Right.

Awesome.

CHAPTER 20

"YOUR FRIENDS ARE *JUST GREAT*."

Stone greeted me with that biting comment as I slid into the passenger seat, shutting the door. I knew what he saw. He knew I knew what he saw. There was no point in arguing. I just sat back and held my bag on my lap. "I told you before, I didn't know anyone before I moved down here."

A few of them were sitting on the steps outside, pretending to talk, but mostly still watching Stone. They waved as Stone pulled from the curb.

"Yeah." His hand flexed over the steering wheel. "Let's talk about that."

Which was code where he said the command and I was expected to confess everything.

Fuck that. I wasn't his bitch. I looked out the window instead.

"Dusty." A low growl from him.

A snap back from me, "Stone."

A second growl. "I care. Fucking hell. I care, okay? I wouldn't be doing any of this shit if I didn't still care about you. Those people didn't give a fuck about you, except the one girl. Not a goddamn one of them, and you're asking me to look away from that? I can't. Me being a guy and caring about a girl, I can't do that. It's not how I was raised."

He cared?

I couldn't.

That statement was swimming around in my head, but I couldn't. Not right now.

I focused on what I *could* process. "There's a big fucking debate that could be had for your last statement, so I'm not sure I'd be all high and mighty over that comment."

"I am trying to make up for that."

Low and quiet and controlled by him. I'd pushed a button and he was reacting, but he was trying to contain it. And I knew that was just another extension of the whole 'I'm trying to make up for that' part.

But still.

I wanted to clip out, wanted to throw it in his face by saying, 'Do better.'

I didn't, but I wanted to. "A movie. A blanket. We shared snacks. Then the next day, I was a stranger to you."

He sighed, his shoulders falling down. "Dusty."

"That was years ago." It was pent-up, and I had to get this out. "You were my best friend growing up. I loved your dog like he was mine. I know you were hurt when you walked away from me. I know you missed my mom, but since then, during those years, I lost my best friend. I lost my mom. I lost my childhood home." I had to skip a beat. He didn't need to know what else I lost before coming here. "And I have now lost my father, my step-mother, my car, and the second home that was never really a home to me. But I got you back? Is that the takeaway for me? The consolation prize?"

He cursed silently under his breath, hitting the turn signal and easing onto the interstate ramp.

"I would give you up in a *heartbeat* to get them back."

Still, he remained silent. A beat. Then, "So would I."

Oh. Damn.

Damn!

That broke the wall. I felt it crack in two, heard it even, and everything I'd been stuffing away and suppressing, I had a second's notice before I turned to him. I knew the tears were already shining in my eyes.

He saw, and his jaw firmed as he reached over for my hand. He kept a death grip on me. "Just let it out. You have to let it out."

The hole inside me was there. His words, my words, had punched a fucking fist through it and I felt as if the roof was caving in. The entire building in me was crashing. I was demolished inside and I'd been holding onto a thin fucking frame to keep me upright. That was gone now, and I was crumbling.

No. It was worse than that.

I couldn't keep it together.

"Stone."

His hand tightened on mine. "Just hold on. I promise."

I tried. I did. I was failing.

But then we were pausing. The gate was opening. And we pulled into his garage.

I didn't have to think about moving. Stone was out of his door and mine was thrown open in a flash. His arms went under me, and he scooped me out. Cradled to his chest, he maneuvered us through the house. Me, I was useless. I couldn't see. I couldn't hear what he was doing until we were in a room, on a bed.

A phone was ringing.

It was silenced.

He moved us both back so he was sitting against the headboard. It was similar to the other night, but this time, crying wasn't enough. My insides were being ripped out. One organ at a time. One tendon being slowly pulled from inside, shredding and being dropped on the floor.

I couldn't handle it.

My dad.

Gail.

All her texts. Her calls. She just wanted to be helpful and I thought she'd been annoying, and now there'd be no more calls. No more texts.

God.

I couldn't... I screamed, the sobs choking me.

A rough hand brushed down my face and I felt Stone's forehead to mine. "What do you need? What do you need right now?" He was breathing so hard. "Dusty. Please. I can't take hearing this from you. What do you need?"

Need?

Not to feel.

I couldn't think. Feel. I couldn't live. I didn't want to live. I needed to go, but I didn't dare say those words. Another scream came out, tearing out of me of its own volition.

I couldn't handle any of this. It was too much.

"Stone," I was sobbing, my hand on his chest. "Stone. I can't!"

I was clawing at his chest.

An invisible hand took a knife and was sheathing at my skin, but it wasn't working. It wasn't a clean cut. And that hand just kept going, digging in, trying to tear me open, and the more it wasn't working, the harder that hand was stabbing me. Twisting.

I was being tortured.

He adjusted me, throwing me up in his arms. A firm arm clamped around my back and his other hand was behind my head. "Dusty. What. Do. You. Need?!"

Finally. His words pierced through and I opened my eyes, to see his. They were wild. He was almost manic, desperate, but the hunger. I saw it in there. It was covered by something else, fear, maybe? Horror, more likely.

His hand dropped to my hip and he was kneading into my skin.

That other hand, the invisible hand, was trying to pry me open. I felt every inch, centimeter, millimeter, and I couldn't live through this.

I just knew it.

I gasped out, "Please. I can't feel. Not this."

"What do you want?" He was almost shaking me from the force of his own need. Savage. His eyes were filling with rage, but he was blanketing it. He was containing it. "Drugs? Alcohol? What do you need from me?"

I stopped just as the invisible hand opened me enough and was reaching in, all over again.

"I can't feel what I'm feeling—"

His mouth was on mine.

Hot. Hungry. Angry.

I gasped, and everything stilled. The world paused and I sat back, dragging in oxygen. A moment of peace, but the hand was coming back for more destruction. I could feel its impending reach and I acted, not thinking. I couldn't do that either, and I almost launched myself at him.

My mouth was on his. Desperate and starving.

He paused, pulling back. "Are you sure about this?"

I crawled up on his lap, my hands going right to his pants and I was frenzied in my movements. That was my response, and he took it as such. His arms swept me up again, he rolled us so he was on top and he paused above me, his eyes on mine.

Blind desire was in there, and I closed my eyes, my mouth searching for his again.

This wasn't gentle. This wasn't romantic. This was an escape and it was ugly and ragged. We were animalistic. There was no foreplay. God. I couldn't have handled that type of touch right now.

I wanted rough. Hard. Almost punishing.

He sat up, his eyes stormy and wild on me, and his hands finished undoing his pants.

I raced him.

I unzipped my pants, lifting my hips and shoving them down. My underwear, too. He leaned down, his hand coming to my thigh, and he helped me pull the rest free. He jumped off the bed, tossing both our pants to the ground, and he went to his night-stand. A condom was pulled out, then he was back.

I didn't give a fuck if both our shirts were still on.

That wasn't the goddamn point of this, but he was back. Condom on. And I reached down to wrap my hand around his dick. He was big and hard, and exactly what I needed to make me not feel. I guided him, almost like his cock was my personal dildo. I caught his grin, but I didn't give a fuck about that either. I was in control of this situation and he was giving me that.

Then, poised at my entrance, we both paused.

His eyes went to mine again. I bit my lip, and he sheathed himself inside.

I lifted, and he pushed, going even deeper, all the way in. Then his body enveloped me. My arms were around him. His around me, his hands sliding down to cup my ass and he lifted me up to him for better access.

Then, so fucking amazingly then, he began to move. And I felt it all. Every movement he made. Everything that I didn't want to feel was gone, suffocated by the enormity of him.

I cried out from the sensations. That peace, it was back. It fell on me, replacing the storm inside me, and I would literally come apart if he pulled away and stopped touching me, but then he began to move harder and faster.

His hand came up, grabbing my hair, and he yanked.

My eyes opened. His face was right there. I should've felt his breath, but he was watching me. His hips surged against mine again. So fucking forceful. So wild and out of control. Exactly like how I needed this to be.

"What do you want?"

I knew what he was asking.

"I need you to fuck me."

His eyes shuddered, but I wasn't done.

I added, "I need you to do it again, and again, and again. You got me?" My words were clipped and to the point. I wanted to pass out from fucking, not from the agony I knew was just waiting to claim me again. This was a Band-Aid. My wounds wouldn't be repaired by a simple fix. He knew that and I knew that, and then he nodded, and we were both agreeing to whatever it was that we were doing right now.

His mouth caught mine again. I allowed it. The sensations were hurtling through me and his tongue in my mouth was helping, but I reached down, took hold of his hips, and I reared to go back against him.

We fucked that night.

There were no nice words. No loving touches.

After the first round, he lay still inside of me. We didn't have to wait long. I waited. He waited. Maybe it was minutes. Maybe it was longer. I was a complete vacuum of nothing until I felt him start to harden again.

I looked at him. He looked up.

Silently, he pulled out. The used condom was thrown in the trash and a new one was put on. He climbed back over me. Seeing the bruises again, I reached for one on his side.

He knocked my hand away.

He was right. I saw the reminder in his gaze.

This wasn't a nice touch kind of night.

His eyes were hard. Well, good. I just hardened everything in me again, and he reached for me, taking my hips and he flipped me over so I was on my hands and knees.

Still no sound. No gasp of surprise from me.

We were almost in a battle now, whoever made the first sound lost, and his hand was rough running down my back. He lined up behind me, and I had a second's notice as his hand spread, his palm flat on me, and he thrust inside.

My head went down.

I would've moaned from the pleasure, but I couldn't make a sound. Not a goddamn sound. This was the lingering element of hatred still between us. Maybe things had thawed. He'd been there for me. He was still there for me, literally right now, but underneath those layers, there was a level of loathing between us that neither of us could see fit to let go.

I didn't know if that'd ever change, but it was there, and I needed it. It gave me a sense of familiarity.

As he rammed back in me, I pushed upright.

Oh no. He wasn't going to punish me that way. I wanted it. I yearned for it. I would probably ask for it, but I was going with him. This was a joint venture, and he wrapped a hand around my waist, his face falling to my shoulder. I felt his teeth scrape against my skin, sending a shiver down my spine, as he kept moving in and out of me.

I reached back, my hand on his hip, and I moved with him.

Our bodies were sensuously rolling as we both knelt upright. I kept up as long as I could until the climax was building, and I fell forward. His arm caught me, holding me so I didn't fall completely down. I pushed up on my hands, on all fours, and I heard a smothered grunt from him.

His hand went to my ass, flexing. He smacked me.

Had he... I twisted around. Those eyes were waiting for me, boring into me, and there was a hint of amusement, but then he hit me again and I almost cursed at him. Now he grinned, just slightly, before he paused, holding both my hips, and he pushed in once more, all the way inside. He held still, rotating around, rubbing everywhere before thrusting slowly back.

I broke. I lost the battle and voiced my pleasure. "Ah!"

A guttural gasp came from me, and my knees shook. My arms gave out. I fell to the bed, but he came with me. A hand on the headboard above me, he began pistoning inside of me, as this round was all about him.

He wasn't giving it to me for me anymore. This was all him. Animals. Both of us.

He came with a roar the same time I did, and he fell down on me. Both of our bodies were shuddering.

I needed a breather, and judging by his panting, he did, too. Still. He lay over me, a hand skimming down my back, curving over my ass. But then he growled, and he was pushing my shirt off me. Yes. That was a splendid idea.

He slipped out and lifted up. I rolled to my back, pulling my shirt up and off me. My bra was next, and I didn't have to say anything. His shirt was off and he came back down. Nope. He changed his mind. Getting up, padding barefoot to his bathroom, and then he was pissing.

The toilet was flushed.

The water ran again. He was washing his hands. And he came back, no shame.

There was none with me, either, not this day, this moment.

His eyes found mine, and he stood over the bed, just studying me as I returned the favor. His eyes almost caressed my body, running over me. Those shoulders. So sculpted and cut. His chest. His stomach. His hips. The V that ran down his stomach and past his groin, it was begging me to touch.

So I did.

Sitting up, I scooted to the edge of the bed, trailing my hand down his muscle.

He moved into me and I glanced up. His eyes were hooded, darkening the more I touched him. He was enjoying this, and knowing what he really wanted, I found him again. My hand circled around him, a good, firm grip, and then I began to stroke him.

He groaned.

I kept stroking.

Another groan, those eyes were almost messy from his pleasure.

I loved it.

And I loved not feeling what I'd been feeling before. Those emotions were pushed aside, and stomped down. They were so far down, I knew I had tonight to bask and take refuge in this momentary shelter, and because I just wanted more of him, I bent down and took him in my mouth.

"Shit," a silent hiss from him. His hands grasped the side of my head, his fingers tangling with my hair.

I took him in deep, sucking on him.

"Oh, fuck."

I kept sucking on him until he began to move in my mouth.

No. This wasn't enough. The angle needed to be better. I withdrew, got up, and shoved him down. Then I was kneeling between his knees, and my mouth was back on him. I didn't look at him to see what he was thinking. I didn't care, but I knew his body was loving my mouth on him.

I opened my throat even wider as he began moving in my mouth, and rising for the best angle, he held my head still as he thrust inside, and our eyes met, held while he continued what he was doing. A full body shiver wracked through me, and I swear it made him come, because he exploded then.

I paused, catching his semen.

He pulled out and shook his head. "Don't swallow that."

Yeah. Fine with me. I was the one padding to his bathroom now. I spat it out, then washed my mouth out, and I stared at myself for a second.

My hair was a mess. My eyes were red-rimmed from the earlier sobbing.

I hadn't worn makeup in days, so my face was just splotchy from the sex and the shit-show before that, but I took note of the rest of my body. I'd gotten thinner since coming here. I hadn't thought that was possible, but I knew I'd lost weight from what had happened before, but no. What was I thinking—my dad, Gail —a sob slipped out before I knew what I was feeling.

But he was there, his hand on my side.

I looked up, almost panicked. I thought I had a night before those feelings would come back. But I started thinking, and that was all I needed. They were unleashed, swimming to the surface at a surprising speed. As if knowing what was going on inside of me, Stone's eyes darkened, holding mine in the mirror.

He stepped up behind me, a firm hand running down my back. He fitted himself there so I felt every inch of him, and his mouth lowered to my shoulder. His eyes were still holding mine captive and I watched, a prisoner, but wanting to surrender to him, needing him to take over, and I was transfixed as his teeth scraped over my skin again.

I gasped, arching my back. A searing spliced through me, almost making me jerk upright in his arms until his hand slid around to my front. His palm was heavy on my stomach. His fingers spread out, and those eyes still watching me watch him, he moved his hand up, up, up, and it encircled one of my breasts.

Then he nipped at my shoulder again, moving to my neck. He ran his teeth over me, lingering where my artery was, but he only swirled his tongue there, and I moaned this time.

I gave in. He won this round.

His eyes flared. Victory surged in him.

He was plastered to me, so I knew he was hard again, but he was bare. He paused, his eyes on mine. "The condoms are all the way in the room. Are you—?"

I shook my head. No. I didn't tell him that I hadn't needed to use birth control for the last year. I hadn't had a period, but he only nodded and he stepped away.

I held myself where he left me, exactly, and I even placed both hands against the mirror in anticipation.

I wanted to watch us. That's what he wanted too, then he was back. He was rolling the condom on, and he saw I was still in the same position. His mouth tugged up in approval, but he stepped up behind me, and there was no warning this time.

He was in, pushing, thrusting, and I was pushing back from the mirror just as hard.

He rode me. I rode him.

It was exactly what I asked from him, and through the rest of the night, he gave it to me. Over and over again. There was a break where his phone wouldn't stop ringing, so after we'd finished that round, he stepped out from the room to take the call.

I lay there, eyes open, staring at the ceiling, and I didn't move an inch. I was naked. I hadn't pulled the sheet over me, and he returned sometime later. I made sure I wasn't thinking when he left, so I didn't know how long he'd been. Could've been seconds, minutes, or a full hour. I had no clue and I wanted it that way.

Then he was back, falling on top of me, again, and I wrapped my arms and legs around him, knowing he'd make me feel other sensations in a moment. And, as he slid inside me once more, he did just that.

CHAPTER 21

SOMETHING DROPPED to the floor with a thud, and I rolled over.

I was disoriented a moment. Where was I? Then the memories came flooding in. I was being blasted by erotic images of me and Stone, and then I looked over. What time was it? I'd fallen asleep in his bed and looked for a clock. It was around eight in the morning.

"Wha—"

"Sorry." He came over, sat on the edge of the bed and knelt back over. He was putting shoes on.

I couldn't make sense of anything. "What's going on?"

I sat up, and looked down. Stone had grabbed one of my bags of clothes and brought it in for me. I pulled on a tank top and underwear. Still. No shame here. We'd violated each other a thousand different ways last night. I didn't move to cover myself, just stared at him, a little dumbfounded.

He finished tying his shoes and got up. Pulling on a hoodie, he grabbed for his wallet and keys. "Okay. I'm off. I have to head in and I'll be gone most the day. You'll be okay?"

He paused, glancing to me.

He added, "I'm not talking about your concussion, because you shouldn't do shit today. Got that? Keep television to a minimum. No reading. Don't exert your brain. Just don't. Trust me."

Great. That left me alone with only thoughts. Not a good picture there.

But, I manned up. "I'll be fine."

"I'm not shitting around. Will you or won't you? I can arrange for that one friend of yours to come and hang out if you need easy company?"

I shook my head. "I'll be fine."

"Okay. You remember the code, right? If you need to leave for any reason, but seriously. Don't. I mean it."

"I know!" I glared. "And I remember."

He stared at me. I stared up.

All the screwing was done. We were back to our normal, almost-loathing dynamic, though I felt myself wanting to say something to push his buttons, make him hate me. You're comfortable in what you know.

He sighed, running a hand down his face. "You're freaking out?"

"No." Fuck. Shit. I sat up, and holy hell, my entire body ached. It was worse than after the coma even. I balked when I scooted to the edge of the bed and stood. "I'll be fine. We fucked. That's it. You helped me out. Thank you for that." I motioned toward his door. "Go and live your big life. I will be fine."

He didn't move, but some of the impatience melted away. The lines around his mouth softened.

What a fucked-up pair we were. I snapped at him and it settled him.

"Go, Stone. I will be fine."

He nodded. "Don't talk to your stepbrother today. If he calls, wait till I'm here. Okay?"

I nodded before he left the room.

I was slower following, going to my section of the house.

I didn't know why he made that suggestion, but whatever. I was so far from thinking about that right now. My stepsister guilt had been dispensed. Jared was with an entire family who wanted him. I'd been fucked by a superstar who was helping me out of guilt. Okay. He said he cared, but I wasn't looking at him with rosy glasses.

This wasn't a romance waiting in the wings.

Maybe more sex. Hot sex. Primal sex. Yeah. Maybe that shit, but nothing else, and remembering all of this, I had two weeks to deal. Two weeks to let my body heal. To let my heart deal with the mourning much as I could handle it, and then I had to make a plan because fuck, I was going to need a job when Stone would send me packing.

I heard the garage opening, the gate opening a second later, but then I was in my room and I almost collapsed on my own bed.

No, no, no. I couldn't do that. I'd think, that led to feeling, that led to wanting the world to swallow me up. Moving. I had to keep moving or doing something. But I was hurting. Nope. Sitting still was worse than the physical pain.

So, what, then? I'd never been into drugs or alcohol, not more than a social wine or something. Cleaning, that's it. I could clean. But no. Stone's house looked impeccable. He must've had a cleaning lady come in on the regular, I was sure of that.

Back to square one.

I washed up, changed my clothes, and by then the bed was beckoning to me again. Phone. I had to find my phone, at least have it by me. Going in search, it took me back to Stone's room. There was a pile of my stuff on his floor, and kneeling down, I scooped it all up and went back to my space. I could snoop, take in what his room looked like, but not at that moment. I didn't have the energy for that.

A yawn left me.

We'd barely slept, so hopefully day one could be passed just by sleeping. Some of the panic subsided, and when I got to my room, I was yawning again. It was the kind that made you tear up, and I dropped my stuff on a chair, digging through it until I found my phone.

Plugging that in, I didn't check the screen.

Day one of actually dealing with my concussion was about to commence. Doing nothing, here I go. I got back in bed, pulled the covers up, and rolled over.

I slept day one away, meandering out to the kitchen sometime that afternoon, and that's when boredom hit me. Not normal boredom. This was the kind of boredom that was verging on panic because I needed something to do or I was going to lose it.

I already had lost it the night before and a marathon of sex had been the result.

An idea took hold standing in the kitchen. Stone liked when my mom baked for us. So, going into his kitchen, that's what I was going to do. It started first with spying a pile of cookbooks in the pantry. I'd been in there looking for water, only realizing later the water would probably be in the fridge, but maybe it was fate. Within an hour, I was sitting in the middle of a stack of fourteen cookbooks.

I couldn't believe Stone had these, and I really couldn't believe he had them stashed away in a corner. Why not use them if you were going to have them? Then I stilled, opening one. First page.

To Stone, I know how much you liked that birthday cake I made for your seventh birthday. Here's the recipe for it. Page 147.
— Sherry

I looked at the next.

Another note.

Stone, those cookies you devoured with Dusty for Halloween that one year you were in fourth and she was in third, the recipe is on page 67. — Sherry

And a third.

Stone, I'm breaking tradition here. I know you liked my baked goods, but I couldn't resist. Remember the sloppy joes that you raved about? I made them for Dusty's tenth birthday. The recipe is on page 183. — Sherry

I looked through a fourth, a fifth.

Sixth.

Seventh.

My heart was pounding, then dropping, until I got to the last cookbook. Every single one of them. All from my mother. Each with a note written from — *Sherry.*

Why?

Why did she do this?

But the note on the last one had me doing a double-take.

Stone,

I know you're off to do great things in your future. I know you feel badly about slighting my daughter. I've come to enjoy our Saturday morning grocery trips, but this is going to be my last note to you. I'm dying and you're officially the first to know, though you won't get this book till after I'm gone.

I have loved you as my own son, and I know Dusty still cares about you. I have a wish for you. If you are ever in a situation where my daughter needs help, please be there for her. She's the silent trooper. She suffers in silence and she doesn't think I can tell. I do. And I know life has ups and downs, and you both will have challenges. Please reach out. Please care for each other. Please don't let this thing between your mother and my husband keep you away.

Life is short. Live. Forgive.
I will be watching over both you and Dusty.
— All the love, Sherry

All the love.

All. The. Love.

I read those words over and over and over and over. I lost track how many times I read them.

I knew she cared for Stone. I knew there'd been a special relationship, but this was more. This was so much more than I thought it was, and it cut me. It cut me deep.

He hadn't even lied to me. I was replaying when I asked him why he was helping me, and he said it. Point-blank. Because of my mom, because he cared for her. Here was the proof. She cared for him back. And my dad and his mom?

What the hell? Again.

What. The. Hell?

Thoughts were flashing in my mind. Bad thoughts. Miserable thoughts.

Like, why'd she have to go?

Why'd he have to go?

Why'd they have to drive on that road? At that time of night? Why'd the deer have to choose to cross the road at that exact second?

Was it me?

Was I cursed?

Did everyone I love have to be taken from me?

My insides were twisting all in a knot, then being knotted again, and again. Bent over, my forehead to the ground, I rocked in a fetal position. Every one of those questions plaguing me, laughing at me, being screamed in my head, taunting me.

It was me.

I was the problem.

I was the connection.

They loved me, and they all died.

I had to go.

Standing.

I put the cookbooks back where they were, and I had one thought. Leave. I had to leave. I wasn't a pity project. I felt Stone's loathing last night. I knew it was still in him, and now it was back and raging inside of me. It hadn't quite left me.

Fuck him.

I was done.

I could do this. Fuck everything.

Numb. I'd go numb. And I'd keep going. That's what I'd do, and one day, I had to hope—one day it would be better. I would be so used to the pain that I'd almost think it wasn't there. That day was my goal to get to.

I went and packed.

I had a goal in mind. I had motivation. It helped, knowing you had to do something in order to survive. Your focus suddenly became crystal clear. I didn't have a ton of stuff here, but my books were the heaviest. I left half my clothes behind. They didn't fit in my bag.

Leaving, I put the code in and hauled ass. I wasn't sure what would set the system off, but I got out of the garage and there was no angry alarm going off, so that was one feat accomplished. The gate was next. I had no clue how to open it, so I tossed my bag up and over, then I climbed. I went slow, but I got there.

Once over, I pulled my phone and ordered an Uber.

The Uber pulled up.

I got in and I just wanted to get as far away as possible.

CHAPTER 22

THE VOICES WOKE ME.

My fan wasn't on, and while they weren't yelling or raised, I could still hear them.

Maybe it was because my body had been waiting, or maybe I was more rested because of the concussion. Either way, when I woke, I rolled over. It was around eleven that night, so maybe the group was back from partying or Stone was here. I was prepared for both.

Grabbing my phone, I checked it first. It was blank.

I paused, frowning. I hadn't expected that, but I still sat up and raked a hand through my hair. I hadn't changed clothes when I got back to my room, so I looked down, remembering that I'd blindly grabbed a different shirt and it must've been one of his. The King's emblem was prominent on the front, the whole name for the team was short for the Texas Kingfishers.

Shit. Oh well. I was already up and moving.

My feet were already in my flip flops, and I had my phone on me, just in case.

I made my way through the basement and to the stairs,

pausing just enough to hear Lisa say, "I'm telling you, she's not here."

"She's here."

That was Stone. He had come, and yeah, he was pissed.

That made two of us.

I went upstairs, rounding the corner in the kitchen until I could see Stone in the doorway.

Lisa was standing in front of him. A guy with her.

That was it. Just those two. I didn't recognize the guy, and both had their backs to me. Not Stone. He saw me right away, and his jaw clenched.

"Is this the concussion? Has it affected your head that much?" He lowered his head, those eyes pinning me in place. A pause, then a bite, "Nice shirt."

Yeah. I should've changed.

I ignored how Lisa and her friend turned to me, surprised.

A second bite from him. "Is this where we finally part ways because I'm getting real fucking tired of this shit, Dust."

Dust.

I flinched, then no. Fuck no. I swallowed some acid and made damn sure my voice came out strong. "I found the cookbooks, Ace."

He flinched at that name. His dad used to call him that, and I knew he hated that nickname.

"What cookboo—" he started to ground out.

I took a step forward, but only one. I stopped, folding my arms over my chest. "You know. The fourteen that my mother gave you."

It took a second, then horror filled his gaze. His head jerked backwards. His nostrils flared. "Fuck."

"Yeah." I clipped that one out now.

"Dusty. Those books, they were a gift..."

"I read the notes."

I was calm. He was frantic. I saw it surging up in him.

And I didn't give a fuck. I was cold. Numb.

I had moved on.

I waited a half second before I drove another nail into him. "I wonder if my dad left you a note, too? Maybe he did? Maybe he explained whatever the fuck happened between him and your mom?"

It came out as an accusation, but it was really a question. If he'd tell me or not, and I waited, bated breath, and when he stepped back, I knew.

He wasn't going to tell me.

Then fuck him.

I didn't need Stone.

We could go back to hating each other.

I didn't need anything.

I didn't need anyone.

Except Stone. You needed him last night, a voice whispered in the back of my mind.

I shut that down, real fucking quick.

"Dusty." Stone's head hung down. His hands went to his hips. He'd lost his fight.

I moved forward, knowing when to capitalize on the moment and I even gentled my tone, knowing it was the last and final nail in our coffin. "You're off the hook."

His head swung back up. "Excuse me?"

"Taking care of me. You said it yourself. You were doing it for her, but you're off the hook. I'm letting you off the hook." Another step forward, but this one hurt. It felt like I was pushing into wet cement, the kind that went to my chest. Still. I took another step, forcing myself. "I don't know what she was talking about, the thing with your mom and my dad, and..." He went rigid. I pushed forward, "Maybe I don't want to know after all.

Maybe I'll find out and I'll hate him, and right now, I can't hate him. I'm still mourning him."

"Dusty." So quiet now. He was giving in.

I was winning.

Another step. This time the cement was almost dry, but I pushed through. I had to. "Thank you for everything, and I mean it. *Everything*."

His eyes darkened. Oh yeah. He got my drift.

I went on, "But I'll take it from here." I reached for the door, my intention pretty obvious, but I paused.

He continued to stare at me. A full thirty seconds. Another thirty.

My heart was pounding, wondering if he was going to let it go, let us go, half fearing he would and half needing him to, and then he jerked forward. My heart jumped into my throat as he circled the back of my neck, dragging me to him. He stopped, our foreheads were almost touching, and I wondered if he was going to kiss me, but he didn't.

"Don't call me when you're needing someone's dick to help chase away the nightmares, Dust."

He spoke quiet so the other two couldn't hear, but his words... they pierced me and my hand fell away from the door, but he was gone after that.

Fine.

Good riddance.

I shut the door after him and threw the lock on.

"Actually, you don't need—" From Lisa.

I threw her a scathing look. "I don't give a fuck."

CHAPTER 23

CONCUSSIONS SUCKED.

I was going nuts by late morning. Everyone had left from the house. I assumed Lisa told everyone I was back because they were quiet, or quieter than they used to be, or maybe they were getting into the swing of school again? Either way, I couldn't stay in my room any longer.

So I cleaned.

All day.

I started in the bathroom. Nothing strenuous, just little things like reorganizing the medicine cabinet and then moved on to the game room...the entire DVD collection that seemed to now be turning into an antique collection was in disarray. Then it was the pile of magazines left in the basement kitchen corner.

Then the towels in the basement closet got reorganized.

Then the stairs needed to be swept.

The floors were vacuumed. The ones that needed to be swept, got swept. Every piece of furniture got dusted.

The entire basement kitchen was cleaned. The fridge was

wiped down, the food put back in neat sections, Lisa's section and mine underneath.

It was three in the afternoon when I finished all that. My stomach growled, so food. I'd eat. I could pass the time with that then, but no thinking. I couldn't handle that. But I knew me. I'd start thinking, remembering, and I'd lose it, so I got my phone and headphones, and I went to task. I was listening to an audiobook when I finished cooking my meal. It wasn't anything fancy, but I couldn't stop once I started.

Finding flour, sugar, enough to bake something else, I started going.

I made a cake. Cookies. Pastries. There was a batch of no-bake cookies waiting to be scooped up when I felt a presence behind me.

Whirling, a scream was already in my throat, but it was Lisa.

She had stopped at the end of the stairs, her mouth hanging open, her eyes big, and her bag dropped from her fingers to the floor. She was taking everything in, and I had every inch of that basement covered with some sort of baked good.

I remembered. Shit.

The flour was hers. Everything was hers that I had used.

"Um."

"Holy Batman, woman." She was still taking everything in. "You made all this?"

"I have a concussion and I'm going through a period in my life right now where I can't think straight. So...this," I motioned around me, "and I cleaned."

She was taking that in, too, her eyebrows raised as her mouth closed. "Yeah. I noticed." She assessed me, her head cocking to the side. "You have two weeks of this?"

"Well." I was redoing the math since the first week was spent in the coma and then at Stone's. "Maybe just a week, actually." Yes! That was right. Stone kept forgetting there was time already spent in the hospital, and those totally counted. "Six days, actually."

My week was looking way better now. I could think in six days. I could busy myself with homework and college again.

My knees almost gave out from relief.

I could call the Quail. I could call Siobhan. I could set up study dates. I could start working. I could busy myself in other ways. Hell to the yes. Halle-freaking-lujah.

"You, uh, need more places to clean or..." She was taking in all the food. "...or cook stuff?" She gestured upstairs. "I know Mia and I have been bitches to you, but we're trying to be civil. Shit's not about you, but anyway. You can go upstairs if you need more to do." She half-grinned to herself. "Don't think anyone would turn down free cleaning and a personal chef."

I should've been insulted? Maybe? She was okay with me cleaning her shit. Lovely. But I was so relieved, to be honest. "You think? They wouldn't get mad at me using their food to cook at all?"

She snorted. "We're in college. You think we have money to cover personal chefs? God, no. We might've been kissing your ass if we'd known all this before." She turned for her room and a second snort came from her. "Hell. When Char comes crawling back, we might not take her at this rate."

Then she was in. Then the door was shut. Then I was alone, remembering I only had this place for a semester.

Nope. Not going there.

One day at a time. Or, well, six days at a time right now. I'll figure the rest out when the time comes.

So, with all that in mind, I took the upstairs to task.

She was right. Savannah and Nicole gave me hugs, and Mia's greeting was a reserved hug, but all echoed Lisa's thoughts. So I cleaned and I baked.

That evening, I had a complete taco buffet made for twenty people. Guacamole. Salsa. Avocado. Multiple dipping sauces. Ground meat. Lettuce. Cheese. Corn tortillas. Soft tortillas. Hard shells. Refried beans.

Day four: I moved to the backyard and began listening to landscaping audiobooks.

Day five: The guys went to the grocery store, restocked everything, and I went to town. Again. That night they had a full pizza buffet spread for them. Pepperoni. Sausage. Taco cheese. Goat cheese. Mozzarella ball cheese pizza.

There were three different sauces to go with the pizzas.

I even shredded parmesan cheese myself into a bowl by each pizza.

They had a Thursday night football party. Eagles were playing Vikings, and I grabbed a slice of pizza and hid in my room that night. Cooking. Baking. Cleaning. Now landscaping. Those things I could do alone, only when I was alone. If people came around, I was gone. Too much stimuli with my concussion.

And I still had two more days to go.

The house was empty on Friday. Texas C&B had an away game, so everyone traveled for it and I had to start thinking what to do to get ready for the next week.

I needed a car for errands. The reason I answered Char's ad was because this house was four blocks from campus, so I could walk, *if* necessary. It was necessary now. So that meant walking back and forth for me next week, and I'd need to call the Quail to set up my hours.

There'd been no communication with Stone. I was glad.

Jared was different. We started texting back and forth, then the last two nights, we'd moved to phone calls. They weren't long, but I was grateful to hear what Stone had said. Jared was angry.

He'd been fixated on Stone. There were no more guilt trips about me taking him on, if I wanted him or not. For going through what I was dealing with, he seemed to be doing better than me. I could hear that he genuinely liked where he was.

I agreed with Apollo's mom and Stone. Jared was in a stable environment there. He wouldn't be with me, but that was another thing I needed to remedy next week. As soon as I could, I needed to travel up there just to see him, hug him, check in with him in person.

That was at the top of the list.

That night, I broke.

I'd been doing good. Going. Not thinking. But with the planning that day, thoughts and worries snuck in, and unlike the last time, I didn't have anything to push these emotions off. I let them in. I felt them. And I cried. I sobbed.

I needed to sob.

Saturday was different. I couldn't stay inside any longer, so I was out. I was walking. And without intending to go there, I found myself at campus.

Then, the library.

Then a back section and I sat there, my headphones on, and I breathed. I just breathed.

I felt an attack coming on. I didn't know why. I didn't know what started it, but it was coming and I had to focus on just getting air in and out through my lungs. That tended to help. I needed my mind to shut down, too, or I needed to leave.

My phone was in my hand.

Stone said not to text. What a bitch I would be, texting him now. I got through my episode last night. I could handle this one just fine.

Not that I could handle it, I would.

I would be fine.

I would be fine.

I would be fine.

I wasn't fine.

My pulse was rising. My vision was becoming blurry. I felt my body heating up, shooting past my normal temp and that wasn't a good sign. Now I was just getting anxiety about getting anxiety or whatever this was. I hated it. I loathed it.

I reached for my phone.

No! I couldn't text Stone.

He'd been helping me because of my mom. He fucked me. I couldn't imagine he fucked me because of her, but I had to deal with this alone. He told me not to contact him when I needed help with my nightmares. This was a nightmare.

I was alone.

No one was coming to help.

And then, as if I had conjured it to happen, my phone started ringing. *Stone calling.*

My breath was becoming more shallow, but when I started seeing stars, I hit accept, putting the phone to my ear.

I couldn't talk.

My throat wasn't working.

I slid out of my chair, my butt hitting the floor, and I leaned forward. My forehead bent over, almost touching the ground. There. I could handle it this way. I could get through this attack like this.

Right?

"Dusty?"

My lungs were rattling.

He cursed. "Where are you?"

They were seizing again. I pushed out, it sounded as a wheeze, "Library."

"I'm at a team thing, but I can be there in thirty. Hold on, okay?"

I should tell him not to come.

I had pushed him away. Straight up. That's what I did. Him being inside of me all night long, I already felt stripped to him. Then finding those cookbooks, unraveling this mother-like relationship he had with my mom and hearing there was some other secret thing going on with my dad and his mom, I hadn't wanted to deal with any of it.

So I pushed him away because I was safe alone. It's what I was used to. No one could hurt me then, but here I was being weak and an asshole, and just so fucking thankful he had called me because I knew my pride was a problem. I wouldn't have reached out. I would've endured, but now I only had thirty minutes to worry about.

Thirty.

I could do that.

Easy-peasy.

But no. I'd have to stand. I'd have to walk out of here because Stone couldn't search the library. He'd be accosted just parking in the lot.

I needed to meet him halfway.

With that thought, I would get up. In a minute. Another minute. Five more. Okay. Ten more.

I was fully paralyzed. I couldn't get myself to stand up, least of all walk out of there. Then my phone was going again. It was a text this time.

Stone: Where in the library?

Me: Second floor. Curled in a ball on the ground.

Stone: I'm coming.

I didn't know how he could.

I tried pushing myself up again, but my body decided not to follow my commands. Curled in a ball, my forehead to the ground, nope. My body was saying it was just fine like this. Stay here. We'll be safe here.

I needed to go...then, a footstep down my aisle. I tensed.

A soft voice, "Dusty? Is that you?"

Siobhan.

She came forward, kneeling beside me. I felt her. "Are you okay?"

No. I was in agony and I couldn't talk, I was in that much agony.

"Dusty." More urgent. More concern. Her hand came to my shoulder.

I couldn't move.

"What's happening to you?"

I was having an episode. Couldn't she tell?

I should be in a mental hospital. They had drugs for this, whatever was happening to me. I couldn't even function on my own in public. This was ridiculous. And I was fully thinking these thoughts at the same time my body was locked up in a fetal ball.

"Dusty!" She began shaking me harder. "You're scaring me."

There was a rush of other footsteps.

She squeaked, whirling around.

"I got her." That was Stone.

"Um." She stood up, backing out of the way.

He moved in, then his arms were around me. He asked in my ear, "Can you move at all?"

A small shake of my head. That was it.

He cursed, but lifted me.

Once I was up, my legs went down and my arms went around him, and I could stand again. It was like he jarred me back to life.

Then he was in front of me. The aisle was too narrow, so Siobhan was behind him. He had on a large black sweatshirt, the hood pulled up, and a hat on underneath. The brim was pulled low, half-masking his face so only his nose, cheeks, and jawline could be seen. His mouth, too.

His so fuckingly talented mouth.

He was raking me in, and whatever he saw had that jaw clenching. His hand tightened on my arm. He demanded roughly, "What do you need right now? I can't carry you out of here. I just can't. Too much attention, so what can I do to help you so you can walk out of here by yourself?"

I touched his face, and I closed my eyes. Leaning in, my head to his chest, I stood there.

Slowly, almost hesitantly, his arms came around me. He held me. And only then did the knot that had a paralyzing hold on me start to unlock itself. My body began to ease, calming down. My temperature returned to normal. I felt my lungs expand.

I waited, past what was a normal time for a hug. But I needed it, and it was helping, and I knew Stone could tell. His hands splayed out on my waist, holding me above my hips. He was just waiting, letting me lean on him. Then, finally, I could talk and I gasped out loud.

His hand came up to the back of my neck. He gripped me, pulling my head back so I was looking him in the eyes.

They were hard, almost dead-like, but he asked, "You done being a bitch?"

Siobhan gasped behind him.

I hadn't realized she was still with us.

I nodded, a small up and down, but it was true. He knew what I'd been doing. I said, but it came out as a whisper, "I'm sorry."

"I get it. What you're going through, I'm shocked you're not a bigger bitch."

I closed my eyes and my head went back to his chest. His hand softened on me, cupping the entire side of my face from my cheek to his fingers behind my neck. His fingers slid up into my hair and he cradled me to him.

"Um, I think..." Siobhan again. She sighed. "I'll call you later?"

I nodded, but my voice would've been muffled against Stone's chest. I was in no hurry to pull away and face her, not how I must've been looking, but I snaked an arm out around him and reached out for her.

She paused, I heard her, and I felt her grip my hand. She gave me a squeeze. "Later, Dusty."

I squeezed her back in response, then she let go and Stone kept on holding me to him. His head was bent down. I was in a back corner, so we were almost in our own section of the library, a moment of privacy before we'd have to go out and face the world.

I just wasn't ready for that yet.

CHAPTER 24

ONCE I COULD WALK on my own, Stone led the way.

I had no clue how he knew where to go, but I went with him. Down the aisle. Through a door. Down stairs that I hadn't known were there. A door leading to the main area of the library opened. I tensed, but a staff member was there.

She nodded, pointing to another door. "Follow me."

I got it then. Stone was snuck in and she was leading us through a hallway that only staff must use, till we got to a back exit door. She opened it, propping it open, and a nice and polite smile to us. "Have a wonderful day, Mr. Reeves."

"Thank you."

Then we were out, and Stone was hurrying toward his truck. They'd allowed him to park in one of their staff slots, too. Genius. But a lot of students were cutting through the parking lot. It was right on the way from the main quad where the post office was and the Quail. It was a shortcut, and a group of guys were going past us. If I were to guess, freshman jocks on their way to a Saturday late breakfast or early lunch.

The group went past us, except one.

Stone kept his head down, waiting before cutting across the sidewalk.

The last guy glanced up, distracted, then swiftly did a double-take. "Holy shit! It's Stone Reeves!"

"What?"

"Huh?"

His friends all drew up short, turning to look.

Stone gripped my hand, but lifted his head to the guys.

At the sight, all of their eyes got big.

"Whoa!"

"Hey, man! What are you doing here?"

"You a student? No. That doesn't make sense."

One of the other guys was studying me, and he nudged his buddy. "News is right. That's his woman." Both were looking at our clasped hands. He stepped forward, wearing a Kings ballcap, too. "You a student here?"

That question was directed at me, and Stone growled. He didn't like that. "You don't direct questions at her."

The guy's head snapped back. All of them stood at attention.

One held up his hands. "Just fans, man. Don't need to be a dickhead."

The one who saw us first laughed. "It's Rampage Reeves in the flesh. That's fucking cool!"

Stone cursed, then forced himself to take a more relaxed stance. "Look, guys. I can't hang out. I gotta get her back. Emergency and all. Hope you understand?"

A few started nodding right away. The one who tried to ask me a question narrowed his eyes and stepped forward. "Nah, man. We may never see you in person again. Sign something for us."

Stone's own eyes narrowed, but they darted to the side.

Oh. Fuck. A phone was pointing right at us.

He bit out a growl. "Enough." He ducked his head down, and

immediately his hand went to my neck, pushing my head down, too. Then he led us to his truck. "Keep your head down. I don't know if that punk got your face or not."

"My face is already out there."

"On gossip sites. Video by a student is a whole different ballgame." His hand flexed over mine. "Sorry about this."

He was apologizing. He was saving me, and he was the one apologizing.

I was such an asshole.

He opened my door. I got in, keeping my head low. And he was rounding, getting in his door. We headed out, but the group of guys had stayed, and every single one of them had their phones out, recording us.

"I'm sorry."

He glanced over, frowning. "For what?"

"You had to come in there because of me."

"I didn't have to do shit. I chose to go in there to get you. I could've sent someone else, you know. I didn't. Maybe think on that, huh?"

I—I didn't know what that meant.

Seeing my look, he started laughing and shaking his head. "All I'm saying, maybe we're not the enemies you like to think we are."

"We were."

He grimaced. "Not quite. I was a prick. You were a nice girl. You got resentful, and I wised up to how much of a dumbass I was. I think that's the best summary for all this shit, don't you?" We were pulling away from the campus, and he glanced back in his rearview mirror. "That's gonna be all over your school's gossip sites. You know that, right? People will figure out who you are."

I sat back. "Maybe I should think about taking a leave of absence?"

His look to me was swift. "You mean that? I thought you were gung-ho about maintaining the 'dream'?"

"That was before I found myself curled up in a ball in the library and I couldn't move." I picked at my nails, picking at nothing that was there, but I was picking at it, nonetheless. Shame and embarrassment was sitting heavy on my chest.

"That was a panic attack."

No. "That was a full-blown meltdown. What if that happened in class?"

"Your school knows what happened. They said you could take a semester off. You'd just have to do summer classes instead." He waited a beat, saying softer, "And my dad paid for the rest of your years."

God. How did I even handle that? I hadn't thought about it before, but the rest? That was a lot of money I owed someone.

And I kept my mouth shut because Stone would say it was his dad paying back a debt to us, but bullshit. I remembered what that last cookbook said.

"What happened with my dad and your mom?"

I had to know.

Stone didn't reply, though. He kept quiet, and I saw he was taking me to my house. He pulled up in my old parking spot, turning the engine off. When he opened the door and got out, I went after him.

"You're not going to tell me?"

He shoved his hands in his pockets, making his shoulders hunch over. "You said you didn't want to risk hating your dad. I won't do that to you."

I gulped. A lump sat in my throat. "So it's something I'll hate him for."

He stopped, turning to look at me. His eyes were kind, and that threw me. Stone was never kind. He was gruff. He could be sweet. He was fierce. He was dead-like, but he was never kind.

He might talk kind, but his eyes never matched the emotion. It was just how he was.

"I highly doubt that."

"Did they have an affair?" That was the worst I could imagine. It would make sense how he was fired.

Stone hesitated.

"Stone." I grabbed his arm. "Tell me."

"There was no affair."

My shoulders relaxed. That was good, but... "What, then?"

"Fuck." He raked a hand over his head. "Can we do this in your house?"

I led the way to the back exit, going down the stairs and opening the door. Once inside, I went into my bedroom and to the door that opened to the rest of the house. Listening, I didn't hear anything, not that I expected anyone to be home.

"Who's all here?" Stone asked, shutting and locking the exit door and shutting the door that opened to where I could either leave or use the bathroom. Once that was closed, I closed mine and we were encased in my bedroom.

My hand fell, lingering. Then I turned the lock.

Stone noticed, his eyes darkening, but he sat down on my bed. Staying on the edge, his hands still in his pockets, he leaned forward. But those eyes, they were tracking me as I moved to the desk, standing, pausing, debating, then going and moving to sit at the opposite end of my bed. My back to the headboard, I pulled my pillow to my lap and hugged it to my chest.

Maybe it was a barrier against whatever he was going to say, a type of armor for the words meant to do damage that he'd volley at me, or maybe it was just against him. I didn't know.

"Tell me." I just needed to know everything because I was sick of 'processing' goddamn everything.

He cursed again, another hand raking over his head. "There was an incident one night. That's all."

"What incident? And why are you evading this question? You don't evade anything."

A half-gargled laugh came from him, one that I had never heard. That really sent my eyebrows up.

His eyes closed. His head hung down, and his shoulders lowered. "My mom drove drunk one night."

"What?"

"Yeah," he bit out. "Not a great defining moment for our family, but I'm starting to learn that that pales compared to what my dad did. But yeah, she drove drunk from wine night with her friends. She was fucking trashed. Your dad was driving home, found her on the side of the road."

"Oh no."

"She was naked. Car was in the ditch. She was barely able to stand."

"Oh *no*." A whole different connotation to my voice.

"He got her home safely. Went back with my dad and they both got the car out of the ditch, too. Then the next morning my mom said that your dad made a pass at her."

"What?! He didn't, did he?"

He shrugged, shaking his head. "I don't know. I can't see your dad ever doing that, and I *can* see my mom trying to make something up to cover up her own embarrassment. She made up that lie and hopefully that's what my dad would cling to and get mad about, maybe her driving drunk would get overlooked. That was her plan, at least. I knew about the accident, about what my mom said. I didn't know my dad fired yours. I swear, but now I'm wondering if that's why your dad got fired. Because of my mom."

I sat there, letting all that sink in.

My dad didn't do what she said. I knew it, felt it in my bones, and looking up, I saw shame on his face. He was ashamed of what his mother had done.

I scooted forward, taking his hand. "Hey."

He shot to his feet, starting to pace. "Don't!"

"Don't what?" I sat back, not prepared for this.

He barked out again, "Don't make this okay? In the grand scheme of things, I still have my parents. You don't. You can't be okay with it."

I opened my mouth to speak.

He pointed at me, his eyes flashing. "And don't say some shit about how it's nothing worse than what my dad did or what I did to you. I get it, okay? I come from a line of assholes. My grand-pops was, too. He was rich and he controlled the fucking town, and he was abusive to my grandma. Everyone knew it. No one said a word. I was glad when he died. Everyone was glad when he died. My dad was an asshole. My mom's an asshole. I am, too. Just like them."

"Stone."

"I can tell that you aren't mad about this, but I know you and I know it's because you have so much shit in your head already, and here I am, putting more in there. Fine. You don't have to be mad, but I am. I'm furious with what my mom did. And I'm furious that your dad got hurt by it, your mom got hurt, and you got hurt. And I can't do anything to fix any of it."

"Wait."

My head was swimming again. I held up a hand. He stopped and I had to ask, "Is this why you're helping me?"

"Jesus fucking Christ! Are you serious with this shit?" He exploded. Full-out. He completely exploded. "What kind of person do you think—" He stopped short. "Wait. Don't answer that. I started because of your mom. Okay? Yes. Me coming and telling you about your dad and Gail, that was me being a fucking decent person. I know you. Who else could tell you? After hearing what my family did to yours, that made me see red. I flew up there. I wanted answers."

"What?"

"You were in a coma. Doctors wouldn't let me anywhere near you for a full twenty-four hours. So after I left you in the hospital, I flew home, missed practice to find out what the fuck was going on. And I handled shit."

"Handled shit?"

"Handled. And yeah, there's bruises on my dad's face and I don't give a fuck how long they're there for. I'd do it all over again. Him paying for your stuff, them both helping with funeral costs and everything—that was a debt massively owed to yours. I am sorry on behalf of whose blood I share. Then me helping you after that, that was because you had been my best friend until I realized what my dick was for and decided I was too good for the likes of a tomboy a grade younger than me. I am sorry on behalf of what a prick I was back then. And yes, me continuing to help you out was because of your mom. Not because I read that note. Those cookbooks didn't get to me until a year ago. My mom had them for me, for some fucking reason, and didn't hand them off. That's when I read the first note. I didn't know your mom wrote notes in all of them. I know now because I read every single one after I got back home from my parents' house, and the ones in the back. Did you see those, too?"

"There's notes in the back?"

He grinned, still grimacing at the same time. "Yeah. Funny ones. Sad ones. I wanted to beat my dad up all over again after I read one in particular."

"Wait a minute, back up...don't you get fined if you miss practice or something?"

"I paid it. Going up there and making things right meant more to me. Don't tell any Kings' fans I said that. They can get rabid." He raised his hands, resting them on his head as he waited for my reaction.

"So this was all because my mom was nice to you?"

His hands dropped down. "You fucking on something for that concussion still? That's what you got from all of that?"

I jumped to my feet. "That's what you said! It was about my mom."

"It started out about your mom. I mean, it started about more than your mom, but yeah. It began because of your mom, but also you. And it became about you—" He cut off, his head moving left to right in a brisk motion. "No. I'm not doing this right now. The whole reason I called you this afternoon is because your step-brother wants to fly down and see my game on Monday. We're Monday Night Football this week. He's coming with his friend, and the guys' parents. Sounds like it's going to be a quick trip for them, and I was calling to see if you wanted to come with them? I can get you tickets."

Oh.

OH!

"Jared's coming here?"

He nodded, his eyes back to being expressionless. "And in case they didn't say something, I wanted to give you a heads-up."

"Are you flying them down?"

"No. The parents are. They reached out about wanting to meet up, see if I'd give him an autograph. I'm just giving them tickets. That's all. They were going to pay someone they know for the guys' season tickets and I told them not to do that." His hands slid back into his pockets. "What do you think? You want to come? Support me?" A faint tug at his lips.

He was teasing.

That floored me.

And I was grinning back. "I had a full meltdown going into my college's library. You expect me to handle a full stadium of fifty-thousand people?"

He shrugged. "That's two days away. I was thinking I could

offer my services for you to 'digest shit.'" And that grin was back, but it was both a smirk and half sensual at the same time.

The fucker.

I laughed. "Sex, huh?"

"Now that we're all good, right? I can offer my dick's services. Happily." He was smiling, and the sight did me in. He was so handsome and attractive and fucking hot all at the same time.

My blood heated.

My pulse spiked, and it was like I hadn't been seriously considering going to a mental hospital moments earlier. My head couldn't get caught up with what was going on. Everything was changing so fast.

I sat back down on the bed, grabbing a pillow. Burying my head in it, I let loose a half-scream and rolled so I was lying on my stomach, turned toward the wall.

I felt the bed decline behind me, and Stone was there. His hand came to my hip. He leaned over me, tugging the pillow away and rolling me so I was on my back, looking up at him. He frowned down. "What was that about? I meant that as a joke."

"I know. It was about me, feeling like I'm totally losing it."

"Oh."

He didn't have anything else to say. I didn't expect a response. That's just how Stone was. He had a thought or a response, he'd give it. He didn't have one, but his eyes were darkening and they were fixed on my mouth.

I stilled.

He didn't.

His eyes lifted to mine and his hand went to my stomach. It flattened there, slipping under my shirt. He paused, now silently asking for permission, and I groaned, biting my lip. He took it as permission and his hand moved farther up, snaking my shirt with it until he paused right below my bra.

He was waiting, gauging what I'd do next.

So was I.

This was different. It wasn't the desperate need to escape before. Everything was different now. My bed. My room. During the day. We did this, there'd be residual effects, but, no. I was stopping myself. I either needed him or I was hating him.

This didn't have to mean anything.

And with that decision in my mind, I was doing something I'd never done before.

I grated out, "I can't handle a relationship." My hands went to my shirt, pausing, too.

His grin turned cocky. "Who the fuck said anything about that?"

"Just sex."

He raised an eyebrow. "You're speaking my language."

I still paused, my mind racing. Was this a good idea? Probably not.

I reached for his jeans, and a second later, his mouth was on mine.

CHAPTER 25

HE WAS inside me when my roommates came home that night. Thrusting in, stretching, he paused. We could hear them traipse across the floor and it was obvious they were celebrating.

"Fuck yeah, biiiiiiiiitches!"

Thud.

"Oh! You fucker!"

"Stop!" Loud laughter. A *clickety clickety.* Someone's high heels.

Clickety clickety—even more high heels.

"Holy fuck. Are they always this loud?"

"They must've won." I wrapped my hand around his arm and pushed my hips up against his. "Um, not to break up this sweet revelation you're having about my party housemates, but can you, you know?"

He grinned down at me, his eyes darkening in lust again. "What?" A slow pull out, then a good rough and quick thrust in all the way to the hilt and he held there, pushing, until I gasped, moaning. "You want me to finish?"

"I'd like both of us to finish, please."

He grinned, then began moving again as his mouth bent down, touching mine.

I was lost.

All the sounds, laughter, shouting, whatever they did up there, it was gone. Stone kept moving in me and it was just him and me, the touch between us.

God.

I gasped, arching my back. My neck was exposed, and with a groan, Stone dropped his mouth down. He was licking, tasting me, and he began moving harder, faster, then pounding until the climax ripped through us both. It sent me over the edge and I yelled out before his hand clamped down on my mouth, but he let out a long and shuddering moan of his own before slumping down over me.

Both our bodies were trembling.

"Hold on! I'll ask her!" someone yelled, the voice getting clearer, and then a stampede sounded down the stairs.

We both froze.

"Dusty! Girl! Dusty Girl!"

Stone leapt, but it was more like he levitated off the bed in a split second and bam! The condom was ripped off, and he grabbed our clothes, the same time checking that the door was locked.

I was stunned at how fast he moved before my shirt hit me square in the face. I grabbed it, moving to put my arms through it. "I forget you're a professional athlete."

He was pulling his pants up just as my doorknob rattled.

We held our breaths collectively, but the door held. The lock worked. Praise to whoever installed that, but then a pounding came on the door. "Dusty! Woman! She who cooks the best fucking pizza in the world."

Stone raised his eyebrow at me.

I rolled my eyes, but I felt the back of my neck heating up.

"We bought more stuff! And we won! We were all wondering if we could bribe you to make us some of those pizzas again? They were fucking fantastic."

"You blushing?"

"No. Shut up." I was. I think even the skin on my stomach was red. Cursing, I scooted to the edge of the bed and looked around for my pants.

Stone cleared his throat. He was fully dressed by now and holding out my pants.

I snagged them, shooting him a look.

"Pizza?"

"What? My mom taught me more than how to bake." I rolled my eyes. "I got better at cooking."

He was quiet a second. "Pizza?"

Was he...yep. He was. "You want to go up there?"

He shrugged. "Why not? They know we know each other."

"But, yeah." I gestured around us. "We smell like sex."

"We'll wash up quick."

We'd spent all day in bed. It was almost a full repeat of the first night, except we ran out of condoms two hours ago and Stone had to run out for a resupply. We did not look how we looked in the library. Our clothes were wrinkled and it was obvious we'd been in bed. A person could tell. Softer skin. Tired eyes. A literal glow, which I knew I had.

"Dusty!" Another bang on the door.

"She probably doesn't know who you are, moron. She will seriously not answer if she doesn't," came a voice from behind him before a door slammed shut.

"Bitch," the guy muttered before raising his voice. "It's Dent, by the way. And I'm in love with your pizza." He laughed to himself. "I could be in love with you, too. You know that, right? Remember the bar? Remember when you ditched me? I know you were thinking I was trying to get back at Lisa, but I swear I wasn't. I was into you—"

Stone unlocked the door and swung it open in that second. A full scowl on his face.

"Ooooh, shit." Dent blinked, shaking his head and stepped back. He'd been leaning on the doorframe. "Oh, wow. Hey, man. Stone. You're like, hanging out now?" He looked at me, and I was still sitting on the bed with my pants in my hand.

He saw me. He saw the pants. He saw the bed. Correction, he saw the state of the bed.

"Oh, whoa. Wow. Oh." A nervous laugh and a crooked grin. "I was just joking, you know? I mean, I'd never fall in love with— fuck. Wow. You two are like doing that shit now?" He stood back, but waved at the bed. "That's awesome!"

I waited, expecting Stone to deny it, or say something to cover that up. Nothing came.

Instead, he deadpanned, "We gotta shower first."

I could die. Literally.

Dent's eyebrows shot up. "Of course." Then he laughed. "Awesome!" He gave me two thumbs up before walking backwards as Stone shut the door, locking it once again.

He took my hand. Not a word was spoken, and he led me to the shower.

We showered. There was some more stroking, but it was quick, and after drying off and dressing, he headed up first. I told him I wanted to do something with my hair, make myself look so it wasn't so obvious we'd showered together.

I could hear a collective greeting as he went upstairs, and knew the instant everyone realized who else had been down here. The entire volume of the house went up five notches.

I was flustered. This was different. This was Stone not hiding he was down here, with me, and it was a full party upstairs. It was already out about us, but yeah, this felt like it was something more than what we'd talked about.

I was at the stairs when I realized I had no bra.

I was *that* flustered, but after getting a bra on, I went upstairs.

I wasn't fully ready for what I walked into. This wasn't a normal party for them, not that I was super knowledgeable on that either, but I knew there was more tonight. The usual crowd was fifteen to twenty. Tonight, there was twenty in just two rooms. I saw people outside in the backyard and people were coming in and out from the front.

I'd stepped into a full-fledged party, and going through the crowd, I didn't have far to go to get in the kitchen. A few girls were coming in the side door, gave me the stink eye, but quickly moved on. I heard one whisper, "There he is! Told you!"

Her friend got excited. Both squealed and I was forgotten.

I did take note of their outfits, because it was so not what I was wearing. They were in halter tops, the kind that had ruffles above the boobs and just underneath, and that was pretty much it for the top. Their jeans were plastered to them. Sleek hair. Makeup on point, and bright red lipstick.

Me. I had on Stone's shirt and my jeans. Granted, my jeans were also plastered to me, but looking at those girls, I knew my jeans didn't have the whole sexy look they were pulling off. And don't get me started on my hair. I'd pulled it up into a quick braid before coming up, but to my credit, it was a messy fishtail braid. Go me. Fishtail braids were always trending, or they should be. They were awesome, which according to Dent, I was fucking awesome.

But back to those girls. As I was pushing into the kitchen, I saw where they were going and who 'he' was.

But I already knew. Of course, I knew.

Stone was leaning against the counter, a water in hand, and he had one arm crossed over his chest. Wyatt, Noel, Nacho, Dent. They were all standing and lounging next to him as if they were all buds. Stone was listening to some other guy talking who was using lots of hand motions, and the girls were on the outskirts, whispering to each other. They weren't the only girls. There were others. Mia, for one. She was curled up next to Wyatt. Her head on his shoulder and his arm around her waist. Noel and Savannah were wifed up, too. He had his arm around her shoulder, but his head was leaning forward, listening to whatever the one guy was saying.

Stone's eyes caught me, and he raked me up and down. A faint grin tugged on his lips.

Before I knew what was happening, he'd said something to the guy. He came over, and just like that, no one else was allowed in our group of two. I went to the cupboard and started pulling everything out I needed. He set his drink on the counter, his back to the rest of the room, and his one hand rested on my back.

"Tell me what to do."

"What?" I pulled out the flour. "You're going to help me?"

"Why not?" His grin was wicked. "Old memories, you know."

Old memories. I almost laughed at that, but saw he was serious.

"Really?"

"I'm here to spend time with you, not them. Not going to lie. I'm looking forward to the pizza, too, but as soon as they're done and cut, we're going to my place." He leaned in, saying into my ear, "I thought maybe I might've missed out on the college parties. I didn't." His hand moved up my back, rubbing between my shoulders. He gestured to the rolling pin I'd pulled out. "Tell me what to do."

"Heeeeyyy!"

Nicole shoved her way through the crowd, coming to the other side of me. Her face was flushed. Her breath was tequila and she was swaying, just barely holding onto the counter. "You've left your room. You've joined society. We need to take a shot for this!"

She whooped, screaming, "I need my tequila."

Dent laughed, swooping in. He bent, tucking down, and as he stood, she was over his shoulder.

She shrieked again, but was laughing.

He smacked her ass. "Excuse us. Nikki's gotta do good on a bet we had between the two of us."

"Oh my God! No!" Her laughter was clearly saying she was fine with whatever he was talking about. "I want to hang out with Dusty. She never leaves her room—OH!" Her eyes were gaping, taking in Stone. Yeah. She was that drunk. She screeched now, trying to scramble upright. "HOLY SHIT! STONE IS HERE! HOLY SHIT!"

Stone shifted closer to me. "Take her out of here?" He was not talking to me.

Dent nodded, burping. "On it." He snagged a beer on his way out, and Nicole kept shrieking the whole way until a door closed.

I stiffened. "You don't think he's..."

Mia clipped out, still in Wyatt's shelter, "He's putting her to bed. It's a wasted Nicole night tonight. Dent's the only one who can get her to actually go to sleep when she's like that."

"Oh."

But I looked at Stone, he shrugged and bent close. "Don't worry about it. Dent seems like a good guy. Crazy with his flirting, but he seems on the up and up."

"You know this how?" I shoved a bowl into his hands.

He smiled, actually enjoying that. "It's a guy thing."

Wyatt started laughing. So did Noel.

Savannah was trying to hide a grin.

Mia was just staring at me, a blank expression on her face. Then she announced, for everyone to hear, "I'm sorry I was a bitch to you. It's what I do. I'm a bitch. Char's a bitch, too. Be glad you never actually met her." And with that said, she pulled away from Wyatt, grabbed her beer and went out to the backyard.

"Well, then." Savannah giggled softly, resting her head on her boyfriend's chest.

Wyatt belched out a laugh, grinning widely. "And on that note, I better go make sure my 'bitch' girlfriend is okay." He opened the fridge, grabbing another beer, and saluted the rest of us. "Onward, my merry pirate friends." He backed up, and just before he was going to step out onto the patio, he held his beer up to Stone. "Fucking kill 'em on Monday! KINGS RULE!"

A huge cheer echoed around him from the entire house, "KINGS FUCKING RULE!" And the second verse to the chant, "THEY DON'T TAKE NO COURT! RULE KINGS RULE!"

Stone was grinning, measuring out the flour we'd need. "Why do I suddenly feel like I'm living the life of *Animal House* mixed with a lot of *Friday Night Lights*?"

Noel barked out a laugh, his hand wrapping more firmly around Savannah's shoulders, pulling her so she was plastered against his front. "Because you are, but it's better. It's more awesome."

Nacho burped. "No. Reeves is more awesome!"

They were all drunk. Jury hadn't been out, but I knew the verdict was in. Every single one of them was drunk.

Stone just laughed, shaking his head. He bumped into me. "Tell me what to do."

So I did.

In the middle of that crazy and hectic kitchen, Stone and I made seven pizzas together. My housemates and their boyfriends stood guard. Mia and Wyatt came back in. Even Lisa emerged, and Nacho had his arm draped around her.

People would come in. Word had gotten out Stone was in attendance, but if they lingered too long, my housemates shifted and literally pushed them out of the kitchen. There were autographs he signed. He posed for pictures, but he never strayed too far from me for too long. And once the pizzas were done, Stone threw them on the counter. He cut a few slices of one, putting them on a plate, then tossed the pizza cutter to one of the guys.

His free hand went around my waist. "Okay. Your turn. We're out of here."

No one argued, but Stone didn't give them time. He was dragging me downstairs, through my room, and true to his word, within ten minutes (that's how long I had to quickly pack a bag), we were up through my side exit and heading to his truck.

A few people in the backyard yelled out his name, but Stone only raised a hand, throwing a general holler back. He didn't stop until we were both in his truck and he was backing out of there.

It hit me halfway to his house.

That night, I was happy. I was actually happy.

Then the smile wiped from my face.

CHAPTER 26

STONE WENT in the next morning to the stadium, but he was back a little after noon. And he wasn't alone.

I was in the kitchen, about to start making food, when in walked the cornerback and quarterback for the Texas Kings. I had a spoon in my hand and it dropped. The clatter seemed to last forever, and all the while, Stone and Jake Bilson and Colby Doubard stood there, waiting for the spoon to stop clattering.

I wanted to avoid watching Stone's games last year, but the truth was that I hadn't.

It was almost unavoidable because his team became one of the best last year, and they were already exceeding their reputation this year so far. Because of that, everywhere I went they were on ESPN or any sports network or channel in a bar, a restaurant, even one time when I was waiting to do my laundry. The desk clerk had highlights playing and there'd been a perfect pass from Colby Doubard to Stone on replay.

I was completely aware of Colby Doubard. All six-foot-three inches, two-hundred-forty pounds of one of the bigger quarterbacks in the league. And I knew this because they talked about it a lot on ESPN. He looked lean on television. He didn't look the same in person. He was large, and after Stone, he was probably one of the best looking guys I'd seen. Ever.

And don't get me started on Jake Bilson.

Black. Shorter, around six foot even. He and Stone were almost the same size, both lean. And those dark eyes were literally smiling while he was trying to hold back a blinding smile. I instantly liked him. I mean, after being speechless and being awestruck.

"Dust, this is Colby and Jake." Stone did the introductions and both stepped forward, shaking my hand.

I was fangirling.

I wasn't used to this.

Stone was hiding a grin. "What are you making?"

"Caesar salad with kale and salmon." I had no clue more people were coming. I had no clue these two were coming.

I needed to start watching Stone's games more. All that happened with my life, I was having another moment about what kind of world Stone lived in. I knew it. I saw the fans' reactions, the blogs, but seeing these two other professional athletes in Stone's kitchen, all three of them looking like they hang out all the time, my stomach was doing double time on the twisting, turning, somersaulting. It was just one big continuous loop.

"You want something else? I can make something else."

He stepped closer, angling my phone toward him. His eyebrows went up. "You been doing some research?"

I flushed. "You like the pizza so much, thought I could make myself useful. Do some cooking for you. Unless you have a chef?"

He was trying real hard to keep from bursting out laughing at my expense. I rolled my eyes, knowing my face was resembling a red sea star. "You're annoying."

Yeah. He lost the battle. He burst out laughing, then hugged me to him, his hand rubbing over my back quick. "Never seen you like this. It's cute."

Jake and Colby shared a look.

I elbowed Stone away, fighting from dropping my eyes to the floor. "So, um, I can make more food. Pasta? I can do a healthy primavera. You have all the stuff here. I'm actually impressed."

Stone leaned back against the counter by me. "I have a girl who comes in and cooks a bunch of meals for me every week. I gave her last week off 'cause you were here." He turned to the guys. "You guys want lunch?"

The two glanced at each other. Both shrugged.

Colby said, "That'd be great. Yeah."

Stone said to me, "Games start in an hour. We were going to watch some tapes beforehand." He was eyeing all the ingredients I'd pulled out on the counter. "You got this? Or you need help?"

It was my last day before heading back to school. Minus the freakout yesterday, the concussion was fading. I was more clear-headed. It took everything I had not to break down and dig into my textbooks, embracing my inner nerd for a bit, but one more day. I was giving myself one more day, and I owed Siobhan a call.

So, trying to stick to that plan, cooking had become my outlet.

He was right. I'd pulled up trying to find what a typical pro football athlete food program was, and it was mostly healthy food, mixed with junk food. Stone was a wide receiver. I wasn't sure, but I found a few programs for what a pro soccer player would eat. I was adapting one of those programs for Stone. Though, hearing he had a girl who did his menus, I wasn't sure how helpful I'd be.

One day at a time.

I was finishing up when he came back to the kitchen. I was pulling out the baked potatoes, adding broccoli over the top with a sprinkle of cheese. His arms came around both sides of me on the counter, and he leaned over me, looking over my shoulder.

"That looks good."

"Hmmm." I turned in his arms, leaning back so I could see him face to face.

He smirked. "You have a crush on my teammates?"

"No!" I laughed. This was mortifying. "But I just wasn't expecting the quarterback and lead cornerback from the Texas Kings to walk into your kitchen. That's all."

"I'm the lead wide receiver for the team."

"I know, but you're you. You're Stone." I smacked his chest with the back of my hand. "I don't look at you like that. You're you. They're...them." Lame. So lame, but true. My face was warming up again. "They're superstars."

He straightened, some of the amusement leaving him. "Colby was a third-round pick. Jake was second round. I was second *overall* draft pick." He was back in my space, pushing me back, crowding me. "You know what that means, right? I was a first-round pick. One other guy got picked before me, and he was the Heisman winner. You understanding where I'm going here?"

I placed my palms on his chest, but he was like cement. He wasn't moving. His heart just picked up pace and I got what he was saying. Still didn't matter.

I shrugged. "What do you want me to say? I grew up with skinned knees and you teaching me the most efficient way to pick your nose. No. You're not a big mega-athlete star to me."

He barked out a laugh. "Shit. That's embarrassing." But he stopped pushing me. "I get it. Just, if you start getting feelings for any of my teammates, talk to me first. Yeah? Since you know." He pushed his groin up against mine, grinding there a second.

There was a hard glint in his eyes, and his jaw clenched for a second. But his voice was teasing, and the grinding made me forget the first two reactions instantly. He forced oxygen out of my lungs, and I was coughing, a rush of heat exploding through my whole body.

My arm curved around his neck. "Jesus, Stone."

He paused, his head reared back so he could see me better. But he didn't move back.

I swear, if he had, I was going to climb up on that counter and lock my legs around his waist. My hand flattened on his shoulder, as if I could keep him in place. But he remained, then he was moving, but his body remained in place.

Both of us shared a grin.

"Someone's awake," he murmured, his eyes growing dark and wolfish. "Fuck." He abruptly pulled back, sneaking an apple from behind me in a bowl. "This between us." He motioned from my vagina to his dick. "It ain't normal. You know that, right?" He moved farther back, leaning against a counter opposite me. "I had a girlfriend in college. A full year. I never felt this shit for her that I feel for you."

Yep. Now my hands were tingling. He was sending shivers all through my body.

"What are you saying?"

He shrugged, but I still saw his jaw clenching again. "Just if you want to fuck someone else, talk to me first. If I'm fucking someone more than once, I don't fuck another girl. No place for that drama in my life. So I'm telling you, I'm not planning on stepping between anyone else's legs. I'd like the same appreciation."

The same appreciation? Was he serious? Did he not realize how broken I was?

I swallowed over a knot, my hands suddenly clammy. "The fact that I'm standing upright as a functioning member of society is remarkable. Yeah. You and me, I get it's not normal, but it's helping me somehow. The idea of even thinking about someone else like that... I'm just standing. That's my main focus right now."

His eyes suddenly cleared, sobering. He stood from the

counter, walking over to me. A sensual look moved into his gaze, but there was more. A predatory look, too. And I *so* felt like his prey, but I stayed. I waited. I watched him come, and I was trembling from head to toe until he was close enough to touch me. As it was, he didn't, but I felt his body heat. That was affecting me in a whole different way, coursing those same shivers all over me, exploding.

"Good. I like you standing." His eyes flashed, growing molten. "I like you in other ways, too, but I want you fighting the most. I need you to fight again."

I swallowed. Noted. He liked me fighting.

Hearing voices coming, Stone stepped back. He was across the kitchen, eating his apple when Colby and Jake entered.

I was in the same room as two—alright, three—professional football players. Jared would piss his pants. Well, no, he wouldn't. He'd act all cool, I'm sure, but I couldn't wait to tell him.

OH!

I turned to Stone. "When's Jared coming in?"

He'd been mid-bite of his apple at my question. "Oh. Uh." He frowned. "Tomorrow sometime?" He shrugged. "Not planning on meeting up until after the game, though. Why? Georgia said you'd been talking to him. When are you going to talk to him again?"

Colby was listening, looking between Stone and me. His dark eyes sparkling. "Who's Jared?"

"Yeah." From Jake, a smirk on his face. "Who's Jared?"

Stone gestured to me with his apple. "Her stepbrother. He's flying in for the game tomorrow night. I'm getting them tickets."

"Yeah?"

Jake leaned against the counter next to Stone, swiping his own apple on the way. "He a big Kings fan?"

Stone grinned, all cocky. "He's a big Stone Reeves fan."

Colby laughed.

Jake rolled his eyes. "Enjoy the spotlight now, buddy. You know Good Ol' Bilson is gonna take it tomorrow night, right? I've got the tapes on Bolston and I ain't letting him get anywhere. All those ESPN clips that rave about you and Colby, they're going to be saying my name tomorrow night." He nodded at me. "Your girl's brother will be my number-one fan. Just see, man." He winked at me.

"Yeah. Okay. You're delusional." Colby puffed up his chest, just as cocky. "Little dude's gonna eat out of my palm. *I'm* the quarterback. I head the whole fucking boat."

Jake snorted. "Right. 'Cause all those pretty runs Reeves takes into the end zone ain't worth shit."

"All those pretty runs come from my pretty hands." Colby's head was up and smiling. "I can do this all night long, baby."

"Baby!" Jake hooted. "Who you calling baby? I don't call anyone baby unless she's under me, or straddling me, and even then—" He stopped, his eyes darting to me. "Uh. Sorry. I mean..." Then he shrugged, throwing back to Colby, "You want to get the right terms, *baby*. I'm sweetheart, not baby."

"Really?!" Colby's nostrils flared, but he had a shit-eating grin on his face.

Stone pushed off from the counter, coming to stand next to me. "Those two trash talk all the time. This is a snippet of the shit they say in the locker room."

"All day, every day." Jake held his arms out wide. He was bouncing on the back of his heels, as if getting warmed up for an actual game.

The oven beeped at that second, and I moved over to pull out the primavera.

"Damn." From Jake. He leaned over me, breathing in the pasta. "That smells fucking good."

"*Looks* fucking amazing." Colby tapped Stone on the chest.

"No wonder you ain't been social lately. Got this to come home to now."

Stone stiffened, his jaw clenching, but Colby didn't notice.

Me, I got light-headed noticing that. I wasn't sure why, but there it was.

He and Jake Bilson kept going back and forth, and as I finished with the food, Stone helped me. Plates were pulled out. Drinks were poured. He asked what I needed for the food, but I was done. We were ready.

After that, the guys insisted I plate first, and they followed behind.

I stood to the side, not totally sure what to do, but Stone came up next to me and motioned with his head. "Games are starting. You need me to bring your drink?"

I didn't know if this was a 'team' thing, if I was 'allowed,' but as the guys headed to the theater room without hesitation, I knew they'd been expecting me to eat with them. Stone noticed my pause and put his plate on the counter. "What's wrong?"

I shrugged, feeling all sorts of awkward. "Those are your teammates. You said watching the games was part of your job. I just figured..." I didn't know what I figured.

No. I did.

I figured I didn't belong.

I figured I was a secret.

The lines around his mouth tightened. "What you and me are doing ain't anyone's business. No. No one needs to know the details, but you're a friend and I don't do well with hiding shit. Lying is way different than just not offering information. Those guys don't know shit about what I'm doing, and despite their ribbing, they don't care. Every guy on the team has a situation, whether that's family, a wife, or something else. We're all just doing our jobs. That's it."

I wasn't sure what to take from that, but I wasn't something he was embarrassed about. I got that part.

"Okay."

Warm sensations were filling my belly up.

"Yeah?"

"Yeah."

I picked up my plate and went and watched two football games with the lead wide receiver, quarterback, and cornerback of the Texas Kings. Then once the quarterback and cornerback left, Stone scooped me up and I watched two more games half-lying on top of him.

All things considered, it was a fucking great Sunday.

CHAPTER 27

"HEY. SO, UM."

This was Siobhan's greeting when she slid onto the seat next to me in class. She glanced around, tucking some hair strands behind her ears. Then, ducking her head, she scooted closer and asked, her voice lowered, "Are you okay? I mean, with the coma and what happened in the library?"

Oh boy. That was a loaded question.

"Yeah. I'm good."

Her eyes were searching mine. I knew she was trying to figure if she should push or not, but whatever she saw must've reassured her because her second question came next, and with a little bit more excitement infused with it.

"So who was that guy in the library?"

I hid a grin. "He was just a guy I know from back home. That's all."

"Really?"

That guy's video had been released the day before. My phone's alert went off last night when we were watching game three. You could hear everything. The guy asking me a question.

Stone telling him no. The rest, and how pissy the fan had gotten. It wasn't a big deal, but I got the alert because it hit on the college's sports page. My name was out there, the other blogs knew who I was, but the college's website hadn't named me, saying it was to allow privacy.

Privacy, my ass.

Just walking through campus, I got thirty people looking at me weird. A guy looked like he was going to approach, say something, but I ducked into the biology building just then. I was hoping it'd all go away and so far, no one blinked an eye at even seeing me in class again. Except Siobhan.

"How are things with Trent?"

She got all red, sitting up, her eyes almost bulging out. And at that moment, Trent slid into the chair on my other side. "Ladies." He paused, as if realizing who I was. "Oh, hey. Where'd you go?"

"Car accident."

Siobhan frowned, her head jerking to the side.

"Really? I'm sorry."

I dipped my head in a slight nod. "Yeah. I'm okay now."

Or I would be. I would be. I would be. I was going to keep repeating that mantra to myself until it was true. For the most part, I *was* doing better. It hadn't slipped my notice that I could handle being in the kitchen with everyone Saturday night. But that was because Stone was there.

If I was thinking far ahead, I'd be concerned. I couldn't depend on him. This thing with us wasn't romantic. I was guessing the friendship was there again. I mean, we slept together the last two nights, Saturday afternoon until my housemates came home, and the other full night before I bailed. So, yes. To say we weren't friends again would be moronic, but romantic... that was different.

I was surviving. He was helping me survive. I couldn't afford to look a gift horse in the mouth, at least not yet.

If he met someone, or if he wanted to stop what we were doing, I'd deal. That was my plan. I'd just deal, but until then, I couldn't stop anything, not even to prevent further heartbreak in the future. It wouldn't matter. I'd crumble now, so, yeah. That's where I was, so I spoke the truth to Trent.

I was okay now. *Now*. Maybe not tomorrow, the day after, but now. Right now, I could stand. I was here.

Trent seemed satisfied with my response, but Siobhan was watching me during class. I was preparing myself for a full interrogation at the end, but the professor called me up and I was saved. My professor wanted to check-in with me, make sure I could handle being back. I told her an abbreviated version that I was fine, I was better, I was ready to learn again. She seemed satisfied, just like Trent, and talking to her caused me to leave much later than everyone else.

I was good.

Or so I thought.

Siobhan was waiting as soon as I turned the corner. "You were in a car accident?"

Trent was next to her, his eyebrows raised, but leaning against the wall with more of a bored expression on his face. He was watching the students go back and forth in the hallway since three other classrooms just emptied, too.

"Yeah," I said in response.

"Is that why you were in the coma? Because of the accident?" She didn't let me answer. Concern flooded her face. She reached out, touching my arm. "I would've been there for you. I'm so sorry. I should've called more. I don't even know where you live. I've been a horrible friend, although we don't really know each other that well. But hey, you have that one friend to help you out, right? I couldn't see his face, but he looked yummy." She leaned in close, lowering her voice. "Real protective and grrr, you know?"

I knew. I *so* knew.

"Hey! You're the chick!" A guy suddenly appeared out of the crowd going past us. He was tall, lanky, a Texas C&B ballcap on his head, and he was wearing a Texas Kings shirt. He shoved his phone in my face. The video on the college's website right there and playing...loudly.

"*...don't direct questions at her.*"

"*Just fans, man. Don't need to be a dickhead...*"

I reacted. I didn't think. I just reacted, hitting his phone away from me. It fell to the floor, breaking, and the guy started to yell, "What the fuck?! You bitch."

"Hey!"

Two guys muscled their way in, blocking me from the phone guy. I had another split-second warning, glimpsing their backs. They were tall and strong, and imposing as fuck. One growled, "Back the fuck off her! You shoved that phone in her face. We saw the whole thing."

The guy started to cower, then his face crunched and he shot back, "She broke my pho—"

The second guy was growling, too. "Let me shove my fist in your face, see what you do. It was a reflex, you little fuck."

The first guy, "Get lost!"

The second guy helped. "Or we'll fuck you up. I know your name, little prick. You play JV baseball. I have buddies on the varsity team. They'll give me all the details on where you live, who your friends are, everything. Get in her face again, and this won't be an empty threat. Got it?"

Nacho.

It took me a second. My heart was pounding so loud in my eardrums. The hallway, the crowd that had stopped to watch, they were starting to swim around me in circles. Faster and faster.

A hand grasped my arm and I heard a female voice, "Are you okay?"

I looked up. That wasn't Siobhan. I was looking up, not down. It was Mia.

I had died. Only explanation for all this.

Mia was in my hell, and she was concerned. Then she shifted, looking at the guys. The second guy was Wyatt. No, wait. Maybe I wasn't in hell. Maybe this was real, and then Lisa was there, too. She wasn't turned toward me, but looking at the guy, instead, and she snarled. "I know Katja. She told me all about your dick. Stay away from our girl or I'll put out a fucking announcement about how much you suck in bed."

Lisa was defending me now?

No. I was wrong again. Hell *had* frozen over. We were all still alive, so that meant hell came up to *us*.

"Whatever. I just wanted to get Reeves' autograph. That's all."

"By almost assaulting his woman? Great fucking idea. I'm sure he'd be happy about that."

But the guy was leaving, along with his buddies.

Everyone turned to regard me then, and Lisa was first, still snarling. "Tell me that shit hasn't been happening all morning?" She gestured down the hall. "I saw the guy recognize you and zero in. What a loser."

Wyatt. Nacho. Mia. Lisa. They all came to my defense, and now they were all taking me in, then looking past my shoulder to Siobhan and Trent.

Wyatt put his hand out. "Hey. Wyatt. You're friends with Dusty?"

A more tentative hand came from behind me, shaking Wyatt's hand, and Trent's voice matched, sounding shaky. "Uh. Yeah. We have class together."

Lisa was nodding to Siobhan. "Dusty's our housemate. We've gotten a little protective of her. Nice to meet you."

Now that the coast was clear, Mia let go of my arm. She was

back under Wyatt's arm, his free hand hanging over her shoulder. And she wasn't looking at me. Her nose and mouth were pinched, as if all of this was beneath her.

Lisa was the opposite. Her hands on her hips. Her eyes still flaring. "I'm fucking pissed! That phone was in your face. It almost hit you. I would've taken his balls if it were me. Is that how it was for you on Saturday? I can't imagine Stone keeping his cool if it were."

There were still people walking by. There were still people standing around, watching. The more they talked, the more I wanted to skip my last two classes and hide in Stone's bed.

"I—" My voice cracked. "It wasn't like that, but yeah. The guys got pissed Stone didn't want to talk."

"I can't imagine. I'd be in jail by now if it were me." Lisa grinned at Nacho, who put his arm around her shoulders. "Aggravated assault and battery. That'd be me."

"Yeah." He tapped her arm. "You don't handle people being in your face that well."

She waved her hand in the direction of where the guy went, a quick and almost savage motion. "I'd hospitalize the guy."

Nacho said to me, "But you're okay?"

Wyatt added, "Want us to call Stone?"

Jesus. They had his number. I wasn't surprised. But I shook my head. "No, no. I'm good."

"We got practice, but the girls could run you home if you needed?"

"Yeah." First time Mia spoke, now looking at me again. "How'd you get to school today?"

More questions. More information. The crowd was still around them, but once they decided to stop dealing with them, it was like poof, they disappeared. But that wasn't how it went, and there were still eyes, phones, and ears all around us.

But this was their world. I was just now a full-fledged member because of my association with Stone.

I said to Mia, "I'm good. I've got another class to head to."

"You sure?" That was Nacho.

At my response, Mia's face pinched up again and Wyatt nodded, an easy grin on his face. "Okay. We got lunch plans. You can join if you want?"

I knew where they had lunch. Varsity football members, their girlfriends, other friends, everyone knew they had lunch in the Quad at the main table. The truth was that this was a normal day to them. Getting this amount of attention, they were used to it. It was like breathing to them. I wondered what they'd think if suddenly no one noticed them, no one thought anything of them.

Because that's how I preferred it, and looking at Siobhan and Trent, I knew from the aghast expressions on their faces, they were like me.

Stone dropped me off this morning. He gave me a number for a driver to come get me if I needed a ride, but I think in the back of my head I'd been hoping to talk to Siobhan. I wanted to make sure things were okay with her since she saw me Saturday mid-freak out. And I'd even hoped to maybe talk her into hanging out at the library.

Georgia texted saying they'd be flying in right before the game. They offered to meet me, but wouldn't be able to pick me up, so I hadn't really known how to plan for the day. Game started at seven. They wanted to meet at six thirty, head in for the seats. That was another name Stone gave me. I was supposed to go to door 8 and give my name. There were supposed to be tickets for everyone. But that was hours from now, and the small wish I had just to pretend to be normal today didn't look like it was going to happen.

Everything had changed.

Siobhan knew. Trent knew. I knew other guys like phone guy

would be in my face. My housemates didn't understand what the word 'discreet' meant, so I had a couple choices to make. Either stay and deal, stay and hide in the library, or leave.

I chose door number two.

Right then and there, hiding in the library seemed the best option.

I shook my head at Wyatt. "I'm good. I'm, uh, I'm going to try to catch up before classes."

"Okay. We'll see you later, then."

He and Mia headed off. Nacho started after them but stopped and looked back. Lisa was still in front of me. She was biting her lip. "We're doing a party tonight to watch Stone's game. Are you..." her eyes swept behind me. "Do your friends want to come?"

I heard a quiet squeak from Siobhan, but was already shaking my head. "I'm actually going to the game."

"Oh!" Lisa's head shot up. "Right." Her face cleared up. "Duh. Of course, you are. It's at home and Monday Night Football. Right on." She punched my arm. "Have fun. I'm jealous."

"Liss!" A shout from Mia.

"Right." She began backing up, but grinning widely. "Have fun. Don't forget the little people." And with that, she turned, laughing at something Nacho said. He didn't put his arm around her shoulder, but he did place it on the small of her back as both hurried to catch up.

Then it was the three of us.

I was ignoring a few onlookers still, trying to adopt my housemates' ways.

Siobhan and Trent were both fixed on me, both pale. Trent kept blinking, chewing the inside of his mouth, and a whole look that he'd just tasted something he couldn't identify kept shifting on his face. His nose was twitching.

Siobhan wouldn't look at me. Her eyes were fixed steadfastly on my shoes.

A deep breath. "I—"

Her head jerked up, blanching. "I have to go!" She began backing away, and once she started, she picked up speed.

She couldn't get away from me fast enough.

"Wha...oh. Okay. I should go, too." Trent started, but he wasn't fast enough.

Siobhan had a good grip on his shirt and she tugged him behind her.

They were almost sprinting away from me, almost as fast as my stomach was sinking to the ground.

Shit.

That'd gone the worst way I could've imagined.

Then it was just me. Again, I was still ignoring any gawkers.

My phone beeped. I lifted it.

Stone: How's the first day back?

Miserable.

Me: Totally fine. It's nice to be back.

CHAPTER 28

LIBRARY.

Class.

Talk to the professor. Reassure them I was okay. I could handle the classwork again.

Library.

Stop. Backtrack. Stop at the coffee hut.

Then Library.

Class.

Again, reassure the professor I'm good to go.

That was the rest of my afternoon, until it was three in the afternoon and I wasn't sure what to do with myself. Not wanting to make Stone's driver come all the way to campus to take me back to Stone's house, be there for maybe an hour and have to drive all the way to the other side of the city, I chose to walk to my house instead.

No one was there. This was one of my greatest mysteries, where were the housemates when they weren't partying? I didn't think Monday at three was party time, especially because they'd be partying in a few hours. That was it. They were probably getting ready for the party, but I had the house to myself. Heading downstairs, I tried to focus and study for the first hour.

I gave up.

I was distracted because in two-and-a-half hours, I'd see Jared again. I had so much guilt for not getting up there before now. An ache was digging in my chest, and lying on my bed, I rubbed that spot. Guilt and regret were going to eat a hole inside of me, literally.

My phone buzzed and I sat up, reaching for it at the same time as I brushed a tear away.

Georgia: We landed!! Jared's super excited to see you. We're going to the hotel now, then we'll meet you at the stadium. Door 8, right?

Me: Yes. How was the flight? I'm excited to see Jared, too.

I wasn't. I was, but I was petrified. My hands were shaking as I typed that text out.

Another buzz.

Georgia: The boys are both bouncing off the walls. They told everyone on the plane they knew Stone and the Kingfishers were going to dominate tonight. Okay! We'll see you at door 8. So excited!

Excited.

My hand never stopped shaking. All the way through taking a shower, changing. The button on my jeans kept slipping. Took me four times to secure it. Then, my hair. My whole arms were shaking now.

A *knock* and my door was pushed open. "You here—oh."

It took me forty minutes just to get my clothes on. I had thirty minutes left to finish dressing before Stone's driver would be outside waiting for me. I'd already sent him the text.

Nicole saw me, saw the state I was in, and came inside. She

shut the door behind her, stood a second, and got serious. "What can I do?"

"My hair," I croaked out.

"Okay." She was eyeing the waves that'd come from my braiding attempts and the hair tie in my hand. "I know what to do." She pulled out my desk chair and turned it around in front of her. Patting it, she said, "Come here. Take a seat."

I did, almost sagging into it.

"Now," she almost hummed under her breath, her fingers making quick work. I felt the tugging, but it wasn't painful. She could've been pulling chunks out and I wouldn't have cared. "I can't do that fancy braid you did the other night, but I do know one trick that my mom taught me. And believe you me, I can rock a waterfall braid like no other. Trust, girl. Trust."

I trusted.

And feeling the braid start to form across the back of my head, I closed my eyes and simply gave in.

The ache was back. My family was no more, except a step-brother I was about to see. I had to accept it all and acknowledge it. I couldn't see him in the half-state of denial that I was still existing in. Grief is a right bastard. Sneaks up on you, blasts you, hits you, pounds you, leaves you wrecked. There's a moment of peace. You never know how long it could last. Minutes. Hours. Days. You're starting to believe you can 'do this' and the bastard comes back, knocks you over with a battering ram. But if you fight it, deny it, ignore it, it's still there. The bastard is just waiting until your shields are down, then he gets you again. Only way to deal is to take the beating, then breathe once he's gone, and wait for him to return because it would get better.

I was rubbing at my chest when I realized what I was doing.

Nicole was finishing the braid. "Hold a second." She disappeared, coming back with a curling iron, hair product, and hairspray. Plugging in the iron, she said, "Gotta perfect the whole look, you know. How my mama taught me."

"Is your mom alive?"

She paused. "Yes." She frowned. "Why do you ask?"

They didn't know.

It was time. "My mom died when I was a senior in high school."

She froze, cursing under her breath. "I—I thought maybe I heard something about that when you and Stone were here, but I wasn't sure. I'm so sorry."

My throat was so dry. My insides felt cracked. "The night Stone came over, the night of my wreck, he'd just told me that my dad and my stepmom had died."

"Holy shit." She drew in a harsh breath.

"My stepbrother is here. He's being adopted by his best friend's family, and they flew down to go to Stone's game. Stone got them tickets. I'm going to see him for the first time since everything happened."

Her hands flattened over my shoulders. "I'm so sorry. I...we had no idea."

I admitted with a rueful grin, "I'm a mess."

A sad smile came to her as she tucked a strand of hair behind the waterfall. "Well, you let me do my magic. This hairstyle, it's something I can do to help."

I nodded, whispering, my throat suddenly clogging up, "Thank you."

"Of course." She touched my cheek a moment before she was back, working on my hair.

Twenty minutes later, I had eight to go before the driver would be upstairs, Nicole stepped back. "You're done!" She was smiling and blinking back tears. I was taking that as a good sign. Slipping from the chair, I went into the bathroom and stopped.

Whoa.

The waterfall braid started at one corner, wound down and around to end behind my other ear. The top was tucked under, pulled into the braid and the rest fell loose at my shoulders. They were curled and shining, and I knew I couldn't have done anything better.

"Thank you." I wasn't thanking her just for the hair.

"Come here." She pulled me in, hugging me tightly before stepping back. "The girls and I, we're here for you. Mia lost her dad two years ago. It's why she and Char got as close as they did. Char's mom died of cancer the same year. Lisa lost a little brother. Savannah, her sister has Down syndrome and is in a nursing home. When I say we're here for you, we are. We all get it. Trust me." She leaned in, still smiling. "Thank you for telling me what's really going on."

Nicole gave me one more hug, and I was back to being a mess, but a good mess this time.

"Okay." She stepped back. "Get dressed and get all hot for your man."

My man.

I sighed after she left.

My man. Her words echoed in my head. Stone and I said no romance. We hated each other, then bam, death put us in bed together, and that's where we still were. And my phone buzzed.

The driver was here.

I didn't have time to ponder that.

———

The driver's name was Morpheus.

I thought he was joking until he took a call and I heard the other person call him 'Morph!' so yeah. Morpheus. He didn't look like the Morpheus I was thinking. He was a young guy, dressed in a button-down shirt, jeans, and black and gold leather dress shoes.

The shoes made me pause, but okay, then.

He picked me up in an SUV, and driving to the stadium, I could tell he'd done that a time or two. He whipped around, used side alleys that I didn't think cars should drive in, and then he pulled up outside of door 8. I hadn't told him I needed door 8, so there you go. The epitome of professional service.

"Here you go." He turned to me, sunglasses hiding his eyes. "Mr. Reeves said you'd go home with him?"

Took a moment, but he was asking me that.

"Uh. Sure. Yeah." I had no clue. But it didn't matter. That felt good, knowing that Stone was planning for that.

And I wasn't pondering that either.

From down the sidewalk, merging out of the crowd of people going for the main doors, I saw Georgia first. She was tall, long black hair. Her complexion was so clear and gorgeous. She looked like Gina Torres from *Serenity*. Her husband was next to her. He was the male version of Gina Torres, and ironically, dressed similarly to Morpheus. Cream-colored button-down shirt. Jeans. Leather dress shoes.

Two boys came from behind, and a little girl.

Apollo. His sister, but my gaze was on Jared.

He'd gotten taller. Could that happen? But yes. The last time I saw him was Thanksgiving the year before. He would've been a junior, and he'd shot up at least another inch, maybe more. He was lean. Wearing a Kings ballcap, a Kings jersey, and Nike shorts, his feet were decked out in the latest shoes. Apollo was dressed the same.

I got out of the SUV, my knees knocking together.

Georgia saw me first. A bright smile showing, she came over and enveloped me to her. She smelled like peaches and citrus. A big squeeze. "Oh, my girl. Dusty." Another squeeze before she stepped back. She wiped a tear away.

Hands on my shoulders, she held me for another moment, just taking me in.

"You are so beautiful." Her hand cupped the side of my face. A sad smile pulling at her mouth.

Her mouth tightened, her jaw starting to shake, and the tears began falling.

Her husband stepped up, sliding an arm around her shoulders, he drew her to him and nodded to me. "It's nice to see you, Dusty."

A pair of arms wrapped around my waist.

I looked down.

Dark curls were there and I had to think a moment. Apollo and Angelina. I couldn't remember how old Apollo's little sister was, but she looked up, a beaming smile. "Hi! Did your mom really name you after dirt?"

Apollo groaned. "Angie, you weren't supposed to say that."

"What? That's what Jayjay told me."

Jayjay.

I knelt down, hugged Angie and whispered in her ear, "No, but that's what Jared likes to tell little girls that he's fond of." I pulled back and winked at her.

I was guessing she was eight because her eyes got big and she started blushing.

Standing, I looked at my brother.

He was fighting back tears.

My eyes were red and my own were coming. I didn't fight them. They fell free, and seeing them, his own started flowing. He was holding a soda in his hand, but it fell and he just stared at it on the sidewalk.

I didn't think he saw it.

I went to him, and in one breath, I pulled him to me. "Hey." I wound my arms tight around him.

He stiffened. His body was so skinny. Tall, but skinny, but damn. His arms came around me, too, and he wasn't weak, like at all. Oomph. He was hella strong. Holy Jesus. He was almost crushing me, hugging me so tight. I felt his body start to shake, and I felt the wetness on my shoulder. I just hugged him harder. The two of us, we were crushing their memories between us. Gail and my dad. Who were they? If we hugged just a bit harder, we'd make them disappear, or bring them to life. Right? That's how it worked?

No. The harder we hugged, the faster the tears fell.

We were all a mess. Except for Angie. She was trying to stop the soda from running free when Jared and I separated.

Georgia. Bud. Even Apollo was having a hard time holding back the tears. Jared's eyes were red-rimmed, swollen, and I could only imagine I looked worse. We all stood in a circle. I wouldn't let go of Jared's hand. Georgia came over, hugged me again. She smoothed her hand up my back in a comforting motion.

And Angie. She started crying because the soda *wouldn't* stop running over the sidewalk.

"Oh dear." Georgia laughed, realizing what her daughter had been crying about. She scooped her up, and her husband helped to clean Angie's fingers.

And Jared, he was just staring at me. "It's good to see you."

Damn.

Oh, yeah. My throat was so clogging up again. "You, too."

Jared ducked his head.

"I have to pee!" Angie announced to everyone. A few people going past heard and snickered. One teenager wrinkled her nose. "Ew."

"Hey, that's my sister."

Yeah. That didn't come from Apollo. The girl stopped, taking

Jared in, and I could see the crush already starting. And I could see why Angie was smitten. Jared was all angry and smoldering and he was cute.

He was going to be a heartbreaker.

The girl said, "Sorry."

When she kept going, Angie snorted. "That was a fake apology. She didn't mean it." She raised her voice, "You don't mean it!"

"Oh, dear God." From Georgia.

Apollo was laughing. "I have to pee, too. Can we, you know, move it along here?"

On that note, I stepped forward and knocked on the door. A security guy opened it. He verified who we were, then showed us inside. A quick trip to the bathrooms, then we were taken to our seats.

CHAPTER 29

WATCHING Stone run out for their game, I'd forgotten what it was like to see the game in person.

It was pandemonium. It'd been like that back home and it was ten times louder now, but damn. In his uniform, those shoulder pads, his hips. Wow. There were emotions going on inside of me, but I was really only remembering how he felt above me and inside of me last night.

Lots of emotions firing inside of me.

My lips were dry. I knew my eyes were hungry, because *damn*. Stone was *hot*. His picture flashed on the jumbotron and his eyes were smoldering, that square jaw firm, a slight scowl on his face, but with his short hair, yes, just fucking hot.

Jared didn't talk much to me after our initial meet-up. He laughed with Apollo. They were either on their phones or pointing to the field. Right before kick-off, he and Apollo went with Bud to the concessions. Georgia moved down and took Jared's seat beside me.

I had a feeling she was going to stay the whole time.

Angie came running next to her, launching herself into her mom's lap.

"Oomph." Georgia laughed, untangling some of Angie's curls. "I was hoping to talk a bit. What are you doing after the game?"

I frowned at her. "What do you mean?"

"Stone offered to meet us on the field if we wanted pictures. We have to head to the hotel and get to bed right away since we fly out so early. So instead of going somewhere after the game, we were just going to go on the field to see him, but I wanted to talk about Jared and his future."

My stomach took a nosedive. "About?"

"The adoption. I wanted to make sure you were still okay with us doing that." She seemed to be hesitating before blurting out, "I know Jared's been wishy-washy, and I think that's normal with what you're both going through."

I didn't respond. I didn't know where she was going with this.

She added, tucking more of Angie's curls behind her ears, "Gail and I talked maybe a year ago. I know they didn't specify in their will where they wanted Jared to go, but she and I talked. She said she'd be happy if we brought Jared into our family."

She was biting her lip, and understanding dawned then.

She felt guilty.

I laid a hand on her arm, and felt her own slightly trembling. "I'm okay with this. Jared, he and I barely know each other. His mom called me a bunch of times. My dad raised him the last few years. The two of us need to get to know each other, but as long as he's happy with you guys, then I'm happy. You guys have a family already. You're established. You have careers. And I know you're amazing parents. It's obvious."

More tears slid down her face. Her mouth was shaking and she pressed her lips together. "You mean that?"

"I do." And I did.

She stopped, looking and watching Stone for a moment. "You and he, are you guys...?"

Oh, boy. I didn't want to lie, but I didn't want to tell her what we were doing.

She added, "No talks about marriage or...?"

Oh! It was all lining up, how she kept talking to me, making sure I was okay with them adopting Jared, and now coming here, asking about marriage.

I sat up straighter and spoke clearly, "I don't know what I'm doing. My focus is getting through one day at a time right now. If you're worried that I might marry Stone and decide I want Jared," she sucked in a breath. I kept on, "I can reassure you that that won't happen. Jared needs a functioning and stable family. I am not that at all right now."

"Oh, honey." Her hand came to my arm.

"You don't have to worry that I'm going to change my mind and fight you for Jared. I wouldn't do that unless I truly believed he'd be better off with me than with you guys, and I don't think that's the case. I'd be hurting him if I made him be with me."

She held still.

The crowd was deafening around us. Hip-hop music was blaring over the speakers. Cheerleaders were dancing. Mascots were walking around, waving to the crowd. The players were finishing their warm-ups, but all that melted away.

Georgia saw me. I saw her.

She was grieving losing Gail, and she was a mother yearning to love another son. And me, she saw me, too. I don't know what she saw, but she did, and a look melted over her face. "Oh, baby." She reached for me, pulling me in. Angie squeaked, but she was in the middle of the hug, and after stiffening, she laughed. Twisting around, her little arms wrapped around me, too. She could only get one of my arms, but she buried her head into me.

I laughed. Georgia chuckled. Angie was laughing, then said, "Your hair is tickling my face."

Georgia released me, sitting back, and I could see how relieved she was. She rubbed a hand up and down my arm. "We're here for you, also. I want to make sure you know that. I am *fully* ready and prepared to step in and be another mom if you'd let me. And that's only if you want that."

I let out a ragged breath, one that I hadn't known I'd been holding. The mom offer was nice to hear, but I was fighting dealing with my own feelings of how good of an older sister I was being. And since Jared wasn't there, I asked, "How's he doing? For real?"

"He's—"

"He's here!"

Georgia and I both froze, but it wasn't Jared saying that.

Angie shoved up on her mom's lap, pointing and waving. She added, yelling, "Jared! Apollo!"

They were higher up, coming down the stairs. Their hands were full of soda and popcorn. I spied a few hot dogs. Pizza. No, two pizzas.

As soon as they got to our chairs, Angie pointed at us. "They were talking about you."

Jared froze, a slice of pizza halfway to his mouth. "Huh?"

Georgia stood up. "Oh, it's fine. Your sister was asking how you're doing. That's all." She reached over, taking some of the food and drinks from him before moving back to their seats. "Come on, Ang. Let's sit over here again."

Apollo came in.

Jared waited, looking up the stairs.

Apollo's dad came next, stepping just past me, and then his son. "Thanks for moving, bud."

"No problem, Dad." Apollo popped the rest of his slice in his mouth.

Jared stepped around me since I was on the end, sinking down next to me.

The players were lining up, readying for the anthem to be sung, and Jared waited for all of that. Once the song was done, the fans were going nuts as the captains were running out on the field, Jared looked at me. "You want to know how I am, you ask me."

"It wasn't like that. Georgia was worried that I might try to take you away from them."

"Why would you?" he bit out, shoving half of a hot dog in his mouth. Two bites and it was gone. "I'm seventeen. Not even a full year and I'm an adult. Who'd want to fight for me?"

He started to turn away as the teams were lining up. The Belves were kicking off against the Kings. Stone was out there, he was primed to catch that ball, but I stopped Jared from totally turning away.

"What are you talking about? I thought you wanted to be with the Montroses?"

He was glaring at the field, his jaw tightening. "Yeah. I mean, yeah." His tone was so biting. I heard the anger there and I knew what Georgia would've said to me. "You're all I have now. I mean, we had to come down here for a game to even see you."

My heart broke. It shattered. There were a million pieces on the ground by our feet.

I didn't say a word. I grabbed him, pulling him to me, and I wrapped my arms around him. There was a hot dog squished between us. I was hoping there also wasn't a drink. I knew there was a bag of chips somewhere, probably his pockets. I heard the squish.

I just hugged him harder.

"I made a decision two days ago that as soon as I could medically travel, I was coming to you."

He stiffened, asking in my other ear, "Really?"

I just hugged him tighter. This boy. He was mine. He was Gail's. Gail had been mine. She'd been my dad's. We were family.

"Really," I choked out. "Only reason I didn't was because Stone said you guys were coming here. Today's the first day I could've come with the concussion."

"Oh." His head bent down, almost shyly. "And I do want to stay with them. I'm sorry I said that."

Okay.

Yeah.

He was confused. So was I. He wanted me, but he wanted them. He was still a kid. Everything is overwhelming when you are seventeen. But I could do this. He could do this.

I framed his face, my forehead falling to rest on his. "You and me." I made sure his eyes were looking in mine, even as I had to pull him down since he was so much freaking taller. "We'll figure it out, but I got you. You got me."

He hesitated, then nodded with me. "Okay. Yeah."

"Yeah?"

"Yeah."

Another hug. This one I had taken Georgia's role and I just wanted to hug him for the rest of his life. I wanted to shield him from everything, take care of him, protect him, love him, guide him, challenge him, but most of all, I just wanted him to be okay. That was job number one.

He pulled back, flicking his hand up at his eyes, his head turned away. He flicked his hand a couple more times before the crowd sat and we went with them. He nodded toward the field. "You and Reeves. He good to you?"

I was having another 'oh, boy' moment, but it was more like an 'oh, shit.' And a laugh pulled from me, hitching up a note. I patted his knee. "He and I... Yeah. We're... Yeah." I noticed the best distraction ever. "Look! They already scored!"

Apollo shot over Jared. "Your boy got the ball and ran it all the way in. One fucking play and touchdown!" He tipped his head back. "YEAH, REEEEEEVES!"

A collective cheer went up around us, but Jared was grinning and laughing with Apollo a second later, and for a moment, just that one moment, all seemed right in the world.

I vowed to have more of those moments with him.

CHAPTER 30

WE HAD three minutes to score.

Kings were down seventeen to twenty-one. Belves scored three touchdowns with the extra point scored for each, and Kings only had two with a field goal. They had possession, but were only at the fifty-yard line. It'd been mostly a running game. We needed something extra.

"We won't get down there if they don't throw the fucking ball!" Jared had been saying the same gripe for the last period. His hands were permanently attached to the top of his head. He kept looking from the game to the scoreboard and back again.

As for me, my heart was permanently stuck in my throat.

Stone kept getting tackled. Over and over again.

A few weeks ago, I would've cheered. Now I wanted to tackle those guys who kept taking him down.

It was our possession.

The ball was snapped back. Colby looked like he was going to hand it off. Their halfback was going past him, and it was a fake! A fake. Cortez, their halfback, tucked it in, but he didn't. He didn't at all. Wait. Where was Stone?

He was breaking through, running down the middle.

NO ONE WAS ON HIM!

He was running, head down.

I jerked my gaze back to Colby. He was looking.

The defensive line was going after Cortez.

It all happened in a split second.

They realized he didn't have the ball. They were looking... Colby's hand went back. He launched the ball.

It was a beautiful spiral and everyone was on their feet. I mean, we were already on our feet, but if we could all jump to our feet again, we were doing it.

The ball was soaring, going, going, going, then going down. And...

Finding his target!

Stone looked back, NO ONE WAS ON HIM. He jumped up, caught the ball, a perfect cradle to his chest, and he was back down and sprinting.

Wait.

A Belves player was zeroing in on him. Their safety saw the play and was coming in fast and hard.

I was screaming. Everyone was screaming.

Twenty.

Fifteen.

Ten.

The safety was right there, angling right at Stone.

He had his arms open. He was readying to tackle Stone, but Stone stopped, pivoted, rotated his hips, and he dove in just behind the safety.

TOUCHDOWN!

I was going nuts.

Everyone was going nuts.

Kings won. There was no time. God. Was there time?

Yes. They had time. Just over two minutes. Anything could happen.

They were lining up. The kick went in. Kings were up now twenty-four to twenty-one.

Jared was groaning, bending over. His hands still attached to his head. I did glance once to make sure he wasn't pulling his hair out without realizing it, but no. His hair was still there. He was saying now, "If they get close enough for a field goal, we're fucked."

We wouldn't be fucked. We'd just go into overtime.

I patted his back. "We'll be okay. It'll all work out." Truth be told, I was as close to vomiting as he was.

They had to hold them, and spotting Jake running out, I was back to screaming.

They lined up. There was the snap, and they pushed it forward, only getting an inch. They repeated this each time, getting a first down, but they were running out of time. They needed to do something. Kings defense was holding them for the most part.

"They're going to throw. They have to throw." Jared now had his ballcap in his mouth. He was chewing on the back strap. "They can't throw." His hand suddenly grabbed my arm and he held tight. "Bolston's been shut down most of the game."

He stopped talking.

The Belves' quarterback dropped back.

Bolston shotput forward, running right up the side. He looked alone... I was scanning the field. He was alone. No. He wasn't. Sprinting to catch up was Bilson.

I tracked back to the quarterback, the ball was already in the air.

Bad déjà vu was filling my mouth full of bile.

No, no, no. Miss. Or interception. Either of the two.

Then it was going down. Just like Stone had done, Bolston

turned, read the ball, and reached for it. It connected...bam! Jake slammed into him. The ball bounced off his hand, then fell to the turf.

The clock was winding down, and as it was nearing the end, Jared heaved a huge sigh of relief. They did a snap, but it was done. The clock ran out. The game was over.

The Kings had won.

Jared used his hat to mop the sweat off his face. "That was a good game." His grin was sloppy, his eyes a bit dazed. "Stone ran in all three of their touchdowns. He's gonna be MVP for this game." His sloppy grin beamed a bit brighter. "He's so fucking awesome."

Yeah, but, "Don't curse."

He only grinned at me.

"WE GET TO GO DOWN TO THE FIELD!" Apollo launched himself onto Jared's back.

Laughing, Jared caught him and they were bouncing up and down. Apollo's fist was in the air.

A staff person came over, showing us to the field.

I felt the attention from people around us. They were assessing who I was, and recognition flared in one person's eyes. He nudged his friend, but I was moving to the aisle. The back of my neck was already hot, and it was only getting hotter.

We were going down there to see Stone.

Cameras were down there. Journalists were down there.

He wanted to give Jared some attention, but there'd be some on me, too. Jared. I saw how excited he was as he moved past me with Apollo. Angie was half asleep, her dad was holding her. Georgia's eyes were dilated from the excitement, too, and she gave me an impulsive hug before following the rest.

My heart fell out of my chest for my brother, and I was just following behind it, trying to catch it back up, but it was now Jared's. Totally.

We were taken to the field. It was how I knew it'd be. Chaos.

Interviews were happening in almost every corner.

A large crowd had formed, and Stone was in the middle. A woman's microphone in his face, the ESPN logo attached. He was nodding, talking, then he looked up, and seeing us, he began grinning.

"Hey!"

That wasn't from Stone. I was turning.

"HOLY FUCK!" Jared couldn't breathe.

It was Colby coming over with his helmet on his side. He nodded to me, smiling, and gestured to Jared beside me. "This the brother?"

Yeah.

I couldn't talk.

I was starstruck again. Just like the kitchen, but on steroids.

"Hmmm-mmm." That squeaked out of me.

Laughing, Colby held his hand out. "Met your sister yesterday. You're Jared?"

Jared couldn't talk either. His hand went out as if he were a robot, and he was shaking Colby's hand, looking at the two hands, to Colby's face, back again. A gargled sound came from him. "Oh, my fuck. You're Colby Doubard. I'm Jared."

"I know. Hi. Nice to meet you." He nodded to me. "Your sister can cook." He said to me, "I'd give you a hug, but I think Reeves would rip my arm off."

A whole burst of flutters kick-started in my chest.

I heard Georgia sighing behind me.

Colby was shaking hands with Apollo and the rest of their family. They took pictures with him. Jake came over and it was almost the same exact response, except Georgia got all flustered, or even more flustered. Her husband leaned down to say in my ear, "She's had a crush on him since last year." He was grinning, and that was another testament to their marriage. There was no jealousy, no insecurity. In fact, he was almost as flustered as his wife when Jake came over to shake his hand. Angie had woken up by then and she was blinking, confused as she turned and was face to face with Jake Bilson.

She started crying.

Everyone laughed.

Then I felt a hand sliding around my waist and I was being pulled into a sweaty and smelly chest, but damn, it was a delicious sweaty and smelly chest. Stone bent down, burying his face into my neck. "Fuck. You feel good."

My heart dipped. It skipped a beat, and those flutters suddenly exploded all over in me.

I pulled back, giving him a glazed-over look. I was trying to smile, but I wasn't sure if it was coming out the right way. "You were amazing."

He looked at me, his eyes darkening. He bent down, saying to my ear, "Can't wait till we get back to the house." Then he was pulling away, but his hand dropped, grazing just slightly over my ass and I knew it'd been intentional. I stepped back, a private smile on my face, so I looked down.

Jared and Apollo were going crazy over Stone. It was the same as with Colby and Jake. Pictures were taken. They got his autograph on everything they had, their clothes, too.

Georgia sidled up next to me. "He's delicious." She was now holding Angie and was patting her back, her head lying over her shoulder. Georgia was taking in Stone. "Wow. You know, we've always heard about him back home. I've met his parents, but we don't run in the same social circles, and I didn't know what to expect. I knew Jared looked up to him, but I was worried. Thought he'd be arrogant, or I don't know. I heard he wasn't the nicest person when he went to school there. Now, seeing him, I'm happy I was wrong." She nodded at me. "I'm happy I was wrong for you, too. I saw how he looked at you. Whatever you two are doing, he's *all in*. You know that, right?"

I stepped back.

I didn't mean to. The response was instinctual, but seeing that Georgia registered it, hurt flashed in her gaze.

Before I could say something, try to rectify that, a hand came around my waist again. I was being pulled back to Stone's chest.

He kept me anchored to him, my face in his chest, as he continued talking to someone beside me.

I could feel his other arm signaling for someone or something. His hand came to the back of my head and he looked down at me. "Just a bit longer. I'll have someone show you to a room to wait in."

I sagged into him, knowing there were probably a hundred images being taken of this moment. Or just one. One was all that was needed. But I couldn't pull away, not even for the life of me, and there'd been no getting around this moment because this was all for Jared.

Georgia touched my arm, leaning into me. "We're going to go. This little one really needs to get to bed and we have to be up by four. It's going to be a short night for us."

I stepped away from Stone's shelter to hug her goodbye. Even Apollo hugged me. Angie wound her arms tight around my neck and said, "Your boyfriend is cute." Then she was back cuddling against her mom.

Jared was last.

His face was a mix of adrenaline, excitement, and now a somberness was edging its way in.

I shook my head and grabbed him for a firm hug. "Nope. Don't look like that. It's my turn to come see you. Okay?" I pulled back, my forehead to his again. "Got it? No sadness. Nothing. Text me later."

He nodded, but he flicked a tear away, then he hugged me back. "Love you, sis."

Oh.

Those words.

I clasped my eyes shut, knowing I would have a cascade of tears falling if I didn't keep them shut. I groped for his hand, squeezing it as he moved back. "Love you back."

With a last wave, Georgia herded her family through the crowd. Then the two of us were left, and Stone bent down. "You okay?"

"I will be."

And I meant it.

CHAPTER 31

IT TOOK about another hour before the door opened and Stone walked in. "You ready?"

I'd been curled up on the couch. He'd had me taken to the same waiting room as before. There'd been a few other people waiting in here, as well, but one by one, they left. The last thirty minutes had just been me, and this couch had started calling my name.

"Yeah. Hi." I gave him a sleepy grin, and however I looked, Stone laughed a little.

He let go of the door, coming inside and moved to where I was still sitting on the couch. He sank down next to me, laying an arm over the back of the couch, and just like that, I wanted to sink back down into him.

A yawn left me, one of those full-body ones, and I was closing my eyes.

"Colby invited us over. I'm assuming you want to head home instead?"

Home.

I didn't have a home anymore.

Suddenly, I was wide awake. "Yeah. I'm ready."

He frowned. "You okay?"

"Yeah." I was peachy, even tried to give him a thumbs up.

"I'm starving. I want to swing through some place for food."

When we left, we walked side by side. Stone was leading me through a maze in the back until we came out into one of their back parking areas. Most of the people were gone, but some still remained. People took note of Stone. Even the people who worked there.

He was special.

That came over everyone when they saw him. It was an invisible sizzle in the air, and it wasn't that he was famous. There was something extra about him, something from his aura that whispered to people to take notice, pay attention, and remember him because he would be a time in history they'd want to always cherish.

Or maybe it was just me. Maybe I knew to take note of these times because they'd always be a memory for me.

Either way, people stood up taller when they saw him. The smiles came quicker. If people were talking when he went past, the second he said hello, their conversation was dropped so they could return the greeting, as if they'd been paying him attention the whole time.

It was the same when we left, when we stopped at the parking lot attendant, when we got food, and this was one night. One day. One weekend in Stone's life. I didn't know how he remained grounded, but he did. He was.

When we went inside his house, he put his food on the counter, his keys next to it. "Want something to drink?"

"Water."

"No wine or anything?"

I shook my head. I'd gotten sleepy on the drive here. He lived a good forty minutes away, and that was after the rush of traffic, and it was close to midnight by now. He poured a glass for both of us, then went to unwrapping his sandwich. Putting it on a plate, he saw my food was untouched. "You're not hungry?"

"No." Another yawn. Good gracious.

"Thought that might've been a power nap for you before."

I eyed him. "I can't believe you're not tired."

He shrugged, placing the second sandwich on his plate. Scooping up his water, he motioned. "Come on."

"Where are we going?"

But I knew. Grabbing my water, I followed him to the theater room. He grabbed a remote, hitting the button and the screen lit up the room. He sank down on the middle couch. His plate was put on the console by his armchair. His water, too. I sat beside him, but a few feet away, my own water in hand.

I wanted to go to bed.

I wanted to sleep.

But seeing him, seeing the restlessness in him, he needed to wind down. Eating and the TV were going to do that apparently. And if I were being honest with myself, I wanted to spend time with him. He scored all the touchdowns for the Kings that night. He was the MVP. He'd been interviewed by so many members of the press.

I was feeling what all those other people felt.

We weren't enemies anymore. I wasn't even sure if we'd been enemies in the first place. There was a dark place in my heart that he contributed to. He knew about my family. He knew what his father did to mine, what I now knew his mother had done to us. But there was one more thing he didn't know. No one knew, and I wasn't sure if I wanted to give it a voice. Ever. Maybe it was a secret better kept buried.

"How was it seeing your brother tonight? Georgia said they couldn't meet after the game. That's why I invited them to the field. You were okay with that, right?"

He was asking in between taking mouthfuls of his sandwich, half watching me for an answer and half watching the ESPN highlights. His team was on there. Him especially, but he turned the volume up when they talked about the other teams. I knew he was already starting to pay attention to their next opponent.

"It was good. He seems to be doing as best as he can be, given the circumstances."

Stone was distracted, so he didn't push me to talk more about it.

I waited, finishing my water, until he was done eating, until he had finished his own water, until I saw his first yawn come over him. He relaxed back, rolling his head toward me and a tired grin tugged at the corner of his mouth. His eyes warmed, taking me in.

"You look nice tonight. I didn't tell you before."

I didn't care about that either, but it felt nice to hear. That's when I made my move.

I scooted over. He started to get up, but I was there, a hand on his chest. I pushed him back down so I was straddling him.

He sank back in the couch, a grin starting. His eyes grew heated and he was taking me in, all of me, in a whole different way than he had thirty seconds prior. His hands went to my hips. "What's this?" But he knew. A low simmer was starting. I felt it. I saw it in him, and he began kneading my hips.

I leaned back, almost looking at him lazily. "Put on some music."

His eyes widened at the command, but he did, reaching for the remote next to us. The lights in the room shifted, going dark, then blaring red as hip-hop filled the speakers. I was assuming he put on a music video, but I didn't look. I only had eyes for him.

This was what I'd been wanting since this morning, since Phone in My Face Guy, every time I hid in the library, when I walked to my house, when I was getting ready, when I called

Morpheus, when I met Jared and we walked into that stadium. And it'd been a slow trickle of torture watching him duck and weave and spin and twist, and being knocked down, only to see him jump right back up and do it all over again.

My hand still on his chest, I rolled my hips.

"I'm going to ride you."

He groaned. "Fuck." He slipped farther down on the couch until he was almost flat. I climbed up and settled back down, feeling him hardening and then closing my eyes, I started.

My body was a wave. A full, sensual wave, and I moved my hips in rhythm, hearing another groan from him, a deeper groan. And I picked up speed. It was like I was riding a mechanical bull, but I was in charge. This was about me having my fun. He could watch. He could enjoy that way, but this was me.

He and I...we'd never been sexually shy with each other. Not the first night, all the positions he'd twisted me into, and I went with everything. I'd never been like that with anyone but him.

He was liberating. He was thrilling. He made me feel confident and sexy, and I was addicted to every time he was inside of me. And speaking of, he wasn't. Not yet. I wasn't there yet, but he was. Reaching between my legs, I opened his pants, then helped him out. My hand wrapped around him, and I stroked him. Slow. Sensual. All the while still rolling my hips forward and back, my body following like I was made of water.

"Jesus, Dusty."

He swallowed just as I rubbed his tip.

I picked up the pace, my body and my hands. But only a half a notch faster. I was tormenting him now.

His hands were holding me tight, as if he couldn't bear not to participate, but also couldn't bear to interrupt what I was doing.

I was weaving a spell, for both of us because I was just as affected as him. My pulse was pounding. My blood was buzzing. I was wet for him, aching, and I wanted to shift over him, sinking down, but I was still rolling. Back and forth until the song changed behind us. We were on song three, this one had a faster tempo and I gave in now, leaning down to graze my lips over his.

His mouth opened, trying to draw me in. I didn't let him, just the graze.

He groaned again. "Fucking hell. What are you doing to me?"

I moved my hand down his chest, then began pushing his shirt up, my hands sliding over his chest underneath. Stone helped with that, ripping his shirt off, and he reached for me, and this I allowed. He went for my bra, and I shook my head, leaning back again, still riding him, but not letting him feel me completely. My hand never stopped stroking over him, but then my mouth was watering and I slipped back a little on his legs, just enough room. I leaned down and took him into my mouth.

His fingers entangled in my hair.

"Oh, God. Christ."

All the way in, and I opened my throat, slipping him in even farther.

He was starting to pant above me.

"You are killing me." He hissed in a breath, a low, guttural moan tumbling out as I touched my teeth to his shaft.

His hips bucked. "Jesus!"

My tongue swirled over his tip. I sucked him like a goddamn lollipop, my head moving until he reached forward, his hands moving to my own pants. I let him. I was getting impatient myself, then he shoved his hand inside, and as I was picking up my pace, his fingers thrust inside of me.

He began moving in and out of me, matching my pace on his dick until he came. I didn't. I was only primed for him. He jerked, exploding in my mouth, and I swallowed. He'd been watching me, his eyes lidded, and seeing that, he let out a low and soft curse. His hands went under my arms and he lifted me. I was back to straddling him, but he didn't push inside me. His fingers slid back in and he sat up, his other hand behind my hip, urging me to keep riding him.

I did. My eyes closed. My head back.

I pumped, back and forth, and once I was going, he tugged my bra off. Just as air touched my nipples, his mouth closed over one, warming me. His tongue swirling around me. He was returning the favor. I groaned, wrapping a hand around his neck, and I started pounding down on his fingers. He slid a third inside, shoving up and up and up.

I was going down and down and down, until the climax ripped through me, hurtling at a breakneck speed, and I screamed. The sensations were pounding me still and I couldn't... I was coming and coming and coming.

"Fuck yeah." He grunted, then he was reaching inside his jeans pocket.

A condom came out. He rolled it on, and I shifted, sitting up so he could put it on.

His hands came to my hips. My hands went to his stomach, and together he went up at the same time I sank down on him.

And we started up all over again.

CHAPTER 32

I WAS FUCKED.

No. Really. I was fucked.

Waking up in Stone's arms for the third morning in a row, I felt my heart do a whole flip, shimmy, and settle. It settled. The whole rolling/riding him last night had been an awakening. Or maybe it was just that grief was starting to fall into the grooves and dips in my heart, letting me feel other stuff, stuff that maybe had been building inside and I hadn't realized it until now. Until I woke up, Stone's arm over my chest, his leg pressed up behind me, his head tucked into my back, and I felt peaceful.

Peaceful.

That wasn't good.

Again. I was *so* fucked.

His arm twitched. His body tensed. He was waking up, and his hand ran up my stomach, finding my naked breast and he cupped me there.

I needed to go over this again because there were more flutters in my stomach than there'd been last night, or like ever.

I might've had a crush on Stone growing up, but him being an elitist prick got that out of my system. Or I thought so because damn, what if that crap never left me? What if it'd been in me this whole time and now him being all nice and kind and taking care of me and giving me all these climaxes, what if all those brought up all of *that*?

"Morning." He moved into me, his hand left my breast, sliding down, down, going past my waist and dipping between my legs.

I groaned.

Oh, yeah. He was bringing all of *that* up right now. As his fingers slid inside of me, I gasped. He was stirring those emotions up. They were like mud that had settled. He was dipping in the water and dirtying everything up.

Then, a second finger slid in, I rolled to my back, and I was gone. Whatever storm he was waking up in me, it was going to happen. Till then, I reached for him as he moved over me and his mouth found mine.

I waited till after I'd made breakfast for both of us, after we'd each had a coffee.

"This can't be a regular thing."

I was so stupid. I was already missing his dick.

He looked up from the counter. His plate was empty. He had a second cup of coffee in front of him, along with a glass of green juice and his phone. His eyes narrowed at me. "*Come* again?"

He smirked.

Yeah. I deserved that, but I was staying firm. "You and me. What we're doing up there, we both agreed no relationship."

"We both agreed not to fuck someone else if we're fucking each other. I like fucking you. Why stop that?"

"Because."

Stellar defense here, Dusty. Freaking stellar.

He cocked an eyebrow up, picking up his coffee. "Because?"

"Because I'm a girl. We feel things eventually." I dipped my head. "And I'm getting better."

A conflicted emotion passed over his face, tightening the lines around his mouth before smoothing back out. He put his coffee back down. "Better how?"

"I'm dealing. I'm not having meltdowns."

"You had one four days ago."

"And that's my point. I'm better, because of you."

His eyes narrowed again, and he cocked his head sideways. "Why change that? Because you're worried you might start feeling something?" He shrugged, grabbing his coffee once more. "Let's end this when that happens."

"It's happening." His eyes lifted back to mine. I added, "Last night. This morning." I turned away, feeling like I was exposing more of myself to him. "It's happening."

I waited.

It didn't matter. Whatever he said, how long he took to say anything, that didn't matter. That's what I was telling myself.

A second passed.

Five seconds.

I stopped counting after fifteen seconds.

I was holding my breath.

A chair scraped against the floor.

Looking, he was walking away. His coffee, his green juice, was left behind.

Well.

That was a nice punch to my face. It shouldn't have been. This was why I said something. He was being smart. I was being smart.

Still. It hurt. It couldn't hurt worse than that, right?

He came back into the room, not looking at me, but turned

halfway to me. His head was down. He was holding his phone, and he asked, "You need a ride back and forth from campus?"

See. My chest squeezed. He was making sure I was okay even after he was kicking me out.

"No. The house is a few blocks from campus. I can walk or get a ride with one of my housemates."

He looked up, his entire face guarded. Nothing shone through. "Get a ride." He left again.

"Okay." God. That hurt to say. My throat was burning.

This was the right thing to do. Right? Then why did I feel so stupid? So foolish? But no. We said no relationship. I knew guys. They could compartmentalize better than I could, or some could. No. Stone could. He didn't have those feelings for me. He liked me in bed. He cared about me outside of it, but he was a rising professional athlete. No way would he want to be tied down in a relationship, and I wasn't ready for that either. What I went through, what I was handling now, a relationship was the last thing for me. Jared. Me. School. Those were my priorities. I bring a guy in, and if that guy was Stone, he'd become everything I would lean on. I wouldn't do any growing on my own. This hurt. All of it, but I needed it.

Stone saw that, or he would've fought me on this.

He would... Wouldn't he?

No. He would. I might've been seeing the nicer side of him lately, but I knew the asshole side of him, too. A total prick. A complete dick. I felt like saying stick just so I rhymed here, but he didn't have a stick. He had a weapon. He had...okay, not helping.

I let out a shuddering breath.

Jesus. This was hurting.

He came back into the kitchen, dressed to go to the stadium. He'd told me he had meetings already, getting ready for their next game. They didn't get the half-rest day because of Monday Night Football.

Good Lord, the way he filled out his shirt, how the jeans molded to his legs, how I knew how powerful those legs could be, especially when he was thrusting inside of you...yeah, again, *really* not helping.

He went past me, grabbing his wallet, his keys. He was putting his phone in his pocket. He went to the door, but paused.

I was waiting. He would open the door in two seconds. He didn't, and then he spoke, "I get why you're stopping this. I know you're doing it for you in the long-run, but I also know you're half doing it for me." A pause. I didn't look back. I remained standing on the other side of that counter, my back now turned to him. "Thank you."

Confirmation.

Right there. He knew he didn't want a serious relationship. That's what I would've needed in my state. We were stopping before we even started.

It was better this way.

I was telling myself that as he shut the door behind him, as he drove out, as I heard the gate shutting behind his car.

I was lying to myself.

CHAPTER 33

THE FIRST WEEK SUCKED.

My housemates thought I was an idiot, and that was putting it nicely. I worried Mia and Lisa would go back to being bitches to me, but they didn't. They weren't friendly. They were just stagnant, if that was the best way to describe them? Savannah seemed quiet, but that was normal for her. Nicole and I spent more time together, actually building a friendship.

We met for lunch on Thursday, and that began our tradition going into my second week.

Siobhan and Trent, they were a mixed bag. Siobhan had moved, so she was sitting on the opposite side of the room as me. I didn't know why. I'd not been fully forthcoming about everything in my life, but welcome to my life. I wasn't forthcoming with anyone, even myself. We'd just started becoming friends. I owed her nothing, really.

As for Trent, he looked at me sometimes. There was the occasional wave, but only when he checked to make sure Siobhan was out of the room, so it was just before she came in or right after she left that he'd glance my way.

Three weeks after the video from outside the library had been posted, I was still getting the occasional 'whassup?' or 'Yo! How's the Rampage doing?' Or the pick-up lines. If Stone Reeves banged me, then I must be quality pussy, one guy actually told me that. Stone had been pictured with a few other girls in the weeks since I left. I knew because I got asked every other day 'what's up with that? You two not boning anymore?'

It was real fun.

But there were good parts. Jared.

I still didn't have a car, couldn't afford to buy one, so I used most of what I had in my emergency fund to fly up and see Jared. I'd gone twice, the second time, I'd gone up on the bus. It took longer, but both had been worth it. I'd gone to his own football game, and Georgia confided after they came to see Stone that Jared begged his coach to switch him to wide receiver.

She didn't ask how Stone was, and I was grateful. I think maybe she'd known not to ask, but I wasn't going to ask about that either. We were both in a no-asking zone, and it suited me just fine.

And now I was standing in the Quail while Joe was looking at me like I was trying to convince him I came from Mars.

"You're shitting me." He was sitting back in his chair, a leg up and his ankle resting over his other knee. His hands were clasped together.

I shook my head. "Nope. I need the money."

"You're coming back now for the job I gave you before your coma and your parents died?"

I gritted my teeth. "Stone didn't have any right to tell you that, but yes. I am. I need money," I said it again. It needed to be said, because I NEEDED money! Like, yesterday. "I used up my funds to go see my brother. I'm still trying to go to college, and no, I don't talk to Stone anymore, so he can't help me. Not that he should've before."

Joe stared at me. Long. Hard.

Cursing, he sat forward, picked up a pen and pointed outside the hallway behind me with it. "Every guy who works here knows Stone. They either love him or hate him. Sports is on the television all the time. The clip of you in Reeves' arms after his one game, that was everywhere. Along with that video in the parking lot. Girls don't know shit. You won't have problems with any of them, unless it's an obsessive fan, but those don't come in here. Your problem is going to be the guys. They'll want to talk to you about him. They'll want to be the next him. You'll be hit on almost from the time you walk in here to when you leave, and you're going to have to be escorted to your vehicle by security because you'll have guys following you, propositioning you."

Was now the time to tell him I'd be walking back and forth from work? I was taking that as a no.

"You're not telling me anything I don't know. I get the comments just walking around campus."

"They'll be worse here."

My gut knotted up. "I need the money."

Another long stare, another low curse, and he threw the pen at the corner of his office. His hands threaded together and he placed them behind his head. "This is not a good idea." He squinted at me, turning his head to the side, his eyes taking on a more assessing look. "Can you change your hair?"

I reached back, grabbing my braid.

I'd never dyed my hair. Trimmed it. Permed it once, but never messed with the colors. It was a honey-blonde color, and in the summer I usually got almost white streaks.

"This?"

He nodded. "Yep."

"You want me to change my hair color?"

Another nod. "Yep."

I was thinking. I was wondering.

What color would even work?

"You want me to darken it?"

He shrugged. "I don't give a fuck. You can make it rainbow color for all I care." He frowned. "Second thought, might not be a bad idea. The guys wouldn't recognize you for sure then." He clapped his hands together, grinning. He leaned forward in his chair, about to get up. "It's decided. Rainbow hair. You won't get harassed every night you work, and I got a server who can do her job without being harassed every night she works. Win-win."

Except I didn't want rainbow hair.

"Um. Okay. I'll see what I can do."

Rainbow hair. I could do it. I was trying to convince myself as I followed him through the rest of the Quail. We were between lunch and before the afternoon early-dinner rush would start in, but I was getting looks. I was getting a lot of looks. Joe was showing me the ropes, where to check in, where to grab my apron and ordering pad. He gave me a menu to take home and memorize, and after my brief orientation, two guys were waiting for me at the door.

Joe saw them, sighing. "It's already starting." He hollered, waving, "Mikey." He motioned at them.

Mikey must've been appraised because he was there and moving them along by the time Joe walked me out the back door. "You ready for this?"

"Yeah."

I had no option. I had to be ready for it.

He stared at me, another shake of his head that I was starting to learn was just a 'Joe' thing. "Okay. I'll have you train with one of my girls tomorrow night, Cammie, but after that, you're on your own. Sink or swim. If you don't swim, you gotta get cut by this weekend."

"I won't sink. I promise." Again. I couldn't. He was underestimating how dire my bank account was. Stone and his dad helped pay for a few things, but they didn't put money in my account. They just took what would've been added debt spread out over the years, which I was now super grateful for, but my present situation was dire.

"Okay. Tomorrow. Be here by six sharp."

I almost saluted him.

CHAPTER 34

I TOLD Nicole about the hair, and the entire house got involved. I have no idea how it even started, but she didn't like rainbow. Dent overheard, asked what was happening, and he wanted pink hair. Wyatt said purple. Noel had no comment. Nacho wanted fire red hair. Mia and Lisa didn't say anything at first, then commented if I had to change my hair, jet black would be the way to go.

I hated all the suggestions.

I didn't even want to change my hair, but Nicole brought a friend to my room that night. She was a hair stylist and she had a light blue in her hair. I fell in love, or I fell in love with it to be a temporary solution because eventually people would move on about Stone and me. So the next day, Joe didn't recognize me. I took that as being successful.

Cammie trained me the first night, but the Quail liked to keep their menu simple. It was relatively easy, just had to make sure to remember all the rules, but no one recognized me. My blue hair had been pulled up in a braid, and by the end of the first night a couple 'regulars' as Cammie told me, were already calling me Blue.

From the job standpoint, the Quail only had a few key drink options for people to order, and the bartenders did the drinks. We could grab a beer or do the tap, but mixed drinks were all the bartenders.

I was ready to go with doing my own thing my second night, and the tips were nice.

The main challenge was walking home after the shift, but I'd walked it the day before and found a shortcut that cut through two blocks. It was a middle alley, so I really only had to walk two blocks, and that alley connected to ours, so it was almost two-and-a-half blocks that I shaved off.

My housemates knew I'd taken a job at the Quail, but none thought about how I got there and back. They knew I didn't have a car. I didn't want to rely on anyone for a ride because that wasn't feasible long-term, but I knew they wouldn't want me walking that late at night. During the day was a different story, but waiting until after closing, after cleaning after closing, and I knew it'd be around two thirty or maybe some mornings it would inch closer to three in the morning when I'd be walking home.

I'd worry about that more later. The first night was fine. The second night was fine.

The third.

Fourth.

Because I was working almost every night. I'd asked for the most shifts as possible, and Joe said I was a good worker. See. Hard working and I didn't complain, I knew he'd be happy that he'd hired me back.

My big snag happened the following Saturday.

"I'm what?"

Joe had called me into his office and he didn't look up. He pointed to the door. "Jer's waiting for you out back. We're doing concessions for the game today or doing one of the concessions. I gotta figure out if I want you in the box or the beer stands."

"But why? We don't do concessions there."

He looked up, dropping his pen. His eyebrows were pinched together. "Not that it's your business, but yeah. I actually run some of the booths over there. But it's Homecoming today and they asked for us to man a second booth. You and a few of the other girls are going over with Jer. It's easy work. Go. Have fun. Be a part of the festivities." He frowned. "Don't you room with half the football team?"

I flushed. The group had started to drop in after practices for a burger. Joe took notice, especially when other people came with them. The Quail did fine already, but they'd gotten busier since Wyatt, Noel, Nacho, Dent, and a few of the other guys were becoming regulars.

"I room with their girlfriends."

He snorted, tossing some papers onto his desk and standing up. "Same difference. Think of it this way, now you can say you were there to support them."

That wasn't that bad of an idea.

"But it also doesn't matter because I'm the boss. As long as you work here, you're doing what I say." He started walking toward me around his desk, shooing me in front of him. "Go, my employee. Go and do my bidding." He leaned close behind me since I'd turned for the door, and whispered, "Go and do your job!"

He reached over me, swinging the door wide for me, and he followed me down the hallway.

I wasn't sure how I felt about this, but like he said, I didn't have much choice.

Cammie saw me coming and flashed me a smile. "Heya. You and me, we're doing the concession thing together."

I relaxed slightly then.

I liked Cammie. She was one of those types of girls who's beautiful in a natural way, but not flashy. Mia was flashy. She could've been on a runway for Victoria's Secret, but Cammie was just as beautiful, just in a more understated way. She was also one of the lead workers for the Quail. Most of the regulars had a crush on her with her caramel-colored curls, freckles, and bright sapphire blue eyes. And I didn't think they were alone. She had a boyfriend at another college, but I had a feeling the moment she was single, Joe himself would be throwing his hat in the ring. He tended to blush when she was around, and get all grrr if a regular was too touchy-feely with her. The bouncers were protective of her, too. They were protective of all the girls, but it was more with Cammie. She was kinda the Quail's sweetheart, and when she worked, all eyes were on her, or most eyes, and I liked that. I really liked that. Helped me stay under the radar even with the guys coming to eat here now that I was working here, too.

"I'm hoping to talk Joe into letting us work the boxes. They tip way better than the beer stand."

"That's where we'd be going?"

She nodded, helping carry out a few bags to the van. I took one and followed behind.

She said over her shoulder, "Yeah. All the hoity-toity people are up in the boxes. They give a twenty-dollar tip for us refilling a beer. Such easy money. We'd be lucky to get twenty for the whole night in the beer stand."

See. Smart and nice. Not many others would bring me along for that type of job.

"Thanks, Cammie." I handed off my bag to Jer, who was waiting by the van.

He tossed it in, then said to me, "You're in your blacks tonight."

Blacks meant we were wearing the Quail's more formal

uniform. Black skirt. White button-down shirt. They resembled a private school uniform, something I'm sure was the point.

Cammie heard. "Serious?"

He nodded. "You ain't working the beer stands. Joe's already ahead of you."

"Nice!" She held her hand up, giving him a high five and turning to me. A wide smile on her face. "Tips for two weeks here we come." Her grin turned slightly goofy at me. "And thank God he's sending you. I don't think I could do a full night in the box with Moore."

If Cammie was the sweetheart of the Quail, Moore was the opposite. Catty. Bitchy. Jealous. She was all of those things, and I'd been able to mostly avoid her, but I knew that time was coming to an end. I heard she had a mission to get into Dent's pants, and it was only a matter of time before she figured out how I knew them. So far she just thought one of them had a crush on me, that was the reason they kept coming when I was on shift.

"Okay, girls." Jer shut the door, going around to the driver's side. "Grab your uniforms. We gotta go. Boss wants us in the boxes before the ticketholders get there."

The game was in an hour.

We needed to curtail it out of there, but after changing in the back, Cammie grabbed me. "Sit." She went to work on me then.

"What are you doing?"

"Sex brings more tips. If you and I both look sexy, that means more money."

She was loosening my shirt. Nothing was showing, but there was a good swell of cleavage showing. She stepped back, studying me, frowning. Her hands went to my hair and she was redoing the ponytail I'd put it in for the night. Going around me, I was slightly impressed at how quick she worked. Not a lot of girls were braid-savvy, but she had put my blue hair in a loose, reverse

French braid. It was meant to look sexily rumpled, and when I saw my reflection in the mirror, I almost whistled to myself.

"Damn. You could do hair for a living."

She grinned, sitting next to me and tugging on a different pair of shoes. "I've got six little sisters and a single mom who works three jobs. Hair duty was like an assembly line in the mornings before school." She finished, standing up and smoothing out her skirt. "Ready to go and make some moolah?"

God, was I.

Going over, Jer pulled up to the stadium, and we were waved in to go toward the back employee parking area. A bunch of buses were back there, too. Hopping out, Jer told us, "Hold up." He opened the back door. "I need help carrying all this inside."

It took six different trips, maneuvering through all the people, even going through the back way and I was sweating up a storm. So was Cammie. She flashed me a smile once we were done, wiping some sweat from her forehead. "There's a bathroom up there we can use to clean up a bit."

I nodded. Sounded good to me.

"Okay." Jer was coming back, holding out two thick, black packets. He handed one to each of us. "Cammie will tell you the pricing, but you guys are your own cash registers up there."

She took hers, frowning. "You're not the bartender up there?"

He shook his head. "Nah. I'm running the beer down here tonight. Another guy's up there, but you'll do fine."

Cammie's frown was telling me otherwise.

Jer kept on, "Close out after the game or when the box clears out. Joe said that's up to you, and come down to the beer. I'll give you a ride back. We'll be closed before you guys anyway, so I'll probably head up to help you guys close out, or I'll be waiting in the van. Check your phones. I'll send word after the game. Joe wants you both back at the Quail for the rush tonight. It'll be nuts."

Cammie nodded, and I didn't tell her until we were going up a back stairway, "I didn't know it was even Homecoming this weekend." I felt stupid about it. I should've known that much.

She laughed, getting to the third floor and opening the door. She held it for me. "I'm not surprised, but that's what I like about you. Some of the guys call you Blue Daze, did you know that?"

She was walking down the hallway, so I was just going with her. "Blue Daze?"

"Yeah, cause you're always in a daze. You're like half here, half not here."

It'd been a week of working at the Quail. Between classes and work, my days were full this past week. So I got it, but she didn't know that I preferred it that way. I didn't want to admit it, but it hurt not seeing Stone, and he'd been my self-medicating way to get through everything else. So yeah, the last week, I'd taken on this zombie-way of lifestyle. I got up. Went to classes. Ate lunch. Studied if I had free time before work, then went to work. I studied any free time I had, but Joe had told me firmly that I needed one full day off from working. That'd be on Sundays, so I already had plans to study the entire day.

Being called Blue Daze, I wasn't too shocked by it. I think I preferred it. They hadn't called me Dusty since the first night. It'd been Blue ever since.

"This is us." She nodded to a door.

A bunch of security people were standing outside. Recognizing our uniforms, the guy opened the door for us, a radio in his other hand.

The entire room was busy, but not with the ticketholders yet. Staff was rushing around, cleaning, carrying food to the back kitchenette area and putting out table coverings. A guy was behind the bar and waved us over. "You girls are the servers?"

Cammie took lead, speaking for me, "We are. How many will be in here?"

"It'll be fucking packed." He was eyeing both of us, slightly concerned. "You both done boxes before?"

Cammie frowned back. "We load up the trays and walk 'em around. We're not in charge of getting the food, right?"

"Yeah. No, you're not." He motioned to the kitchenette area. It was being turned into a buffet. "You guys have to watch the food. When a dish gets half empty, let me know. I'll call down for more to be brought up. Mixed drink orders go through me, too. As for shots or beer," he motioned to the fridge behind him, under the counter, and the tap. "You guys can pour that stuff yourself. You know pricing?"

"Eight, ten, twelve for the beers." Cammie was half-telling me at the same time. "Bottles are..."

"Twelve."

She whistled. "Homecoming inflation rate?"

He grinned. "Pretty much. Shots are five even."

"Five?"

He shrugged. "They're getting the cheap shit here, but they don't need to know it. Oh, and we're only offering these types of shots. Nothing else. We're a box suite, not a fully functioning bar." He slid over a piece of paper, and taking it, I saw it was a cheat sheet for what we offered and the prices.

I tucked mine into my pocket.

"No." He reached behind, grabbing some black aprons to tie around our waist. "Use these."

They were short, but they would blend in with the skirts. I tied mine on, put the cheat sheet in there, the money on the inside pocket, along with a small pad of paper and a couple of pens. My phone went in the other pocket.

"We good to go?"

Cammie glanced to me. I nodded, and she spoke for both of us. "Load up the first trays. We're doing champagne?"

"Yep." He reached around, then swung right back. His hand extended. "I'm Ben, by the way."

Cammie laughed, shaking his hand. "I'm Cammie and this is Blue." She gestured to me.

He laughed, shaking my hand, too. "That'll be easy to remember." He went back to filling the first glasses when he said, "Oh. These are high rollers, so stay extremely professional. No flirting. Nothing like that. The team's new GM asked for these guys to come as a personal favor to the team."

Cammie nodded. "Who is it?"

He was back to filling the glasses when he said, almost casually, "The local Kings. Some of their star players and family. And their coach."

Cammie's eyes whipped to mine, but I'd heard. Every. Word.

My life flashed in front of my eyes because this news, well, consider it like a bomb dropped and it just exploded at my feet.

CHAPTER 35

"HE WON'T RECOGNIZE YOU."

Cammie must've known more than I realized, because as soon as Ben dropped that revelation, she pulled me into the bathroom. She immediately began changing my hair all over again, and she was giving me her version of a pep talk. "Your hair is totally different." She reached into her bra and pulled out a contact case. "Here. We'll change your eyes, too."

She was twisting it off, and two green contacts were being pulled out. "Ever had contacts before?"

"What?" I grabbed her wrist. "No. Stop."

"They're not prescription. You'll be totally fine, just maybe not look him in the eyes when he's here. Yeah?" She shoved the case at me, then reached back into her bra and pulled out a makeup case. "I can contour your face so you're barely recognizable."

"No. It's not him."

She was readying, opening her makeup, tilting my head up.

"No. Stop." I grabbed her wrist and stepped back. "I didn't change my hair because of him. I changed my hair because of everyone else. Those people in the box, if they recognize me it's not the end of the world. It's the guys in the bar, back at the Quail. They're the ones who hassle me."

"Oh." Pity formed in her eyes, and I turned away.

I didn't want that. I never wanted that look.

But stepping back to the mirror, I did wash up a little bit. Carrying everything inside had made me sweat, so after, I felt more refreshed. Cammie hadn't moved, just watched me. I went to the door, saying, "I'll see you out there."

She didn't respond or nod, but I opened the door and stepped out.

Ben was waving me over, his eyes a little frantic. He pointed to his watch. "They're coming up soon. Any minute."

Okay.

I could do this.

Picking up the tray, I went to wait at the door and smoothed a hand down my front, just to help ease my anxiety, but I was good.

This was a normal day at work.

I was still telling myself that as Cammie came out of the bathroom. She picked up her tray, standing beside me. And we heard people coming down the hallway. They were nearing, getting closer. Louder. Louder. Even louder. They were right outside the door.

It was opening.

I could do this.

They walked in.

It was the Kings' coaching staff first. I recognized them.

A player, Colby. He picked up a champagne glass, said thank you, ran his gaze over Cammie, and moved inside. He hadn't recognized me.

A few more players, some family members. Or I was guessing. A wife. Girlfriend. Colby didn't have a date. That was interesting. I couldn't remember if he was married or not, but then

Cortez came in, the Kings' halfback. Jake was behind him, his arm around a woman. Both picked up champagne glasses, said thank you, and moved on.

No one recognized me.

I slipped behind Cammie, going to the bar. Ben was ahead of me. He had a tray waiting for me, so I picked it up and returned in line.

Head up. Eyes forward. A nice and polite smile on my face. Professional. We were here representing the Quail, but we were also here for the tips.

The door closed, and I kept waiting.

My stomach was in knots.

I was expecting him to come in any second.

Still longer. We waited.

Cammie was done, so she murmured, "I'm going to start the walk-throughs."

I nodded. I had three glasses on my tray. "Should I wait?"

She opened her mouth.

The door opened.

But it wasn't who I'd been worried about.

It was worse.

My eyes met hers first, and the polite greeting I uttered, saying, "Welcome!" died in my throat. I knew this woman, had known her all my life. She'd seen me when I laughed, when I bled, when I cried, and she'd been the reason for some of those moments.

Barbara Reeves stepped through the door. She was still slender, but always had been. Her hair was cut short, still a dirty blonde, and she had it styled so it glistened and had good volume. She was dressed how rich people dressed. A white sweater that I knew without touching it, would be the softest material I'd ever touched. She was wearing tan khaki capris and sandals that were woven up her legs. For middle-aged, she was very chic and sophisticated, and I knew I never would be able to pull an outfit like that off, regardless of my age. She was very earthy and woodsy and natural, but I knew she probably spent a fortune to look like that.

Crystal earrings. A diamond bracelet on her wrist.

She was still just as beautiful as ever.

And she picked up a champagne glass, a frosted smile on her face, but she winced as she took in my hair. "Thank you, dear." She moved right along, not recognizing me just like everyone else.

Ben had moved out from the bar just then. He handed Cammie a full tray of champagne and switched over my last glass, then gave me a tray of appetizers instead.

I held them up, seeing that they looked like a gourmet version of pigs-in-a-blanket.

Barbara had seen and she paused, coming back a few steps. Her eyes were trained on the appetizers, and I knew her. I knew she was hungry, knew she wanted them, but knew she was right now battling herself in her head because she so rarely ate.

So I smiled, my hold steady, and I said clearly, "I mean, it's not *lasagna*, but it's still a little treat."

Her eyes lifted to mine, and she narrowed them, but any confusion she might've had left because in the next breath, Charles Reeves stepped in behind her. "Let's go, honey. Ooh. Those look delicious." He swooped in, grabbed a champagne, then grabbed two appetizers. "Damn good."

He smiled at me, at Cammie, and at Ben who had paused at my statement.

I was forgotten, and Barbara moved forward, her smile turning plastic once more. It was the type of smile she reserved for us, for the 'less thans.' I was the help and I was beneath her, but I'd always been beneath her.

God.

I sucked in a shuddering breath.

Gail.

My dad.

My mom.

They were gone, but this woman, this man, they were still here. I wished I had said more, but the moment was gone. She would recognize me if I drew attention to myself.

My tray was starting to tremble.

I was going to lose it. I felt it coming at me like an out-of-control freight train.

The food was going to fall to the ground, and everyone would look, and everyone would say 'how disgraceful.' And I'd be fired, or at the very least, they'd look down on me even more.

"I got it." Cammie's voice was a soothing whisper right next to me, and she took the tray. As soon as her second hand had ahold of it, I stepped back and drew in a rasping breath. Her smile upped in wattage, and she took over.

I needed a minute, just a minute.

"Blue," Ben hissed at me from the bar.

I held up a finger, knowing it wasn't steady, and I started to move behind Cammie.

Stone's dad had been talking to the head coach. As soon as both men cleared the door, Stone was there.

He was there.

I halted, freezing in place, and he rolled right in.

Not a look my way.

He saw Cammie, dipped his head in a greeting, and went right past her, too.

Her smile was frozen, and she looked to me once he was past us. Her eyes were almost bulging. And mine, I couldn't look away from him.

He looked so fucking good.

I never took a minute. I couldn't get myself to leave the room.

Through the game, a part of me wanted Stone to recognize me.

I wanted him to pull me aside, touch me, hold me, say the nice and comforting words I knew he would, but the other part of me knew that couldn't happen.

My head was messed up. There was no clear thinking with me, and that was translating to my heart. I used to hate the guy, for God's sake. What? A few kind acts, a few amazing nights, a few times he'd made my body bend and shudder and quake from exquisite agony, and that was enough to make me fall for him?

I didn't think so.

A few weeks couldn't and wouldn't erase the damage from all the years before.

Or, at least, that's what I was telling myself the one time I stepped forward to take Stone's emptied glass. He didn't look up, not once. None of them did.

To their credit, I kept my head down, and I knew over the last four weeks, I'd lost another ten pounds. It wasn't intentional. It was just grief. A different form of grief over the loss of Stone, but grief, nonetheless. My housemates kept the house stocked with food, and every now and then, when the feeling hit me and if I had time, I'd go and whip up a feast for them. The guys especially brought over extra ingredients for me, and if they saw me heading to the basement empty-handed, they'd signal. A full plate would be put in my hands. I used to fight it, but once Nacho leaned in and said gruffly, "Let us care. Okay?" That shut me up and I couldn't deny that I now had a soft spot for Nacho. I had a soft spot for all of them, even Mia and Lisa. They were my people. My tribe. But here, here I was out of my element surrounded by these people and their families.

There were no breaks to watch the game, but I did keep an eye on the scoreboard.

When Wyatt scored, I stepped into the hallway to send a congratulations text. I did the same thing for all the guys if they did a play or helped in a big play. It was my way of letting them know I supported them back. My people. My tribe.

The game was winding down. Texas C&B was up thirty-one to ten and the box was emptying out, as well. No one got too loud. Most everyone watched the game, cheered them on, and returned to conversation in between. A few of the coaches headed out first. The families went after them, especially the two who brought a couple younger children in with them.

Jake went out with his date. His arm was fully resting around her shoulders.

Cortez was next. He hadn't walked in with anyone, but he spent most of the game either talking to Stone or spending time at a table of women. He walked out with one of them now, holding her hand. Charles and Barb were after them. Stone was right after them. His mom was turning around, and I overheard them making plans to have dinner later.

It didn't hurt.

I was trying to tell myself that.

What was I expecting? For them to talk about me? Mention me since they were at the same school I attended? But nothing. And that wasn't realistic. Stone helped because he said he cared, but it was initially because of my mom, because he hadn't known what his parents did to mine, and then it was about righting some wrongs. So, no, I shouldn't have expected them to talk about me. Why would they? Bringing up my past only muddied their future.

His parents only helped because Stone made them. That was just the truth, and I needed to get over it. And I was trying to do that as I moved around the box, picking up the remaining dishes after everyone had left.

Cammie scooped up some of the emptied platters. "They

called downstairs and could do with some help getting everything taken down. I'm taking these down. I'll be back for another load."

Ben was right behind her. "Me, too." His arms were full of booze, though.

I nodded. "Got it. I'll finish picking up."

Both nodded, and then it was just me.

A toilet flushed.

Shit. I heard the sink in the bathroom turn on, off. The drier started. The door opened, and Colby walked out.

He stopped, scanning the room, craning his neck to look into the other section of the box.

His eyes found me after, and stark determination flared. He started for me.

I turned, reaching for more emptied dishes.

"Hey." He stopped beside me. "Is that other girl gone?"

"Cammie?" I kept my head down.

"Yeah. She take off?"

"No. She just took a few things to the catering section."

"Oh. Good." He sounded relieved. "What'd you say her name was? Cammie? Does she work with you here? In the catering section?"

He was interested in Cammie.

The surprise and the relief mixed with a thread of warmth. Colby was a good guy. Cammie deserved a guy like him, but her boyfriend. I didn't know much about her boyfriend, just that he wasn't here and she was tight-lipped about him.

"Uh...she has a boyfriend."

Colby laughed, snorting. "Is he a professional athlete?" I could hear his arrogant smirk. I didn't even need to look up.

"I don't know." I moved around him. Most of the glasses had been picked up. I headed behind the bar. Ben was cleaning them before putting them away, so I put my bin on the counter and started emptying the small dishwasher.

Colby followed me, standing on the other side of the bar. "Look. I'm serious. I'm interested."

"For what? A hookup?"

He was silent.

Jesus. He was.

I looked up, glaring. "Are you serious? Cammie deserves more than th—"

I messed up. Bad. Terribly.

The second I looked up, recognition flared over his face and he took a step backwards. "Holy fuck! Dusty?" He was looking me up and down, taking in my blue hair. Shock was soon replaced with concern. His eyebrows pulled together, and his face softened. "You've lost weight."

Shit.

Shit.

Shit!

CHAPTER 36

SHIIIIIT, Colby.

"Don't say anything."

His eyes flashed, and he shook his head, already backing away.

"Colby!" I started after him.

He held his hand up, his phone in it. "You know I can't keep quiet about this." He frowned, taking me in again, and regret flaring a second. "I'm sorry, but I'd want to know if it was my girl."

With that, he was gone.

And I was so fucked.

He was probably making the call as he left.

I didn't have long. I needed to get out of here as soon as possible.

I finished cleaning the rest that was left, then grabbed my phone. Ben was coming back right as I was heading for the door.

"Hey..." He trailed off, seeing me. "What's wrong?"

"Nothing, but I gotta go."

What was I doing, though? Really? No. I could go back to the

Quail. Stone wouldn't remember it. He'd only hear I was working here, not there. He might not follow me, and then I really stopped myself.

It didn't matter.

Colby would call Stone, but nothing. Nothing would happen. He might come. He might get in my face. He might issue threats about me eating, or something, but that'd be it because in the long run, he left. I spoke the words, but he was the one who utilized it. He put it into action.

So, with that decision, I stayed. I helped clean up the rest, and it was much later on when I was heading back to the Quail. Ben took the last round of dishes with Cammie, and there'd been no room in the van. It was fine. I told them I would walk. I could do with the clear air, to be honest.

And in all that time, nothing happened.

Not one text. Not one call. Not one Stone showing up in the box.

It really was done.

I was just turning the corner for the road leading to the Quail when my phone started buzzing again.

Cammie: Dude! Colby Doubard is at the Quail! Oh. Are you coming? Joe's pissed. We told him you were walking, but he doesn't believe us.

Cammie: OMG! Colby Doubard just asked for my number.

Cammie: OMG OMG OMG! Colby Doubard just asked me out!!! He left already, but he asked me out!!!

Cammie: Shit. Double shitter let's all take a dump together shitter. Kyle will be so pissed.

I scrolled through the rest.

Joe: Cammie arrived ten minutes ago. Where are you?

Ten seconds later,

Joe: If you have an emergency, I need to know what it is.

Two seconds later,

Joe: Just let me know if you're okay.

Joe: Reeves called me. You're good.

Stone.

My heart jumped up in my throat.

Whatever Stone was doing, he wasn't here and he was leaving me alone. That's probably all he was doing, knowing I needed time and that I'd be fine and he was just covering for me.

Still.

Should I text him?

No. I wouldn't. It was better to leave it alone. And with that decision made, I had five hours of shift I could still cover.

I texted Joe.

Me: I'm almost there, just walking. I'm fine.

Five minutes later, I was coming up the back alley for the Quail. I could hear all the people in the front, the line extending past where I was coming up, and I was just to the back door when a hand grabbed my wrist.

"I don't think so."

I was pushed against the building.

My heart stopped. I'd like to say dread filled me or panic started, but that would've been a lie. The first thought and emotion that flashed through me was finally!

Finally, he came for me.

Finally, he sought me out.

Finally, he remembered me.

Finally, he cared.

But here was how messed up I was because while I wanted him to be here for me, and I knew he was, I knew he was only here because Colby called him. He was here to 'check up on me.' I could just imagine the phone call from his teammate. Stone wasn't here because he had feelings for me, or at least the feelings I wanted for the long term or the feelings I needed from him to even have a fighting chance.

He was here because he cared, just not enough.

Be happy with what he's showing you. That thought flashed in my head, too, and I wanted to give into it. I wanted it so badly that my teeth were aching, tears were coming to my eyes, but I couldn't. I just couldn't. I would not survive.

He was in my face, and my God, he felt amazing. His eyes were angry. His jaw clenched. His hand had a cement hold on my arm before he shifted, placing both his hands on either side of my face. "Got a call earlier."

"I'm sure you did." I was resigned. He was going to go through it all, and I was already folding. If he kept at this, I'd be in his bed by tonight. And I'd hate myself for it.

Weak.

He shifted closer, lowering his head so he was peering at me eye level. "Got a call saying that the girl with the blue hair, that I hadn't looked at her close enough." He touched my hair. "Apparently, none of us had looked at her hard enough, but why would we? Different hair. You've lost weight. More pale." He skimmed me up and down, a sneer tugging at his lip. "What the fuck have you been doing to yourself?"

Anger surged up and I smacked his hand away. I seethed, "You don't get to stand there and judge me."

His eyes flashed again. Hot. "Yeah?"

"Yeah." I was in his face now because fuck him.

My body was craving him.

My heart was aching for him.

But my pride, yeah, that was raging. It was like in high school when he walked past me in the hallways because I wasn't good enough for him. Seeing his parents, him, serving them, old fucking times.

"You don't get the right to sit up on your high horse and judge me on the ground. You don't get that right, Mr. I'm So Fucking Talented and I have the whole fucking world at my feet. Mr. My parents' marriage might be a sham and unhappy, but we got a house and we got land and we got money to insure we never have to go cold or hungry. You don't have that right because you might have shitty parents, but you still have paren—"

His lips were on mine.

God.

I folded. My knees dipped. My arms wrapped around him.

I gave in, for three seconds.

One. Two. Three. So fucking heavenly, and I could've died and felt satisfied with life, but it was just for three seconds and then reality set in and I shoved him back.

"Get off of me!"

He was right back, his hands in fists, hitting the building beside me. He snarled, "Why? Goddammit, tell me why. One fucking good reason!"

"Because you're not the long game."

He flinched, as if I'd slapped him.

And to hell with it. "Because I could fall in love with you, and I know that you don't love me. You'll never love me. I'm a body you think fondly of, and if you care anything about me, give me that much honesty."

He turned his head, that jaw clenching over and over again. His hands were still in fists beside me, but he wouldn't look at me.

That. Right there. That was the truth for me.

Every word I said was real. I didn't have to play the guessing game anymore. I didn't need to torment myself because it was all the truth.

I spoke another truth, one I needed from him. "Let me hate you."

A second flinch. He sucked in his breath, and his eyes closed. His head reared back.

I had to hate him. Maybe it's why I hated him all those years before, because I had to, because if I didn't there was just the vast hole of his rejection.

A part of me was waiting for his response, and I hated that, too.

Hated that I still needed his acceptance, that I couldn't just walk away.

I wanted his rejection.

I was praying for it.

I could muster the strength and keep going.

I needed his rejection, because then I could walk away, once and for all.

"I served your mom today."

He tensed, but looked at me. A wall came down over his face.

My words were soft but chiding. He knew what was coming wasn't going to be pleasant. It wasn't going to be healing. Oh, no. He knew. He knew what was coming next would make him hate me. Oh, yes. We were going back there.

If he wasn't all in, then he was all out, and I was going to fucking shove him all the way out.

I was going to make him hate me.

I was going to make us enemies, once and for all.

I pushed off from the wall, an inch between us, and I taunted him with my words, "You said you didn't look hard enough, but she did." I raised an eyebrow. "She looked me in the face. She looked me in the eye. She saw my hair, and guess what her reaction was? She was disgusted by me."

He drew in a shuddering breath. His head lowered, his eyes were closing.

I was right there, right in his face. "I was beneath her. I was the dirt under her shoes, the *dust* on her expensive furniture, and you know what's funny? I'm so used to it, that's what I prefer now. I can't remember when she tried to teach us to cook. I don't remember that woman anymore."

"Dust." A low warning from him.

I didn't care. My breath was on him. I knew it was and I was doing everything I could to make him snap. "That woman back then, she hadn't been the waste of space that she's become now. Does she even mother you? Is she proud of you? Does she see a trophy son? Are you the reason she stays in their pathetic marriage? Drinking. Driving drunk. Lying about it. That's just the stuff she did to destroy my family, what'd she do to destroy yours?"

His hand flashed out, wrapping around the back of my neck. "Stop it."

I laughed, knowing I had the upper hand. "I haven't even started."

I felt how cruel my smile was. Good.

I was going to torture him. I would haunt him. I would say the words that he only thought, but never wanted to hear out loud. I would give him that gift, and he would goddamn loathe me for it.

"She's an alcoholic, Stone."

"Shut up."

"She hates her life."

"I said to *shut* up."

"She hates your father."

He started to look away.

I grabbed his face, holding him in place, and I leaned forward, pressing a soft kiss to the side of his mouth. "Do you wonder if she stays with him for his money? Or is it really just you? If he didn't have the money, if you didn't have the notoriety, would she leave?"

He was rigid and still and I could feel how his body was turning against me.

I kissed the other side of his mouth. "Do you wonder if she would've left you with him long ago if you guys were poor? If your family would've changed places with mine?"

"Jesus," he grated out, starting to pull away.

I was on him, both my hands locked behind his neck. He couldn't get away from me. I was a leech on him now. I was sucking the will from him and I was filling it with something toxic instead. I was infusing him with poison.

"What about your father?"

"Stop." He reached behind him, took my hands, and thrust me off of him.

I hit the wall, and I felt alive. Maybe for the first time since being in his arms. I laughed, seeing the torment clouding his face.

I leaned forward, dropping my voice to a whisper. "Be honest. You got the call from Colby and what? You couldn't leave because of your parents? I'm right, aren't I? You were with them, catering to them, giving them the royal treatment, and you knew if you left to come for me, your mother would have questions. She'd want to know the answers, and I bet you anything that you couldn't come to me at the stadium because Mother Dearest would've had a fit. And I bet you even more that she hates that you made your father pay for my schooling, that you made them both pay for my parents' funeral costs, that they had to pay for all of that because your mother is one twisted sick piece of fu—"

His hand wrapped around the back of my head again, this time knotting in my hair, and he jerked me to him. "I would be very careful what you're about to say to me. Very. careful."

Good.

He was starting to hate me.

One more shove.

It was a boulder balancing on the edge of a cliff and I was going to knock that fucker completely off.

"Did you know that your dad gave me a ride home one night my senior year?"

I was lying. I didn't care.

His body never loosened. It remained rigid and unmoving, but I felt his hand flex on the back of my head. His eyes were growing half wild, dilating, a panicked look edging in there. I knew it because I was putting it there, because it's the same emotion I hadn't stopped feeling since she got cancer.

"I was working at your parents' supermarket and my car wouldn't start. It was the beginning of November, so temps were bad. Mom was already in Hospice by then. We knew the house was going on the market for a short sale, so I didn't want to bother my dad. But your dad saw me walking home and he pulled over."

"Dusty," he clipped out. He started shaking his head. "If this is a lie, I swear to God..."

I kept on as if he hadn't said a word, "He offered me a ride. Insisted on it when I refused." I pushed against him, my body rubbing over his and I felt him hardening. "Said he'd drive behind me the whole way if I didn't get in the car, so I got in."

His hand was holding the back of my head captive, but I had everything else in check. Drawing a hand down between us, I grazed over his cock, feeling it jerk against his jeans at my touch.

"You know when you meet someone and they want you? But you don't want them? It's plain as day to you. They might not say anything to you, but it's in their eyes. They track you everywhere you go."

A low curse word slipped from him.

I turned my hand around, fully cupping him and he grunted, but he didn't move away. He didn't release his hold on me either.

I leaned into his left ear and murmured, "That's how your father was the whole ride home. He could barely watch the street. He kept looking at me, his eyes running the length of my body. He liked what he saw. He wanted what he saw. He wanted more than what he saw. He wanted to touch me. He wanted to taste me. I can't help but wonder now, like father, like son?"

He yanked on my hair, whipping my head back. "You are such a bitch."

I started to smile, my hand still cupping him, and I ran my thumb down the side of him, but his mouth covered mine. I surged up, my hand going to his jeans and I started to draw his zipper down. His tongue thrust in the same time my hand snaked inside his jeans, finding the opening of his boxers and I had him in the palm of my hand.

"Hey...oh!"

Bass ripped through the air as the back door of the Quail opened.

Joe stood there, taking us both in. "Uh. Sorry." He started to close the door, but paused and grimacing, he looked back. "I need Dusty to come in and work. We're slammed."

I took a breath, my chest rising against Stone's and falling as I released it.

Play time was over. Knowing it and feeling it, Stone moved his mouth to my ear, the one closest to where Joe was standing. He spoke in a normal sounding voice, "Take your hand off my dick."

"Shit." From Joe.

I did so, releasing him, but my thumb ran over his tip as a parting goodbye.

"Pull your hand out of my pants."

I did so, half-laughing as I felt his hand flexing to cup the back of my head.

"Now." He nipped at my earlobe with his teeth. "Zip me up."

I moved so I could use both hands to close his pants. Once I was done, Stone pulled my head back to his and he had one last hot and demanding kiss for me. Releasing me, he stepped back. "She's all yours." He was staring right at me as he said those words and I got the message.

He walked away, his back turned toward the line at the end of the alley. And he put his hands in his pockets, his shoulders hunching forward, pulling his shirt to outline his back, and I almost called him back. I almost gave in to him, told him it was a complete lie, but my teeth sank into my lip because I couldn't.

He was done.

CHAPTER 37

I WAS NOT proud of what I did. But it was necessary.

I was flicking a tear away when Cammie came over, her hip bumping into mine. She turned so her tray of drinks was angled away and said to me, "I'm still on a high about that delicious quarterback, but we have to process that later because that entire table came in and asked for you."

I followed her gaze, and I had to smile, something I never thought I would've done a month ago. The table was full of housemates and their boyfriends, i.e., the football team. Just like with Stone, all eyes went to them.

She saw and her eyebrows went up. "You know them? They're going to be the rowdiest group here."

Was Cammie not here when they came in? I tried to remember, but I don't think she was.

"I live with half of them. They'll be fine for me."

Both her eyebrows shot up. "No kidding?"

"No kidding."

She eyed them again. "Tell 'em congratulations for me. They kicked some Homecoming ass today."

I scooped up the tab from my emptied table and patted her arm. "I sure will, and they sure did."

She laughed as I moved past her, tucking the bill and tip in my apron and pulling out an order sheet. I was getting good enough where I rarely needed it, but one just never knew. Coming up to the table where Wyatt, Mia, Noel, Savannah, Nacho, Lisa, Nicole, and Dent were sharing, along with two more tables around them that housed the rest of the football team along with more of their party friends, I gave 'em a big smile. "Congratulations, guys!"

They threw up their arms. "Heeeey!!"

The rest of the bar thought *I* was cheering *them* and they all joined in, yelling out congratulations.

Once they died down, Nacho leaned toward me. He was the closest and his beefy arms were resting on the table. "You watched our game." He looked happy about that.

"I did."

Wyatt had pulled his phone out and he read from the screen, "Nice fucking tight ass. Tell Mia she did good picking you for your second score from the thirty." He was beaming as he looked up at me. "You're awesome."

I tipped my head back, laughing, and actually enjoying it for once. "Thank you, and I meant what I wrote. You guys did really great today."

Nicole asked, "Why didn't you sit with us?"

Oh.

That.

I was wincing on the inside. "Because I was actually working. One of the boxes, but I could still see. I made sure to see."

She frowned, but didn't respond.

Mia's eyes narrowed. "What box?"

Fuck's sake. Really?

I shrugged. "Just one of them."

"There's just two boxes that get servers during games. The coach's box, which a bunch of the Kings' players and families were using today, or a TV exec box. Which one were you in?"

Why did she continue to hate me? I thought we'd moved past this. But I lied through my teeth, "Must've been the exec one. Funny. I thought they seemed a bit Hollywood."

She pressed her lips together and I knew what she was thinking. Liar. Yeah, well. I was. I didn't care.

"So, what'll everyone have?"

They gave me their orders and I weaved through the crowd to go put it in. Mia must've followed me, because as soon as I got to the register, she was next to me and scowling. "Why'd you lie?"

I paused, eyeing her. She was glancing over her shoulder. One hand on the counter by the register and the other tucking a strand of hair behind her ear. She moved as Cammie had to get behind the bar. Kneeling down, Cammie shot me a look.

I shrugged, but Mia was back to scowling at me.

"What do you mean?'

"I know you were in the other box. I know Ben from class and I ran into him after the game. We chatted. He told me about a blue-haired girl helping him today. That was you."

"So?"

I finished putting in the order and went to fill a pitcher of beer. Mia waited, going right with me.

"So?! So, you shouldn't have to put yourself in a situation like that. I looked up Stone's parents. His mom looks like a bitch."

An argument could totally be made here, be one to know one, but I moved to another table and gave them the new pitcher, pulling the empty one. All eyes went to Mia, because she was one of the blessed and holy people. She just didn't get it in that moment. All eyes would be on me until she and the entire table left, but they'd had my back the last month. I could make Stone hate me, but I didn't have it in me to make them hate me. There was no point.

Then it hit me what was actually going on.

Mia was worried about me.

Mia. Bitch Mia. Bully Mia. Mia who I thought would've laughed if I had killed myself when I first moved in, that Mia. Now she was the one following me around at my job, interrogating me why I put myself in that situation.

A wave of emotion swept over me and I put the emptied pitcher on a nearby table. Ignoring the 'hey!' from the girls there, I grabbed Mia in for a hug.

She stiffened, her hands coming to my side. "What. Is. This?"
Yes. She said it just like that.

I just laughed, hugging her tighter before stepping back and picking up the empty pitcher again. "Nothing. Just felt a hug coming on."

She backed up, her mouth fully sneering at me. "Well. Don't." She shook her arms as if to get the touch of me off of her. "Wyatt's the only one who touches me."

She cared. She totally cared.

She kept backing up, then stopped. Her face cleared before growing determined again. "Next time you have to work a box at a game like today, ask who's going to be in it."

Okay. Let's play this game, too.

I asked, starting to grin, "And what, then? If I find out it's someone like today?"

"Refuse." Duh.

My grin grew. "And if my boss says I have no choice?"

Her mouth flattened. Her head pulled back. She'd never thought of that scenario and gave me a shrug. "Then quit? They'll hire you the next day. I mean, look around." She waved a hand. "This place needs you. It's a mess."

I let out a full laugh now.

Mia rolled her eyes and turned to go back to her table.

Cammie sidled up next to me, a tray under her arm. "You know Mia Catanna?"

I did her one better. "I *live* with Mia Catanna." I moved to go and take more orders because this was my job and this was my new normal. And I loved it because for some reason, everything fell into place and it hit me that night.

I would be okay.

CHAPTER 38

BOY, oh boy. Times had changed.

All of my housemates and the rest of the football team stayed until the bar closed. And apparently, when everyone is celebrating, when everyone is loose and relaxed and happy, there's a contagious feeling that takes over entire crowds. I could say that because I was in the back of my house. I was sitting at the picnic table, squished with Joe on one side, Cammie on the other. Ben had even been called and he was sitting at the end of our table.

We had Dent and Nacho debating the dangers of going keto during the off season, even for a month to trim pounds, and the rest of my housemates were either spread around the backyard or in the house because here I was. Antisocial, newly orphaned college student in the midst of one of my housemate's infamous parties. I knew tonight was extra special because I'd even glimpsed some of my classmates from my genetics class in the corner.

"It's ridiculous!" Dent cried out, half rising from his side of the table. "Why the fuck would you want to trim weight and in the off season, no less? You're a defensive lineman. We need you in your weight class."

"Because Coach thinks I need to trim."

"Not like that!" Dent was very concerned about this potential diet. "Your body will rebel and you'll lose muscle mass. This is the stupidest idea I've ever heard from you. Lean meat. Carbs in moderation. And fruits and vegetables. Stick to your protein drinks, too. Or hell, have you talked to the team's nutritionist? What'd she say about this?"

Nacho's shit-eating grin was enough to convince me he had no intention of going through a keto crash diet, but it was funny to see Dent get so worked up.

Cammie leaned down to me, then. "So, these guys? Really? They're all your roommates?" Her tone was awed, but she was trying to hide how awed she was. That told me she was *really* awed.

"It kinda was this horrible miscommunication, but we've all grown on each other. Sort of like a clam and two shells."

"I'll say." Nacho had overheard. He pointed at me. "I love clams. They look like dicks. And you guys haven't lived until you've tasted this girl's cooking. She does a full pizza buffet that's out of this world. I don't know what you're going to school for, Dusty, but you should be going for culinary school. You could be one of those Michelob chefs."

Dent burst out laughing, holding his sides. "It's Michelin chefs. Michelin. Not the beer, you dumbass."

"I'm not the dumbass thinking a starting defensive lineman is going to do keto on his off season."

Dent stopped laughing. Frowned. And shot to his feet. "What? You were lying the whole time?"

"I was messing with you, not lying."

"You fuckhead." He stalked off, going into the house. Lisa

called after him, but he ignored her. She frowned, holding a beer, but turned back to the group she'd been talking to.

"He gets so worked up about everything." Nacho was now griping, but he stood and was going after him.

Lisa said something to him, too, and he only gestured into the house. She sent me a frown, wavering, then came over. She moved to the edge of the table where I was. The rest of the conversation halted. That's just what happened when these guys approached. Lisa didn't notice, her eyes only on me. "Those two fight or something?"

"Nacho was gonna do the keto thing. Dent believed him. Got upset when he found out it was a joke."

Lisa rolled her eyes. "He's so sensitive sometimes." She migrated back over to her group, sipping on her beer the whole time.

I didn't recognize the others at the table besides Joe, Cammie, and Ben.

Joe groaned, hunching over the table. "I shouldn't be here. I'm a grad student and I manage the Quail. I should go, be irresponsible somewhere else."

Ben grinned at him. "Or maybe you should stick around, see if you can get lucky?"

Ben held his beer up over the table. He said as Joe clinked it with his, "That's the way to go, man. It's only Homecoming once a year, and we blew the Stallions out of the water this year. We should celebrate."

Cammie was watching the two, her own faint grin tugging at her lip. "Look at you both, bonding and having a good time."

Ben nodded, saluting her with his beer. "Thanks for the invite." He scanned the backyard. "I know Catanna from school, but she's never invited me to one of these parties."

Cammie gestured to me. "Don't thank me. Thank our hookup here."

"That's not me. The guys were just at the bar and said, "Everyone head over.""

She laughed. "Right, because the last time they did that, staff were included in the invite?"

I had no idea.

Joe leaned closer to me, the four of us pulling in to form our own group at the table. "They've never done this. I'm older than everyone here, but even I've heard about the infamous 'football house' parties." At my confused look, he clarified, "This is the football house, not because the actual team lives here, but because most of the team are always hanging out here. You've got connections, girl." He whistled, leaning back. "And you basically lied at your job interview."

"I have no connections."

The door was shoved open, slamming against the side of the house. It was loud enough that everyone paused in their conversations and looked over. Wyatt was there. He was looking, and seeing me, he waved. "Dusty Girl, come here! We just got back from the grocery store."

I groaned, but I stood up. "You think if you buy the materials, your personal chef will come?"

He barked out a laugh as I walked up the patio steps. His arm came down around my shoulder and he walked with me inside. "There's our awesome little funny chef, making a *Field of Dreams* reference. We could do with a few more."

Noel and Savannah were unpacking the groceries.

I murmured, "Just call me James Earl Jones." But even though I was grumbling, I spied the fresh cilantro and arugula, and I was already thinking about some fancy Mexican recipes. I nudged Wyatt's side before he dropped his arm. "Tell me the truth. You guys only like me because I can cook a mean meal, right?"

I started laughing, but he saw the look on my face and sobered up real quick. "You serious?"

"Nah." I was.

Wyatt went back to smiling from ear to ear and he squeezed my shoulders, leaning down so his chin touched my shoulder. "Whatever you make, we will worship. You're the Boss, Dusty Girl." He squeezed my shoulders once more before holding out his hand and half-burping, "Beer me."

A beer materialized from the crowd and was placed in his hand.

He winked at me before leaving. "God. I love this place."

He was already gone when Savannah and Noel finished unpacking everything. They paused next to me. Noel was reaching inside the fridge and pulling out a beer for both of them when Cammie came in, pushing her way through the crowd. She ducked her head, putting a strand of her hair behind her ear that was already there, and she seemed to shrink in size somehow. A hand resting on the counter, she waved with her other one. "Hi. I work with Blue."

Savannah looked at the beer in Cammie's hand.

Cammie's laugh hitched up a note. She put her beer on the counter before rubbing her hand over her pants to dry it. She lifted it back for Savannah. "Sorry about that. Cammie again." Her cheeks were pinking.

I'd never seen Cammie like this.

She was the picture of cool, calm, and confident. And she was gorgeous, just as beautiful as Mia or Savannah. But Savannah glanced at me. Noel took a step back, the fridge shutting, and he leaned a hand on the counter behind her. He was letting her run the show.

As if she needed a second to weigh the options, she put her hand in Cammie's, shaking it. "It's nice to meet you. I'm one of

Dusty's roommates." She couldn't pull her hand away quick enough, and inclined her head toward me. "Blue?"

"'Cause you know." I flicked my own hair back over my shoulder, going back to grabbing a bowl to wash the cilantro in. "So, who wants to help chop some tomatoes?"

"Cammie."

Ben had come in, standing beside her.

"Oh!" Her eyes were wide. "We were going to take off. Joe left. Ben said he'd give me a ride home. You working tomorrow?"

I shook my head. "It's a study day for me, all day."

"Joe wouldn't put you on the schedule seven days in a row."

I griped. "You'd think he'd want to. I'm way better than Moore."

Ben grimaced. "I was worried he was going to send her to work the boxes today."

Cammie flicked her eyes up. "You were better than Moore before you were even a waitress, and if you're not working tomorrow, I'll see you Tuesday. I'm off on Monday." She nodded to Savannah and Noel. "It was nice officially meeting you guys."

She and Ben both held up a hand as they left, returning through the back door again.

Savannah helped with the food. Noel helped her help with the food. Lisa. Mia and Wyatt. Nacho and Dent. They all came to the kitchen, wandering in. They formed a casual-looking wall to keep everyone out and gave us a pocket of normalcy within the raging party.

Once the food was done, I did what I usually did.

I scooped up a small plate for myself, setting everything out for everyone else. I cooked. They cleaned up. That was the deal, and this time when I slipped to the basement, put my food in the fridge down there, and headed to my room, I had a weird sense of familiarity.

I was starting to enjoy living here.

I was thinking about that when the basement door opened and footsteps hurried down the stairs. I figured it was Lisa heading to her room, but it wasn't her who said my name. "Dusty."

I turned back.

Siobhan stood there, her hand still on the railing, one foot on the ground and the other still on the last step. Her eyebrows were arched high, her mouth slightly opened, and then she closed it, her chest rising and falling. "Wow. Okay. I'm here. I didn't..." She stepped down that last step, letting go of the railing. Her hands folded in front of her and she looked to the ground. "Trent's roommate goes to the Quail a lot. He said you were working there now and I've been meaning to come in, say something, but I just haven't. We were there tonight, actually trying to be normal college students. Heard the general invite, and here we are."

"You got past my roommates." I took a step toward her, indicating upstairs. "They keep the basement sectioned off for a reason."

"Yeah. I, uh, I slipped in through the garage. Speaking of, I don't know how long I have. I think one of your roommates saw me and looked like they were coming over, probably to lock the door or something. Listen." She was speaking in a rush, her words almost melding together, but now she paused. Oxygen in. Oxygen out, and she started again, "I heard the rumor and I'm not talking about who you're sleeping with or now who you live with, but the one about your...about where you...there's an article out about you and I'm sorry. I just wanted to tell you that I'm sorry."

"An article? You mean the ones from over a month ago about Stone and—"

"No." She started backing up, reaching for the railing behind her. "Not an old one. It came out today."

Burning.

My insides were on fire.

My throat was singed, and it was spreading. Fast.

"What are you talking about?"

"You don't know?"

"I've been working all day."

"Oh." She actually went up a step, backwards. Her eyes were clinging to mine, but her hand looked like it was glued to the railing. Another step. She wasn't stopping, but she couldn't look away. There was a desperate gleam in her eyes, and she began sweating. "Oh, no. I shouldn't have been the one to tell you. I'm really sorry."

The door swung open above her and Lisa's voice snapped, "What the hell? Get out of there. Basement's off limits."

One last look at me. The flash of pity and apology wasn't sitting well with me, and I turned, hurrying into my room. My own door shutting almost the same time as the other as she'd rushed upstairs. I sank onto my desk chair and powered up my laptop. Whatever was there, it couldn't be that bad.

It wasn't a recent one.

Unless someone had spotted Stone and me in the alley, but it was dark there. No one could've seen us. We were so far away, and if they had recognized Stone, they would've shouted something. There were no windows from the other building or even from the Quail. Not in that alley.

About my parents?

I felt dizzy just considering that.

I typed in the date and my name and then sat back as the results came in.

I felt sick. My stomach was churning.

Stone Reeves' Childhood Sweetheart Stalked!

No, no, no.

My heart was pounding.

I knew what was coming, and no. No.

I clicked on the second article below it. *Restraining Order Filed by Stone Reeves' Girlfriend.*

It wasn't about my parents, but it was worse. It was so much worse.

It was the very reason I came here.

CHAPTER 39

IT WAS ALL OVER.

I read the article and his name was given. The details of everything was there. The history. The attack. The stalking. That he wasn't in prison anymore.

What?! He wasn't?

Panic crashed over me, pressing me down.

He was supposed to be given five years. At least five. He was released a week ago. One week ago.

I'd been walking back and forth from the Quail during that time. I worried about local dangers, never considering he could've... I choked out a sob. This was too much. One week? Really?

He was coming.

I just knew it.

I didn't care about the time, I grabbed my phone and pulled up the detective's cell. Officer Henry. He'd been the one who 'handled' me the most during the case. Hitting call, I pressed the phone next to my ear and I focused on not passing out.

"It better be a goddamn emer—"

"Why?"

That word gutted me. I was stripped, vulnerable, and all the underlayers of trauma and baggage, it was all hanging out. Anyone could see. I had no problem with him hearing.

He was quiet a second. I heard rustling, a sigh, and a soft, "Shit."

"Shit, indeed."

"You heard, huh?"

"An article is out. An article! Why am I learning about this through the media?"

"Look." His voice was calm now, more alert. As if he'd pulled on his armor and he was prepared to handle a difficult client. Client. What a funny word. Maybe a difficult victim? If that phrase could even be put together. How could a victim be difficult? Strip away what made them a victim, and there'd be no reason for them to be 'difficult.' He said further, "I didn't let you know because he's not going to find you or harm you."

"How do you know? He was obsessed!" Shoving out of my chair, I began to pace my room. Back and forth. To the door, the dresser, to the other door, back again. A sweep by my chair. I was going in a clipped, tight circle and I couldn't stop myself.

"He's dead."

I stopped. Everything stopped. My heart stopped.

Had I heard that right? "What?"

"It's not been released, so I'm not surprised the article didn't report it, but he was killed tonight. Bar fight." A sad chuckle. "He went to Rick's, mouthed off about Stone Reeves, and it was his luck that members of a nearby charter of Red Demons were passing through. They stopped for a drink, took offense to what he was saying. Guess they're Reeves' fans. He got hit too hard in the parking lot, and he's gone. We're waiting to notify his aunt before saying anything, but to be honest, no one up here will care."

East River Falls was a small community. A stalking case didn't get much attention. The two-day court case got even less attention, but every moment of that event changed everything for me.

I almost fell down on my bed, my hands shaking. My legs were trembling. I was sweating profusely. "Oh my God." I breathed out, making my nostrils flare. I drew in oxygen, focusing on that, remembering my breathing exercises. "He's really gone?"

Another sad chuckle. "He's gone, Dusty. You can come back if you wanted. He had no family here. No friends. By the end, you were his only obsession. It's done."

It wasn't done.

I pressed my palm to my forehead, as if trying to ward off the impending headache before it even started. "A classmate found me tonight and said she was sorry. She read the article. Stone's name was attached. It's not going to be ignored. It's going to get traction."

A swift curse from him.

But it was done. Everything was done.

We were quiet a beat.

"I heard about your parents. I'm real sorry. I know you've already lost so much."

"Yeah." There was nothing else to say, just...yeah.

"Listen, we can try to put a cork on any leaks coming out from here, but you know how it is. Now that a celebrity's name is attached, press will be calling. There's always someone needing money, but I'll have a talk with the lead on your case. Maybe we can shift things around to make sure nothing of yours gets out there any more than it already has been."

Another shuddering breath released from me. "Okay. Thank you. That'd be helpful."

"Not right what you've gone through. Not for someone so

young, someone just starting out, but that's how it goes sometimes."

"Yeah."

"If you need anything, give me a call, but as for him, that's all done. He's dead. You can draw comfort from knowing that."

We hung up.

I couldn't remember if there'd been conversation after that. *He's dead.* Those words were echoing in my head. This time, this loss was welcomed. I slid down to the floor, my back to my bed and I rested my elbows on my knees. I bent forward. The phone fell to the ground. The party was still going on upstairs. I could hear the muted bass, the sounds of footsteps over my ceiling. Doors opening, closing. People outside. People inside. But in my room, in that basement, I had been given a sanctuary that I hadn't expected to be granted.

Tears rolled down my face, but I let them. I didn't fight them. They were tears of relief, just complete and utter relief, because the fear I hadn't given energy to, had ignored since coming to Texas, was gone and it'd been so compressing that I hadn't even known it was there. An invisible elephant on my chest and poof, it was gone.

This time, I actually smiled.

Bang! Bang! Bang!

I jerked. My heart lurched in my chest, too.

Someone was pounding on my exit door.

Bang! Bang! Bang!

"Let me in, Dust! Now."

I had nothing in me to keep him away. Shoving to my feet, I was through the door, then to the door that separated us, and I unlocked it. He was pushing his way inside. I shut the door behind him, and he locked it.

He stood there. A black hood pulled over his head, and I knew he would've walked past the party, hunched forward. He would've kept to the sidelines, trying to merge with everything else so he didn't draw attention.

We took each other in.

He saw the tears on my face, cursing softly.

"Is it true?"

I frowned. "You know?"

"You have a stalker?"

I shook my head. "No. Not anymore." I whispered, "He's dead."

He frowned. "What?"

But my God. Stone was here. I felt as if I'd just been given life back. I was trying to remember the reason I wasn't touching him, why I wasn't kissing him, and then I stopped thinking.

I went to him.

I couldn't fight anymore.

He straightened, another curse falling from his mouth before he reached for me. His hands came to my face and he surged for me at the same time I went to him. We met in the middle, lips on each other, and nothing but a blur. A long and blessed and sensual and pleasurable blur happened after that.

Clothes were shredded.

I was being lifted up.

My legs were around his hips.

He turned a fan on in the background. Noise to drown out our noise, drown out the party above.

We were on my bed.

Hands were clawing for the other, raking, digging in.

I tasted him, his tongue inside my mouth and mine was rubbing against his, exploring him.

He was over me, pressing me down.

Then, I opened my legs and he was inside of me.

And for the life of me, I couldn't remember why he hadn't been there this whole time?

———

"I was lonely when I went to school."

I didn't wait for him to ask. It wasn't long after we finished, after we both rose to wash up, pulling on some clothes, and without talking about it, we got back in bed. He started to pull me against him to rest on his chest, but I held back. This was going to be difficult, and I needed to be able to think clearly or I wouldn't say it all.

"I'd already been lonely, and when I went away to East River Falls, I didn't have good standards to measure people by. A cute boy flirted with me in orientation. My heart started fluttering. When he sat by me in our first class together, I was already crushing on him. When I found out he was a football player, I was gone."

Stone moved on the bed, and because I worried he was about to touch me, I hurried, my voice only a rasp, "He flirted with me a lot the first two weeks of school. It was nice. It was less lonely. I didn't have a lot of female friends. There were girls there and a few of us tried to get together, but we were all in the same boat. We were there because we didn't have money for a better school. All of us were working. Most had full-time jobs. Most didn't even live there. They commuted. That was the one thing I felt guilty about. I could've commuted, but honest to God, I couldn't handle being in that apartment with my dad anymore. He never talked. He worked and he existed and so did I. The place was so empty and cold after she died. He met Gail the week I left for school, so I think we were both trying to move on, to fill the void, just in our own separate ways."

"Dust."

I closed my eyes. A tear leaked out.

He couldn't say my name like that. I wouldn't be able to keep going if he did.

"His name was Mark Ranger, and I thought he had the coolest name ever. He was *a* Ranger. He came from the Rangers up north."

"The trucking company?"

My heart sank as I remembered. "That's what I thought. That's what he let me think, but he wasn't from that family. It was just a coincidence. He was the big man on campus, or that's what he wanted. He thought it, so he made it happen like that. Mark was the starting quarterback. I swear, his head, his ego, they just got bigger and bigger and bigger. We were a couple by Thanksgiving. I loved going to his games. I felt important." Not how I felt at home. "People knew me. People saw me." I wasn't invisible there. "I thought I was in love with him by Christmas, and that's when it turned. Everything turned."

Pain sliced me.

"He wanted to meet my family. That was the last thing I wanted. I didn't even want to go back there, much less bring someone else with me. The fighting started then. He didn't like that we were meeting his family and not mine, but he didn't have family. I found out later it was a work buddy of his. He was an older guy, and Mark had something on him. Mark grew up in the foster system. He blackmailed this guy's entire family. They had to act like they were happy and adoring, meeting the girlfriend for the first time."

Stone cursed, moving on the bed.

I kept on, wincing at how hollow I sounded, "He began pressuring me for sex."

A savage curse from Stone now.

"The first time was fine. I wanted to. I thought I loved him, but it wasn't enough. Then things got bad, and I couldn't stay with him anymore. So I ended things."

"Are you fucking serious?"

"You're nothing."

"You're fucking white trash."

"He researched me. I have no idea how he found out, but he did."

"Don't think I don't know about your old neighbor? Stone Reeves."

His laugh still made me taste acid.

"Were you fucking me while thinking of him?"

"I left him, and that night he broke into my apartment. I had a roommate by then, a girl from one of my classes, and she called the police."

I could smell the acid.

"I filed a restraining order, and it worked for a while. Until it didn't. He became obsessed. He was obsessed about *you*, that I knew *you*, that he had to live up to *you*. He kept taunting me, how he was better than you, how he was going to drive down here and beat you up. He was going to come and break your leg so bad that you'd never play football again. And then, in his warped delusion, he was going to take your place. He wanted *your* life."

I was in my bed again back there. The window was open. It was summer by then.

"He broke in again, but this time my roommate wasn't there to call the police. She'd moved home by then. Her family was scared for her."

My voice broke.

I was not going to tell him about that night. I would never tell another living soul, but I could recount the aftermath.

"I had a dolphin paperweight on my desk. It was a gift from Gail, and when he was in my room, I focused on that paperweight. I *only* saw that dolphin. I vowed to myself. I vowed that night that if I survived, I'd find the best marine biology program I could and apply to get into it. I'd go into that program and I would study them save *them*, just like how they had saved me."

Stone jerked on the bed, but I didn't look.

"They arrested him the next day. He never got bail and he's been in prison ever since. Or I thought he was until I saw that article tonight. I called one of the officers before you got here. He told me that Mark was dead. Bar fight. He was mouthing off about you and some of your fans took offense." I turned now, saying before I saw him, "Apparently you have some dangerous fans and..." I stopped talking.

He was completely white, his eyes glazed over, glued to me, and his fists so tight blood was seeping from his palms.

"Stone!" I was over to him in a flash. "Oh my God! Oh my God!"

He couldn't hurt his hands. Not his hands.

I ran to my bathroom for a first-aid kit I stashed there. Bringing it back, I didn't ask. I didn't speak. I tended to his hands as he sat on the edge of the bed and he let me. The cuts weren't too bad. He had crushed a pin in his hand. I didn't know where he got it from. I don't think he knew it was there either, but his eyes never left me as I finished cleaning his hands.

Some antiseptic, dressings. His hands would be okay.

I ran a hand down the side of his face, smoothing his hair back. "You're going to be so tired for tomorrow."

"I don't give a fuck about how tired I am," he grated out. His eyes flashing hot and fierce.

"I do."

He grasped my hand before it would've fallen away. "I don't have words for you right now. Colby sent me the article. I was sleeping. I didn't hear my phone go off, so he called me. I was starting to chew him out, but he told me to stuff it and check my texts. Said I would want to know as soon as possible. He was right. I read that article and the next thing I know, I'm in my truck, heading over here. I don't remember leaving the house, or the drive over. I was just here. I was in a blind panic. If you got hurt? If you were taken away from me?" His voice cracked.

"Stop. Sssshhh."

"If anything had happened to you." He cut himself off. "Something already did happen to you." He looked up, his eyes haunted. "If I was the cause for that…"

I shook my head, my thumb running over his mouth to silence him. I didn't want to debate what had or hadn't set off that guy. I didn't even want to think his name. He'd already taken up too much time and energy between us. Tomorrow, I promised myself. Tomorrow we'd figure it out. We'd talk about it more, but not anymore.

I leaned down, my hair cascading around us and my lips met his.

I loved him. I knew it then.

"I'm fine. Everything's fine," I murmured against his lips.

He held onto me, framing my face, searching me. "I left you before. I gave you space. I'm done with that. Fuck whatever you think. Just fuck it. Fuck this enemies shit between us. That's done. Got it? I'm not walking, not again. I can't—"

I kissed him.

I silenced him this time.

It was me. It was my turn.

I didn't hide. I let him see me. I let him feel me, and he was right. We were done with that. Then he tugged me down on his lap, and he rolled us over on the bed. When we fell asleep, he was still holding me and it was perfect.

CHAPTER 40

STONE

I SAT on the edge of the bed the next morning, actually just five hours later.

I needed to go. I needed to go to my home, start my day. I needed to head to the stadium. I needed to get ready. We had a game tonight, but as hard as I tried, I couldn't leave. My ass wouldn't leave that fucking bed and I couldn't stop watching her.

She needed sleep. Not me. I was fucking wired.

This asshole, some asshole, hurt my girl.

Because that's what she was. Mine.

She was no one else's and I should've shut that shit down long ago. I knew why she walked. I got it, and a part of me wondered if she was doing the right thing, but fuck that. No more. I was done staying away. I was done keeping quiet and not making her talk. We needed to talk. Talking. Shit. We barely talked. We fought, then we went to bed. That's how we communicated, and I was trying to tell her all the ways I cared for her. I needed to show her, not just say the words, but she was asleep and I had to leave and do my job.

Except I couldn't make myself leave her room. I couldn't even get off the bed, and I needed to get off the bed. I'd be fined so damn much money if I didn't show, but every cell in my body was screaming at me to curl back in her bed, pull her into my arms, and never let her go.

Never ever let her go again.

But, shit. I raked a hand through my hair.

I couldn't do that. I was a professional. We played through everything. Wind, sleet, rain, pain, blood. We showed up. We played. We dominated.

He was dead. I was trying to tell myself. She was safe. I could leave, do my job, and scoop her back in my arms afterwards. Her. Me. Our bed. Yeah. It wasn't my bed anymore. It was ours. She just didn't know it.

Shit. Shit!

I had to go. I had to, but God, I didn't want to go.

Moving around the room, I went to wash up before dressing, but I wasn't going out her side way. Hell no. I went the other way, not expecting anyone to be up. I'd been in college, but I hadn't partied like these guys. I rarely partied. I footballed. That was it. I did football, and if I wasn't footballing, I was training to football or thinking about footballing. Football was my life. These guys, they were different. They were more normal. If they were planning on pro, they had one last year to get their shit together. But that wasn't my issue.

Going up to the kitchen, I hadn't expected anyone to be up.

Someone was up.

A girl was at the counter making toast. She turned, yawning, but seeing me, she shrieked. "Oh, my Jesus!" She pressed a hand to her heart, giving me a shaky smile. "I wasn't expecting a guy, and then it's a guy, but it's not just any guy, it's you, and yeah. Still getting used to seeing you around here."

She was the nice one, the one Dusty liked. I was trying to remember her name.

"Nicole?"

"Yeah. Hi." The toast popped up and she took one, waving at me before putting it on the plate and reaching for the butter. "I suppose you're on your way out? How's our girl doing downstairs? She seemed tired last night. I mean, more than usual considering how much she's working."

I had started to walk past her, letting her talk, but hearing the last few words, I paused.

The girl was still rambling, her back to me, still buttering her toast. "Between you and me, I worry about her. She's not gotten a car and she doesn't think we notice, but she's walking back and forth from campus. That means she's walking after her shifts, but she's got some hang-up about asking for help. I don't get it, but she's prideful. So, yeah. My uncle has a car in the garage. There's no insurance on it, but I was thinking I could ask him to get some and she could drive that. We could say it's the house's vehicle, but poof—like magic—it's always available only for her." She turned, the toast done on her plate. "What do you think?" She was smiling at me.

She took one look at me and that smile was wiped clean.

I was barely keeping my shit together as it was, and now to know this.

She'd been walking. No, fuck that. She was working. A lot, from what this one was saying, and she was walking?

I grated out, "How far is campus from here?"

She swallowed, getting with the program and cluing in how close to the edge I was. "Her job is four blocks away. I think she cuts through somewhere, maybe a side alley, so it might be less. I'm not sure."

Fuck that. Fuck this girl. Fuck her fucking roommates. And fuck me, for letting her go when I knew I shouldn't have.

Fuck. Just fuck.

"How long has this been going on?"

Another swallow before her head bobbed down. "Uh. A week? No. More than that, I think. Maybe two?"

"You don't know?" I ground that out.

"No. I'm sorry."

I was gone. Dusty was going to have a car in her spot by the end of the day and before then, Morpheus would be on her curb. If she walked, he would follow. I didn't give a flying fuck how pissed she might be about that.

She had had a goddamn stalker.

My thoughts went rampant thinking about that piece of shit. I wanted to find him again, murder him with my bare hands and stuff his desecrated bones back into the ground, and I wanted to repeat that process all over again. Over and over and over until I got justice for Dusty.

I had no clue, no fucking idea.

A stalker. A goddamn motherfucking stalker.

If I'd known, shit. I would've wanted to go at him, wrap my hands around his throat, but fuck. I couldn't go back in time. The piece of shit was dead, but I could go forward, and I interrupted the nice roommate. She was still talking.

"Where's Witkerson?"

She'd been pouring orange juice into a glass, and at my growl, she jumped. Juice spilled all over the counter, but flinching, she swung those wide eyes to me. "Uh. What?"

"Noel. Witkerson. Your school's QB 1. Where is he? I know he sleeps here."

"Oh." She was flustered, her cheeks getting red. "Savannah's room is upstairs on the right, but..."

Yeah. Yeah. Don't go up there. They're sleeping. She didn't know I didn't give a shit.

I stalked up the stairs, lined up there were two bedrooms and I saw the bathroom door open. I went to the right and I didn't give 'em an option. I was hoping they weren't going at it—but I'd seen that shit before, so no big deal—because I flung the door open.

The girl screamed.

Witkerson jumped out of bed, wild and panicked, but saw it was me and he swore, grabbing for a pillow to cover his nuts. He remembered we both spent most of our lives in football locker rooms and dropped the pillow. Crawling back in bed, he lay back down. "Tell me this is fucking important, man. You're interrupting my sleep time and my time with my girl."

"She had a stalker."

"What?!" the girl squawked, bolting upright.

She had a shirt on. Thank God. I didn't want to see her girls. Any normal day before today, I might've looked if they were presented to me because fuck, I'm a guy...but not this day.

"It's why she came down here. A stalker."

The QB I sat up, suddenly all serious and yeah, he better be.

I clipped my head at him. "You're here. You're here when I can't be. That piece of shit is dead, but there might be others. Her name, her face, it's getting out there. And she's mine. I ain't keeping quiet about that anymore. She's going to get more attention, more focus, and that brings haters. Bitch catty women and dirty perv assholes. Sick fucks, too. She and I haven't talked, she doesn't know the lengths I'm going to, but I'm going to them. If she stays here, and if she chooses, I'll be here most nights, but I'm going to try to get her to my house. But if she stays, you're on duty. Got it?"

"Wait." The girl was looking between us.

The QB nodded. "Got it."

"What is going on here?"

"Good. I'll have a guy parked out front all day. He's her ride. She ain't walking anywhere alone today and tonight. There'll be a car of her own here by end of the day." I bit out and turned for the door. "I got a game, then I'll be back to either sleep here or collect her for my place."

The girlfriend jumped up in bed, but I had turned already. Caught the movement out of the corner of my eyes, glimpsed something white on her legs and figured she had pants on, too. Again. Not caring. This was today, not yesterday, not a month ago. Things were different today. Everything was different. I was staking my claim and I wasn't going away. Hell to the fuck no.

I pounded the doorframe. "See you later. Remember what I said...watch her."

And because there was an unwritten guy code and my job was to pick on the younger bucks, I pounded on the other door. "Don't forget to pull out, Harrington!"

There was a scream in there, too, and then from him, "Shut up!" He groaned. "I was fucking sleeping, douche."

I pounded the door a second time, laughing, then I was down the stairs and out the front door. I had a block to walk to my Jeep and a game to get ready for.

CHAPTER 41

STILL STONE

I WAS JACKED. I was hyped. I was ready to tear heads off bodies.

Morpheus was currently camped out on Dusty's street. He was given orders to grow roots if he needed, and if she walked somewhere and refused the ride, he was supposed to be her personal shadow. And I had a call in to my manager. A brand new Honda HR-V would be parked in her spot by tonight, and the keys were getting hand delivered to her door. I texted with her and found out her plans were to study at the house. Perfect. She said her roommates weren't having a party, so it'd just be the girls, their guys, and my girl all watching my game. I told her to wait for me that night. I was coming for her.

Her response:

Dusty Girl: Ready and waiting.

That made me laugh, but onto the game. I had a job to do.

We were in the locker room, music blaring in our head-phones. Russ, his Flute song, was blaring in my ears, and I was there. I was on the field. I was running, dodging, losing the other motherfuckers. The ball was mine. It was coming right for me.

It was another extension of my body, just no one else knew.

That was my job. I'd teach them. I'd school the fuckers. They'd know by the end of the game, each time I ran into the end zone and not once, twice, three times. Four. Five. I'd keep going all day long, all night long. I could score in my sleep and pity to the fools who didn't believe in me. They'd be schooled real quick.

"Yo." A hand appeared in front of me.

I reached up, meeting it with mine, and Colby was there, pulling me up to my feet.

We were in this together.

This game. Him and me. There's nothing like the dynamic between the guy who throws the ball and the guy who can catch it, especially when no one else can catch him. That was me. That was what I got paid to do. We were going to go show everyone again, because you know, they all needed reminding.

His eyes were ready.

He was amped up.

So was I.

We go out and we win. We got paid to do this shit, and after the coach had his say, after we ran to the field, after the anthem, the coin toss, the kickoff—it was my turn.

Colby came up to me on the field. His fist to mine. "You ready?"

I gave him a nod back. Fuck yeah, I was ready. I was salivating over getting out there, doing my thing.

He grinned, reading me right. "You're in a mood today."

Another cocky smirk from me. Fuck yes, I was. I was gonna score here. I was gonna win here. Then I was going home to get my woman. But all I did was tell him, "Throw it to me. They won't expect a long throw to me on the first play. And trust me, they won't be able to catch me tonight."

He studied me a second longer, then nodding. "Okay. Yeah. I'm seeing that. Let's do this."

He called the play as we were lining up. Everyone knew. I didn't have the headphones any longer, but that music was with me. It was in my head and I tuned into it, remembering it, and I envisioned how this play would go.

Ball was snapped and I was off.

Pumping.

Running.

Lighting up the field.

Then I was right there, right on target, and Colby had already seen it all. The ball was in the air, and holding back, reading that —yes, yes, yes. It was right on point. I kicked off more speed, saw three players heading for me. Saw two of mine coming to cover, and with a quick spin, I was around one guy and going full force.

The ball sailed, so pretty, and it was a perfect play.

A perfect throw.

I didn't have to jump, move, none of that shit. I just ran and that ball fell into my arms. I was cradling it like a baby as my foot came down in the end zone.

That was our first score.

There was no celebration. I was doing my job.

I tossed the ball to the ref, ran to the side and pointed at Colby, who was running diagonally with me. "That was the first one."

He dipped his head. He knew my mood. He knew what to be prepared for this game. It was the first of many. He said, "Got it. My arm's ready. *You* be ready."

There wasn't even a question. I'd been born to do this shit.

All night long, I be scoring. All night long, I be winning. All night long, because I was Stone The Rampage Reeves.

Tonight was a Rampage Game.

DUSTY

"Stone Reeves is on a Rampage tonight." The announcer was excited, smiling wide, turned to the other announcer with him. Both in their suits, with the crowd cheering behind and beneath them. "I love these nights. We don't get them all the time, but every now and then..."

The other announcer finished for him, smiling just as big, "Every now and then we get a treat to watch Stone The Rampage Reeves perform, because that's what he's doing tonight. He's performing. He's giving us a show."

"He is, indeed, and it's a pleasure to watch."

They kept on, moving to talk about Colby and how the two together were magic, but we were at halftime and my stomach was growling.

Nicole heard, sitting next to me. "You know, we did order pizza."

It wasn't the first hint she gave me that night, but I couldn't eat. Everyone was being so nice. They hadn't invited anyone extra for the game, saying it was just the roommates and the guys, which translated into Dent, Nacho, Wyatt, and Noel. They hadn't asked me to cook, but I almost wished they had.

My stomach was in knots. All I could feel was dread.

What would I do if they talked about me during the game? It was so unlikely, but that article got traction and it'd been building. Every now and then, they might gossip a bit about the player's personal lives, and especially if it spread into the legal aspects of the law. I didn't think they would, but you just never knew. And because of that, I hadn't wanted to watch the game, but I also couldn't not watch the game. Stone came over. I didn't even know if he slept after I finally passed out, but last night had been different. I felt it.

He knew everything.

Everyone would also know everything.

It was all out, no reason for secrets. I had nothing else to hide and Stone stayed. He remained next to me until he had to leave for his game.

I was giving in. It was Stone. It was all Stone. I was in love with him. I refrained from spilling those words last night, but it'd been so hard. I had to bite down on my lips. I drew blood.

But tonight, those words would come out because I knew what was going to happen.

Stone was coming for me.

I had a bag packed. I wasn't going to make him stay here. I didn't want to stay here myself, not tonight. Tonight was special. Tonight was different. We'd go to his house and we'd make love. I would take care of my man, but those words, they'd come out.

I would have to see what his reaction would be then, but I just knew that I was done hiding. I couldn't anymore.

All the shit was coming out tonight. Let's hope I didn't have another loss tomorrow to get over, because I didn't think I could. Not this time. There was no walking away, or moving on, or just dealing. I'd be shattered forever. The question was if I was lining up my own undoing or not.

CHAPTER 42

DUSTY GIRL

I WAS CURLED up on the couch, in the corner, hugging a pillow, when Wyatt switched the television to watch the extras on the NFL channel. He turned it to the press conference section, and after a bit, the Kings' head coach, Stone, and Colby walked in, then sat behind a table.

The first question was to the coach. How'd he feel the team did, considering they blew the other team away with a thirty-eight to seven score.

Second question was to Colby: What did he do to prepare for tonight's game?

The next was to Stone, a similar question, and they each answered a few more before it happened.

They all seemed at ease. Stone kept his head down, leaning forward. Colby was the opposite, head up but leaning back. The coach was forward and head up. He was meeting the questions head on, and then the last question.

"Stone, going forward into the next week and preparing for the Horns, do you think you'll be distracted with the reports of your girlfriend's stalker? And how is she doing?"

Stone's head whipped up, and he was *pissed*.

Not pissed. Furious. Livid.

His jaw clenched. Fire blazed from his eyes, and he started to shove up, but his coach put a restraining hand on his shoulder.

"Damn," from Wyatt.

"Oh, shit," from Dent.

"Fuck."

The last was from Nacho. Me... I couldn't breathe.

Stone looked ready to leap over the table and tear the guy apart.

Colby jerked forward in his seat, his eyes immediately going to Stone.

But the coach acted first. He stood up, clearing his throat. "I think we're done for the day. Thank you, folks."

He lifted his hand and Stone shoved up, his hands in fists. He didn't wait for Colby to lead the way out, he whipped around him and was gone within a second. Colby paused before following, and the coach just lowered his head, his hand finding his hip, a clipboard in hand as he trailed at a more sedate pace.

"Shit."

Nicole's the one who swore softly beside me. She patted my leg. "I'm sorry."

"It's not a mainstream press conference. Most of that stuff will get printed only in sports blogs."

That was from Dent. He was trying to reassure me, but it didn't matter. It was out. I hadn't thought I'd be brought up, but there was always one person, one article that wanted to be more scandalous than the others, and the headline with Stone's name and stalker would get clicks. I would've clicked on it myself, but this was *me*. This was *my* life.

I had to deal.

The biggest damage had already been done, and that guy was dead.

I could handle whatever else came out.

I was in my room, on my bed, dressed and just waiting, when my door opened. It was the one to the rest of the house. Stone came in, shutting the door behind him. He didn't turn the lights on, but I heard him turn the lock before he stopped to take me in.

It was a few hours later. His hair was wet. He'd recently showered. No sweatshirt this time, just a Kings shirt and a hat pulled low. I loved that look on him. Loved how it highlighted his square jaw, how when he clenched it, he made me salivate, my body starting to ache.

I almost sighed. "I wanted to hate you."

The air around him had been restless, edgy. Like he wanted to fight, but had no target to take it out on. It grew calmer, more pensive at my statement. He didn't come over. I wanted him to come over, but he sat on the edge of the bed, leaning forward. Elbows on his knees, but his head was turned to me. He was watching me.

He was waiting. Listening.

"I knew you'd be like a god down here, and I wanted to hold onto that hate from when we were kids. 'Cause I did. I hated you so much. Because of him, because of his obsession with you and what he did to me. He got worse once he found out about you, but it wasn't you. You're talented. I mean, you're so talented, but my head, all the crap I went through, I was half-blaming you for him. But it was never you. It was him. He was sick, and I never wanted to burden my dad with what I went through. That's another reason I never went home. I didn't want to take that to him, but coming down here, being here, being with you, coming out on this end of the whole process, it hit me tonight."

My heart squeezed, but it was a good squeeze. It was the kind of squeeze you only got to feel a handful of times, and maybe not even then, if you weren't lucky.

"I am so fucking proud of you."

His head lowered.

I kept on, whispering to the dark room. "I am proud that I know you, that I knew you before, that I've seen you bring yourself to this stage of success. Most guys, with your family how it is and was, most guys might not get here. They might party, drink, not be so focused. But you. You were *only* focused. That's what you did when you left me behind, isn't it?"

His shoulders rose, paused, and dropped. I heard a soft swear from him.

Yeah. Yeah, I was right.

"You focused. You trained. You sacrificed. I know you didn't party. It was always football only, wasn't it? All to get here, to get where you are today."

His voice was low. "I didn't know what I was doing." His tone grew rueful, regretful, "Maybe. All I know is that it was never because you were beneath me. I was in sixth grade. I think I knew it could've been you and I looked into the future and I knew you'd pull me. I wouldn't be so focused, whether it be school or football or... You would've tempted me. I would've wanted to be with you all the time, experienced life with you, and I knew I couldn't. I knew even then that I'd have to decide which way to go, and I couldn't go the route that you traveled because it would've been all you. Training. Football. I needed that. I needed to leave, get out of my house. We had money, but we had shit for happiness. Money gives you security. It just pads the walls so you can wallow in how fucking unhappy you are. My mom's been dying a little bit every fucking day. You're right. What you said. She is an alcoholic. My dad—he's not a bad guy, he's just... All he cares about is maintaining their life. He's blind to anything else. Keep the company going. Grow it if possible. Keep my mom alive, literally, and that comes in different forms, but not believing your dad, trying to make your family go away, that's what my dad was doing. He was trying to keep his family together, though he was wrong. He was fucking wrong, and trust me, he's seen the light." He moved to me, his arms coming down on both sides of me. He was looming over me now. "I'll never let another person hurt you."

His eyes were glowing, almost glittering from a small bit of moonlight shining through my window.

And they were kind. I saw how kind they were, and my heart folded. I was gone. Donzo. The L word was coming and I couldn't stop myself.

"I fucking love you."

Him.

It was him who said it, and he said it fiercely. He said it as if his life depended on me knowing it.

My heart was folding all over again, jumping up, doing a skip, hop, and a somersault, and my knees were just boneless. I could've melted into the bed.

I raised a hand, cupping the side of his face. "You do?"

I had a tear there. It was falling. I was helpless from stopping it from falling.

"Yeah." Just as fierce, with every bit of conviction as the first one. "I fucking love you." His hand raised, cupping the side of my face, but mine was steady. His was shaking. "I love you so much that it's ripping me apart, knowing what you went through. Knowing I couldn't be there to help take some of that pain away, but I can't go back in time. I wish I could. You have no idea how much I wish I could, but I can't. All I can do is make it right from here on out, from today and forward." His head dropped. He moved more over me, his forehead resting on mine, and he whispered again, so fiercely that I swear it was starting to heal old haunts. "I love you and I want you to let me love you and I want to make you mine. My woman. Just mine. All mine. I don't care what you want. I can't let you be someone else's. Mine, babe. Mine."

He was waiting, not letting himself fall down on me, but I just pulled him the last bit toward me.

I needed him. "I was going to tell you that I love you. That I didn't care what you were planning for your future, because I am your future and that I loved you and that was that, but you beat me to it."

"You do?"

I was smiling and I nodded. "Yeah." My hand applied more force, still holding his cheek, and my thumb rubbed down over his mouth. "I love you."

"Thank fuck."

"Thank you for the vehicle."

He chuckled, running his hand down my arm, then curling around my hip. "Yeah, babe. You need some wheels. You need to be safe."

And because I needed to know, "You were dating, when we were, you know. Those other women—"

He shook his head. "No dates. Group events. Things for the football team, fundraisers." He cupped both sides of my face, his fingers sliding into my hair. "There's been no one since you. There couldn't have been. My dick stopped working unless I only thought of you."

Best. Words. Ever.

But shit. I cupped his hands, holding still. "I have my own confession. That thing I said about your dad—"

He cut me off again. "A fucking lie. I'm not stupid. My dad's a lot of stuff, but he's not dirty like that."

I had tensed, then let out a breath. "You're not mad?"

"Oh. I was furious when you told me, but I knew what it was. You were pushing me away for a final time." He grinned. "Good thing I don't give a shit when it tends to come to you. You're mine, Dust. You can't push me away, not anymore."

Right.

I thought about what he said earlier. Safe. I was more than safe now. I had some grief to get through, but I felt a clearing in the sky. Light was shining down. I would be happy. He already made me happy.

And that was everything.

EPILOGUE

LIFE CHANGED AFTER THAT, but for the better. It was something I wasn't used to.

As for my stuff and what all happened to me, a few people brought it up on campus. Not many, though. Less than what I expected and more than what Stone wanted. Siobhan had resumed being my friend. It was a slow-go at first. It meant something that she came to the house, she found me, she apologized, and she further apologized for staying away one time during a study session.

"I was hurt. You didn't tell me you knew him and all the people you live with. They're just so not what I am, and I felt insignificant. I felt foolish." Her head bent down. She was picking at her pen. "But I thought about it and realized you didn't need to tell me. You didn't owe me anything. I was insecure, and it was all me. Not you. You were this 'big' person and I had no clue. Thought you were like me."

"Like you?"

"Small. You know?"

I covered her hand with mine and squeezed. "You're not

small. No one's small, and it doesn't matter who you know. That doesn't make you not small. I *am* like you. I just know a few people you don't, that's all."

She looked like she had more to say, but Trent came back to the table then and we went to studying.

My housemates, they were ecstatic.

They went to a couple of Stone's games. Stone went to a couple of their games with me, Colby and Jake, too. I was learning that the three of them had a friendship dynamic that I didn't think I'd ever understand. Colby and Jake razzed each other. Stone was quiet, but somehow, the three were always so in tune with each other that it was a little freaky. Stone told me later that that wasn't normal. Guys on the teams didn't get close to each other. It was a job. People showed up. Did their job. Went home to their family. A few times, a couple guys might get close, get friendly, but with the threat of being traded to a different team always looming, most didn't let themselves get super attached.

It was too late for him, Colby, and Jake. They were attached. Cortez came over to Stone's house a few times, too. He was like an appendage, like an arm to the body of the three.

Noel. Wyatt. Nacho. Dent. The four lost it every time the three or four of them sometimes showed up.

Colby had started mentoring Noel.

Stone sometimes gave Wyatt pointers, but I could tell there was something there. The pro-ballers were a little detached from the college footballers. I didn't know why, except Jake made one comment that they shouldn't be partying as much as they were. Colby and Stone didn't rebuke him. They both just got a nod and that was it. Made me wonder if maybe my housemates weren't as dedicated as they should be, but Colby mentioned they had one more year before the Combine.

No clue what that meant, but again, the other two just nodded and said nothing else.

"You're fidgeting."

We were driving in his truck, and he was right. I kept playing with my hands, moving around in the seat. I was not comfortable, and I'd try to get comfortable and I just kept doing that. It was a whole cycle. Over and over again. Cursing, I stuffed my hand under my leg. I was about to do the same with my other hand, but Stone reached over. He grabbed my hand, laced our fingers, and threw me a smile. "Okay. Let's not get hasty here."

I laughed, and it was enough, just enough. No. It was perfect because it calmed some of the nerves.

We were driving to Acquiesce, a more upscale restaurant that bordered on a club. I'd heard about it. Stone mentioned it in passing, that we should go because we'd never been on an official date. I relayed the name of the place to Nicole, and she and Savannah went apeshit, claiming how prestigious the place was. Mia'd been walking through the living room, overheard our convo, and paused to give her two cents. "I've been there. It's cool. They have dancers." That'd been it. She kept moving, reminding me of the first time I met her and thinking she was a gazelle in human form. Her long legs striding forward, but moving as if she were delicately prancing. It worked for her. Me. I'd look like a goose trying to pretend it was a flamingo. Just couldn't pull that one off.

But I was nervous because one, it was our first 'out' date together. People knew. Blogs knew. Half the male population on campus knew, and not because of me, because of their love for Stone. This was different, though. Felt different, more official, and I was sweating buckets. Hence, the fidgeting.

"What's in your head?"

I tried to pull my hand from Stone, but he only tightened his grip and squeezed me back.

"Stone."

"Tell me."

He was swinging into the parking lot, and it was a circle drive-up thing. There was a line of cars in front of us, and they had valet. Stone was glancing around, making sure he didn't have anything expensive laying out. Wasn't supposed to happen with valet, but let's be real. It happened. I just went right back to fidgeting and smoothed my hand down over my dress.

I was wearing a pink dress that Savannah insisted on. There was a sheer covering up my top, with green beading that made it look like I was wearing a fairytale garden. The bottom was pink tulle and she'd thrown on a long necklace of white beads at the last minute. I'd done away with the blue hair, and my hair was now dyed back to my dusty blonde color. I thought it was appropriate. It was up in half curls and a half braid. According to Mia, the only housemate who'd been to Acquiesce with Wyatt because they had dinner with his parents there, the dress was perfect. I wasn't sure, or I hadn't been until now. Stone was wearing a nice button-down shirt and nice jeans. He could've stepped off a yacht in Cannes and fit right in, but the couple in front of us got out of a fancy car and I settled even more. The woman had on a gold sparkling dress, top to bottom. Diamonds dripped down her neck, so yeah. I was probably underdressed.

"This place is a different level of fancy."

It was our turn next, and he pulled up, but when the valet opened his door, Stone didn't get out. He was watching me. "You don't want to go here?"

"I didn't say that."

"It's in your voice. I can tell." He looked around, cursing, and motioned to the guy. "Sorry. Change of plans."

"What are you doing?" I asked as the valet nodded and stepped back, helping Stone shut the door at the same time, and then we were moving forward, pulling back onto the highway.

"You don't want to go there. I can tell. I'm sorry. Asked around. Everyone said to take you there, said all chicks would want to go there. I should've known. You're different." He sighed. "Thank fuck you are."

I should protest, have him turn back, but he was right.

"Besides." Stone threw me a wolfish grin. "Pretty sure we'd have our pictures sold to a gossip site." He reached for my hand, our fingers sliding against each other. "Way you look, we would've been put up somewhere."

The paparazzi buzz had settled, too. Mostly because we never went out. Stone didn't have the time. If he wasn't at practice or traveling for away games or at the stadium in meetings, he was watching tapes at ~~home~~ his place. We divided our nights. The nights before my early morning classes, we were at my place. All the other nights, we were at his, so I almost thought home—my home—but it wasn't. And that was moving too fast. We weren't there, but as his thumb started rubbing over the top of my hand, I started wondering if we were actually already there.

I definitely felt like I was.

It wasn't long before I saw where he took us.

We pulled into the parking lot of the Quail.

I shot him a look. "Way to keep a low profile."

He laughed, parking and getting out of his side. Coming around, he opened my door and helped me down, saying, "Your school knows who you are."

A fact he'd been a part of since he kept coming to the Quail when I was working. He'd stop in, get food, give me a kiss, and then usually head out. Or he'd come in with either Colby, Jake, or both of them, and they'd sit a while. His presence wasn't as big of an uproar. There were still a few whispers, some looks, maybe one person asking for an autograph or a selfie, but for the most part, he was right. He'd blended in, and he was also right because as soon as we walked in, a collective laugh came up from the corner booth. My housemates were all sitting there. It seated twelve, so the adjacent booth had the rest.

Nicole slid out and came over, a beer in hand. "What happened to the date?"

Stone's arm came around my shoulder. "This is it. We'll do fancy for Valentine's Day, but till then, this is what my girl wants."

He was right, and I was grinning, feeling weird about smiling so much, but it was what it was.

"Well." Nicole's tone turned into a warning. Her face grew somber real quick. "Then I should prepare you…"

"Is that her?!"

Coming out of the bathroom, behind Mia, was another just-as-beautiful-looking girl. Charcoal black hair. Pert nose. Tiny chin. A dimple on one side. Flashing green eyes. Megan Fox look-a-like. She stepped around Mia, her hair being tossed over her shoulder. She was finishing drying her hands and she came forward, walking as if she owned the Quail, the whole college, and the whole world.

"Hi!" She held her hand out, but her eyes were raking in Stone. "I'm Char. Finally nice to meet you."

Char.

Oh.

Shit.

Char.

Nicole sighed beside me. "This is Char, Dusty."

"Dusty. I just love your name. It's the best ever." I didn't shake her hand quick enough. She transferred it to Stone, upping her smile wattage. "Hi! I'm Char." Her eyes widened and she took a step back. "Holy shit. You're Stone Reeves. Aren't you?"

Stone looked at her, her hand, me, and shifted back, placing a hand in the small of my back. That was his cue he wasn't engaging. This was all me, but he was there to support me.

I eyed Nicole. She was flashing me an apology. She wasn't saying it, but it was there in her eyes.

A double dose of 'oh, shit'.

"You're back."

Char was frowning at both Stone and me, but put her hand back to her side. "Yeah. I'm back." She gestured to the booths behind her. "Got a cheap ticket and flew back, surprised everyone just as you guys left. They weren't expecting me and voilà." She indicated the bar around us. "We're here to celebrate."

I caught sight of Wyatt and Noel making a point to drink gulpfuls of beer.

That eased some of the knot in me, but Nicole wasn't saying anything. Mia had followed to stand behind Char. She looked more constipated than normal, but knowing Mia, this could've been her trying to be supportive of a friend she was still hurt by. It was also a show of solidarity and she was there. Yeah. That's what that look relayed on her face.

Savannah just had her mouth closed tight, her arms folded over her chest. She was sitting back in the corner. Noel on one side. Wyatt on the other. Lisa hadn't gotten up. I noted that. How'd I miss that?

"And," Char was talking as if none of what I was noticing was happening, as if everyone was happy-go-lucky to have her back. "Don't worry. I won't kick you out of my room, not just yet. You can take a couple weeks to look for a new place. My family has an apartment here, downtown. I'll stay there. And I'm not joining C&B until next semester so it's not like the commute's going to be a nag. I'm sure they'll all come see me half the time."

I didn't want to move out.

I knew it then, and hearing that I'd have to, I didn't want to. I wanted to keep what Stone and I were doing. Maybe in the future, we'd have that conversation, but it was too soon. Living together was serious, and I wasn't ready. I was enjoying what we had.

As if feeling my turmoil, Stone had enough. He asked her, "Who's your man?"

"What?"

"Your man. You got a man?"

She blinked, taken aback by how blunt he was being. "No."

"Who's your handler then? Who handles you in this group?"

"Uh." She looked behind her, and hearing that, Mia stepped forward, but she was still frowning.

"I think I do."

Stone frowned. "You don't sound so sure."

She was eyeing Char before a look flashed over her. Her face cleared and she was set. "Because you can't come back and declare it's your room again. You left us. Like, completely. We had no clue what you were doing, where you were, until the day before Dusty showed up. And we didn't make it super easy for her to be in the house."

Stone's hand pressed on my back. He shifted, standing closer to me.

Mia still just looked so annoyed. She said to me, "I said it before, but I'm so sorry for being such a bitch. Now I care about you and I worry about you and you," she turned to Stone, huffing, "you better be good to her or I will hurt you. Somehow. Lisa and I will both hurt you. We're the vengeful ones in the group. Sav's the prim and proper one, and Nicole's the nice one. Char was just the bitchy one of us, but not anymore." She turned to her old best friend, now on a roll. Her head went higher. The Greek goddess look was coming back as she straightened to her full height. "You're back. Fine. Welcome home, but not in the house. We got Dusty now, and we're not letting her go. You, we can work on being friends again if you apologize for what you did to us." She twisted around, looking at Savannah and Lisa. Both were watching. We were within hearing distance, a fact that Char was noting, too, because none of the others were speaking up. Guys either. Her face was getting more and more pale as Mia went. And Mia wasn't done. She added, nodding to herself, "Right. Yes. It's decided. You left us in the lurch. You don't get to just come back. As long as Dusty wants the room, and she's got the basement room."

Char winced, sucking in her breath. "No!"

"She gets to keep it."

She finished, and no one said a word.

I didn't look, but I could feel Stone's amusement. He didn't like hearing they'd been not so nice to me, but everything else, he'd been keeping in his laughter. Now he ducked down, saying softly enough so only I could hear, "Colby and Jake would've sold a jersey to witness something like that. Who's this chick again?"

I elbowed him but fighting my own grin.

"You guys hated on me dating Brian."

Now it was Char's turn, and she'd snapped back. Her face was filling with color.

I had to give her props because she'd bounced back quick. She'd been pale up to the last second Mia stopped talking.

"That *again*?!" Mia rolled her eyes.

"Yes, that again. I loved him and you and Lisa were riding my ass, saying what a dick he was, saying I shouldn't date him. You know how that makes me feel? Great supportive friends, huh. You made him dump me because of your bitching."

Lisa was pushing out of the booth, a finger in the air, and she was coming in real hard. "Brian Caldriona is an idiot and he was not worthy of dating you. And he proved that fact. He rebounded by banging Vallia Cortega."

Char sucked in her breath again. "He didn't."

"He did."

She looked at Mia.

Who nodded, her hand resting on her hip. "He did. Week after you left for Greece, he went through half her sorority house."

Another sucking in of air. "That piss ant. He knows I hated her. That's why he banged her."

"See." Both Lisa and Mia. At the same time.

Char's mouth pressed together, fury was tightening her face. "But whatever. I can destroy him before lunch tomorrow. You. Me. Us." She waved between the three of them. "I need you guys back. It was so hard being in Greece without you guys. I mean, yeah. My new boyfriend chartered a boat for us and they had chocolate-dipped strawberries and would make us truffle fries at our request, and their coffee was divine and the wine and cheese, don't get me started, but I didn't have you guys. I needed you guys."

Nicole tugged on the back of my dress, motioning to go back a few feet.

Stone read the situation and leaned in. "Grabbing a table just for us, some beer and food. Find me?"

I nodded. That was always easy. He'd be surrounded by at least a couple guys. It happened every time. They all wanted to talk football, and especially with Stone Reeves.

Nicole indicated the girls. "Don't worry about Char. Those three will make up, probably tonight. They're halfway there, but Mia meant what she said. We'd all talked about it a couple weeks ago because Char sent an email, hinting she was coming back. We took a vote. Three to zero, but not about if we'd kick you out for her. It was if we'd find a room somewhere in the house for Char. Mia was the holdout because she didn't vote. She didn't know what she wanted." Her eyes trailed past my shoulders, going to the girls again. "Looks like she decided. Char's not in until she majorly kisses ass. Between you and me, Char will be our sixth roommate by next semester. That's just how those three are, hot and cold, but usually always hot together. And again, that room is yours for as long as you want it." She turned, finding Stone and nodding at him. "Unless you and he are moving in together?"

I wasn't ready. I just wasn't ready.

"I think if that happens, it'll be later, much later. Like senior year later."

"Good." Nicole seemed relieved. "I have to ask. It's been on my mind, but I know you're going for marine biology, but I don't know. Your cooking, it's fucking phenomenal. You could go to culinary school and be a personal chef. I mean, you got the hookup." She went back to watching Stone, who, as I knew would happen, was now talking to two guys.

Had I thought about being a chef? Yes. Stone suggested the same thing a week ago, but the marine biology thing stuck deep in me. It was my vow, and who knew. Maybe I'd do both at some point. I didn't know, but I didn't have to make that decision.

I had time.

I had lots of time.

And I felt good knowing that.

Instead of answering Nicole, I went over to Char.

She stopped talking, blinking at me. "Yes?"

"You owe me a full month's rent." I narrowed my eyes. "And if you don't pay, I can make your life hell."

Her mouth opened but held there.

Mia clamped a hand on her arm. "Don't even think it. We will back her up in a heartbeat, Char."

Char's mouth closed. She nodded to me. "You'll get the check tomorrow."

"Good." I grinned at the rest. "Now, excuse me. I'm going to go sit with my boyfriend."

And that's what I did. As I went, I heard, "Blue!" Looking over, Joe slid a beer toward me. I reached out a hand just in time, and the mug slid right into my palm, splashing a little. He tipped his head. "Nice to see you enjoying life right now, but can you take a shift in two days? You never answered my text."

A second laugh from me. I was letting more and more of those out. "Thanks, Joe. And yes. I'll cover the shift."

He held up a hand, leaning down to hear another customer's order.

As I got to our table, Stone already had a beer in hand. Cammie was bringing over a tray of food and a couple of waters. A basket of fries and I already knew there'd be two chicken sandwiches with them. "Heya! How's the date?" Her amusement was evident, and as I slid onto a stool on the inside of the table, right next to Stone, she tapped my arm. "Let me know if you need anything. I don't work tomorrow, so we should grab lunch, yeah?"

I nodded. "Sounds good."

It was more than good. It sounded perfect.

Stone excused himself and moved so he was facing only me. He blocked out the rest of the room. He leaned over, resting a hand on my hip and reached forward to grab a fry.

"That all okay back there?"

I looked. Char, Mia, and Lisa were still talking, their heads pressed tightly together. Nicole had returned and Dent put his arm around her shoulders. Savannah was snuggling against Noel's side, and I knew my answer.

"Yes. It's all good."

Yes. Mushy. Me.

I didn't care.

I reached up, my finger under his chin, and I said, "Come here."

He flashed me a grin, bending, and his mouth fit over mine just how it should've been. Perfectly.

EPILOGUE AFTER THE EPILOGUE

The alarm went off, and I was up.

"Fuck, babe." The covers moved and a muscled arm came over me, pulling me back down into his warmth.

I would not be deterred. No way. No how.

Even if that warmth and that muscled arm was connected to my husband. We'd been married four years now, and to say our journey had been smooth sailing would've been a lie. Not between us. Well, we still fought.

Stone and I would never not fight.

We fought. We bickered. Then we had hate sex (it wasn't really hate sex, but I still liked to use the term), which turned into hot sex, and then make-up sex, and well—

"MOM!"

There was our reward.

"Fuck. Babe."

I grinned, but we heard the door slam into the wall. The door was already open. We didn't sleep with our bedroom door closed, and we didn't let Grayson's door remain shut either, so why he hit the floor running every morning and why he had to shove the door open when it was already open was beyond me.

Stone muttered, sitting up and running a hand over his face, "We've already fixed three holes this month. It's time to take the doorknobs off."

That was another battle on our hands.

We wanted to take Grayson's knob off his door, but his door wasn't the only door he slammed open. That meant we'd have to take all the knobs off the doors, ours included and to say Grayson was hyper and unpredictable was an understatement. There was no rhythm or reason to why he fell asleep, how long he'd fall asleep, or more specifically how long he'd remain asleep. That meant we never knew which doorknobs we could actually lock, say...if we wanted to have any forms of sex stated above. He was also an expert at escaping anything. No crib held him. No fence contained him. Tables and cupboards weren't too scary to him. The kitchen became his personal gym, and yeah, it was panic-inducing and I almost had three heart attacks when he first began crawling. He went straight to climbing and the kid was not normal.

I blamed Stone. Those were his genes.

Bare feet were running down the hall. A pause. Then, a big heave (even though our door was already open) and wham! The door flew back into the wall. In its place, our three-year-old not-quite-human child stood. His chest heaved again, his cheeks got big, and, "DAD! IT'S TIME TO GO SEE THE TURTLES!"

Stone sighed and lay back down. His arm came over his face. "*Fuck*, babe."

I fought back a grin.

Grayson's eyes got big, and he pumped his legs, then launched himself. He landed in between us, but not quite on the bed. Grabbing the blankets, he pumped again, and then he grappled up. Another battle on our hands. We were not allowed to help him with these challenges.

Our kid was going to be either a professional athlete or an adrenaline junkie. Either way, I was going to be having heart attacks the rest of my life. I was just resigned. But this morning, knowing why we were awake, my own excitement was bubbling to the surface. I couldn't help myself and I scooped him up, rolling so he was on his back, in the middle of the bed with us.

"Mom!" He squirmed, trying to push my tickling hands away. "Stop!" But he was giggling, and I only upped the tickle monster even more.

Stone grinned, dropping his arm. His hand came down and he joined in.

Grayson was shrieking and kicking to get back up. "Stop! You guys! Stop. The turtles."

That was only cuter, and soon he was shrieking so loud I was pretty sure we didn't need coffee or alarms to wake the rest of the house occupants.

"Fuck, guys."

"Language." It was a reprimand from me, but there was no heat in it.

Standing in the doorway, his hair messed and standing upright, a hand idly itching his chest was Jared. He yawned, his hand moving to rub his jaw. "Some of us need our hearing for the rest of our lives, you know. We're not all already washed up and hall-of-famers."

Stone only grinned. "Washed up?" He raised an eyebrow. "We won the Super Bowl last year." And there was talk they'd do it all over again the next season.

Jared started laughing, then his face went slack. "Fuck!"

"Jared!" There was more heat in that one this time.

He grimaced. "Sorry. Forgot about the game today."

Our day was packed.

We were off to watch the baby sea turtles hatch, and we were running out of time. We had forty minutes to get in the vehicles. Twenty minutes to get there, and that was not counting any stopping time for coffee or pee breaks. Another thing Grayson loved doing. Peeing. The higher the stream in the air, the better, and he got a kick out of it no matter how old he was. I wasn't holding my breath he'd grow out of that one either.

But Jared was thinking about a scrimmage at his future law school. He'd gotten accepted, but once they found out who his brother-in-law was, his faculty advisor asked if Stone and a few of his teammates would participate in a charity game with a bunch of their law students and football alumni. It was going to be televised and Jared was earning major points that not only did Stone say he'd participate, but so were Cortez, Jake, and Colby. There were a bunch more too, including Apollo, who had flown in the previous night just for the game.

"Is Apollo up?"

Jared shrugged, yawning again. "Not a clue. We got in late, so I doubt he's going to see the sea turtles."

Grayson gasped. "No way! He has to come!"

This was apocalyptic in his eyes.

Another door opened across the hall, and Apollo stepped out, the whole shebang in repeat. Hair messed up. Yawning. Jaw rubbing. Chest itching. And he added a new one, rubbing his eyes before grinning at Gray. "Hey, little dude. No way am I missing a hatching." He smirked, glancing at me. "It's like we don't see a dozen others over the summer."

Now that was apocalyptic to me.

I huffed, shooting upright. "Excuse me?!"

I missed the shared grins from all the guys except my little dude, who leaned into my side, glaring at Apollo with me.

Jared rolled his eyes, but smacked his brother in the chest with the back of his hand. He nodded at me. "Respect my sister, man. There can never be enough sea turtle hatchings to watch and help."

I felt it coming. A fight. I was gearing up. The steam was rising.

If they were going to mock my need to do whatever I could to help the ocean and any and all marine sea life, then—

Both Jared and Apollo started laughing.

Jared gestured to me. "Relax, sis. We've helped stranded whales with you. We've volunteered at sea otter hospitals, at sea turtle rescue and rehabilitation centers, and yeah, we've gone to protest environmental bills with you in D.C. The next step is flying to Japan to help the dolphins over there. We love the creatures as much as you do, but damn, I need some coffee before being there at five in the freaking morning."

He headed off, Apollo right behind him.

Grayson had perched on the edge of the bed, taking in the exchange, but Stone moved. His arm curved around my waist and he pulled me back down to him.

"Mom, Dad."

Stone started to roll over me, but paused and lifted his head. A fond and adoring smile softened his face. "Do your pops a favor and go wake up Grandma Barb. Yeah? Grandpa Chuck might need an extra yell in the ear, too. Flying in for the visit probably made him extra tired. Right up here. Right in here." He pointed to his own ear, winking.

Gray's eyes got big, and he shoved off the bed, jumping down with a thud which he didn't feel at all. He was off and sprinting down to the main floor because that was where Stone's parents liked to sleep. Their bedroom was off by the kitchen, and relatively more quiet until everyone decided to eat, but they liked being closer to the coffee machine. That was my guess.

"That wasn't nice." I grinned up at him as he looked back down at me.

His eyes were already darkening, taking in my eyes, my lips, remaining on my lips, still on my lips, and then he rolled completely over top of me. Our door was wide open. We had two recent college graduates in their own showers. Our little dude was downstairs and currently doing his best impersonation of a human alarm clock, but nope. He nestled in, grinding into me, and my mind turned off.

Sea turtles who?

He grinned, dropping his head and kissing my neck. "You and my mom seemed good last night."

I frowned, a hand to his chin and I lifted his head up. "Excuse me?"

Another grin. His hand slid around my waist, sliding up my back, but I knew it would move down. He said before that happened, "You two cooked last night together. Don't think I didn't notice. Kept expecting the house to burn down."

I was annoyed.

I scowled. "Are you kidding?"

"No, babe. That's not a joke."

Ah. Screw it. He was half-right to worry.

It'd been a long road for Barb and Charles (now Chuck once Grayson was born), but we were at the place where we could cook an entire meal for hungry teammates, college students, and three-year-olds together and I was happy. When Stone let them know we were serious, they hadn't been pleased. They warned him off me, saying I'd turn around and finish blackmailing them exactly how Gail had started.

I'd been furious until Jared happened, and how he heard, I had no clue. He wasn't saying.

He was the one who went up to her at the end of his basketball game. Sweaty. Had been one of the two star players for that game, and when Barb went up to him to congratulate him on the win, he asked her if she said what he heard she said. She stammered, stepping back. Her neck and face went beet red. Charles had been there, and he stepped back, coughing, uncomfortable. There'd been two other couples with them, and the women looked aghast. One of the husbands coughed, laughing, but Stone got a phone call that night.

It'd been loud and long, until Stone said, "She's going to be my wife one day. It would be smart for you to change your attitude." That was it. He hung up, and he didn't take another call from her for six months.

Barb and Charles changed their attitudes.

But then it was on my end, and I had to get over everything they'd done to my family and me.

So that'd been another long journey of ups and downs.

But we cooked a meal together last night, and there'd been wine, and while Barb cut back on hers, I upped mine so we met in the middle. It was a wine-compromise, and it worked. It also helped that they adored Grayson, and I knew they were hoping for another four grandchildren. Not two, not one more. Four. Chuck told me one night after too many bourbons.

So yes, we were all a work in progress, but things were getting smoother. Much, much smoother.

They also earned bonus points because not only could we hear them getting up to start the coffee, but they'd been adamant they'd attend the hatching, too. I also heard Barb asking Stone one night if it was true that an octopus changed colors when they slept.

I yelled from the other room, "They also come to say thank you if you save their lives. It's true. Youtube it."

I said now to Stone, "She's been trying. It helps."

He lifted his head from my throat. "Babe. She's been kissing your ass for years now."

I was growing heated, but not in the bad way. I shrugged before twining my arms around his neck. "There was a lot of stuff she needed to kiss my ass about." Then I grinned. "Now shut up and give me a proper good morning kiss before we go off to shield baby turtles from frigate birds."

So he did just that.

And after Stone carried me to the shower, behind a locked door, we were quick but panting when we finished just in time to dress and dash downstairs. Jared was shaking his head. Apollo was smirking, again. Grayson was dressed and jumping up and down. Barb and Chuck were at the door, having helped to get everyone ready and dressed and fed.

Barb held out two coffees for us and a bag. "Those are toasted bagels for you both. Now we must go or we'll miss the hatching."

We were off.

We got there in time.

The babies were just crawling out, starting their speeding for the ocean, and people lined the way for them. With Stone's arm around my shoulders, with Grayson leaning against both of us and standing on our toes, and with both of my brothers with us, and yes, even with Grandpa and Grandma there, I was happy.

I tipped my head back.

Stone gazed down, those eyes reading my need and he bent his head.

His lips touched mine, and then I raised up and told him we needed to stop for a pregnancy test on the way home.

If you enjoyed Enemies, please leave a review!
They truly help so much.

A bonus prologue scene is on my website if you'd like more Dusty and Stone!
www.tijansbooks.com

THE LETTER

Baby girl, this is your mother.

I know I've given you explicit instructions to trace this into your yearbook, but they're my words. That means this is from me, my heart, and my love for you.

There's so many things I want to say to you, things I want you to hear, to know, but let's start with the reason I'm having you put these words in your senior yearbook.

First of all, this book is everything. It may be pictures, some names of people you won't remember in five years, ten years, or longer, but this book is more important than you can imagine. It's the first book that's the culmination of your first chapter in life.

You will have many. So many! But this book is the physical manifestation of your first part in life.

Keep it. Treasure it.

Whether you enjoyed school or not, it's done. It's in your past. These were the times you were a part of society from a child to who you are now, a young adult woman. When you leave for college, you're continuing your education, but you're moving onto your next chapter in life. The beginning of adulthood. This yearbook is your bridge.

Keep this as a memento forever. It sums up who you grew up with. It houses images of the buildings where your mind first began to learn things, where you first began to dream, to set goals, to yearn for the road ahead. It's so bittersweet, but those memories were your foundation to set you up for who you will become in the future. Whether they brought pain or happiness, it's important not to forget.

From here, you will go on and you will learn the growing pains of becoming an adult. You will refine your dreams. You will set new limits. Change your mind. You will hurt. You will laugh. You will cry, but the most important is that you will grow.

Always, always grow, honey. Challenge yourself. Put yourself in uncomfortable situations (BUT BE SAFE!) and push yourself not to think about yourself, your friends, your family, but to think about the world. Think about others. Understand others, and if you can't understand, then learn more about them. It's so very important. Once you have the key to understanding why someone else hurts or dreams or survives, then you have ultimate knowledge. You have empathy.

Oh, honey.

As I'm writing this, I can see you on the couch reading a book. You are so very beautiful, but you are so very humble. You don't see your beauty, and I want you to see your beauty. Not just physical, but your inner kindness and soul. It's blinding to me. That's how truly stunning you are.

Never let anyone dim your light.

Here are some words I want you to know as you go through the rest of your life:

Live.

Learn.

Love.

Laugh.

And, honey, know. Just know that I am with you always.

And my last word, look.

Look for signs from me, because I'm giving them to you. They're everywhere.

I love you, my sweet child. You will grow and you will go through hardships and happiness, and every single time, I am there with you.

Always, always love you so very, very much, your mother.

ACKNOWLEDGMENTS

Writing this book was during a particular important stage of my life. In writing these acknowledgements, I need to mention this because I'll always remember it.

Having said that, I want to thank my editor, my proofreaders, my beta readers, my author friends, and of course the members in my reader group! Thank you guys for always being there, always supporting, and always inspiring me.

Thank you Crystal!

Thank you Kimberly!

Thank you my Bailey.

TEARDROP SHOT

Lucas is busy forking his new girlfriend, but if you're feeling vengeful, I can pop in my dentures."

Those were the words I heard as three things were happening at once.

One, I was just dumped.

The message was being delivered from Newt, my boyfriend's —no, my very, very recent ex-boyfriend's—grandfather, while I was standing on his doorstep.

Two, my phone started ringing.

I glanced at it, half hoping it was Luc-ass, but it wasn't.

I gulped because the person calling was a blast from my past, like my way early past before Lucas, before the guy I was using Lucas to get over, before even him. That far back, and while the person calling me was a guy, he wasn't a romantic guy. At all. It was more the group of people he represented, a group that I left in my dust years ago.

So, hence the gulp, because none of them had called for at least six years. Give or take.

While both those events were hitting me at once, the third was what shirt Newt was wearing—my Reese Forster shirt.

I pointed at him. "You stole my shirt!" And because I was getting flooded with everything happening, the question blurted out of me. "If an owl could talk, what accent would it have?"

My neck was getting hot, furiously hot.

Newt was the one in front of me, so I was dealing with him first.

Who did he think he was?

A thief, that's what.

I loved that shirt. I lived in it. Slept in it. Drooled even. I did so many things in that shirt. And there was no way he could claim it wasn't because the collar was ripped. I put it there, one time in frustration when I watched Forster get the ball stolen from him during the West Conference Finals.

Reese Forster was the Seattle Thunder's star point guard. They had other star players too. In fact, their team was stacked this year, but it was Reese.

It was my shirt of him.

I got it the first year he was drafted, when he was nineteen, and while my obsession with basketball had waned over the years, my obsession with him had not.

I kept up on his stats. He was lined up to have one of his greatest years this next season.

Goddamn. I'd have to get a new shirt. Maybe a jersey even?

"Is that a no on the revenge sex?" Newt countered.

"I hope your dentures get glued to the bottom of someone's saggy ass and you have to go to the emergency room to get them removed. You old fuck!"

I stormed off after that, but my phone kept ringing.

Shit.

Looking down, seeing a name I never thought I'd talk to

again, I faltered in my storming away. I couldn't lie, even to myself because I wasn't sure how to proceed.

Too many things were all converging at once.

But Luc-ass.

Was I devastated? No.

Was I annoyed? Yes.

Lucas and I bonded over our love of Reese Forster and he'd been the first guy I could tolerate in over a year so I was using him. The whole mantra of getting under someone else to get over someone—well, I'd been trying to test that theory out with him.

It hadn't worked.

So no, I wasn't crushed about Luc-asshole's cheating. I mean, it made sense. In a way. I could never bring myself to practice human corkscrewing, as he'd put it. He'd tried selling me on role-playing opening a bottle of wine.

I'd be the wine bottle, and...

Ring!

Okay. It kept ringing.

In the past, the very distant past, if they tried calling, it was only once.

They'd call. I wouldn't answer. They'd leave a voicemail, which I usually deleted. There'd been a few I had kept saved in my mailbox and depending on how much I wanted to suffer, I might listen to them over a box of wine and Cheetos.

This was different.

He called. He called again.

He kept calling.

Oh boy.

Taking a breath for courage, my thumb lingered over the accept button. I mean, why not? The day had already gone to shit. Might as well add another to the pile.

But if I was going to answer it, I was going to do it my way.

"If you had to pick an alcoholic drink to be the title of your autobiography, what would it be and why?" Pause. A breath. Then, "Heya, Trent."

Read more about Reese and Charlie in Teardrop Shot.
He's an NBA star, and she's a mess.

For additional sports romances, check out Hate To Love You, Ryan's Bed, or my Fallen Crest Series!

9 781951 771096